DATE DUE		
SEP 04 2009	DEC 08 2012	
MAR 07 2010		
JUL 17 2010	JUL 30 2013	
APR 28 2011		
JUN 24 2011		
OCT 06 2011		
MAY 25 2012		

Girl in a Red Tunic

ALYS CLARE

Girl in a Red Tunic

HODDER &
STOUGHTON

First published in Great Britain in 2005 by Hodder and Stoughton
A division of Hodder Headline

A Hodder & Stoughton Book

1 3 5 7 9 10 8 6 4 2

A CIP catalogue record for this title
is available from the British Library

ISBN 0 340 83113 8

Typeset in Plantin Light by Hewer Text UK Ltd, Edinburgh

Printed and bound by Mackays of Chatham Ltd, Chatham, Kent

Hodder Headline's policy is to use papers that are natural, renewable
and recyclable products and made from wood grown in sustainable
forests. The logging and manufacturing processes are expected to
conform to the environmental regulations of the country of origin.

Hodder and Stoughton Ltd
A division of Hodder Headline
338 Euston Road
London NW1 3BH

in memory of my father
Geoffrey Harris
1915–2003
I will always love you

Stetit puella
rufa tunica;
si quis eam tetigit
tunica crepuit.

A young girl
in a red tunic:
the tunic rustled
to the touch.

From *Carmina Burana: cantiones profanae*
(Author's translation)

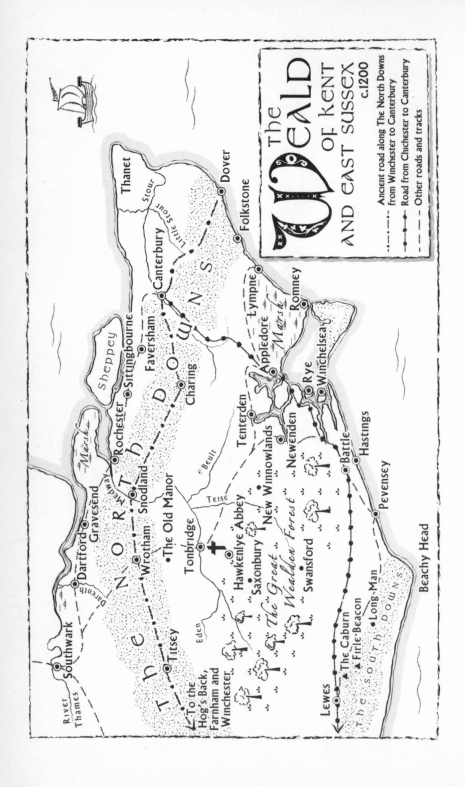

The **Weald** of Kent and East Sussex c.1200

- - ·-·- Ancient road along The North Downs from Winchester to Canterbury
- •••• Road from Chichester to Canterbury
- - - - Other roads and tracks

River Thames

Southwark

Dartford

Gravesend

Darenth

Titsey

To the Hog's Back, Farnham and Winchester

Eden

Wrotham

Snodland

Rochester

Sheppey

Sittingbourne

Faversham

Medway

T h e   N o r t h   D o w n s

The Old Manor

Tonbridge

Teise

Beult

Charing

Canterbury

Little Stour

Stour

Thanet

Dover

Folkstone

Lympne

Appledore

Romney Marsh

Tenterden

Newenden

Hawkenlye Abbey

Saxonbury

New Winnowlands

The Great Wealden Forest

Swansford

Rye

Winchelsea

Hastings

Battle

Pevensey

Lewes

The Caburn

Firle Beacon

Long-Man

The   South   Downs

Beachy Head

Marsh

The Family Tree of Helewise, Abbess of Hawkenlye Abbey

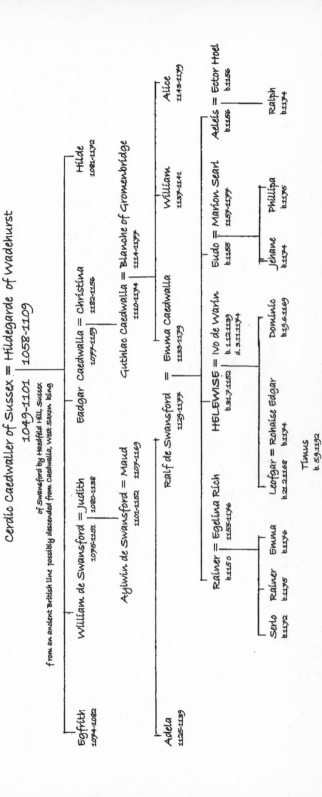

Cerdic Caedwaller of Sussex = Hildegarde of Wadehurst
1049-1101   1058-1109

of Swansford by Hatfield Hill, Sussex
from an ancient British line possibly descended from Caedwalla, West Saxon king

Egfrith
1074-1082

William de Swansford = Judith
1076-1151   1080-1138

Eadgar Caedwalla = Christina
1077-1159   1182-1156

Hilde
1081-1172

Adela
1125-1139

Aylwin de Swansford = Maud
1101-1152   1107-1169

Guthlac Caedwalla = Blanche of Gromenbridge
1110-1174   1114-1177

William
1137-1141

Alice
1143-1159

Ralf de Swansford = Emma Caedwalla
1129-1177   1133-1179

HELEWISE = Ivo de Warin
b.31.7.1152   b.1.12.1139
  d.3.11.1174

Eudo = Marion Searl
b.1155   1157-1177

Adelis = Ector Hoel
b.1156   b.1158

Rainer = Egelina Rich
b.1150   1155-1176

Leofgar = Rohaise Edgar
b.21.2.1168   b.1174

Dominic
b.15.6.1169

Jehane
b.1174

Phillipa
b.1175

Ralph
b.1174

Serlo
b.1172

Rainer
b.1175

Emma
b.1176

Timus
b.5.9.1192

PROLOGUE

November 1193

He had to wait until it was dark and everyone was asleep. He watched her for a moment, his distress at what she had done competing with his love and his anguish. She began to relax – at last! – and he listened as her breathing deepened. Then he stood up and stepped quietly away.

Outside it was bitterly cold. The night was clear but the moon was not yet up. He had no need of a lantern; he could find his way well enough by starlight and it was better not to have unnecessary illumination for this deed that he must do before dawn. Furtively he made his way to the ramshackle outbuilding where he had left the handcart but, knowing only too well what was waiting for him, he hesitated at the door. But all the hesitation in the world wouldn't make it go away. He hunched into his leather jerkin and wound his muffler more snugly round his neck then, spitting on his hands, wrenched open the flimsy door and picked up the cart's handles.

The load was heavy. A dead weight. Grunting with the effort, he pulled the cart backwards out of the outbuilding then turned it and headed off across the yard and off down the track. The most dangerous few yards were while he was still visible from the house; if she saw him, she might—

But he made himself stop thinking about what she might do.

Soon he had passed out through the gateway and reached the deep shadow that the winter-bare trees cast on the path.

That was better – he felt safer now. He pushed on, feeling the sweat breaking out across his back, and gradually the forest loomed up ahead of him.

It would be Martinmas in a few days and the forest floor cracked with beech mast and acorns. By long tradition, the people were allowed to turn their pigs out under the thickly growing beech and oak trees of the woods to fatten them before they were slaughtered and their salted meat laid down for the winter. The act was doubly necessary, for not only did the people need the meat to see them through the time when the Earth slept; in addition, killing their livestock meant they would not have to bear the cost of feeding the animals through the lean months. The ever-hungry hogs loved the abundant feed and needed no encouragement to gorge themselves.

He thought about hungry swine as he heaved the handcart up the bank and beneath the beech trees that lined the forest fringe. His own animals would be ravenous by now – almost starving, he fervently hoped – for two days ago he had rounded them up and penned them into an enclosure that he had made out of stakes driven into the forest floor and securely joined together with hurdles. As he made his arduous way along the track, soon he could hear them.

It was an awful sound. The screams and cries sounded as if someone were being cut to pieces.

He felt sick. No, he must not give in to it! He took a steadying breath. The nausea receded.

His axe was on the cart, together with a heavy mallet, and he could feel his long-bladed knife stuck in his belt. He had spent a long time honing it on the sharpening stone and now it was as keen as the finest razor. The three tools ought to make quick work of what he had to do. He would place the axe's sharp iron blade carefully in place and then bring down the mallet on to its back with all his might, so that—

The nausea rose up again and this time he could not swallow it back. Putting down the cart handles, he turned and, bent over, hands on his knees, vomited up his paltry stomach contents – he had barely eaten all day – into the dry grass and bracken beside the track.

Eyes streaming, he wiped his mouth on his cuff, picked up the cart handles again and pushed on. Somewhere out in the mysterious darkness he heard a wolf howl. He had never felt more wretched in his life. He wondered yet again if he was doing the right thing. No, not the *right* thing, for this deed could not be right, even to the most liberally minded man. The question was whether what he was doing was in truth the only way out of this desperate trouble that they had fallen into. There was still time to turn back, to take the terrible chance of that other option, although soon that choice would be gone for ever. He thought hard, noticing with a strange detachment that even as he thought, he went on pushing the cart, as though his deeper self knew full well there was no turning back. No, he told himself firmly after some moments. I know what I *should* do but I cannot, for failure would be the end; the risk is too great. Although it is against everything that I feel, everything I believe in, I must go through with what I have set out to do.

As resolved as he would ever be, he quickened his pace and hastened on beneath the trees.

The ravenous swine must have smelt him – or his burden – some time before he reached the secret, hidden grove where he had penned them and, with one voice, they set up a terrible, unearthly sound that would have stopped him in his tracks, had that been an option. By the time he emerged into the glade, the starving animals were pushing up against the sides of the pen, making the hurdles bulge outwards in one place. With a muttered curse, the young man put down the cart's handles and hurried over to where he had laid the surplus building materials. Grabbing a couple of stout posts, he picked up his mallet from the cart and hurried over to the weak spot in the pen's wall. Swiftly he banged the posts into the spongy forest floor. The hurdle ceased to bulge and he breathed freely once more. The sudden sweat of fear-fuelled exertion cooled on his back; not only would it have ruined his gruesome plan had the swine escaped, he also had a fair idea of what they might have done to him.

For they were desperate. For a man such as he, who cared deeply for his creatures, the state to which his need had driven them was dreadful to witness. He stood staring into the pen and noticed that one of the pigs – a skinny young boar which had been the runt of the litter – was dead. Its fellows had begun to eat it.

He stood frozen with horror.

Then he gathered himself and fetched the cart, wheeling it as close to the pen as he could. The screams of the swine were nearly deafening now. He folded back the sacking that wrapped the cart's heavy burden and an overpowering, slaughterhouse smell rose up. The squealing instantly intensified.

The young man stared down at the bloody body. The victim had been around thirty, short and wiry, and his pale skin looked almost transparent in death. His sparse hair had been red and he had blotchy freckles on his face.

I know what I must do, the young man thought. I must use my sharp knife to carve the meat from the bones – no, carve was not the right word; from somewhere he recalled that the act of cutting off flesh was known as flensing. Well, I must do that, and then I must use my axe blade and mallet to detach the limbs from the torso.

Slowly he drew his knife. The pigs, as if they knew what he was about to do, shrieked in impatience. He put the bright blade to the white skin of the corpse's thigh and cut a thin slice of flesh. Gritting his teeth, he picked it up and flung it into the pen, where it disappeared instantly amid a cacophony of yelping squeals. He stared down at the wound he had made; it was not bleeding and he wondered why. Because he's been dead too long, he thought. There won't be that great pulsing out of scarlet that frightened her so when he—

No. He must not think of that. He put his knife to the thigh again and cut another slice, which followed the first into the pen. But the swine were wild now and those two tiny morsels served not to satisfy them but to increase their desperation. The young man did not see but his intelligent animals had found another weak spot in the hurdle wall and several of them were pushing against it, driven to a frenzy by the food that was so close.

He was about to nerve himself to cut deeper when there was a loud cracking sound and, as a portion of the pen wall gave way, thirty starving, screaming pigs hurled themselves at him. He maintained just enough presence of mind to realise that the gravest danger was while he stood by the cart and he jumped out of the way as the lead pig – a vast sow – leapt for the meat meal that he had provided.

He used the animals' fierce fixation on what lay on the cart to his advantage, hurrying away to the encircling trees and climbing up on to the lowest stout branch of an oak. From there he watched in horror as the swine attacked the dead man. They had overturned the cart in the first attack and now the corpse lay splayed out so that several pigs at once could get to work on his four limbs. Then the big sow opened her mouth wide and plunged her sharp incisors into the bloated stomach. The stench that filled the air made the young man retch but seemed to drive the swine to greater heights; fighting each other for the prime cuts, they plunged their snouts into the wide cavity in the dead man's belly and ate his innards in a matter of moments.

★

It seemed to go on for hours. The young man, body aching, sick at heart and numb with horror at what he had done, sat in his tree and waited until the swine had finished. There were various awful noises – the lapping of blood from the forest floor, the crunch as a pig's strong back teeth bit through bone – but eventually the sated animals wandered away and silence fell.

He climbed down, flexing his stiff muscles, and went across to the pen. He would dismantle it and pack the hurdles and posts on to the cart first, he decided, while he plucked up courage to inspect what was left of the body. The pen came to pieces readily – he had done such tasks many times before – and before loading it on the cart he removed the sacking that had wrapped the corpse. It was now ragged and full of holes where the swine had gnawed away the bloodstained areas. He bundled it up and stuck it away at the back of the handcart; when he got home, it would follow the dead man's clothing on to the fire that he had stoked up before he left.

At last he knelt down to see what the swine had left. There was not very much: the dome of the skull with one empty eye socket; a few dark-coloured and rotten teeth; part of the solid pelvis; a single overlooked finger with a blackened, broken nail. The young man carried these remains a few paces deep under the trees, where he dug a shallow pit and buried them. They might stay hidden, or else some carnivorous predator – he remembered the distant howl of the wolf, and there were plenty of foxes in the forest – would discover them and consume them. Either way, he did not think it likely that the bone fragments would come to human attention.

Or so he fervently hoped.

Back in the glade, he spent a long time scuffing up dead leaves, beech mast and other forest floor detritus until he was satisfied that there was nothing to distinguish this glade from any other.

He filled in the pen's post holes with earth and made sure that the bloody ground was well covered. The moon had risen some time during this endless night and, although it was only just over the half, there was sufficient light for him to work by.

I can do no more tonight, he decided at last. I will return tomorrow, in the daylight, and do then whatever further covering-up is necessary.

He picked up the handles of the cart. It was heavier now and he realised that he was aching all over and almost exhausted. Then he straightened his back and set out on the long road home.

I

Helewise, Abbess of Hawkenlye, was in a troubled state of mind. She tried to rationalise it by admitting to herself that she was very tired. The pressure to come up with yet more money towards King Richard's ransom had been relentless and wherever she looked she saw evidence of the terrible punish- ment which a king's arrogance and folly had inflicted upon his people. Even Hawkenlye Abbey, favoured as it was by its special place in Queen Eleanor's heart, had not been excused from providing what seemed a vast sum. Fortunately, with the invaluable help of the intelligent and quick-witted Sister Emanuel, Helewise had just about managed to raise the money from the Abbey's revenues and they had kept hold of their treasures.

Hawkenlye Abbey possessed two extraordinary items. One, the Last Judgement tympanum that had pride of place over the great West Door of the Abbey, it would have been difficult (although not impossible) to take down and sell. The other treasured possession was the walrus-ivory carving of the dead Christ supported by Joseph of Arimathea, reputed to be a gift from Eleanor herself; the nuns' and monks' secret prayers must have been heard, for the ivory remained safely locked away in its usual place.

Helewise was deeply concerned, too, for the ageing Eleanor. On the one hand, the huge effort that she had made to gather together the ransom that would buy her favourite son's release had filled her with restless vitality and apparently boundless energy; on the other, it had to be remembered that she must be well into her seventh decade. The English, who knew and loved her, saw her only at a distance and believed her blessed by God with eternal youth. Helewise, however, honoured by being the Queen's hostess whenever she graced Hawkenlye Abbey with a visit, knew better. Queen Eleanor had recently made a swift overnight stop at the Abbey, dashing from one place to another – the explanations had been terse and Helewise, distressed by the Queen's pallor, had not absorbed the details – and her fatigue had been tangible. Such was Eleanor's preoccupation that she could not relax, pacing up and down in the best guest room even as she nibbled at her food and sipped warm, spiced wine from a goblet kept especially for her use. It was her usual custom to pray with the community when she was with them, but she passed up every opportunity, spending the hours of prayer closeted with her ministers in secret conversation.

Reviewing these her concerns, Helewise tried to convince herself that their sum was surely enough to trouble anybody, even a nun who had risen to the rank of abbess and ought to be able to discipline herself to her duty and the pressing needs of her life of devotion. For this was her problem: try as she might to lose herself in prayer, to still her mind and open her consciousness so as to receive God's voice, she could not do so. She realised that she had previously taken for granted the ease with which she had formerly emptied herself for God; now this facility seemed to have abandoned her and she did not know what to do.

She had spent a long time with her confessor, Father Gilbert. He had given her but modest penance for the pre-occupations and the wandering thoughts that kept her mind too busy to hear the word of God; she would have preferred a heavier punishment and was secretly denying herself half of the daily food ration. But when the formality of confession was over and the two of them spoke as the affectionate friends that they were, he had been kind to her and said that he understood her predicament only too well, suggesting that it was something that afflicted many people in Holy Orders from time to time. His advice had been simple: keep trying, keep asking for God's help, and sooner or later He will hear you.

But she had not yet told Father Gilbert what it was that persistently and exclusively occupied her mind. He would have to know soon, she was well aware, if the sorry situation did not mend itself. She redoubled her efforts, spending so long on her knees that her work piled up on the heavy old oak table that served her as a desk and she had to labour long into the night to catch up. Then she would drag herself to bed, exhausted with the work and the emotional strain, hoping against hope that the dream would not come back.

But it did.

Not every night; sometimes she would wake refreshed and filled with hope. But then, the next night or the one after that, those powerful, emotional images would be there again and all the things that she was trying so hard not to think about – had no *right* to think about, having forfeited that dubious pleasure when she left the outside world and became a nun! – would come crashing back.

Now, sitting at her table with one of the Abbey's huge account ledgers before her, she sat deep in thought, distracted, studying the end of her stylus with unfocused eyes. Her feet were numb. It was a bright November day but the lack of cloud had allowed the cold to penetrate. Usually one of her nuns would slip into her chilly little room at the end of the cloister with a hot stone wrapped in flannel, but she had discreetly ordered them not to; suffering feet like ice was part of her self-imposed penance.

I must bring myself to speak to Father Gilbert again, she

told herself firmly. It is no good continuing to try on my own –
I need help. Perhaps if I tell him about my dreams and why it is
they disturb me so, he will talk it all over with me and rid me of
my problem.

She went on sitting there.

Yes. I'll go and see Father Gilbert straight away.

She did not move.

Then, with a gesture of despair, she flung down her stylus,
folded her arms across the great ledger and dropped her head.
In a fierce whisper, she muttered, 'Oh, how I *wish* Josse were
here!'

But Josse, as she well knew, was far away.

In the afternoon she begged a basket of dainties from Sister
Basilia in the refectory and set out for Father Gilbert's modest
little house. It was quite a walk and she threw herself into the
exercise, shoulders back, basket held firmly in one hand and
the other arm swinging powerfully. Her numb feet grew warm
and soon the heavy woollen cloak that Sister Euphemia in the
infirmary had insisted she wear began to make her sweat. As
she marched, puffing slightly, she rehearsed what she would
say to the Father.

After trying out several different approaches, each of which
sounded as contrived as the rest, she decided that the only
thing to do was to give him the unadorned truth.

Which, a short time later, blushing and hesitating in so
uncharacteristic a manner that Father Gilbert was gravely
concerned for her, she did.

Father Gilbert walked with her back to the Abbey. They had
been talking for what felt like hours and Helewise was feeling a
great deal of relief; after her initial awkwardness, the Father's
sympathetic ear had made her confession relatively easy. Filled
with a new hope that her dreams really would go away now

and leave her in peace to do her best in this life that she had chosen, she would have broken into a run from sheer happiness had Father Gilbert not been with her.

As they went in through the Abbey gates, Sister Ursel, the porteress, was greeting some visitors. They were a group of three: a young man, a pale-faced, nervy looking woman and a child of about a year. Father Gilbert went forward to greet them. It did not often happen that he was in the Abbey when visitors arrived and he intended to make the most of the opportunity to hear news of the world outside his own small domain. He turned to Helewise, saying, 'My lady Abbess, come and speak to the newcomers and—'

But the words died on his lips. Helewise, her face even paler than that of the young woman now being helped down from her horse, was staring with fixed eyes at the young man. He was staring right back and, for anyone sufficiently observant to notice, there was a remarkable similarity between the two pairs of eyes. Helewise put out a hand and began to say something. Then she fainted.

She came round quickly to find herself lying on the hard ground with her head on Sister Ursel's soft lap; the sister was stroking her superior's forehead with a gentle hand and murmuring anxiously, 'There, there, my lady!'

Struggling to sit up, feeling very foolish, Helewise accepted the helpful hands offered by Father Gilbert and Sister Ursel and got to her feet. The young man was still staring at her, concern written all over his handsome face. Before anyone else could speak, he strode over to stand before her, took hold of both her hands and said, 'Oh, God, Mother, you're not ill, are you?'

Mother. Oh, dear God, it was so long since she had been addressed like that in the real, waking world! Squeezing his hands so hard that he winced, she said, 'No, Leofgar, I am well.' And, opening her arms to him, she hugged her son in an embrace that she did not want to end.

There was at first no opportunity for private talk and Helewise had to hold back her impatience. But her mind now raced even faster in its search for explanations. She urgently needed to know why it should be, by what miracle it had happened, that this son of hers should now appear in the flesh when, for the past two weeks or more, she had been dreaming of him. Hearing in her sleep his calls for her help, so real in her dreaming mind that, awake, she had been able to think of nothing else.

The Hawkenlye community threw itself into a bustle of preparations to welcome this son of their Abbess. Helewise found a moment to slip away by herself into the Abbey church where she offered up a prayer of thanks. 'This was not the help that I expected, Lord,' she whispered, 'but it is a far better answer to my prayers than I could possibly have wished for.'

Putting aside for the moment any thoughts of just why her son should have chosen to seek out his mother after so many years, she gave herself up to gratitude that he had.

Helewise had known of her son's marriage to Rohaise Edgar, the daughter of a friend of the knight to whom the young Leofgar had been page and then squire before, on maturity, taking up his inheritance from his late father. Leofgar was the elder of Helewise's two sons and lived on the manor that had been Helewise's marital home. His brother Dominic, sixteen months his junior, was a soldier in Outremer and had not seen either his family or his homeland for eight years.

Leofgar and Rohaise had married when the groom was twenty-two and the bride just sixteen. Their child – a willowy little boy named Timus – had been born two years later; he was now aged fourteen months. These were the bare facts known to Helewise when, feeling as nervous as a girl, she allowed Leofgar to escort her from her room across to the refectory for the welcoming meal. As they took their seats at the head of the long table, Rohaise got up to greet Helewise. There was a strange expression on the girl's face, Helewise noticed, and she was still ashen. Perhaps that was her normal colour, although the rich brunette hair neatly dressed beneath the small veil and the dark brown eyes – huge, and circled in grey as if the girl did not sleep – made this seem unlikely. The deep russet shade of her gown seemed to increase the pallor. Trying to put her concern out of her mind, Helewise responded to her daughter-in-law's politely formal words and, putting both arms on the girl's thin shoulders, raised her up from her deep bow of reverence.

They sat down to eat and then, as Helewise had been secretly longing to do, she took her grandson on to her lap and began to make his acquaintance.

Quite early in the evening, Rohaise asked if she might take Timus to settle him for the night, adding that she would like to retire too, if that was acceptable. Assuring her that it was, Helewise gave orders for the girl and the baby to be shown to the guest accommodation that had been prepared for them.

As if by tacit agreement, the members of the Hawkenlye community quietly faded away and Helewise and her son were left on their own. There was a half-full jug of mulled wine left over from the meal and Helewise, having summoned Sister Basilia to pick it up and bring two clean mugs, led Leofgar out of the refectory and along to her own little room. Silently thanking whichever nun had foreseen this event and placed a small brazier in the room, Helewise pulled out the visitors' stool and set it before her table. Dismissing Sister Basilia, who bowed and tactfully retreated, closing the door behind her, Helewise poured wine into the two cups then, seating herself in her throne-like chair, said, 'Now, Leofgar. Tell me why you are here.'

Watching him intently, she saw his brief smile, there and gone in a flash. 'What is it?' she demanded.

'Oh – this is so strange,' he replied. 'I haven't seen you for years but you're just the same. Anyone else's mother might have asked other things in the first private moment with her son. How are you? How are things at the Old Manor and are you managing all right? Are you happy?' Briefly his face clouded, then, with an effort, he grinned. 'It's only my beloved mother who goes straight to the point and demands to be told the purpose of my visit.'

'It does not mean that I am not eager to ask all the other questions,' she countered swiftly. 'We learn here to be brief, son. It is simply that I have asked the crucial question first.'

He nodded. 'Yes. I see.' Then, drawing a deep breath, 'Rohaise is not herself and has not been so, in truth, since Timus was born. At first she was euphoric – she greatly feared giving birth and was overcome by her relief at having survived the delivery. But soon she changed. She is fearful all the time, she worries that she is not a good mother; she frets when Timus is out of her sight but is impatient with him when he is at her side. She does not sleep well and I feel that she is deeply unhappy, for she weeps constantly and finds no joy even in the brightest day. And we—' He stopped. Then, with a quick glance at Helewise, he lowered his head and muttered, 'She has turned away from me because she fears another pregnancy.'

Helewise, shocked to her core that her direct question had received such a brutally frank answer, was momentarily speechless. Then, feeling the waves of need pouring out of her son and coming straight at her, she knew she must respond. Not ready to comment on what Leofgar had poured out, she said, 'And the little boy, Timus? He is well?'

'He—' Leofgar hesitated. 'Yes, for the most part. He—' Again he stopped and when he finally spoke, Helewise was quite certain that what he said was not the first response that had come to his mind. 'He's overly timid at times and he clings.'

'Clings?'

'Yes.' Leofgar shifted impatiently on the small stool. 'He refuses to let go of my hand, or he'll bury his face in his mother's skirts.'

'He's little more than a baby,' Helewise said gently.

'I know! You asked me, so I'm telling you!'

Nineteen years fell away and Helewise was in the parlour of the Old Manor, her former home, face to face with a furious, indignant six-year-old trying to evade a justified punishment for having kicked a sharp-edged stone at his little brother. She had demanded furiously why Dominic's cheek was bleeding and Leofgar had said, because the stone hit him. When she had cried out, oh, how can you confess such a thing? he had replied with those exact words: *you asked me so I'm telling you.*

But that was then, she thought, a variety of emotions coursing powerfully through her. And this is now.

She said carefully, 'What help do you ask of us?'

She could plainly see the relief in his face; it was as if, she thought, he had expected to be ordered to give more explanation and was very glad that this was not the case.

'We who live out in the world hear tell of the Hawkenlye nuns and monks and always the tales are good,' he said quietly. 'I am proud that my own mother heads the community and I am happy each time I hear your name spoken.'

His eyes met hers and she inclined her head, acknowledging his compliment. 'I am fortunate in my hardworking and devoted nuns and in my monks who selflessly tend those who come to take the cure here,' she said. 'If indeed we have achieved a sound reputation, then it is to them that the credit is due.'

'You're the chief, though,' he observed.

'I know, but—' No. It was not the moment to go into that. 'So, you believe from what you hear of us that we can help you?'

'You must,' he muttered, 'you're my only hope.'

She was horrified at his desolate tone. 'You forget God,' she said quietly. 'Have you not asked God's help?'

'I have. I've done what our priest tells me to do and I've prayed till I can pray no more, and when no help comes he just says it's because my faith is insufficient and if I really believed God can do it, I could raise your table here without moving a hair.'

'Oh, dear.' Yes, Helewise thought, I've heard that argument many times before. She tried to suppress the reaction that it had scarcely been either appropriate or helpful in her son's case.

He was gazing intently at her table as if he were indeed trying to move it by faith alone. With a smile she said, 'Give it up, Leofgar. I don't believe a caring God concerns himself with jumping tables and I'm quite sure he is more interested in all the other ways in which we demonstrate our love for him.'

Leofgar returned her smile. 'I wasn't trying to move it, I was just thinking that I recognised it.'

'You do,' she said shortly. 'It used to stand in the long hall at the Old Manor and it had been in your father's family for generations. By rights I suppose it should be yours but actually I'm rather attached to it myself.'

'You keep it, Mother, I don't want it!'

He spoke fervently, and she wondered why. 'Do you not care for it?'

He grinned. 'Too many memories of being taught my lessons. That priest who used to come to instruct Dominic and me had a habit of rapping our knuckles with a stick.'

'No doubt you deserved it.' Helewise had vivid memories of

just what a task the poor priest had had to engage Leofgar and Dominic's attention, especially on bright days when their hounds used to sit outside the door and howl for their young masters to come out and take them hunting.

Leofgar had got to his feet and was peering closely at one corner of the big table. With a smile, he pointed and she could see two initials faintly carved, an L and a D. Funny, she thought, I've sat staring at this table all these years and never noticed that my naughty sons marked it . . .

But these happy reminiscences were dangerous, for her at least, and in any case, presumably nothing to do with the reason why her son had sought her out. 'About Rohaise,' she said gently, and instantly the smile left Leofgar's face. 'Would you like our infirmarer to talk to her? Sister Euphemia is wise and very experienced, but she is also kind and loving. She may be able to help.'

Leofgar looked as if he thought that was a forlorn hope. 'Thank you, Mother,' he said politely, if not very enthusiastically, 'that would be good. Maybe Rohaise would open her heart to someone whose opinion she respected.'

Which suggests, Helewise thought but did not say, that she has neither opened her heart to nor respects you, her husband. And that, she discovered, hurt. She put out her hand and took his. 'Sister Euphemia knows a great deal about women and their babies,' she said encouragingly. 'She was a midwife before she was a nun and I often think that she shows her most skilful and devoted face to sickly infants and troubled young mothers. Whatever ails your Rohaise, if anyone has ever experienced anything similar and can offer help, then it is Sister Euphemia.'

Leofgar said quickly, 'Timus is not sickly, he's—' But yet again he did not continue; whatever he feared might be wrong with his son, clearly he was not ready to share it with his mother.

We are getting nowhere with this discussion, Helewise thought. It is time to conclude our talk and make a decision, before Leofgar's distress becomes more than he can cope with.

'It is late,' she said, getting to her feet. 'Let us find our way to our beds and seek the comfort of sleep.' She placed her hands on her son's head and added softly, 'I shall pray for you and for Rohaise, that the night brings you rest and the morning, hope. God bless you, son, and keep you safe.'

Briefly Leofgar closed his eyes to receive her blessing. Then, opening them, he said suddenly, 'Mother, why did you faint when you saw it was me? You said you're not sick, so was it just the surprise?'

She laughed. 'Son, I very rarely faint and certainly do not do so when faced with a surprise, even one as extraordinary as seeing my son after so long. No, it wasn't that.'

'What was it, then?'

She looked into his wide grey eyes and almost seemed to see in them a reflection of her own. 'In fact it really was no surprise.' She made herself give a light laugh, as if to suggest that she did not speak seriously. 'You see, son, I have been dreaming. When you arrived, I was on my way back here with our priest, with whom I had just had a long and helpful talk during which I described those dreams in some detail.'

She paused, trying to make sense of something illogical. He said, 'Go on, Mother. Describe them to me, too.'

'Oh. Yes, very well. I kept seeing the same scene and it has been affecting me so much that during the day I have not been capable of keeping my mind where it belongs, on my work and on my prayers. That's why I talked it over in such depth with Father Gilbert, because I realised I was wasting God's time all the while I was closed to his voice.'

With an impatient sigh, Leofgar said, '*What* did you dream?'

Her eyes on his, she said, 'I dreamed of you. You were a

child again and you were calling me, over and over again. You desperately needed my help and I could not reach you to give it.'

Her words must have affected him for he lowered his head so that she would not see his face. Then, his voice tight with emotion, he said, 'I do need you. I kept thinking about you and once or twice when – well, when things were really bad, I would call out to you.' Raising his head again, he whispered, 'I can't believe you heard me!'

'I did,' she assured him. 'And I shall do all that is in my power for you and your Rohaise. We will help you, Leofgar. I promise you that.'

Then he was in her arms and at long last she could provide the wordless, loving comfort she had so yearned to give him.

2

Josse d'Acquin was on his way home. The November day was fine – bright sunshine sparkled off the frost and the ground was dry and good for riding – and Horace, his horse, who was fresh and well rested, felt eager and full of energy. But Josse was depressed, exhausted and too low in spirit to appreciate the beauty of England in the late autumn.

He had spent the past few weeks in the East Anglian port of Orford, having received a peremptory summons to hasten there with all speed on a mission of vital importance. The messenger had enjoyed being mysterious – when Josse had pressed him for details, he had smugly laid a grubby forefinger to the side of his large nose and shaken his head, murmuring just loud enough for Josse to hear that he was sworn to secrecy and would not break his oath if his very life depended on it – but in fact there was little need for the drama because Josse knew full well why they had sent for him.

How, indeed, could the matter be secret, when it concerned the entire population of England?

King Richard was a prisoner of the Holy Roman Emperor, Henri VI, and he would be held captive until his loyal subjects stumped up a ransom of 150,000 marks, not to mention the two hundred hostages who would have to give up their free-dom in return for that of the King. The King's elderly but vital mother, Queen Eleanor, had thrown herself into organising the collection of the ransom – there had now been three levies and still the money fell woefully short of the required sum –

and the people of England had given till they could give no
more. The first fine fervour of generosity had quickly faded;
many had not felt it at all and those who had and who had
unquestioningly given as much as they could were now
beginning to regret it. The whole business was fraught with
difficulties: the quick-witted, the crafty and the downright
dishonest had evaded the earlier levies, and some of the
collectors had proved less than trustworthy and had run off
with what they collected. It was rumoured that King Richard
was beside himself, frustrated to the very edge of sanity and
driven to composing mournful self-pitying poems and miserable songs bemoaning his fate.

By October, 100,000 marks had been amassed and locked
securely away in huge iron-bound chests stored, under heavy
guard, in the crypt of St Paul's Cathedral. When the Emper-
or's envoys arrived in London to check on progress, they were
sumptuously entertained and then sent on their way, the
money solemnly handed over into their charge. Richard, with
freedom beckoning, wrote to his mother commanding her to
meet the remaining terms of the ransom and bring the rest of
the money and the hostages to the Emperor in person; he
commanded that Walter of Coutances, the head of the council
of regency, accompany her. They were, he ordered, to present
the most magnificent spectacle that they could muster; the
captive King, after all, had a point to prove and a reputation to
repair.

The Emperor had indicated that, provided all the terms of
the ransom were met in full, he *might* be prepared to release his
prisoner on 17th January next.

Queen Eleanor, on receipt of her son's command, had
wasted no time in making her preparations. An impressive
fleet was assembled in the ports of Orford, Dunwich and
Ipswich and, as money, treasures, hostages and the King's
regalia were steadily transported east ready for shipment, she

ordered a guard of reliable and steadfast King's men whose chief duty was to ensure the safety of the various valuables while they remained on England's soil.

One of those sturdy men was Josse.

The duty had been frustrating, exhausting and fraught with difficulty. The King might be absent but it seemed to those working so desperately on his behalf that his angry, restless spirit watched over them, always hurrying them, always ready with a harsh word and an impatient cuff across the face when there were mistakes and delays. Josse was billeted at Orford Castle, an extraordinary building put up by Richard's father, King Henry II, who had taken pride in its strange eighteen-sided shape and its three stout buttressing towers. The old king, Josse reflected one bitter morning when the harsh east wind carried horizontal drops of spiteful, freezing sleet, never had to stand outside his precious castle for three hours checking the contents of an apparently endless cart train.

He could have borne the cold, the frustration and the inefficiency; he could even have ameliorated the last two, had he had the heart. But, like everyone else, his enthusiasm had waned. The people of England had to ransom their King and bring him home, aye, no mistake about their duty there. But they didn't have to *like* it.

Josse was embarrassed now by the fervour with which he had initially clamoured for King Richard's release. He seemed to hear his own voice railing at his uncle, crying out against the terrible humiliation of the King of England being walled up in a foul dungeon, and he heard his uncle's anguished reply: *it is not to be borne!* But that was then, when the outrage was news and did not as yet have a price upon it. Now, nearly a year later, Richard's subjects knew just what it was costing them to get him back and were privately wondering if he was worth it. What's he ever done for us? people muttered, quite openly, as if they didn't care who heard. Comes a-hurrying over four years ago for his coronation, fills his coffers with England's wealth then off he goes on crusade, and *that* was a waste of time and money if ever there was one since the Lionheart didn't capture the Holy City as he'd promised. Didn't so much as set foot in it, so they said, but sat on his horse looking down on Jerusalem and crying his eyes out like a child denied a plaything because God hadn't seen fit to allow him to deliver the city from His enemies.

Then, to cap it all, King Richard goes and gets himself captured, would you believe it, by some upstart duke who promptly hands him over to the Emperor! To the people of England, it was almost inconceivable that their King, who had set off with such a force of arms that it had taken thousands of ships to carry everything (the tale had grown in the telling), could have been taken against his will. What of all his soldiers? What of those companies of heavily armed men guarding him? Couldn't they have prevented this disaster that was making beggars of everyone? Josse could have explained to them, had he been of a mind, that the King had been separated from his main force of arms and was virtually undefended; that, having been shipwrecked south of Trieste on his way home from Acre, he'd had little choice but to opt for the overland route, despite the fact that it took him into the territory of his mortal enemy, Duke Leopold of Austria, where his merchant's disguise had been penetrated and his capture had swiftly ensued.

But Josse was as tired and dispirited as everyone else and he didn't bother.

Now, his guard duty done – he had been relieved by a company of eager knights whose youth and innocence made him feel very old – Josse was heading for home. He thought – he *hoped* – that it was merely a product of his state of mind, but in reality he felt far from well. His throat ached, he had a congestion in his chest that produced a constant, phlegmy cough, and his limbs ached. Horace plodded steadily along beneath him, well-behaved and calm, and Josse sat in the saddle and dozed.

He made a couple of overnight stops, then crossed the Thames estuary and went on with his journey. He still felt ill; a concerned serving woman in a tavern outside Colchester had given him a hot drink which she said would ease his cough but instead it had made him vomit, which had caused his throat to hurt even more. Riding miserably towards the North Downs, he had an unexpectedly cheering thought: he would not go home to New Winnowlands; he would turn aside and instead go to Hawkenlye Abbey. The infirmarer there was an old friend and he had more faith in her healing powers than in anyone else's on Earth. She would fuss over him, tuck him up in a cot with clean sheets and a hot stone at his feet, cover him with warm woollen blankets and spoon medicines and remedies into his mouth. Her nursing nuns would glide calmly up and down the long infirmary, giving him serene and caring smiles and occasionally pausing to put a cool white hand on his hot forehead, and he would lie there being looked after until he felt better. Clucking to Horace, he kicked the big horse into a canter and hastened on his way.

The solicitude with which he was received at Hawkenlye was all that he had envisaged. Sister Euphemia, reaching up to place the envisioned cool hand on his forehead, studied him briefly and then gave a quick nod. She summoned a nursing nun – to Josse's delight it was young Sister Caliste, a favourite of his – and gave orders for him to be put to bed at the far end of the infirmary 'where it's more peaceful'. However, given the sharp look that she gave him when, amid his effusive thanks, he broke off to cough, he reckoned that his placement away from others had more to do with her concern that everybody else currently sick at Hawkenlye Abbey would not end up coughing too.

It was odd, he mused, following Sister Caliste's slim, up-right form down the long ward, how some sicknesses could pass from one person to another. Things like a headache or the pain of a sprained wrist, for example, you kept to yourself, but coughs, fevers and inflammations of the lungs seemed to jump from body to body as if some malign and invisible spirit bore them through the air . . .

They had reached the curtained-off recess where he was to be cared for. Sister Caliste tactfully turned her back while he took off his heavy cloak and slipped out of his tunic, shirt and hose and, dressed only in his thin undershirt, crawled into bed. The sheets were as cool on his hot skin as he had dreamed they would be and he just knew that as soon as his blood cooled down and the shivers began, Sister Caliste would return to cover him with a warm blanket. With a smile she disappeared between the curtains, but presently she returned and made him drink a concoction that tasted almost as bad as that of the Colchester serving woman. The only difference was, he re-flected as at last he gave in to sleep, was that the Hawkenlye infirmarer's medicine worked the other way round: it didn't make him vomit and it did stop his cough.

He slept, dreamed and dozed the day away. Sister Caliste came to see him briefly now and again, once bringing him some savoury broth and a couple of times giving him more of the medicinal draught, although he detected that the subse-quent doses had been watered down and were less potent. Once he opened his eyes and thought he saw the Abbess's face staring down at him but it could have been a dream; the Abbess seemed to feature quite regularly in his dreams. Later, when it was dark, he was given a cool drink and someone – he thought it was Sister Euphemia – said a prayer over him whose main point appeared to be to ask God and His angels to watch over Josse until the morning. Then, with that most comforting thought in mind, he slept again, this time long, deep and dreamlessly, and he did not wake up until morning.

He realised straight away that he felt better. Much better, in fact; the heat in his skin had gone and so had the sore throat. He tried an experimental cough and managed to produce only a small amount of phlegm. Aye, he was on the mend, no doubt about it. He noticed that he was very hungry and, as if she had been waiting outside the curtains for him to appreciate this fact, Sister Caliste appeared bearing a bowl of porridge and a cool drink.

As the infirmarer had done the previous day, she put her hand on his forehead. Smiling, she said, 'Your fever has passed for the time being, Sir Josse, although it may return later in the day, that being the way of fevers.'

'I feel quite well,' he assured her. 'I'd like to—'

'Get up?' She smiled again.

'You have learned to read men's minds in the course of your nursing training, Sister,' he observed.

'Oh, no. Sister Euphemia has that talent, but not I. If I guess right, it is only because I learn through constant repetition. Sir Josse, nine people out of ten want to get up the first morning they wake to find their fever gone.'

'But you do not let them.' He was depressingly sure of it.

'No,' she agreed, taking the empty porridge bowl from him and straightening his sheet and blanket, 'because if we were to do so, they would spend a happy hour or two believing themselves recovered, then come creeping back to us with their hot, aching heads in their hands and feeling more ill than they were in the first place.'

'Oh.'

His mournful monosyllable made her smile again. 'Do not worry,' she whispered, putting her sweet mouth close to his ear, 'I think I may safely assure you that you'll be up and about tomorrow.'

Then, with the suggestion of a wink that, in a fully professed nun, was highly daring, she was gone.

Sister Euphemia came to have a thorough look at him later in the morning, ordering him to open his mouth widely so that she could look down his throat, making him give a cough or two, putting her ear to his chest to listen to his breathing and smoothing the hair back from his forehead with her hand as she tested him for fever. What she observed must have reassured her for she allowed his curtains to be drawn back. He would have liked her to stay and talk to him – as yet he had not even begun to catch up on what had been happening in the Abbey since his last visit – but she seemed preoccupied and he guessed she had too much to do to waste her time gossiping with him. With a nod of approval, she left him.

Now that he was able to observe the comings and goings in the main body of the infirmary, time passed far more quickly and interestingly and he found that being confined to bed when he felt well was not so bad after all. He was puzzled, though, because although both the infirmarer and Sister Caliste had given the strong impression that they were very busy and had their minds on other things, it did not appear that there were all that many patients in the infirmary needing their care. As always, there were plenty of nursing nuns calmly going about their duties and Josse would have thought that this was in fact a relatively quiet time. He firmly squashed the small, peeved voice that said, one of those nuns ought surely to be able to spare a moment of her time for me . . .

As the morning wore away – he had earlier watched the nuns troop out for Tierce and now they were coming back from Sext – he wondered how soon he might see the Abbess. He believed, although he did not know for certain, that it was her custom to visit the infirmary at least once each day, probably more often if there were very sick patients who needed the comfort of her presence. She does not spare herself, he thought, she—

There was a small stirring at the infirmary door; three nursing nuns paused in their work to bow and an old woman's quavery voice called out from a bed just beyond the entrance, 'God bless you, my lady!'

The Abbess Helewise had arrived to visit the sick.

Josse waited patiently for some time for his turn. The Abbess had worked her way steadily up the long ward in his general direction, stopping to speak to what patients there were, but then, when it seemed she must surely come on to him, she turned and went back the way she had come, striding down the room and disappearing into a curtained recess like the one in which Josse lay but at the far end of the infirmary.

She was in there for some time.

Then at last she emerged and marched even more swiftly back up the ward and straight to his bedside. She took his hands in hers, raised one of them to touch it briefly to her cheek and said, 'Sir Josse, forgive me that I come to you last. There were pressing calls I had to make and I was reassured this morning that you are much better.'

'No need for apologies, my lady,' he replied, managing to give her hand a squeeze before she withdrew it, 'for as you say I am no longer sick and others must take precedence.'

'Not in the least!' She looked quite shocked, the grey eyes widening. 'I saved my visit to you until last so that I would not have to hasten away.'

Feeling himself grin with pleasure like a boy given an unexpected and undeserved treat, Josse said, 'Then pull up that stool, my lady, and let us catch up with one another's news.'

She insisted that he speak first and so he told her all about the summons to Orford and the tedium of guarding the ransom, the miserable, apprehensive hostages and the King's treasures. She was the only person on Earth to whom he would have confessed his disenchantment with the whole business of Richard and his confounded ransom. His impulse to confide was justified; as soon as he had spoken – lowering his voice to a conspiratorial mutter – she whispered back that she felt exactly the same and was filled with compassion for the people, especially the poor, who, because of their sovereign's carelessness in allowing himself to be captured, were having such a struggle to buy back his freedom.

They stared at each other and he had the feeling that she was as grateful as he for a trusted friend to whom it was possible to speak the truth. Confirming his suspicion, she said quietly, 'What a relief, Sir Josse, to stop the pretence, even though but briefly; I fear it must be only for this moment.'

'Indeed, my lady, and in truth we must not repeat these words.'

'Will the ransom be sufficient?' she asked.

He sighed. 'They say the sum falls short of the demand, but the Emperor speaks of a release date so we can only hope that he will settle for what is on offer.'

'It will be better than nothing,' she said thoughtfully.

'Aye, and we'll all breathe more easily if we know the deal is done and the King is on his way home.'

'It will be a great weight off all our minds,' she agreed, and he knew without asking that she referred not to having King Richard back in England but to the definite cessation of the alarming, ruinous levies.

There was silence between them for a time, the sort of easy silence that old friends fall into when they have finished discussing one topic and are not quite ready for the next. Then he said, 'What of life at Hawkenlye, my lady? I observe for myself that there are not too many patients here in the infirmary, yet for all that there is an air of preoccupation among the nuns, as if something worries them.'

She shot him a glance. Then, after a short pause, said, 'All is well with us here, Sir Josse, and I thank you for the enquiry. My nuns and monks are busy, as always, but that is what they are here for. We have fewer pilgrims coming to take the holy water in the Vale, but that is on account of the cold and not, I am sure, because our shrine loses its attraction. Those who do brave the winter weather are greeted with extra rations of food and the luxury of a small fire at night. And, of course, the kind attentions of Brother Firmin and his companions. Otherwise' – there was a vaguely panicky look in her face as she cast around for a way to complete her brief account – 'otherwise, as I said, all is well.'

He waited. After a moment, she looked up and met his eyes. Very gently he said, 'Now why not tell me the truth?'

3

She wondered why she had ever thought she would not confide in him; hadn't Josse been the one person she had so much wanted to talk to when her dreams had troubled her so? Although her conscience still frowned at her inability to keep thoughts of her son and his family's problems from intruding when her mind should be on greater things, she did not think it would be *wrong* to confide in Josse. She had, after all, prayed for God's help in almost the same moment as she had wished for Josse's presence, so maybe a part of God's help had come in the form of sending him.

Anyway, as soon as Josse spoke those words – so kindly, with such compassion for her in his brown eyes – she was lost.

'You perceive what has not been put into words for you, Sir Josse,' she said. 'I ought not to burden you with my private concerns when you are so poorly but—'

'Private concerns?' he snapped, interrupting her. 'Please, tell me straight away, my lady, what ails you?'

'I am well, Josse,' she said, putting her hand briefly on his. 'Better than you!' She tried to make a small joke.

'Nothing much wrong with me,' he said gruffly. 'Sister Euphemia herself drew back the curtains which isolated me from everyone else and Sister Caliste assures me I'll be on my feet tomorrow.' He glared at her, but the fierce expression was denied by the tenderness in his eyes. 'Now, what is the matter with you?'

'It's not me, it's my son.'

His eyebrows shot up. 'Your son?'

'Yes. You knew, I believe, that I was a wife and a mother before I came to Hawkenlye?'

'Aye, my lady. I knew. But—' He shrugged, as if what he was thinking could not be put easily into words.

She did it for him. 'But you cannot now imagine that one in my position was ever other than you now perceive her?'

He muttered something that sounded like *all too easily* but she must have been mistaken.

Wishing only to move the conversation on and spare them both further awkwardness – for he was giving a very good impression of an embarrassed man and her own composure was shaky – she said hastily, 'Actually the problem really lies with my son's wife, but such is his love for her that her problem is his, if you see what I mean.'

'I do. Please, go on, my lady.'

'They were married three years past and in September of last year, Rohaise gave birth to their son, whose name is Timus. According to Leofgar – my son – Rohaise has suffered in a variety of ways since the birth.' Noticing that Josse was looking even more embarrassed, she said frankly, 'Sir Josse, I do not speak of that sort of problem. The illness, if that is what it is, is of poor Rohaise's mind.'

Josse had such an open face, she reflected, watching him with amusement despite the seriousness of the subject under discussion; when she reassured him that they were not going to have to talk about some bodily malfunction of Rohaise's but, rather, a mental one, relief had swept through him, swiftly displaced by guilt that he should feel pleased that Rohaise's difficulty probably amounted to something a lot more serious than some temporary disorder in her reproductive organs.

'I am sorry for her,' he said as the flush faded from his cheeks. 'Sorry for all of you. She has seen Sister Euphemia?'

'Indeed.' Helewise nodded in the direction of the long

infirmary ward. 'Rohaise was exhausted after the journey and did not sleep well last night, so Sister Euphemia has brought her in here and is keeping her under observation. She – Sister Euphemia – had a long talk with the girl this morning and then gave her a sleeping draught.'

'The girl is in the recess down there?'

'Yes.'

He nodded. 'And you went to see her just now.'

'I did,' she agreed. 'She was deeply asleep and did not stir while Sister Euphemia quietly told me of their earlier discussion.'

'Does the infirmarer detect the nature of this illness of the head?'

She paused, collecting her thoughts. What Sister Euphemia had told her was still too fresh in her mind for her to have digested it. I shall share it with Josse, she decided, and see what he makes of it.

'Sister Euphemia has had many years' experience of new mothers,' she said, 'and has what can only be a divinely bestowed ability to gain a young woman's confidence. She did not tell me the full story that Rohaise told her, but she assured me that what she did pass on formed the most important elements. Oh, Sir Josse, poor Rohaise! She has not smiled since Timus was six weeks old!'

'Why? What happened?'

It was an obvious question but had no clear answer. 'Rohaise cannot say. She began to feel anxious about almost every facet of the baby's well-being, doubting her own ability to protect him, to look after him, to love him, in short to mother him adequately. She started to believe that her milk would poison him and, despite the fact that she had milk in plenty and had previously been enjoying feeding him, she engaged a wet nurse and bound up her breasts to stop the milk.'

'That is not unusual, is it?' Josse asked.

'No, not at all. It is Rohaise's reason for her action that is unusual. And that isn't all,' she hurried on. 'Sister Euphemia could get little more out of her, for she appears highly suspicious of us, as if she fears we are testing her fitness to be a mother. But what she did say before she fell back into her silence – she hardly speaks at all, Sir Josse! – was that she is in constant terror of someone coming to take Timus away from her.'

'Has she any reason to think they will?'

'I do not know. I can't imagine that any decent soul would make such a threat but I will ask my son. He is with Rohaise at the moment, sitting beside her with Timus on his lap watching her as she sleeps, but I have asked him to come along to meet you presently.'

'I look forward to that meeting with pleasure.' He spoke courteously but he was frowning, apparently thinking hard. Then he said, 'Does Sister Euphemia recognise the symptoms of whatever it is that affects Rohaise?'

Helewise felt herself smile. 'Yes. I am wrong, I'm sure, to take such comfort in her words, for in truth she urged me not to and said there was no certainty that she guesses aright. But she did admit that she had observed such irrational fears and such ongoing lowness of spirit in other mothers.'

'Did those other mothers recover their serenity?'

Trust Josse, she thought, to put the arrow in the bull's eye. 'Sometimes,' she said. It was the very word that Sister Euphemia had used.

As if he too found it unpromising, Josse just said, 'Oh.' Then, after a pause, he said, 'In summary, then, my lady, your son has brought his wife here to Hawkenlye because she is unwell.' He hesitated, as though not sure how best to speak his thoughts. Then he went on, 'Forgive me if I speak too bluntly, my lady, but is it, would you say, Hawkenlye's great reputation as a centre of healing that draws him rather than the identity of the person who is its Abbess?'

It was a roundabout way of asking something that she had already asked herself. Modesty ordered that she meekly agree with him and say, *Oh, of course it's because of our healers, he didn't come here with any wish to see me!* But modesty had never been her greatest strength and when, as in this case, it fought with maternal emotion, there could only be one winner.

Staring down at her hands, lying still and folded in her lap, she said, 'He was calling for me, Josse. I heard him in my dreams and I was so very troubled because hearing my son's voice, even after so many years, took me straight back to my previous life. I felt so wretched when I could not concentrate on those things that make up my present existence, but I could not help myself. I'm a nun!' she said in an angry hiss. 'I'm Abbess here and all these people depend on me! I've no business returning to the sentiments of my past, it is surely wrong!'

Apparently ignoring her little outburst, he said, his voice low and full of warmth, 'Did you verify that your son really did call out to you in his trouble?'

She found that she dared not risk speaking so she just nodded.

After a time Josse said, 'You once said to me, my lady, at a time when I felt myself to have been betrayed and was greatly distressed, that the act of childbirth turns a wife into a mother and there is no going back.'

She gave a small gasp; she remembered the conversation very well, and also the tense and emotional circumstances under which it had occurred. She whispered, 'Yes.'

In the same gentle tone, he said, 'Your words gave me great comfort then, Helewise. Hear them again, apply them to yourself and take the same comfort, for I am quite sure that God wouldn't have bestowed on the world the immeasurable gift of maternal love had He not intended his children to benefit from it.'

She felt tears spill from her eyes. Trying to be discreet, she turned her head so that her coif hid her face while she wiped them away.

Josse said, far too bracingly, 'And what of the little boy? Timus, was it?'

An absurd chuckle almost broke from her at the obvious distracting ploy. But then she thought about her grandson and no longer felt like laughing. 'He is too quiet,' she said. 'He was never very vocal, my son says, but now he makes no attempt at speech.'

'Is that not normal in so young a child?' Josse looked as if he were trying to recall if it was; no doubt, she thought, he was envisaging all those nephews and nieces of his.

'Children speak when they are ready and in some it is sooner than in others,' she replied. 'For sure, I never knew a child to speak proper words much before a year and a half to two years. But most little ones try out their voices, Sir Josse! They make sounds and begin to string them together and sometimes they make up what sounds like a language of their own, although of course it is nothing but nonsense.'

A vivid picture came powerfully into her head. She tried to dismiss it.

'What of your own boys?' Josse was saying. 'I ask because I'm thinking that these matters of how soon a child walks and talks may be similar in the father and his son.'

Oh, he was trying to help and she was more than grateful to him, but his innocent question was making those remembered images from so long ago so lifelike that she could smell the sweet lilac blossom and feel the tiny hands clutching hers. 'My sons were always noisy, the pair of them,' she said. She noticed absently that she sounded as if there were something con-

stricting her throat. 'Dominic spoke early, but he had his
talkative elder brother to copy.'

'And Leofgar?'

She could no longer fight her memories. 'It was Leofgar of
whom I was thinking when I spoke of the nonsense language,'
she said. 'He was so eager to speak that he even made sounds
in his sleep. Ivo claimed he was snoring but I said he was trying
to communicate with us. Oh, and he used to make every other
sort of sound, too – he'd laugh at almost anything, he was such
a sunny, cheerful child.'

The nun that she now was commanded *enough*, and
abruptly she stopped.

As if he were reluctant to bring her from the happy past to
the distressing present, Josse waited a moment before he
spoke. Then he said, 'What does Sister Euphemia have to
say about your son's child?'

She went back to studying her hands. 'She says he is afraid.'
She looked up hastily and met his compassionate face. 'And
before you ask, afraid of what, I have no idea!' Then she shot
to her feet and said, 'Wait here. I will fetch Leofgar and the
child and you can judge for yourself.'

Josse watched her tall figure stride away down the infirmary.
He lay back on his pillows, momentarily exhausted by the
tension. She's feeling very guilty because she's putting a
mother's natural instinct to care for and help her child above
her duty as a nun, he thought, trying to make sense of it all,
and in addition to that she's frantic with worry about her
daughter-in-law's fragile mental state and her grandson's
dumbness.

Great God, he reflected, no wonder she's so distressed.

He was just making a solemn promise to himself that he
would do all that he could to help her when he saw her coming
back. Now there was a tall young man walking beside her,

carrying a small child dressed in a short blue tunic and thick hose.

As they approached, he wondered if anyone else had had the same thought: that these three people were so alike that, even had you not known them, you would have guessed that the same blood just had to run in their veins. Leofgar was taller than his mother but shared her broad shoulders and her upright bearing; his hair was dark (and Josse knew full well that Helewise's was reddish-fair) and his skin had the same golden glow. The little boy's colouring was light, like his grandmother's, and the well-shaped mouth, although now set in a solemn line, looked as if it were made for smiles and laughter.

What pointed them out as close relatives, though, was their eyes.

Struggling to sit up, Josse held out a hand to this sad man who was the son of his dearest friend and said, 'I am in my infirmary bed and you are troubled, young Leofgar. This is no time for lengthy and formal introductions – I shall only say that I'm Josse and I'm delighted to meet you.'

Amusement filled Leofgar's eyes – making him look even more like his mother – and, taking Josse's hand, he said, 'The delight is all mine, sir. My mother has told me all about you.'

Not all, Josse hoped. That would be too much for anyone to absorb in a few hours and anyway he fervently hoped that the tenderest parts of *all* remained his own secret.

'And this is Timus?' Josse turned to look at the child.

'Yes. Timus, say hello to Sir Josse,' Leofgar commanded.

But the little boy was timid and hid his face in his father's tunic, turning his head only a fraction so he could look at Josse out of the corner of his eye.

Josse remembered a trick that had once amused one of his nephews. Making sure that Timus was still looking at him, he raised both hands and, with an expression of deep concentration, pretended to wrench off his left thumb, tucking it down into the palm of that hand. Then he put his right hand behind his left and, sticking up the thumb, slid it up and down as if it were the detached left thumb.

Timus had come out of hiding now and was openly staring, eyes wide with fascination. Then, as Josse looked with exaggerated and horrified amazement at his wayward thumb, suddenly the boy laughed.

The sound was so sweet and so infectious that, almost without realising it, the three adults began to laugh too. But then Leofgar said, 'You are a magician, Sir Josse. That is, I believe, the first time in a week that my son has laughed.'

Josse gave him a vague grin; he was busy with the next trick. As once more he held up his hands, Timus struggled round in his father's arms to get a better view; Leofgar, with a raised eyebrow at Josse, who nodded, carefully placed the child down on Josse's bed. Josse caught Timus's eye and said softly, 'Watch.'

Frowning and narrowing his eyes as if he were having trouble seeing, Josse threaded an imaginary needle. Then, wincing in pretend pain, he stuck the imaginary needle through each of the fingers of his left hand, starting with the little one and ending with the thumb. He gave the invisible thread a twitch, which brought all his fingers snapping together, then, pushing hard and going 'Ouch!', he pretended to push the needle into his left ear and pull it out of his right. Then, as if a thread really did run from his bound left hand through his head to his right one, he pulled his right hand down and simultaneously raised his left, repeating the manoeuvre several times and beaming broadly in triumph.

Timus, who had been watching open-mouthed, clumsily copied the gesture. Then, pointing at Josse, who had now stopped, he said quite clearly, 'More!'

Josse was smiling again, and one glance at Helewise and her son – whose mouths had dropped open just like Timus's entranced by the trick – made him laugh aloud. 'This is the child who does not speak?' he said quietly; Timus was kneeling on his lap now and trying clumsily to make Josse's hands do the trick again. Looking down at him, he added, 'Well, whatever ails him that makes him opt for silence, it is not because he can't speak.' Staring up at the mother and son before him, he said, 'Is it?'

And as Helewise quietly shook her head, Leofgar's face took on an expression of deep joy as he said, 'No. Oh, I must tell Rohaise as soon as she wakes!' Looking over his shoulder down the ward, it was clear to Josse where he wanted to be. Josse said, 'Off you go. Timus will be quite safe with me. If his grandmother' – he shot a look at Helewise – 'has to be off and about her duties, I shall be glad of this little man's company. I have a few more tricks yet and, if I remember children's ways aright, the first two amusements may bear a repetition or two.'

'Thank you, sir.' Leofgar gave him a graceful bow, then turned and hurried away in the direction of his wife's bedside.

Josse knew she was looking at him even before he raised his head to check. 'How did you do that?' she breathed.

'It's quite easy really, you only *pretend* there's a needle and thread and—'

'Sir Josse, do not joke!' But she was smiling as she spoke. 'You have a rare gift with children; your brothers' sons and daughters are fortunate in their uncle and you would appear to be a natural—'

She stopped, and he could tell that she was confused. Well, perhaps what he guessed she had been about to say was a little personal, but he wouldn't have minded.

He watched the little boy crawling across his bed for a moment or two. Timus seemed to have made himself at home and instinctively Josse put out a hand and gently took hold of the child's ankle, in case he went too near the edge and fell off. 'Do you feel reassured a little, my lady?' he asked.

'I do, Sir Josse,' she replied. 'I do not dare to hope that this minor miracle you have brought about means that all Timus's troubles are behind him but, as you said, we now know that he *can* utter sounds if he wants to.'

'Aye,' Josse agreed. And he thought, but did not say, that the next question was surely to ask why Timus did not want to speak. Or to laugh; he wondered if Helewise had also noticed what her son had said when Josse's first trick had met with such a response: that it was the first time *in a week* that the little boy had laughed.

Which surely implied that he had laughed – perhaps also made the normal speech-like sounds – up until a week ago. And that suggested to Josse that something must have happened to make him withdraw into silence.

He realised that the Abbess was watching him intently and he almost asked her if she was thinking the same thing. But then her expression seemed to close up and, straightening her back and folding her hands away in the opposite sleeves of her black habit, she said in a voice that brooked no argument, 'I must be on my way. There is much for me to attend to and I can spare no more time here.'

'Very well, my lady,' he said meekly.

'I—' She was staring at the child and he could see the longing in her eyes. 'You will tell me if he speaks again?' she asked.

'Of course. Don't worry, he'll be all right with me.'

'I know,' she said softly. Then, lifting her chin and adopting a determined scowl, she strode away.

Leaving him to remember, too late for now, that they had forgotten to ask Leofgar whether there was any foundation to Rohaise's fears that somebody wanted to take Timus away from her. I must not forget, Josse told himself firmly. It may be important . . .

He studied the child, who had discovered Josse's large feet

under the bed coverings and was trying to twist them side-
ways. I wish I could ask you, Timus, he thought. I wish I could
say, what's been happening in that home you share with your
worried father and your frightened mother? Does the lady
have good reason to be so afraid? And what was it, little one,
that made you so suddenly stop laughing?

He could feel a headache beginning above his eyebrows.
When Sister Caliste arrived with his herbal drink – she must
surely be due on her rounds soon – he would suggest, as
tactfully as he could, that she take Timus away and allow her
convalescent patient to have a well-earned sleep.

4

It was night and Helewise was dreaming again.

She had gone to sleep thinking about Josse's quite unexpectedly easy and natural way with children and uppermost in her mind had not been the extraordinary reaction he had evoked in little Timus. It had been the thought – which in truth was never very far away – that Josse had a child of his own and he did not know it.

The daughter whom Joanna de Courtenay had born him would be about a year old now. Rumour of mother and child had reached Helewise occasionally: they said Joanna had been living as a herbalist deep in the Great Forest. They said she lived hidden away in a little hut and that she talked with the Wild People. They said she made simples and potions and would help anyone who came a-knocking at her door. If they could find it. They said she lived high up in a tree and could charm the bees and the birds and talk to the animals in their own strange tongues. Then, in the spring of the year, there was a whisper that she had gone away. Helewise had discreetly tried to find out from the Abbey's own herbalist, Sister Tiphaine, who always seemed to know more than a good nun should about the goings-on among the mysterious and pagan forest people, if this rumour were true. Sister Tiphaine had looked her Abbess right in the eye and said calmly, 'She may well have left, my lady. But she will be back.'

Which had not answered the question in any satisfactory way at all . . .

★

For all that her thoughts as she fell asleep had been on Josse's child, it was her own sons who flooded Helewise's dreams. The first image was one that had disturbed her sleep before. She was young, dressed in a sunshine-yellow gown that she had made from an expensive length of French silk brought back by her indulgent father from a trip to a trading port on the south coast. She had reason to remember that gown very well and there was not one single detail of it that she had forgotten. But, in the way of dreams, the chronology was not quite right because she had worn that gown when she was a fast-maturing girl of fourteen (she had been so proud because she and her nimble-fingered nurse had had to let out the bodice to accommodate Helewise's richly rounded breasts) whereas, in the dream, she was wearing the yellow gown at a time after she had given birth to both her sons.

And there, too, dream time played tricks because the sixteen-month gap between them had disappeared and, as if they were twins, she fed them together, one held tenderly in the crook of each arm. Milk ran from her freely and in her sleep she turned and moaned softly as the never-forgotten feeling of let-down surged through her breasts under the linen sleeping shift. In her dream she sat on a grassy bank beneath a spreading willow tree and Ivo, kneeling before her and kissing her bare feet, took her toes in his mouth even as her hungry sons took her nipples and he sucked and licked them as if they were coated with honey. *My Flora,* he said, breaking off to look up at her and give her a wink, *my Queen of the May.* Then Leofgar turned from a suckling baby into a boy of five and stood in front of her, feet firmly planted in the green grass, demanding an apple because he needed the core to throw at a huge rook that was eating the corn. Dominic, also growing from babyhood to childhood in the blink of an eye, stood with her in the cool kitchen of the beautiful rambling old manor house that had been her marital home and helped her make

Alys Clare

gingerbread men with black, dried-fruit eyes. Then she was a girl again, newly married and wearing the red silk gown that had caused such problems because her new father-in-law gave it to her as a wedding gift – he must have noticed her generous breasts because she did not have to let *that* gown out at all – and she loved it, yet the more straight-laced members of her large family sniffed their disapproval and said that scarlet was a dangerous, pagan colour and only worn by wanton women. Elena, the old nurse, had just smiled and said *Never you mind, my sweeting, it'll be a lucky colour for you because it belongs to the Old Ways and the Great Mother, and she'll see how you honour her and she'll keep you fertile.*

Elena had known. She always knew . . .

Helewise woke lying on her back from a dream in which Ivo had been making love to her. Shocked at the response that was still coursing through her throbbing body, she got silently out of bed, crept along the length of the dormitory to the little recess at its far end where, breaking the ice on a basin of water, she sponged herself down until her flesh was bright red and she was shivering like a wet hound.

She tiptoed back to her bed but, not yet daring to risk more dreams, fell to her knees beside it and prayed to God to restore her peace of mind and her serenity. After quite a long time, she got back into her cold bed. As sleep took her once more, she seemed to hear a voice that could have been Josse's or Ivo's saying, quite kindly, *No good praying for that, dear heart, not until this trouble is past.*

But the voice disappeared in the deep dark of profound and dreamless sleep and she forgot all about it.

She was awake before the summons to Prime and was already praying in the cold, dark Abbey church when the rest of the community quietly filed in. As the office began, she gave her heart, mind and soul into God's hands and promised to do her best, humbly asking His forgiveness if her concentration wavered but begging Him to understand that the circumstances were a little unusual.

Then, determined to complete a session of hard work before anyone else popped up with a claim on her time, she hurried away to her little room and firmly shut herself in.

Josse woke up a long time after the Abbess. He had slept soundly and was relieved to discover that yesterday's headache had quite gone. His fever had not returned the previous evening and he was very much hoping that he would be allowed to get up today.

Sister Caliste brought him porridge and a hot drink, then the infirmarer came for her customary check. She pronounced him well but warned him not to overdo it and to return for a nap in the afternoon. Then a young nun in the white veil of the novice brought him his clothes – someone had kindly washed out his linen – and, with relief, he dressed and set off to see what had been happening in the outside world while he lay abed.

He went to see Horace and found that as usual Sister Martha had been spoiling this guest in her stables. Horace looked half asleep and very well-fed and Josse, thanking Sister Martha for her care, made a mental note to make sure he found the time to take the big horse out for a ride to remind him that he had been put on this Earth to bear Josse and not to stuff himself in a warm, sweet-smelling stable.

At the back of his mind since waking had been the Abbess's son and his family. He had formed a vague plan of offering to talk to Leofgar and perhaps also Rohaise in an informal sort of a way to see if they unwittingly revealed rather more of what was going on than Leofgar as yet had told his mother. But he did not feel he could do this until he had talked it over with the

Abbess; accordingly, soon after the community had emerged from the Abbey church after Sext, he went to find her.

His tentative tap on the door elicited an unusually curt response: she barked, 'Yes? Who is it?'

Surprised that she had not heard the jingle of his spurs and guessed who it was, he said, 'It's me.'

Her voice warming by several degrees, she called out, 'Please, come in, Sir Josse.'

He did so, closing the heavy door behind him with exaggerated care as if she now suffered his headache and he did not wish to cause her the pain of a loud noise. When he looked at her, he wondered if he might by chance be right, for she was pale and had greyish circles under her eyes, as if exhausted.

He said without thinking, 'Try not to worry. I'm sure that between us all we can help them.'

She gave him a wry smile. 'Thank you, Sir Josse. I was not actually thinking of Leofgar at that moment. I had just managed to turn my mind fully to these reports from our outlying properties out in the Medway valley and I was at last making progress.'

Until you brought my son and his problems right back to my attention, hung unsaid in the air.

'I'm sorry, my lady.' Josse was contrite. 'Er – can I help?'

It was a foolish question and he knew it before it was confirmed by her ironically raised eyebrow. 'With the reports? I think not, and indeed I would not wish such a task upon a friend since the writing is all but illegible and the content, once deciphered, deadly dull.'

'I did not really mean help you with your work.'

'I know, Sir Josse,' she said gently. 'I was teasing you.'

Teasing was a good sign, he decided. Teasing meant she wasn't as bowed down by her anxiety as he suspected. 'I thought maybe I'd have a talk with your son and his wife,' he said as casually as he could, which didn't sound very casual at all. 'I have yet to meet the lady and, if she's awake and feels adequately restored, perhaps she would appreciate a visitor.'

The Abbess had put her stylus down and was looking at him with affection. 'Forgive me, Sir Josse, I quite forgot to ask after your own health, but if you are up and about, I would guess that you are recovered.'

'Aye, my lady, thank you, but the infirmarer has summoned me back for an afternoon sleep.'

'You must have it,' urged the Abbess. 'It is rare for Sister Euphemia to be so indulgent, so make the most of it.'

He grinned. 'Very well.'

'And as to your proposal to speak with Leofgar and Rohaise, I think it is an excellent idea. I have been to see Rohaise this morning and she is well rested. Sister Euphemia has suggested another undemanding day – she is still concerned at Rohaise's pallor – but I am sure that a visit from you would brighten her up. You may find Leofgar with her but I believe he intended to take Timus out for some fresh air.'

'It might be a happy chance to catch her on her own,' he mused. 'Do you not think, my lady?'

She gave him a conspiratorial smile. 'I do, Sir Josse. Indeed I do.'

He found Rohaise sitting in the little curtained recess that was a copy of the one in which he had been cared for at the other end of the infirmary. She was dressed in a warm woollen gown in a russet shade, over which she wore a sleeveless tunic edged in fur; her dark hair was neatly braided and partially concealed by a small, stiff white veil held in place by a plaited cord of silk. She sat on a low stool at the foot of the bed and she was sewing a hem in what appeared to be a very long length of white linen.

Standing with his head through the gap between the curtains, he said, 'Lady Rohaise, may I come to talk to you? I am Josse d'Acquin.'

She had raised a startled, wide-eyed face to him at his first words, as if her thoughts had been far away and he had made her jump. But, as he identified himself, her expression relaxed and, putting her sewing aside, she stood up.

'Please come in, Sir Josse.' Her voice was low-pitched and attractive. He stepped between the curtains and into the recess. She pulled another stool forward from where it had been set back out of the way beside the wall and invited him to sit. As she resumed her seat, he did so.

'You are the very exceptional man,' said Rohaise, 'who not only is a good friend of the Abbess, my mother-in-law, but also performed the miracle of making my little boy laugh and speak.'

Overcome by her praise, he muttered, 'Hardy *speak*, my lady. It was but the one word.'

'You cannot know what that one word means to me,' she said urgently. 'I wish with all my heart that I had been there to witness the moment, but I was sleeping. They gave me some drug that rendered me senseless,' she added tonelessly.

He wanted to go on talking about the child but her words seemed to imply criticism, and he leapt to Hawkenlye's defence. As kindly as he could, he said, 'They are skilled healers here, Lady Rohaise. Put yourself in their hands, I do urge you, and they will do their very best for you.'

Her dark eyes met his and his kind heart shuddered at the misery he saw in their depths. 'I am not sure that I can be helped,' she said. She sighed. 'There has been too much . . .' Her voice trailed off.

'Too much?' he prompted.

She did not respond, instead reaching out her hand for the sewing. 'I asked for something to do,' she explained, 'for when my son is not by my side I worry about him. I worry even when he is with me, now, and I fear that it will take more than hemming sheets to stop me.'

'Why do you worry so?' Josse asked gently. 'Your boy is healthy, is he not? Some parents would say that, offered the choice, they would prefer a quiet child to a boisterous one.'

'Oh, Timus can be as boisterous as any little boy,' she replied quickly. 'Sir Josse, he used to—' But, as if someone had put a hand over her mouth, she stopped.

'Can you not confide in me, my lady?' Josse asked. 'I am here to help; you have my word on that.'

She gazed into his eyes, her needlework forgotten in her lap. 'I am not a fit mother,' she whispered. 'Timus deserves better, for I fear that I contaminate him a little more with every day. I stopped feeding him, you know. My milk was bad for him and he was better off with Adela. She stopped coming to our home too, you know. *She* knew. She saw it all.'

The poor woman makes no sense, Josse thought, deeply concerned. Making up his mind that the best way to respond was with the prosaic and everyday, he said, 'Well, once your boy was weaned, he had no more use of a wet nurse. Isn't that so?'

'Oh, yes.' She sounded dreamy, as if her thoughts were far away.

'I do not believe that you can possibly contaminate your own child, my lady,' Josse pressed on. 'It is clear that you love him.'

'Is it?' She almost snapped out the words. '*Is* it?'

'You have brought him here in order that help be given to him over these strange silences of his, have you not?'

She gave him a tiny smile, enough to put a faint dimple in her gaunt cheek and give him a glimpse of how pretty she might have been under other circumstances. 'Coming here was my husband's idea, Sir Josse,' she corrected him. 'He told me – went on telling me until I was so tired that I silently screamed at him to stop – that this was a good place where they would help me. *Me*,' she repeated, emphasising the word.

'He thinks, like everyone else, that I am in dire need of help because I am an unnatural woman who cannot raise her child.'

'I am sure that is not so!' Josse protested, but even as he spoke the words he was wondering whether there might not be some truth in Rohaise's pitiful accusations against herself. Then, like a blessing, he remembered the Abbess's report on her talk with the infirmarer. 'They tell me,' he said, lowering his voice and leaning closer to her, 'that quite a lot of young mothers have feelings such as yours and that many get better.'

Damnation! He hadn't meant to say that, to imply that some did not! 'That is,' he hurried on, 'things quite naturally improve as the child grows and thrives, and – well, all turns out for the best in the end.'

It sounded lame even to him. He was not at all surprised when she turned cool eyes on him and said, 'So I have been told, Sir Josse. But it is a different matter to be *you*, out there where things make sense and normality rules, and to be *I*, who am forced to live in this nightmare world that threatens me.'

'But threatens you with what, Lady Rohaise?'

He wondered afterwards if he had spoken too urgently, for she seemed to flinch, then her eyes closed and two huge tears rolled down her sallow cheeks. Then she bent her head over her sewing and began to weep.

With the horrible sensation of having done more harm than good, Josse got up, summoned one of the nursing nuns – it was Sister Beata, who might not have had the cleverest brain but certainly had the most generous heart – and asked her to look after Rohaise. With a worried little frown, Sister Beata wiped her hands and hurried into the recess, where she crouched down beside the weeping young woman and enveloped her in soft, loving arms, muttering kindly as the girl turned her wet face into the nun's bosom.

Feeling utterly redundant, Josse slunk away.

★

With nothing better to do, he remembered his resolve to exercise Horace and he fetched the horse from the stable. Trying to allow the bracing autumnal air to take his mind off his failure with Rohaise, he kicked Horace into a canter and then a gallop and they pounded along the track that led around the forest, the horse's big feet sending up flying divots of frosty earth. After a while they slowed to a canter, then a brisk trot, until finally Josse drew the horse to a halt and they turned back towards the Abbey.

They were not far from the gates when Josse spotted the figures of a man and a small child. The man was crouched down beside the small and well-wrapped figure of the boy and as Josse drew closer he saw that Leofgar was showing his son how to make a skeleton leaf.

'. . . gently, now, don't damage the veins of the leaf – there!' Leofgar was saying as he held up the child's clumsy attempt. 'That's very good, Timus, we'll take it home as a present for your mother.'

The child caught sight of Josse before his father did. With a smile of welcome that went some way towards making up for Josse's failure with the boy's mother, Timus pointed and said, 'Man!'

Spinning round, Leofgar's wary expression instantly relaxed into an ironic grin as he saw who it was. 'I should have guessed,' he called, 'you being the only person who inspires my son to speech.'

Hurrying to cover the remaining paces between them, Josse slid off Horace's back, keeping tight hold of the reins in case the horse should frighten the child by a bit of innocent curiosity; the disparity in their sizes suggested this might be unwise. Then he went to greet them. With a nod to Leofgar – Josse could not for the moment think of any suitable reply to the young man's comment – he knelt down beside the child and opened his arms for a hug. Timus rushed straight up to

him and snuggled against his chest, grasping a fold of Josse's
cloak and pulling it over his head. Josse, thinking it was a game,
began to laugh but Timus turned a solemn face up to him and
whispered something that he did not understand.

'What was that, Timus?' Josse asked. The little boy repeated
the word, which sounded like *hide*, but still Josse did not quite
catch it. Leofgar made as if to remove his son from the nest he
had made of the cloak against Josse's broad chest but, to
Josse's surprise and faint dismay, the child cowered against
him and would not be budged.

'If you will lead my horse, I'll carry the lad back to the
Abbey,' Josse said, trying to make light of the strange occurrence.

Leofgar was not fooled. 'It is not as it seems, Sir Josse,' he
said softly.

'I was not making a judgement,' Josse protested.

Leofgar smiled thinly. 'No? The smallest part of you was
not saying, see how this silent child pulls away from his father
into the protecting arms of a near-stranger! Does this not
suggest that the child fears the father?'

'I do not believe that.' It is true! Josse told himself. But
whether he believed it because of Leofgar himself or because
he was Helewise's son, he did not dare think about.

They walked slowly along the track towards the Abbey
gates. Horace walked obediently behind Leofgar, and Timus,
still snuggled in Josse's arms, put his thumb in his mouth and
with the other hand reached out and delicately took hold of a
strand of Josse's dark hair, which he twiddled with small, deft
fingers.

The silence between the two men was hardly companion-
able and Josse was relieved when Leofgar broke it. 'May I risk
a confidence, Sir Josse?'

'A—?' Josse played for time while he thought rapidly. Then
he said, 'I would be honoured to hear anything you would wish

to say to me privately. But I cannot give my word that I would not repeat it to – to another.'

'To my mother,' Leofgar said calmly. 'Yes, I know. I think, though, that I must speak anyway.' Not giving himself further time for consideration, he plunged on, 'Sir Josse, there are several reasons why I have brought my wife and son here to Hawkenlye. The first you know, for it is no secret that I wished to consult the excellent infirmarer and her nuns not only about my mute son' – he shot a swift and loving smile at the sleepy Timus – 'about my hitherto mute son but also about my sick wife. This we have done. The other – no, if I am to be honest with you, as indeed I wish to be, *an*other reason is because my wife feels threatened at home.'

'Aye, so I am beginning to understand,' Josse said. 'She seems—'

But, with an apologetic smile, Leofgar interrupted him. 'Forgive me, Sir Josse, but I must explain before we— Well, hear as much as I feel able to say, if you will.'

More mystified than ever, Josse said, 'Gladly.'

Again the smile, and this time Leofgar's expression was grateful. 'Thank you. Sir Josse, I am the son of a nun, an Abbess, a woman who stands high in the esteem of the Church, and what I must tell you may displease her when she comes to be told of it. Part of my reason for speaking initially to you is that I would be pleased to have your advice on *how* my formidable mother is told.'

He paused, apparently waiting for a response, and Josse said, 'I usually find that the direct approach is best. But I will listen and if I can make any helpful suggestions, I will.'

Leofgar nodded. 'I am grateful.' He took a breath, then said quickly, 'Sir Josse, back at home the clergy have come to know of my wife's state of mind. Our parish priest has prayed for her and with her and still there is no improvement. He has decided, in his wisdom, that my beloved Rohaise has suffered the misfortune of having a changeling put in the cradle. You understand what that is?'

Memories of half-forgotten folk tales were surfacing slowly in Josse's astonished mind. A changeling, he recalled, was the name given to a fairy child substituted for a human baby. Hardly crediting that a priest should believe such superstitious nonsense, he said grimly, 'I understand, aye.'

'Father Luke tells Rohaise that it is not her fault she cannot be a proper mother – which, as you will imagine, does further damage to her desperate lack of confidence – because the child she tries to care for is not the product of her own womb but an evil spirit, planted in our baby's cradle for some malicious and secret purpose of the dark world of the spirits.'

Josse, stunned, noticed that in this alarming Father Luke's version, the innocent 'fairy' had become 'evil spirit'. Dear God alive! 'Go on,' he said.

'He tells us – tells Rohaise especially, for it is she who constantly turns to him for help – that the real Timus is now the captive of the spirits and that only our true and deep penance will make Father Luke's stern God relent and send our little boy home.'

There was a silence as Leofgar finished speaking. Then Josse burst out, 'You cannot believe this rubbish!'

'I, no. I grew up with my mother's version of what a loving God does and does not do and, besides, I'm too old for fairy stories. But I'm afraid to say that Rohaise, despite her intelligence, is inclined to half-believe what her priest tells her.' He shot a dark look at Josse. 'As you will understand, I am sure, the Church and I are not friends at present.'

Josse put a hand on the young man's arm. 'Do not judge them all by this one misguided man,' he urged. 'And do not hesitate in telling your mother, who will, I've no doubt, share your disgust at your Father Luke's tactics.'

Leofgar sighed. 'I'm afraid that's not all,' he said. 'Father

Luke eventually lost patience with us and commanded us to remain in our own home while he made the necessary arrangements. He does not feel we're trying hard enough in our prayers, by which he means, I guess, that he suspects that I for one disbelieve everything he has told us and am on the point of encouraging Rohaise in rebellion against him.'

With a chill feeling around his heart, Josse said, 'For what was he making arrangements?'

'Not what, who. For him,' Leofgar mouthed, jerking his head at his sleepy son. 'Father Luke was coming for him. He was going to take our boy and lodge him with the monks, in the hope that their chilly hearts and strict discipline would frighten the changeling into fleeing back to his own kind and allowing the human child to return in his place. We left to come here just in time, shortly before Father Luke was due to arrive to carry out his threat.'

He watched Josse closely, as if trying to gauge a reaction. Josse, caught off guard, realised that he was scowling ferociously and hurriedly he smoothed out the expression, at the same time clutching Timus more closely as if afraid some lunatic, wild-eyed priest would spring up and try to wrest the child from his arms there and then.

Observant eyes missing neither response, Leofgar said with a grim smile, 'I have the feeling, Sir Josse, that I've found an ally.'

'You have, lad, you have,' Josse said fervently.

Leofgar laughed suddenly, a happy, relieved sound. 'Then will you please do me one more favour and help me explain to my mother that the holy church is after us and we're on the run?'

5

Time passed.

To the casual glance, Hawkenlye Abbey maintained its air of calm, each day slowly unfolding to revolve around the seven offices that punctuated the hours from dawn until dusk. But the calm was an illusion and maintained entirely by the discreet and silent hard work that went on without ceasing beneath the surface.

The cold took a grip like a wolf's teeth on the bones of a carcass. Helewise, observing the additional burden which this imposed on both her nuns and monks and on the wider community centred around the Abbey, ordered that fires be lit wherever there was – or could be contrived – a safe hearth in which to set them. The Abbey had a vast store of wood, gleaned by the industrious lay brothers over successive seasons from natural wastage in the huge forest right on their doorstep. Vowed as they were to poverty, the devout souls of Hawkenlye accepted shivering through the winter as part of the gift they offered to God. However, their Abbess was sensible as well as devout and appreciated that her nuns and monks would be little use to those they were there to help if they were all so cold that they could not function.

Word spread, as word always does, that there was comfort to be had at Hawkenlye for those who went asking and there was an abrupt increase in the numbers who came to seek the various sorts of solace that the Abbey offered. Pilgrims arrived at the shrine in the Vale and at times the mood down there was

more like a holiday than a self-denying and arduous experience for the sake of the visitors' souls, with excited children
slithering across the frozen pond and adults collecting around
the braziers swapping tales of hardship as they drank their hot,
thin soup. But Helewise turned a blind eye and suggested to
Brother Firmin that he do the same. Her sanction was more
than enough for the soft-hearted old monk, whose instinct all
along had been to welcome the cold and the hungry in the true
spirit of his master Jesus, even if it was patently obvious that, at
this time anyway, the cold and the hungry had come for food
and warmth rather than for the precious holy water so dear to
Brother Firmin's heart.

Up at the Abbey, people began arriving at the infirmary with
a variety of complaints ranging from coughs, colds and chills
to damaged limbs caused by falls on icy paths. But the biggest
problem was bellies that ached because there was nothing
in them and hadn't been for days. Hungry people, as the
infirmarer observed with compassionate anger, all too readily
fell victim to any ailment that tried to seek them out.

Josse gave up his comfortable berth in the infirmary and
moved to his usual lodgings down with the monks in the Vale,
where he was welcomed like a long-lost brother and enjoyed a
morning of informative gossip with several of his particular
friends there. Brother Saul, working like three men to make
room for all the visitors, was heard to mutter that God must
have had His holy ear cocked Saul's way because hadn't Saul
been praying as hard as he knew how for an extra pair of
hands, particularly ones that belonged to someone as strong,
capable and willing as Sir Josse?

Rohaise seemed to be responding to Sister Euphemia's
dedicated attempts to help her, although whether it was the
herbal remedies or the infirmarer's store of wisdom and
loving-kindness that was making her better it was impossible
to say. But, away from one, at least, of the dark spectres that

she had believed were stalking her back home at the Old Manor, her spirits lifted considerably and, as her terrors receded, her intelligence and practical good sense were able to come to the fore. Like Josse, she did not need prompting to realise that there were no beds now in the infirmary for the undeserving; she vacated her little recess, moved her few belongings to the guest room where Leofgar and Timus had been put up and announced to Sister Euphemia that she would really like to help and what could she do for her? Sister Euphemia was not one to refuse such an offer and soon Rohaise could be seen, her russet gown covered by a white apron, busy on the many basic nursing tasks within her admittedly limited ability. But someone had to do them, Rohaise reasoned, and if she was that someone, then it left the skilled nurses free to get on with more exacting tasks.

Sister Euphemia watched and took note. As Rohaise's colour and mood improved with the more she had to occupy her mind and her hands, the infirmarer observed to the Abbess that possibly a part of the young woman's problem all along had been too much time in which to think up fanciful notions. Had Helewise not recently had a certain conversation with her son, she might have agreed; as it was, she took Sister Euphemia aside and quietly told her what had happened back at the Old Manor.

'The priest did *what?*' the infirmarer hissed, scarlet with indignation.

'He suggested to Rohaise that poor little Timus is a changeling and that her real son has been spirited away.'

Sister Euphemia was shaking her head in disbelief. 'And we're told to obey these priests and any nonsense they cook up without question,' she muttered, not quite far enough under her breath for her superior not to hear.

Helewise, however, decided to let it pass. It would have been difficult, she realised, to criticise dear Euphemia for expressing a sentiment which she herself was fighting so hard not to let take root in her mind.

'You really think that Rohaise improves?' she asked instead.

Distracted from her muttering, Sister Euphemia stared along the infirmary to where Rohaise was crouching down beside a very old woman and, with infinite patience, encouraging her to take sips of broth from a small wooden spoon. The sips were so tiny, and the woman's rate of drinking so slow, that it looked as if Rohaise would be there for some time, but that did not dim the encouraging smile on her face.

'Aye,' Sister Euphemia said, 'she's improving all right. Next test'll be to see how she is with that lovely little grandson of yours, my lady.'

The little grandson was having a wonderful time.

Fourteen months was too young for him to have any understanding of the things that had happened back at home; all he knew was that his mother had cried a lot and his father had looked angry. Or worried. Or very upset. Or all three at once. Nobody had had much time for Timus and he had been sad and lonely even before—

He did not think of that. He couldn't even if he wanted to, because something in his mind had blocked it off. He remembered that there was something that had been very, very frightening but he did not know what it was. He had been afraid to utter the chattering sounds that he used to make in case . . . In case what? He couldn't remember that, either. And he had *really* been afraid to laugh because not only was there nothing to laugh at, but also someone might hear him. He could not quite think why, but he knew that must not be allowed to happen. His mother and his father had been so strange that he hadn't wanted to be with them and no funny things had happened like they usually did, such as his father making silly faces and pretending to be a horse. Then they had come here, to this big place with all the women dressed alike in black and white, and the big man in the bed had done that funny thing with his thumb and Timus had giggled. Nobody had been cross with him; in fact the big man had done another trick and Timus had been so entranced that he'd said the one word he could say: *More!* That had been all right, too, and the big man was now just about Timus's favourite person and he sought him out whenever he could so that the big man would pick him up – Timus wasn't very good at walking yet and could only manage a few tottering paces at a time – and the man would cuddle him in those strong arms. Timus felt really, really safe with the big man. The big man was *nice*.

Today it was very cold and Timus's father had wrapped him up in lots of bulky clothes before letting him leave the room where they were staying. Then they had gone out into a long alley with pillars along one side and his father and the big man had helped him with his walking. His father put Timus on the ground and told him to walk to the big man, which he did. The big man picked him up and said 'Well done, Timus!', then put him down again and told him to walk back to his father. Timus did this several times and realised that he was taking a few more steps each time. Then he missed his footing and sat down quite hard on his bottom, which didn't hurt at all because of all the clothes he was wearing, but his father said it was enough for now and he and the big man took Timus off to the place where they served the food and he had a hot drink and a sweet cake with currants in it. The cake was so delicious that he would have liked another and so he tried out his word again: 'More?' But the fat lady with the black veil and the white cloth round her red-cheeked face looked very sad and she shook her head and said sorry but one was all she could spare. Timus felt sad that she was sorry and he gave her a big smile and reached up to take her hand, at which two big tears welled up in the fat lady's eyes and she said, 'Oh, the little love! And to think that anyone could say he—' But the big man gave her a nudge and she stopped what she was saying.

And Timus still didn't get another cake.

The Abbess might believe that what her son had confided in her remained a secret known, apart from Leofgar and Rohaise, only to Josse, the infirmarer and herself. But the very air of Hawkenlye seemed to have the ability to pass on whispered confidences and within a day, almost everybody knew that some well-meaning (most nuns were tolerant people when it came to the clergy) but misguided priest had told the Abbess's poor daughter-in-law that her little boy had been snatched by evil spirits who had left one of their own in his place. Virtually all the nuns – and several of the monks, who soon heard the tale too – found some excuse to have a peep at the child and not one of them saw anything but a normal, smiling, healthy little *human* boy. Their sympathy would have been engaged even had the child not been their Abbess's grandson; since he was, the emanations of love that surrounded the little boy wherever he went served only to increase the incomprehensible but very lovely feeling that life, quite suddenly and unexpectedly, was all right again.

If only he could have a little more to *eat* . . .

Food was uppermost in Timus's grandmother's mind as she sat in her room wrestling with herself as she tried hopelessly to make one bag of flour do the work of four. She had just returned from yet another round of the Abbey and seen for herself what she could no longer ignore: the underlying cause of Hawkenlye's sudden popularity was that the people outside its walls were slowly starving and had come for help to the only place they could think of.

Helewise got up and went to the door. Opening it, she checked that there was nobody nearby, then she shut it firmly and for a few self-indulgent moments, stood in the middle of the floor and gave vent to her feelings, addressing an imaginary King Richard and telling him exactly what she thought of him. 'It's your fault your people are going hungry,' she said in a suppressed but still furious hiss, 'and it's this hunger, that *you've* brought about by demanding more than they can afford to give you, that's making them even more susceptible than usual to the maladies of winter. And you're not even here to witness the results of your own folly! You couldn't quell that adventurous, crusading, foolhardy spirit of yours, could you? And see what it has led to! Sire,' she added as an afterthought. Pausing for breath, she went on, more quietly now, 'Some of them have got nothing left, my lord King. They come here and throw themselves on our mercy, yet we too have had to give more than we can spare, so that now, when we have such need of our emergency supplies, the cupboard is bare.'

Abruptly her anger faded. With slow, tired steps, she walked round to the far side of her big table and sat down heavily in her chair. Then, drawing towards her the fat ledger in which every item brought into or out of the Abbey was recorded, she once more went through the list of supplies that had to last through the winter. It still amounted to the same result: not enough. Not nearly enough. Already her nuns and monks were on short rations and what she was about to do would not be welcomed by hungry, hard-working people who needed more food than they were currently receiving to get them through each long, arduous day.

But the decision could not be put off any longer. Acting now, she reasoned, might mean that some of the people at present wondering whether it would be a good plan to make for Hawkenlye while they still had the energy would change their minds and stay at home. Their numbers might be few but even that few could make the crucial difference between the Abbey's surviving or not.

Don't think about *not*, she commanded herself firmly.

Then she drafted out the order and, a little while later, set about putting it into action.

The initial reaction of the Hawkenlye community to being told that their food rations were to be cut by a quarter so that more could be given to the desperate poor was fairly predictable. They might be vowed nuns and monks but they were people too, and people running on far from full bellies at that. But the dismay and the grumbling soon passed; Helewise ordered a special service in the Abbey church and gave thanks to God that a good harvest meant enough food at the Abbey for them to be able to give some away. She made sure not to mention just how much of that good harvest had already disappeared to raise funds towards the King's ransom; it would not have been the moment and in any case, everybody had a pretty good idea anyway.

The mercy visits began that same day. Pairs of nuns, usually a fully professed and a novice, went out carrying wicker baskets full of bread, flour, strips of dried meat, one or two apples and some small folded packages containing Sister Tiphaine's sovereign remedies for the most common winter ailments. They also carried little phials of the precious holy water from the miraculous spring in the Vale; given Hawkenlye's reputation, which was founded originally on that same healing water, these were perhaps the most beneficial gifts of all.

Each pair of nuns was accompanied by a couple of the stronger and tougher lay brothers to act as bodyguard; rumour had it that there were ruffians and desperate men lurking in the fringes of the Great Forest and it was not wise to take any chances. Hunger makes beasts of men and someone who was dying of starvation might very well not have the usual scruples about attacking unprotected nuns carrying food to desperate peasants. Josse and Leofgar volunteered their services and

Helewise gratefully accepted; the two of them, together with Helewise's favourite lay brothers, Saul and young Augustus, formed the nucleus of her bodyguard force and made countless excursions each day.

Josse had begun to think of returning home to New Winnowlands; he was fully recovered from his fever and his would be one less mouth to feed if he left the besieged Abbey. But he realised that the Abbess badly wanted him to stay. For one thing, she suspected – and he had to agree – that they had not yet got to the bottom of the strange events that had brought Leofgar and Rohaise running for the safety of Hawkenlye. The Abbess and Josse had talked over the matter and decided that all they could do was wait on events and hope that either Rohaise or Leofgar would break their silence and confide in someone, hopefully Helewise or Josse. To this end, Josse was spending as much time as he could spare with Leofgar and little Timus, and Helewise made sure that she made room in her busy day for at least one visit to her son and her daughter-in-law.

The other reason why the Abbess did not want to lose Josse just yet was because his strength was such a boost to the morale of the nuns and lay brothers engaged on the mercy visits. Some of the homes that they visited were little more than hovels and presented a pitiful sight; constant repetition of the experience of misery made even the most courageous souls begin to waver. But then there would be Josse, riding up on Horace at just the right moment, offering a bundle of firewood to a frozen family and leaping down to cut up logs with his powerful arms and a sharp axe. Then he would make them all smile as, with exaggerated delicacy, he gave two tired nuns a leg-up on to Horace's back, pretending to close his eyes in shock if either showed so much as a bare ankle.

And, of course, riding out with the bodyguard meant that Josse spent much of each day with Leofgar, which gave him the time to study the younger man without Leofgar noticing. Or so Josse believed.

When the mercy visits had been going on for a week – Josse and Brother Saul had discovered that it was possible to extract roach and rudd and sometimes a large pike from the pond in the Vale and now smoked strips of admittedly fairly unappetising fish were going out in the baskets – the Abbey received a visitor who, at first sight, was neither sick, wounded nor starving.

He was, however, cold and so Helewise took him straight away to warm himself by the small fire that was kept burning in her room. As Gervase de Gifford, lawman of Tonbridge, swept back his fur-lined cloak and removed his heavy leather gauntlets so as to hold his hands to the flames, Helewise summoned a nun and ordered hot, spiced wine, and only when it had arrived and been poured out did she finally ask de Gifford what she could do for him.

'It may be a case of what I may do for you, my lady,' he replied. 'Oh, this is good!' He held up his cup in a silent toast.

'Much watered down, I am afraid,' she said apologetically. 'Like everyone else, we have had to draw in our belts.'

'Yes, I have heard of your nuns' visits to the worst-off families,' he said. 'It is what I would have expected of Hawkenlye.'

She bowed her head. 'In truth, we do what we do in part for our own sake, in the hope of keeping to manageable proportions the influx of visitors constantly arriving here to seek our help.'

He nodded his understanding. 'I have heard too of the way in which your numbers here have swelled.' He finished his wine and, when she went to refill his mug, shook his head with a smile. 'No, my lady. Thank you, but I will not have more if you do not join me, and I know full well that you won't.'

She smiled and replaced his mug on the tray. There was plenty of wine left in the jug and she was grateful for de Gifford's forbearance, which would mean that at least two people would later have a drink with their food that they hadn't been expecting. Then, indicating that he should sit down by the fire and resuming her own seat, she said, 'Now, tell me why you are here.'

He paused as if collecting his thoughts and then said, 'It may be nothing but I can't stop thinking about it, which is why I've come. One of my more sharp-witted officers overheard a conversation yesterday in the tavern in Tonbridge. It was between two men, one of whom is a ruffian well known to my officer, which was why my man was listening in to what the fellow had to say. The ruffian's companion was a different class of man altogether – better dressed, well spoken, obviously of more substantial means than the other.' He frowned as if still doubting whether he should be wasting her time telling her this.

'Do go on,' she prompted. 'You believe that what your officer overheard concerns us here at Hawkenlye?'

'Perhaps.' He gave her a wry grin. 'The two men spoke of a missing person – a man, apparently a friend or possibly a relation of the ruffian. The well-dressed man was telling him not to worry and that the missing man would turn up. The ruffian said no, he wasn't satisfied with that, he was going *up the hill'* – here he caught her eye to make sure she appreciated the significance of the words he had emphasised and she nodded that she did – 'to see if *he,* by which presumably he meant the absent ruffian, had gone where they reckoned he'd been heading.'

'I see,' she said, working it out as she spoke. 'Two men are trying to find a third, who has apparently come up here to Hawkenlye.'

'Not necessarily,' de Gifford said quickly. 'Other roads lead uphill out of Tonbridge, although I grant you that it's usually the Abbey that people of the town are referring to when they say up the hill.'

'Yes.' She was still thinking hard. 'What I don't understand is why you felt the necessity to warn us that the ruffian's friend, or whatever he is, was coming here. Do you think he is dangerous?'

De Gifford studied her. 'I mentioned that the ruffian in the tavern was known to my officer.'

'Yes.'

'He is also known to me, and so is his usual companion. If it is he who is missing and is the man to whom the other two referred, he's called Walter Bell and he is the ruffian's brother.' De Gifford's clear green eyes met hers and he added softly, 'Walter Bell is the more violent of the brothers. He has committed murder, although circumstances were such that he was never put on trial for it. Had he been, I should have done my utmost to see that he hanged.'

She felt a chilly finger of fear creep up her back. 'And Walter Bell may be on his way to Hawkenlye,' she whispered.

'Yes, my lady. Of course, he may not be, but I felt it only right to warn you.'

'Yes, I understand, and I'm grateful. What should we do?'

He hesitated. 'Well, it's difficult because we have no idea why Walter Bell would come to the Abbey. It could simply be that he's sick, or reckons it would be the best place for a free meal.'

'Not a very substantial one,' she remarked. De Gifford's practical and undramatic reasoning was helping her to regain her composure.

'Or on the other hand,' he was saying, 'perhaps when Bell's brother said he was coming to Hawkenlye because that was where they reckoned he'd gone, the *he* in fact meant someone else.'

Something in his tone warned her and, fearful again, she said, 'Who might that be?'

'My lady, please do not look so alarmed, for this is but conjecture, but my officer said that Bell's brother seemed to be furiously angry. It did just occur to me whether the *he* whom he might or might not be following up here to Hawkenlye could be not his brother but the person whom he holds responsible for his brother's disappearance.'

He said it is but conjecture, she reminded herself as she waited for her rapid heartbeat to slow a little. Then she said, as calmly as she could, 'As you are aware, the Abbey is full of people at present. How can we possibly hope to isolate which of them is in danger from this man Bell?'

'His name's Teb,' de Gifford supplied. 'A nickname, presumably, but it is how he is known.'

'Teb,' she repeated. 'Teb Bell. Is there any point in asking around, do you think? To see if mention of the name raises a response in anyone here?'

De Gifford shrugged. 'Possibly, my lady. It can surely do no harm, and we might be able to warn the man whom Teb Bell is after, if I have reasoned correctly and this whole miserable tale has not caused you needless anxiety.'

'Better safe than sorry,' she said stoutly.

He smiled briefly. Then, looking at her with what looked like a slightly awkward expression, he said, 'Er – I'm wondering, my lady Abbess, if it might be a wise precaution to ask Sir Josse d'Acquin to come over to Hawkenlye, just until this business is cleared up.'

Now it was her turn to smile and hers was more wholehearted than his. 'No need,' she said happily, 'I'm pleased to say that he's already here. You have but to wait until he returns from this morning's second mercy visit, and then you will be able to talk to him yourself and tell him all that you have just told me.'

★

Josse returned and was briefed by de Gifford. Having as he did such favourable memories of the sheriff and trusting that the man was not causing a fuss about nothing, Josse agreed that they should begin asking all the people currently making use of the Abbey's various services if the name Teb – or, come to that, Walter – Bell meant anything to them. In particular, whether it brought fear into their eyes. Leofgar and Brother Saul offered to help, and Saul said he would enrol the assistance of some of the other lay brothers; there were, after all, an awful lot of people to ask . . .

But in the end they had got no further than interviewing the first dozen or so pilgrims down in the Vale before they were overtaken by events.

Two nuns, Sister Anne and Sister Phillipa, were on their way back from the tiny hamlet of Fernthe, accompanied by Brother Erse, the Abbey's carpenter, and a young lay brother called Peter. They had met with a slight accident when almost within sight of the Abbey; Peter had tripped on a tree root and sprained his ankle. Erse had been of the opinion that, with the support of his stout shoulder, the lad would be up to hopping back to the Abbey if they gave it a while for the pain to subside but, not wanting the nuns to take a chill while they waited around in the cold, he urged them to hasten on to Hawkenlye. It had seemed unlikely that they would meet with any mishap so close to the Abbey's walls, especially as their baskets were empty and no longer a target for hungry thieves, but if they did, Erse told them 'to holler as loud as you can and I'll come running'.

They did as he suggested, as confident as he that nothing unexpected would happen.

But it did. They rounded a curve of the track that ran along beside the Great Forest and walked straight into a body hanging by a rope from the branch of an oak tree. Sister

Phillipa had the presence of mind to try to lift the man and take the weight off his neck; a good idea but in fact quite pointless since he had been dead for some time. Poor Sister Anne's terrified screams echoed not only back to Erse, who dumped Peter on the ground and, habit flying up round his thighs, raced to help; they also echoed faintly in the cloisters of Hawkenlye Abbey, where people looked up in alarm and wondered what on earth had happened now.

It would not be very long before at least some of them found out.

6

Josse and Brother Saul were first on the scene. They had been speaking to a young family who had just arrived at Hawkenlye and they had run the distance from the Abbey gates up to the forest fringe with the speed of anxiety; Sister Anne had a scream to equal the last trump. Leofgar, who had been in the stables trying to get some of the icy, caked mud off Horace and his own horse, raced after them. Everyone had been too busy to notice, but Leofgar looked if anything even more tense than when he and his little family had arrived.

Josse hastened to relieve Sister Phillipa of the weight of the body and Saul climbed up the oak tree and tried to undo the knot that bound the rope to the high branch. Leofgar, who had put his arm around Sister Anne to comfort her and in the hope of stopping her piercing screams, looked up briefly and, catching Saul's eye, took a sheathed knife out of his belt and threw it to Saul, who deftly caught it. He sawed through the rope about two hands' breadths from the knot and instantly the full weight of the body descended into Josse's arms.

Josse put his fingers to the throat and his ear to the gaping mouth, from which a blackened tongue protruded. As his senses confirmed what he already knew, Josse shook his head.

He sensed that someone had come to stand close beside him and Sister Phillipa's low voice said, 'Did I not succeed in saving him, Sir Josse?'

He laid the dead man carefully on the ground and, taking off his own cloak, spread it over the horrible spectacle of the ruined face. 'Had you happened upon him soon after the rope tightened, your resourceful and brave action might well have helped, Sister,' he replied. 'But he is already cold and his limbs begin to take on the stiffness that follows death, so we must assure ourselves that any action we tried to take to save him came far too late.'

'Sister Anne and I did not set out by this path,' Sister Phillipa murmured. 'Had we done so, we might have been in time.'

Josse looked at her and noticed how pale she was. Shock, he reminded himself, can manifest itself in other ways than in hysterical screaming. Straightening up, he took hold of Sister Phillipa's hand, which was cold and clammy. Thinking quickly, he leaned close to her and whispered, 'Sister, we must get Sister Anne back to the Abbey for she is beside herself and is in need of the infirmarer's calming draught. Will you see her back, if Brother Saul and Leofgar go with you?'

'But that means you would be left alone with the body, Sir Josse!' she exclaimed. 'I will stay with you, for two together will be better than one alone.'

She was courageous, there was no denying it, and he admired courage; indeed, he would have welcomed her company. But he did not want her to stay out there in the cold with him for the length of time it might take Saul to arrange and dispatch a party with a hurdle to fetch the body. 'I will be quite all right, Sister,' he assured her gently. 'I have stood vigil by the dead many times and they do not frighten me.'

Her eyes met his. A very small smile touched her lips and she said, 'And you would rather not have the additional worry of a woman who might pass out on you.'

He grinned back. 'I have no fear of that, Sister. But you have had a disturbing experience and I would be reassured if I knew that you too were on your way to being tended by helping hands.'

She bowed briefly. 'Very well, I will go.'

Brother Saul and Sister Anne had already started off down the path and now, for the first time, Josse looked over at Leofgar, about to ask him to take Sister Phillipa's arm and help her along after them. What he saw quite surprised him, for Leofgar was almost as white as Sister Phillipa and he was staring down at the body as if he could see straight through the thick cloth of Josse's cloak and was still studying the blackened, distorted features of the dead face. Perhaps, Josse thought, it is the first time he has seen violent death. Perhaps, despite the fine example of bravery set by Sister Phillipa, he cannot control his reactions. Well, if so, the sooner he puts distance between himself and the corpse, the better.

'Leofgar?' he said.

The young man slowly turned his head towards Josse, although his eyes remained fixed on the body. 'Yes?'

'Leofgar, please take Sister Phillipa back to the Abbey.' This time Josse put a little asperity into his tone and to his relief Leofgar responded. As the young man stepped around the corpse and approached the nun, his features seemed to unfreeze and he gave her a comradely smile. 'Come, Sister,' he said, holding out his hand for hers, 'Sir Josse is right, there's no need for more than one to stay on guard here. Let's help each other back to the sanctuary of the Abbey walls.'

She took his hand and Josse watched as the two of them strode off down the path, quickly catching up and overtaking Brother Saul and Sister Anne; Leofgar called out something, perhaps an assurance that he would alert the community to what had happened, and then he and Sister Phillipa, still rather touchingly holding hands, broke into a trot and hastened away. Leofgar might well have reacted like a green young lad on seeing the body, Josse mused, and I can't really blame him for it was not a pleasant sight. But he's pulled himself together, no doubt of that, and I am sure he will not falter again.

Josse put the matter out of his mind. There would be only a brief time before the hurdle bearers arrived to take the body away and he had work to do. First he inspected the ground beneath the branch from which the body had been suspended, but it was hard with the dry cold and, in any case, any informative footprints there might have been had been obscured by the lightly shod feet of the two nuns, by Saul's sandals and by the boots of Leofgar and Josse. No help there, he decided. Then he went to look around the trunk of the tree. There were the prints of Saul's feet; he had broken the thin ice on the edge of an all but dried out puddle and the marks of the hobnails on the thick soles of the lay brother's sandals had made a sliding pattern in the mud.

There was another footprint too.

Josse hurried back to the dead man and studied his feet. He wore filthy boots of poor quality leather and the uppers had pulled away from the soles in one or two places. The backs of the boots were trodden down, as if the man had been in the habit of pushing his feet carelessly into them. Grimacing at the task, both because it took some force and because the man stank, Josse pulled the right boot off the dead foot. Then he carried it over to the base of the oak tree and compared it with the footprint there.

Interesting.

He laid the boot down beside the corpse – putting it back on the pale, naked and filthy foot would take time that he did not have and, besides, the infirmarer and her nurses would in any case soon be stripping the corpse in preparation for burial – and then he spat on his hands and shinned up the tree. He edged gingerly along the branch and, at the point where the knot was still tied to it, settled himself securely, winding his legs firmly together beneath the branch and, holding on with one hand, bending down to inspect the knot.

He traced the way in which the rope had been tied. That was

interesting, too. Then he spotted something else. Leaning down, he teased out the small but revealing thing that was caught up in a strand of the knotted rope and carefully tucked it inside his tunic. He pushed himself back along the branch – funny how it seemed to be even further from the ground now that he was up there – and as he slid back down the oak tree's trunk, he heard the hurdle bearers coming along the track.

Later, he and the Abbess waited together in the infirmary, outside the recess where Sister Euphemia had ordered the lay brothers to put the corpse. She would strip the dead man, she had said, have a preliminary look at him and invite the Abbess and Josse to join her when she was ready. She had just sent Sister Beata to fetch them and, as they waited there, the curtains parted and the infirmarer stood back to let them approach the cot where the body lay.

There was a strong smell of rosemary, combining refreshingly with some other flowery scent that Josse thought was geranium.

'We've washed him,' Sister Euphemia murmured. 'He was lice-ridden and I didn't want the little devils spreading.'

'Quite so,' said the Abbess. Josse, glancing at her, did not miss the swift expression of disgust that momentarily crossed her face. Then, like her, he turned his attention to the dead man.

The flesh was white and sparse; he had been a lean man, not very tall. Josse stared at the skinny arms and looked for several moments at the hands and wrists. The limbs were stunted and the legs slightly bowed, an effect often seen, Josse reflected, in the bodies of the poor who had never had quite enough to eat. Sister Euphemia had discreetly placed a folded sheet across the man's lower trunk so that his groin and genitals were concealed; Josse raised the corner of the sheet and had a quick look, which told him little other than that the man had had gingery body hair and had not been circumcised. Replacing the sheet, he turned to stare at the head and face. The head hair had also had a ginger tinge, although less pronounced, and the man had been in the process of going bald. With a nod to himself, as if privately noting that some earlier possibility had just turned out to be true, Josse looked at the bulging eyes – Sister Euphemia had managed to close them – and finally at the open mouth with its protruding tongue.

Noticing the direction of his attention, the infirmarer said, 'He had rotten teeth, Sir Josse. They'd have given him gyp, I shouldn't wonder.'

'Hm.' Josse hardly heard; he was thinking. He put his hands either side of the head and, raising it from the cot, moved it gently around, from side to side, then backwards and forwards. Again he said, 'Hm.' Then he pulled out the small object he had found in the strands of the rope and put it on the cot beside the dead man's head. Looking up at the infirmarer, he said, 'A match, would you say?'

With a soft exclamation she bent to look more closely. She sniffed at the dead man's scalp and picked up the few strands of ginger-brown hair that Josse had laid beside the head and sniffed them too. She felt the head hair – still damp from her own recent ministrations – and then the stray strands, rubbing at them between her fingers. Then, replacing the loose hairs on the cot and carefully wiping her hands on a clean piece of soft white linen that smelt of lavender, she said, 'Aye, I reckon so.'

The Abbess, who had silently been watching, said quietly, 'Where did you find the hair, Sir Josse?'

'In the knot of the rope.'

'The knot—' She swallowed. 'You mean the noose that was around his neck?'

'No,' he replied. 'The knot that bound the rope to the tree branch.' She frowned, as if she knew that this was significant but had not yet worked out how. Since he was in much the same state, he added, 'There is much here to puzzle us, my lady.'

'Indeed,' she agreed. 'But our first task must be to try to establish the poor man's identity, since surely someone, expecting his return, must soon miss him and wonder where he is.'

'Aye. I had thought, my lady, of sending word to Tonbridge to ask de Gifford for his help?'

He turned the suggestion into a question and immediately she nodded. 'Oh, yes. I could send one of the lay brothers, or . . .' She looked at him enquiringly.

'I should be happy to go,' he said, picking up her thought. 'I will set out immediately.'

If Gervase de Gifford were surprised at having to return to Hawkenlye so soon, he gave no indication. As he and Josse rode back up Castle Hill towards the Abbey, Josse did what he could to answer de Gifford's questions. He had already asked the sheriff whether any man had been reported as missing and de Gifford had said no, not as far as he knew.

Although neither man had spoken the thought aloud, Josse guessed that de Gifford was wondering the same thing that was occupying him: whether the dead man could be the absent Walter Bell. Arriving at Hawkenlye, they gave their horses into the care of Sister Martha and then went straight across to the infirmary.

The corpse lay alone on its cot behind the curtain; Sister Beata stood just outside the recess, as if to ensure that the idly curious should not be allowed to approach. Seeing Josse and de Gifford, she parted the curtains for them and stood back to let them enter the recess. Josse smiled his thanks and the sheriff paused to speak a few muttered words; it sounded, Josse thought, as if he were commending the care with which the dead were treated by the infirmary nuns, for Sister Beata gave

a little bob of a bow and whispered that it was ever the
Abbess's and the infirmarer's wish that due respect be given.
Then, appreciating that he was keen to proceed, she stepped
back and let the curtain fall behind the two men, leaving them
alone with the corpse.

Josse observed de Gifford studying the dead face. After a
moment he said, 'Is it Walter Bell?'

The sheriff looked up and his green eyes were clouded with
doubt. Then, unconsciously echoing Josse'e earlier remark, he
said, 'There's a mystery here.' Speaking softly so that nobody
but Josse would hear, he went on, 'It's not Walter, it's his
brother Teb.'

Josse and de Gifford went next to report to the Abbess and
Josse listened as, with admirable brevity of which the Abbess
seemed to approve, de Gifford outlined what he had just
discovered.

'Yet it was Teb whom you suspected was coming to
Hawkenlye to search for his brother Walter, the one who is
missing?' she asked.

'Yes, my lady.'

'Are the brothers similar in appearance?' Josse asked.

The Abbess nodded. 'That was to have been my next
question.'

'You are both wondering, I would guess,' said de Gifford,
'whether my officer mistook Teb for Walter and it was in fact
Teb who was missing and Walter who was looking for him.'

'Aye,' Josse replied.

'There was a strong resemblance between them, yes, and I
wish it were that simple.' De Gifford gave a sigh and ruffled his
hair vigorously as if trying to stir his brains into action. 'But it
was Teb in the tavern. My man was in no doubt of it.'

'And you trust your man.' Josse made sure that there was no
note of enquiry in his voice; he was in any case quite sure that

de Gifford would not use men whose judgement he questioned.

'I do,' de Gifford agreed.

'Teb Bell is dead, then,' the Abbess summarised, 'and Walter, we must assume, is still missing.' She looked intently at de Gifford. 'Were the brothers close, would you say?'

'Close?' De Gifford thought for a moment. 'Their lives were lived closely, my lady, for, as I told you, they were engaged in the same villainy and as far as I know they shared the same miserable hovel of a dwelling. But if I am correct in thinking that you are asking whether there was affection between them, then I can only say that, although I may malign them, I would doubt it. May I know why you ask the question?'

She shrugged and, to Josse's eye, appeared suddenly diffident. 'It seems that I am following a fruitless path but I wondered if the dead man – Teb – could have discovered that his brother had in fact died and had taken his own life because the loss was too great to bear.'

'But, my lady, he—' Josse began.

She misinterpreted his protest. Turning to him, diffidence changing smoothly to righteous indignation, she said, 'Sir Josse, deep love is not the prerogative of the wealthy, the honest and the educated. Despite what the sheriff says about the Bell brothers, it is perfectly possible for a poor man, even for a thief or a murderer, to love his brother!'

Josse bowed his head. 'Forgive me, my lady Abbess, but I would not dream of denying it. That was not what I was about to say.'

'Oh.' She looked slightly ruffled. 'Then what were you going to say?'

He glanced at de Gifford, then back at the Abbess. 'It is perhaps only to be expected,' he began, 'that the assumption will be made that a man found hanging at the end of a rope in an isolated spot has died at his own hand. In many such cases, I believe this is found to be true.'

'But not in this one?' de Gifford put in.

'No,' Josse agreed.

'How can you be sure, Sir Josse?' the Abbess asked.

'Because of two things,' he replied. 'Firstly, I discovered a footprint at the base of the oak tree and, when I compared it to the dead man's boot, it did not match. Neither did it match the footprints of those of the Hawkenlye community who found him, cut him down and brought him here. It's possible, I accept, that someone else came along before Sister Anne and Sister Phillipa arrived and that this someone made to climb the tree to cut the man down but for some reason thought better of it. Perhaps he heard the sisters approaching and decided to run for it before anyone decided that his presence at the scene pointed to his guilt.'

'You reason logically,' de Gifford commented. 'However, my inclination is to think that the footprint at the base of the tree is more likely to have been put there by whoever strung Teb Bell up. What is your second thing?'

'I found a strand of hair entangled in the rope, just below where it was knotted around the branch,' Josse said. 'Sister Euphemia and I are agreed in our opinion that it belonged to the dead man.'

'Does that not rather point to his having made the knot himself?' the Abbess asked.

'Again, it is possible,' Josse allowed. 'But I also noticed faint marks on the dead man's wrists, marks that I believe were made by his having been tied with perhaps the very rope later used to hang him. I may be wide of the mark, but the scene that I see is this. Teb Bell is making his way to Hawkenlye, where he believes he will find news of his brother Walter. He is, let us say, concerned for Walter and he fears some harm may have come to him. Well, perhaps it has. Perhaps Walter has been attacked and killed and perhaps the killer, knowing about Teb, is lying in wait for Walter's brother to come looking for him. Along comes Teb, perhaps armed with a knife or a stout stick—'

'He usually carried both,' de Gifford put in.

'Very well! Along comes an armed Teb and the assailant, knowing as well as you, Gervase, about the cudgel and the knife, plays for safety and jumps him from behind. He slings a rope round Teb's neck – and it's then that the strands of hair become entwined – and perhaps loops another bit of the rope round Teb's wrists so as to render him helpless. Then he pulls him across to the oak tree, throws the free end round the branch and, before Teb can do anything to save himself, hauls him off the ground so that he strangles to death. Then the killer climbs the tree and ties the rope in a knot, with the thought in mind that anyone recognising Teb will think what the Abbess just suggested. That Teb Bell hanged himself, perhaps from grief that his brother Walter cannot be found and is presumed dead.'

'A clever murderer,' de Gifford said slowly.

The Abbess did not look convinced. 'Sir Josse, could that not still be what really happened – that Teb Bell took his own life – despite the two contrary indications that you describe to us?'

'No, my lady.' He looked sadly at her, wishing in that moment that he could agree and say yes, suicide *was* the more likely verdict. 'For there is one more thing. You saw the body, did you not?'

'You know I did,' she said, her voice barely audible. 'You and I stood together beside his cot after Sister Euphemia had prepared him for us.'

'And did you observe his neck?'

'I – yes. There were the marks of the rope.' She lowered her eyes. 'It was quite dreadful.'

'Aye, and I'm sorry to make you see those images again.' Had de Gifford not been present, he might have gone to stand by her side and given her a brief, reassuring touch on the shoulder. 'But there is a reason for my insensitivity,' he plunged on, making himself ignore her distress.

'And that is?' She spoke from behind the hand that momentarily covered her mouth.

'I implied just now that a man who is hanged by being hauled off his feet by the rope around his neck will, in all probability, strangle to death. If, however, that man climbs to a height and then flings himself off it, the rope round his throat will probably break his neck.'

There was silence in the room. Then de Gifford said, 'I take it that the branch was sufficiently high but that there was no broken neck?'

'The branch was high enough, aye,' Josse said heavily. 'And no, as far as I am able to tell, Teb Bell's neck wasn't broken.'

De Gifford gave a sigh. Then he said, 'It is as you fear, Josse. We are looking for a murderer.'

Josse turned to him. 'Aye. And, unless we find or hear word of Walter Bell alive and well, it may prove to be the case that this unknown murderer has killed more than once.'

7

Gervase de Gifford requested a second look at the dead body; he did not say so but Helewise guessed that the wished to verify for himself what Josse had said about the rope marks on the wrists and the neck not having been broken. He was gone for some time – Josse went with him – but then she heard the sound of their boots in the cloister outside her room and called out to them to come in.

'I have seen all I need to see, my lady Abbess,' de Gifford said. 'It is as Josse described and I shall be able to give evidence as to the manner of death, should the man's killer be appre-hended.'

'And do you think that he will be?' she asked.

He gave a faint shrug, elegant, as were all his movements. 'I cannot say. At present, with so little information to help us that we do not have even so much as a starting point, I have my doubts.'

She was about to comment on that but Josse forestalled her. 'Would it not be an idea to look for the missing brother?'

'For Walter.' De Gifford glanced at him. 'Yes, Josse, I've already thought of that. As you will recall, I came up to the Abbey to warn the community that Walter Bell might be on his way here. But this was not the only place I was searching for him. My men are asking after him in other areas too.'

A thought had struck Helewise and, as soon as de Gifford had finished speaking, she expressed it. 'Have you surmised any valid reason why Walter Bell should have wanted to visit the Abbey?' she asked him. 'I do not recall that we discussed that aspect in any great depth before.'

'Indeed not, my lady, and as to his purpose here, I can still only guess.'

'Was the man sick?' Josse demanded. 'Injured, perhaps?'

'We wondered, but if that was his reason for coming then for sure he did not arrive,' she said quickly, 'for there is no man who resembles the dead brother at present being treated in the infirmary.'

'Aye, and no pilgrim who bears the Bell features down in the Vale,' Josse agreed.

'In which case,' de Gifford said slowly, 'we must conclude that either Walter Bell did not get to Hawkenlye – perhaps was not even making for here in the first place – or that he is here but does not wish us to know that he is.'

'You mean that he's spying on us? Spying on someone here?' Helewise asked. 'That perhaps he wishes to do harm to one of our community or one of the many people currently taking refuge here? You suggested something similar before when you spoke of Teb Bell planning to search *up the hill* for the missing Walter and you implied that both brothers might be after a third party.'

'Yes, my lady.' De Gifford looked solemn. 'That's exactly what I mean. It is why I originally came to warn you. I was worried then but I confess that, after today's discovery, I am now even more anxious.' He looked at Josse, who was standing frowning heavily beside him. 'I find the picture that you painted for us, Josse, quite plausible. Walter may indeed be dead and the same man who murdered him may have been the killer of Teb. But what if Walter is still alive? What if he suspects someone sheltering here at Hawkenlye of having killed his brother? It is, after all, no great distance from the Abbey to the place where we found Teb. Walter is, as I have told you, a violent man. Even if he did not bear any strong love for his brother, I do not believe he would leave Teb's murder unavenged.'

'It comes back to finding Walter!' Josse exclaimed in exasperation. 'There are so many ifs and maybes that I see no other way forward.'

'I agree,' de Gifford said decisively. 'I shall return to Tonbridge now, my lady, with your permission –'

'Of course.'

'– and see if there has been any word or sighting of Walter Bell. If I make haste, I shall be back in my own home by the time darkness falls.' He gave Helewise a deep bow, Josse a rather sketchier one, and then he was gone.

'He is a man,' Josse observed into the silence left in de Gifford's wake, 'who seems always to move with elegance and deliberation, yet there is a vibrant energy about him that belies that impression.'

'I too have marked it,' she agreed. 'We are lucky to have him.' She smiled suddenly. 'Remember Harry Pelham?'

'God's boots, aye!' Josse gave a tut of remembered annoyance. Then, apparently noticing the blasphemy, mumbled, 'I apologise, my lady.'

'Your apology is accepted,' she murmured. Then: 'What should we now do, think you, Sir Josse? Is it worthwhile to make another check of our visitors to make quite sure that Walter Bell is not among them?'

'That was my thought,' he said, nodding. 'And I've thought of something else; it is too late for further investigation tonight, but tomorrow, with your leave, I'll take Saul and Gussie with me and have a good hunt through the nearer reaches of the forest, in case Bell is out there living rough while he plans his next move.'

'Yes, I will gladly give you leave. But' – she met his earnest brown eyes – 'I am happy that you restrain your impatience and do not propose starting your hunt today.'

He smiled. 'I admit that I am tempted, but it would be fruitless because in the fading light we would miss anything there was to find. Oh!'

'What is it?'

'My lady, I would like to ask Leofgar to be of my search party, if you agree. In all the drama of today's events, he has slipped from my mind. But he would be an asset, of that I am sure.'

She too had forgotten about Leofgar and his family. 'Sir Josse, I am glad you reminded me. I have not yet made my daily visit to Rohaise and her child nor had the opportunity to speak to Leofgar. And yes, by all means ask him to join your hunt!'

She found Rohaise in the guest chamber preparing Timus for bed. Rohaise sat by the small fire, the child well-wrapped in a blanket on her lap, and she was cuddling him to her as she softly sang a lullaby. The scene was so heart-warming – and it was so good to see Rohaise acting just like any other mother – that Helewise contented herself with a brief smile and a nod to Rohaise before quietly closing the door. Timus, she could see, was almost asleep and a visit from his grandmother might stimulate him back into wakefulness. I will make time for a proper talk with both mother and child tomorrow, she promised herself. As she went off in search of her son, she was already looking forward to it.

She could not find Leofgar at first, but then one of the nuns said she thought she had seen him going towards the stables. Helewise was surprised, but then recalled that he had taken the duty upon himself of looking after Josse's horse as well as his own; perhaps he had gone to groom them ready for tomorrow. He had always loved to be with horses, even when he was far too small to groom them . . .

Dwelling for a few self-indulgent moments on the pictures that her memory provided, she then firmly dismissed them.

She made her way to the stables, wrapping her arms around herself against the penetrating cold of the approaching night. Somebody was within; she could hear soothing whistling and the rustle of straw. She called out, 'Leofgar? Is that you?'

There was a moment of stillness and she was suddenly very afraid. Suppose it was not her son in the stables but Walter Bell, armed with a cudgel and a knife . . . ?

But then there was more rustling and her son's voice called back, 'Yes, it's me, Mother. I'm – er – just finishing grooming Rohaise's mare.'

Faintly surprised, for surely the mare had not been out anywhere that day to become dirty, she was about to comment but then Leofgar appeared from out of the end stall and, approaching her, gave her a swift hug.

'What was that for?' she asked as he released her.

'Oh – nothing.' He did not meet her eyes.

After a moment she said, 'It's getting cold. Let's return to somewhere warmer. I will order some wine and—'

'Thank you, but Rohaise is waiting.' He led the way out of the stables and they set out across the courtyard side by side. 'We're both rather tired.'

'Yes, it's been a wearying day.' She tried to speak brightly to disguise her disappointment; it was unreasonable to expect him to put a cosy chat with his mother above settling down snugly with his wife. 'Rohaise is being a great help in the infirmary,' she said. 'Sister Euphemia reports that she has a gentle hand and a kind manner with the sick.'

'I'm glad she's being useful.'

Helewise had intended that her remark should be the prelude to a brief comparing of notes between them concerning Rohaise's state of mind; she was keen to know whether Leofgar too saw an improvement. But his somewhat curt reply made her realise that he did not think now was the moment and reluctantly she abandoned the plan.

'You are useful too,' she said instead. 'I understand that you have been riding out with Sir Josse and the lay brothers helping with the distribution of food to the needy.'

'I have.'

'And has Sir Josse asked you yet about tomorrow's search?'

'Search?' He stopped and stared at her. In the darkness it was hard to see his face properly. 'What search?'

'The dead man found this morning is apparently brother to a missing man called Walter Bell. Gervase de Gifford – he's sheriff of Tonbridge – has reason to think that Walter Bell was on his way here to Hawkenlye and he is looking for him. Sir Josse is to hunt through the forest fringes tomorrow morning to see if there is any sign of Bell and he suggested that you join him.'

Leofgar did not speak for a moment. Then, with a sort of sigh, he said, 'I see.'

Before Helewise could work out whether his reply meant he would or would not agree to be part of Josse's search party, Leofgar had taken her arm and was saying something about its being too cold to linger out of doors. He escorted her back to her room and then, with a bow, turned and hurried away in the direction of the guest chamber where Rohaise awaited him.

Helewise, her thoughts and emotions threatening to overcome her, gave him long enough to reach the chamber and then left her room and walked quickly across to the Abbey church. Vespers was long over and there was nobody there; she fell on her knees and prayed both for the ability to understand and therefore help her son with whatever was troubling him so deeply, and at the same time for the grace to put him out of her mind so that she could concentrate on being a good nun.

'I hope, dear Lord,' she whispered, 'that you can work out what exactly I am asking you for, because I do not think that I can.'

Smiling ruefully to herself, she got up and set off to find her own bed.

Most of the people living in, being treated or sheltering at the Abbey that night slept soundly, for it was a cold, still night and the best place to be was warmly wrapped in blankets on a straw mattress, preferably with a low fire burning down gradually not too far away.

But three people hardly slept at all.

As soon as he had eaten his meagre breakfast, Josse took his mind off his still-growling belly by immediately setting about organising his search party. Brother Saul had found woollen cloaks for Brother Augustus and himself, and he accepted the two stout sticks that Josse handed him without comment. Gus, on the other hand, could not conceal his satisfaction; 'If we're to hunt down a violent man,' Josse heard him whisper to Saul, 'then old Sir Josse here's quite right and we ought to be able to defend ourselves.'

Grinning tolerantly at the 'old' – Gussie could be no more than seventeen, and anyone over thirty would doubtless be so described – Josse observed Saul's reluctant muttered reply, although he could not make out the words. But Gus said, 'Saul, you only need carry the stick and look as if you mean to use it. If there's any thumping necessary, I'll do it.'

It was as well that Josse already knew Augustus and had learned a little about the youth's good nature. Otherwise he might have found such eager anticipation of *thumping* quite disturbing in one who lived in an Abbey, even if he was but a lay brother. Still smiling to himself at the exchange, he led his party up the path to the Abbey and went in search of Leofgar.

He was not in the guest chamber. Nor were Rohaise or Timus; nor were any of the young family's belongings. Running across to the stables, Josse found that Leofgar's horse and Rohaise's mare had also gone.

Wondering just how he was going to word the announcement, he went to find the Abbess.

She said, as people so often do when given tidings they would prefer not to hear, 'Are you quite sure?'

'Aye. Quite.'

She did not press him for details, bless her, but just sat there behind her great table as if turned to stone. His heart going out to her, he said, 'My lady, I am quite sure there is some simple explanation.'

She rounded on him furiously. 'Such as what?' Then, instantly regretting the little outburst, added, 'I am so sorry, Sir Josse. I did not mean to shout at you.'

'It's all right, I understand.' Again he had the impulse to go and stand beside her and give her a comforting touch and this time, with no de Gifford to witness, he did so. For some time she sat in her chair and he stood with his hand on her shoulder. Then she said weakly, 'What shall we do?'

'Hm.' He had no immediate answer; he had not been thinking ahead, contenting himself for that short time with trying to reassure her by his touch that she had his unquestioning support. Now he said, 'Well, I suppose we should try to guess why they left in the night without telling us they were going. It suggests—' He stopped. There was no tactful way of saying what was in his mind.

'It suggests guilt,' she murmured. 'Does it not?'

'Well, I'm not sure that I think . . .' But he had always been honest with her. 'Aye. It does.'

'Why should they be guilty? Concerning what? What can they have done?' Her distress was palpable.

'One thing occurs to me, my lady.' He was not at all sure if he should say what it was, but then again he had to say something.

'Yes?' she said eagerly.

'It isn't much!' he protested, distressed by the sudden flare of hope in her eyes.

'Please, tell me anyway.'

So he did. 'Yesterday when we found Teb Bell hanging from his tree, I noticed that Leofgar seemed badly affected. He was pale and sweaty-faced, despite the cold, and could not take his eyes off the body.' She made as if to speak but he hurried on. 'Now naturally I can't say for sure, not knowing his background or his history, but I wondered if maybe it was the first time he had come across violent death. Many a time I've noticed a reaction of this sort, my lady, when a young man first looks on an ugly death, and indeed it's nothing to be ashamed of. Most of them over-come it and learn the courage to accept what they must accept.'

She said, after an uncomfortable pause, 'You believe my son to be a coward, Sir Josse, and you think that his absence this morning is because he did not want to be among your party hunting for the probably violent Walter Bell.'

It sounded even worse when she put it into those particular words and he hastened to qualify what he had said. 'No, I am sure he is not cowardly; all I meant was that it takes some young men longer than others to get accustomed to the dirtier side of life. But he rallied, your Leofgar, he pulled himself together double-quick and got busy looking after Sister Phil-lipa as soon as I asked him to.'

'That is something to be thankful for,' she said ironically.

'I've thought of another possibility,' he said, hardly register-ing her brief comment. 'The lady Rohaise was in a sorry state when they arrived, was she not?'

'Yes, although she seems to have improved. The work in the

infirmary has been good for her, I believe, and she seems more at ease now with her little boy.'

'Aye, well, that all goes to suggest that this time I may have come up with the right answer!' he said eagerly.

'Which is?' She was, he noticed, watching him with something that looked like indulgence.

'Let's assume that Leofgar too has seen the improvement in his wife,' he said, the words rushing out of him, 'and he decides that if they stay on here now that this wretched business with the Bell brothers has started, there's every chance that poor Rohaise will get anxious and worried and she'll fall back into her former misery. What do you think of that?' he demanded triumphantly.

But to his dismay he heard her murmur, 'Oh, dear!' Then she said, 'Dear Sir Josse, you are trying so hard and I appreciate your kindness. You ask what I think of your suggestion, and I have to reply that the answer is, not very much.'

'But—'

'If their departure were for such a very understandable and indeed logical cause, then why did they run away in the middle of the night without telling us? Leofgar had only to say that he feared for his wife and son's safety all the time there was the risk of a violent ruffian in the vicinity and we would have said, of *course* you must go home! Wouldn't we?'

He had to admit that it was so. Moving away from her and returning to his usual place on the opposite side of the table, he said, 'What do you think, my lady?'

Her brow creased into a frown. 'I do not know what to think. I wish that I—' She stopped. Then, looking at him, holding his eyes, she said very quietly, 'Sir Josse, I have scarcely seen my son for more than fifteen years. I knew him as a baby and as a small child as well as any woman knows her son, but after that I – well, I was widowed and it was best for my sons' own sakes that I took certain steps to ensure their futures. So I – homes were found for them with men of equivalent rank and position to that of my late husband and off they went. And then I came here.' She dropped her head and seemed to be engaged in an intent study of her folded hands. 'You ask me what I think of my son's strange behaviour and I have to say that I have no answer. I no longer know what or who he is and I cannot even make a guess as to why he has fled from the Abbey as if the devil himself were on his heels.'

Josse had never really thought about the Abbess's past. There had been hints – she had once or twice mentioned her late husband and made the occasional reference to mother-hood and the birth of her sons – but this was the first time that she had spoken with such power and, it had to be said, such emotion about her past life. Wondering whether or not it would be diplomatic to pursue the subject – oh, surely he should, for did she not need some kindness, some reassur-ance? – he said tentatively, 'My lady, you sound almost as if it is a matter for regret that you have lost your former closeness with your children.'

'It is,' she said baldly.

'But is it not the case with the sons of many men and women, that they are sent from home when young and trained for knighthood by other men? It happened to me and I did not suffer.'

'Yet you remained in contact with your mother. I know you did, Josse, you told me how she insisted you spend time with her kinfolk in Lewes.'

'Aye, that's true,' he agreed reluctantly.

'And when your brother Yves came here that time, you and he spoke with such love of your late father that I knew full well you had all been close.'

He had forgotten her prodigious memory. And the fact that, in pursuit of the truth, she was relentless. Even when –

perhaps especially when – the truth was to do with some
accusation she was making against herself.

'The past is the past,' he said eventually. 'Maybe you will
have to live with your regrets about what was done long ago,
my lady. But must they be allowed to affect what you do in the
present and what you plan for the future?'

Slowly she looked up. Then, her grey eyes full of tears, she
said huskily, 'I keep seeing him as a child. Both of them, and I
see Ivo too. All this time, ever since I had those dreams when
Leofgar was calling out to me, I've been unable to control my
thoughts. The pictures from my own past flood into my mind
and I can't shut them out. And I still dream so vividly, about –
well, about things that a nun should not be dreaming of.'

'We cannot help what breaks out into our dreams,' he said
reasonably, 'or, if there is a way, I do not know what it could
be.'

'I dream of Ivo and me when we were young,' she murmured. 'It is *wrong*, Sir Josse!'

'You were his lawful wedded wife,' Josse said. 'Surely there
is no shame attached to that?' He thought she was about to
speak but she seemed to change her mind. 'And it is not as if
you kept your past a secret when you presented yourself here
and took the veil, is it?'

'I . . .' She hesitated and he thought he saw a faint blush rise
in her pale face. 'They knew I had been married, had borne
two sons and was widowed, yes,' she said. 'As you say, nobody
protested that any of that made me unfit to be a nun. The
Abbess at the time questioned me carefully over the provision I
had made for my children, but everything had been meticu-
lously arranged and she found no fault.'

'What provision had you made?' He asked the question
despite himself; he was very curious to know the answer.

She paused for some time. Then said, 'Leofgar went to a
great friend of Ivo's. He was to stay there and receive his

training as a page and then a squire until he came of age, upon which he would take up residence at the Old Manor. That was Ivo's family home,' she added, 'and it was, of course, Leofgar's inheritance as the elder son.'

'And your other son?'

'Dominic was not all that much younger than Leofgar but he was—' She swallowed. 'He was closer to me, the one who always wanted to be with me. He was less of an adventurer than his brother, although ironically it is he who has grown up to be a soldier who fights in faraway lands. He – I sent him to live with my brother and his wife and Dominic quickly became like another child in their happy home.'

'You did what was best for them.' He believed it; knowing her as he did, she could not have done otherwise.

But she said only 'Perhaps.'

After another lengthy silence she wiped the last traces of tears from her eyes, mopped her face with her sleeve and stood up. Taken by surprise, Josse said, 'My lady? You are going somewhere?'

'Of course I am.' Determination written all over her, she strode round her table and made for the door. 'I would love it if you were to accompany me, Sir Josse, provided you think you can be spared from the search for Walter Bell.'

'Saul and Augustus can start without me,' he assured her. 'But where are we going?'

The expression that she gave him suggested that she thought he should have known without asking and, when she spoke, he realised that he should have done. 'To look for Leofgar and Rohaise,' she said. 'We'll search for them in their home, that used to be mine. We're going to the Old Manor.'

8

Helewise sent word to Sister Martha and both Horace and the golden mare named Honey were saddled and waiting by the time she and Josse had collected what few belongings they were taking with them and were ready to leave. Helewise had dressed herself in an extra layer of warm underclothes – a fine woollen shift and petticoat – and she had found her heavy travelling cloak. Josse, she noticed, was also well wrapped up against the cold.

Sister Martha, eyes betraying her curiosity, saw them to the gate and watched them set off. Helewise turned Honey's head to the right, instinctively knowing which way to go; Josse, catching her up, said, 'How far away is this Old Manor, my lady?'

I should have told him, she thought. It is discourteous to have virtually ordered him to accompany me without telling him exactly where we were going. 'It lies in a small hamlet in the shadow of the North Downs,' she said, turning round in the saddle. 'As to how far . . . a morning's ride, perhaps a little more. I will take us along lesser-frequented tracks, Sir Josse, if you do not mind, for I prefer not to ride down through Tonbridge and possibly have people speculate and guess at our purpose.'

'No, I don't mind,' he called back. 'Lead on, my lady.'

They had been riding for some time when something occurred to her. 'Sir Josse!'

'My lady?' He kicked the big horse and trotted up to ride beside her.

'You speculated that perhaps Leofgar left as he did because he did not want to be a part of your search party.'

'I was wrong, I am sure of it,' he said quickly.

'Never mind. What I wanted to say is this: I found my son in the stables last night and I realise now that he was probably getting everything ready for the family's secret night-time departure. Did you tell him yesterday about the search party?'

'No.'

'I thought not because I did tell him, as we left the stables, and to judge from his reaction I would have said that he had not known of the plan before.'

'Therefore he did not leave because he feared helping us search for a violent man,' Josse concluded. 'There, my lady. I said he was no coward.'

For some time the happy thought cheered her. But then she recalled all her other worries and the fleeting lightening of her burdens was gone again.

Although she had once covered the journey in the opposite direction, Helewise had never travelled the route from Hawkenlye Abbey to the Old Manor; nuns did not habitually leave the convent for visits back to their former homes for, once within the order, that was considered to be their life and reminders from the past were not encouraged. Returning to your previous existence to care for a sick parent, for example, turned your mind from where it belonged, with God and in His service, perpetually His to command.

So it was strange, she mused as they rode along in the feeble sunshine, that she knew the way without hesitation. They left the main route down Castle Hill towards Tonbridge soon after leaving the Abbey, branching off to the right and descending into the wide Medway Valley down a track that was mostly used by drovers trying to get their herds up on to higher – and therefore drier – ground. They crossed the river some distance to the east of Tonbridge. It was as well, she thought, that the weather had not been wet recently because the marshy areas either side of the river would have been impassable if the ground were anything but bone dry and hard with frost. She turned north-west on the far side of the Medway and soon the long ridge of the North Downs rose up before them.

I must, she decided as once again she made a slight change of direction with barely a thought, have made this journey many times in my mind . . .

But she was not sure that she wanted to dwell on that. The idea that she had mentally and unconsciously made her way back to her old home, perhaps with regular frequency, suggested that her detachment from her former life was not as complete as she had always believed.

They came into a small settlement with a wide green and a pond – there was nobody about and Helewise concluded that the inhabitants were wisely tucked up in their homes, sheltering from the cold – and rode on up a long, gentle rise towards the Downs.

Then the great line of oak and chestnut trees that sheltered the Old Manor from the east wind came into view. Helewise kicked the golden mare into a smart trot and then a canter and, with her veil flying in the breeze and the sound in her ears of Horace's big hooves pounding the hard ground as Josse raced to keep up with her, at last she was approaching her former home.

And unbidden into her mind – impatient, as if it had been lying in wait for this moment – came a powerful vision of the first time she had set eyes on the place . . .

★   ★   ★

She is a bride – a very young although fully mature bride – and she wears rustling scarlet silk; her new father-in-law's wedding gift. She rides a neat bay mare whose name is Willow. She is excited and her blood races lustily through her body. It is a morning of high summer and her husband of slightly less than two days rides beside her.

She turns to look at him and the invitation in her laughing grey eyes is all that it takes. He kicks his chestnut gelding and comes up alongside the bay mare. Without a word he reaches out with strong arms and catches his bride around her waist, easily lifting her from her saddle and swinging her across so that she sits in front of him astride the chestnut horse. She leans back against his broad chest and a sigh of desire slips from her open mouth. He puts a hand on her jaw and turns her head so that he can reach her lips with his own. He kisses her hungrily and she responds. She wonders, as the kiss goes on and she feels their excitement mount, whether they might pause a while and, in the shelter of those big trees over there, make love . . .

But he eases his mouth from hers and, opening her eyes, she sees that he is looking not at her but ahead. There is a light in his face that she has not seen before. Then he says, 'Sweetheart, let's wait until we're home.' Nodding towards whatever it is that he stares at with such deep pleasure, he says, 'Look. We're nearly there.'

She looks.

And sees a stone house perfectly sited; a gentle fold of the Downs rises up behind it and there is dense woodland screening it from the track that goes on up the hill. To the right – the east, and therefore the direction of the most spiteful winds – there is a copse of oak and chestnut; these are the very trees under which she has just been contemplating a short session of passion which, she now appreciates with a chuckle, would hardly have been suitable since the trees are actually rather close to the house.

The dwelling consists of a long building which she guesses is the great hall; it is a good size and it sits over an undercroft

with a stout wooden door and one or two tiny windows. A
stone stair leads up to the main entrance of the hall. To the
right of this long, low construction is what she assumes to be a
solar block. This too has an under storey, whose door, she will
soon discover, gives on to a stone-walled room built half into
the ground and off which a winding stair leads to the rooms
above. The Old Manor, she can already see as she rides up to
it, promises to be a magnificent home . . .

'My lady?'

It was not Ivo calling; it was Josse. Shaking her head and
dismissing her reverie, Helewise turned to him. 'Yes?'

He was, she noted, looking slightly anxious. 'Oh – you
stopped and looked for so long that I wondered if you had
mistaken your way and brought us to the wrong place.'

She smiled at him. 'No, Sir Josse. I am sorry but I was
remembering the first time I came here.'

'Ah. Oh.'

He's embarrassed! she realised. He thinks I've forgotten our
present purpose and am lost in my past! Dear Lord, but he is
not far wrong. Gathering Honey's reins in firm hands, she said
decisively, 'Let us go up to the house and see if we can find
Leofgar. The sooner we can speak to him and find out why he
left in such a manner, the sooner we can be on our way back to
Hawkenlye.'

Now Josse looked simply surprised, presumably at her
lightning change of mood. 'Very well, my lady,' he said.
But she noticed that he continued to eye her with a certain
amount of suspicion, as if – the whimsical thought quite
surprised her – he feared that she might suddenly change
into somebody quite different.

She rode the short distance up to where the gates of the Old
Manor stood open and, with Josse beside her, went on into the
courtyard. Josse called out, 'Halloa! Halloa the Old Manor!'

At first there was no response. The main door to the hall was firmly closed and remained so. Helewise turned to look towards the solar block, but the door into the undercroft was similarly shut fast. Josse called again, but still there came no reply.

'My lady,' Josse said softly, 'I am beginning to think that either your son does not wish to see us or else he is not here.'

'There must be someone about!' she said, copying him and keeping her voice low. 'Leofgar and Rohaise may only have a small staff but they certainly do not live in this place all by themselves. There must surely be house servants and grooms and such like.'

Josse dismounted and handed her Horace's reins. Then he paced away to the end of the long building that housed the hall and disappeared round behind it. He must have seen the smoke from the kitchen fire, she decided – she too had spotted it – and he has guessed what I know. That, if there are indeed servants here, they'll be round the back.

Presently Josse returned. With him was a slim young man aged somewhere in the mid-twenties. He had smooth dark hair and was dressed in a cheap-looking but clean tunic and neatly darned hose. His sturdy boots were well-made and had been recently buffed to a shine.

Josse, walking a pace ahead of the young man, said, 'My lady, may I present Wilfrid, who is in charge here in his master's absence. Wilfrid, this is the Abbess of Hawkenlye, your master's mother.'

Wilfrid went down on one knee on the hard-packed earth of the courtyard and said, 'You are most welcome, my lady Abbess, and what hospitality I can offer you is yours to command.'

'Thank you, Wilfrid.' She took the hand that he held out to her – it was clean, even down to the fingernails – and dismounted; Josse silently took Horace's reins from her and collected Honey's as well.

Face to face with her son's man, Helewise studied the pleasant, open expression and the regular features. He reminded her of someone and, bearing in mind where they were, it did not take her long to decide who; his father had been manservant here before him. But she must get on with the matter in hand; deciding that there was no use in prevaricating, she said, 'I had hoped to find Leofgar and the lady Rohaise at home.'

Clearly puzzled, Wilfrid said, 'They have gone to Hawkenlye Abbey, my lady. Did you not receive them there?'

She glanced at Josse, who gave a faint nod of encouragement; he too, it seemed, had formed a good opinion of Wilfrid and was, she thought, urging her not to hold back from telling the whole strange story. Or, at least, telling as much of it as she knew. 'We did,' she said after a moment. 'But then they departed and we had assumed they were heading for home.'

'They have not arrived, as you see, my lady.' Now Wilfrid was looking worried. 'When did they set out?'

She hesitated. Then, with a rueful smile, said, 'In the middle of the night.'

Silently she applauded Wilfrid's discretion. Instead of asking the question that he must have been longing to ask – *why on earth did they do that?* – instead he said quietly, 'Perhaps they are even now on their way and it is merely that you have overtaken them.'

She hadn't thought of that. 'Sir Josse, is it possible, do you think?' she asked, turning to him.

He was frowning hard. 'We came by a route other than the main way, did we not?' he asked.

'Yes, but the main way would, I believe, have been more direct and therefore quicker. If they came that way then they should already be here.'

'Aye, my lady, so I appreciate, but what if Leofgar too took a less frequented and more roundabout road? After all—' He made himself stop.

But she guessed what he had been about to say: after all, a man who creeps away under cover of darkness is unlikely then to ride home along the best-used and most public road, especially if that road takes him through a populous market town and over one of the busiest river crossings in the south-east of England.

'Yes, I understand your meaning,' she said quietly. 'And Wilfrid is right in saying that they may well be still on their way home.'

'My lady, I would be delighted to offer you hospitality,' Wilfrid said quickly. 'Will you and Sir Josse not come inside? I will light a fire and food will be prepared for you while you wait for your son to arrive.'

It was a kind offer, she thought, and her opinion of this man of her son's rose a little more. And indeed, what else was there to do but wait at the Old Manor and see if Leofgar turned up?

'Thank you, Wilfrid.' She exchanged a look with Josse, then said, 'We would be very pleased to accept.'

Wilfrid turned and gave a whistle and a boy of about eight came running round from behind the house. 'This is my lad,' Wilfrid said. The lad gave the visitors a big grin. 'We're teaching him the care of horses. Here, Simeon, take these two and make sure they want for nothing.' With a formal bow he took the two sets of reins from Josse and solemnly handed them to his son who, despite his small stature, gamely took them and, making an encouraging clucking sound with his tongue, led the horses off behind the hall. To the stables, Helewise remembered. The smell of sun-warmed hay fleetingly filled her nostrils and there was a memory of laughter; then it was gone.

'Please, my lady, Sir Josse,' Wilfrid was saying, 'follow me.'

They climbed the steps up to the main door, Wilfrid going

ahead. He opened the door and, stepping back, waved his hand to usher them inside. Little had changed, Helewise saw: new hangings over that far door that was always draughty; a different table at the far end of the room; a careful and clearly recent repair to the huge iron-bound wooden chest that stood against the wall opposite the door. Otherwise it was very much the place she had left eighteen years ago. Her eyes went to the section of wall on the far side of the room, beyond the sooty stones where the fire would soon be burning in its central hearth; Wilfrid was already busy with flint, straw and kindling. There on the wall, in the place where it had always been, was the ancient shield of the Warins, Ivo's kin. Dark with age now and blackened by the smoke of a thousand fires, the device could still just be made out. A bear, long-clawed and fierce, stood on its hind legs against a background of deep blue sky and soft green grass on which there was depicted a tiny castle flying a long red pennant.

The fire began to crackle and Wilfrid pulled forward two high-backed, carved oak chairs. Then he excused himself, saying he would see about some refreshments, and Josse and Helewise were left alone. Josse paced slowly away down the length of the hall, touching the old stones, smoothing his fingers across the shiny surface of the table, looking everywhere.

Helewise stared into the fire . . .

⋆   ⋆   ⋆

She is in the hall and her new husband is impatient with the servants who bustle around them, telling them to hurry up and bring this meal they've prepared. But it is clear that there is no malice in his words for the fat woman and the slim young man who serve the food are clearly amused and trying not to laugh out loud. She has a sudden fierce hope that Elena will be happy here, that she will like the fat woman and the slim young man, for where she goes, Elena goes; but it is important to Helewise that her old nurse settles in this new place to which her young mistress has brought her. She hears the fat woman say something to the dark young man, not quite quietly enough, but although it is a ribald remark and the fat woman should not really have made it, the young bride is so glad that she did because it's just the sort of earthy, crude, rude thing that Elena would say.

The meal is served, eaten and cleared away in record time. At last the servants melt away into their own quarters at the back of the house and Ivo takes Helewise on to his lap. She puts her arms around his neck and kisses him passionately, gasping between kisses 'I've been waiting – hours – and hours – to do that to you!'

His hand slides inside the bodice of her red tunic and his fingers cushion the warm, smooth roundness of her breast, taking the nipple in gentle fingertips and playing with it until it stands erect. 'And I this to you,' he says huskily.

She is sitting astride him now and she feels his hard penis push against her. A moan of desire escapes her and she whispers in his ear, 'Is this where you mean to bed me, husband?'

He laughs. 'Oh, aye, wife. I shall fling you on to the clean rushes and ride you like a man on a wild horse until you cry for mercy!'

'Until I cry for more,' she corrects him, greedy for him, hungry to have him . . .

*   *   *

'Are you hungry, my lady?

Wilfrid was addressing her. Wilfrid, who so resembled his father whom she had just been seeing again in her mind's eye as the slim young servant he once was.

She was not hungry at all; far from it, for her stomach felt as if it were tied in knots and she sensed the onset of a slight queasiness. But Wilfrid, or someone, had prepared a platter of cured strips of meat and bread generously buttered, and in these times of hardship she knew she must not refuse. 'Thank you, Wilfrid' – she was very relieved that, despite the tumult of her memories, her voice sounded perfectly calm – 'I should like to take a little food.'

He held out the platter and she helped herself, then watched as he did the same for Josse; he, she noticed, had considerably more of an appetite. Then Wilfrid offered them some watery beer – 'I'm sorry that it's not better quality but, like every household, we're not able to offer ale of our usual fine standard at present' – and they both drank. When they had consumed all that they wanted, Wilfrid took away the leftover food and the beer jug and once more disappeared down the passage that led to the kitchen quarters.

Josse went over to the door and stood looking outside, as if by staring down the track he could somehow make Leofgar and Rohaise appear. He was, Helewise had observed, unusually quiet and she wondered if his silence might be out of respect for her and her memories. If so, she would really rather he chattered away to her on virtually any subject under the sun, her memories being almost more than she could cope with.

To encourage him to talk to her, she said, 'How long, Sir Josse, should we give them, think you?'

He turned from the door, closed it – there was a cold wind blowing in – and came back to the hearth where she sat, throwing himself down into the other chair. 'I have been thinking, my lady, that it may be that they travel only by night. If indeed they have a need to keep their journey a secret, then maybe they rode out from the Abbey and then, when dawn broke, found a place to hide themselves away out of sight for the hours of daylight, planning to set out again once it is dark.'

'But why should they want to disguise the fact that they are returning here?' she asked. It was all so strange! 'They *live* here. Why be furtive about their homecoming?'

He stared at her. He looked worried. 'I am thinking more and more as time passes that they are not coming home,' he said neutrally.

She felt instinctively that he was right. What, indeed, was the point of a furtive flight in the middle of the night only to ride away to the one place everyone would expect to find you?

'I think,' she said, 'that I must agree with you. Wherever Leofgar has taken his wife and child, he is not bound for here.'

Josse was looking at her sympathetically. 'It will be dark soon,' he said. 'Do you wish to set out for Hawkenlye and try to reach the Abbey before nightfall?'

She thought about it. Then: 'No. For one thing, the journey will be easier' – safer too, she thought but did not say, if indeed this vicious ruffian Walter Bell is abroad – 'in the morning. For another thing, if we stay for the night then we shall be giving Leofgar a little longer to appear.'

He gave a small bow of acknowledgement. 'It is your choice, my lady, but I think that is a wise decision,' he observed. Standing up again, he added, 'I'll find that Wilfrid and request that he arranges accommodation for us.'

She and Josse were made as comfortable as it was possible for unexpected guests to be made in the midst of a hard November when nobody had much of anything to spare. Josse said he was quite happy to bed down by the fire and Wilfrid found him a straw mattress and a couple of blankets. Helewise, for reasons of her own, would greatly have preferred the same but both Josse and Wilfrid looked quite shocked when she suggested it and Wilfrid protested that he had already arranged that a bed be prepared for her in the smaller of the bedchambers on the upper floor of the solar block.

At least, Helewise thought as, later, she wearily climbed up the winding stone staircase, I have not been put in the main bedchamber. Nevertheless, she was quite sure that she would be powerless to withstand the flood of memories that would assault her the moment she lay down to sleep.

As indeed she was . . .

★   ★   ★

Ivo has been teasing her about taking her there and then down on the rushes, in the hall where she sat on his lap and so aroused them both, but she knows full well that he isn't serious because he has already shown her the sleeping chamber. He led her up to the larger of the two rooms that open off the solar soon after they arrived at the Old Manor and he showed her the big marriage bed made up ready for them. Someone – perhaps the jolly fat woman whose name, she now knows, is Magda; perhaps Elena – has placed a sweet-smelling garland of lavender and rosemary on the pillows. It is because this bed is so very inviting that Ivo and his bride have been so desperately impatient to get into it.

Now, at last, it is time. Down in the hall Ivo stands up with Helewise in his arms, intending to bear her off up the spiral stair to their bedchamber. But Helewise is no lightweight – she is only a little shorter than Ivo, although not nearly as broad in the shoulder or deep in the chest – and, with a shout of laughter, he has to admit defeat and he sets her on her feet. But there is in truth no need for him to carry her to bed; she cannot wait to be there and she runs ahead of him up the stone steps, holding his hand and dragging him behind her.

Up in the bedchamber, a soft summer breeze stirs the light hangings and makes the rose petals that float in the bowl of warm, scented water set out for their use skim across the surface like tiny pink boats. Ivo tears off his tunic and tries to remove his undershirt without loosening the strings that fasten the neck, and he almost throttles himself. Helewise, breathless with both laughter and lusty excitement, helps him and then positions herself before him and stands quite still so that he can untie the laces that fasten down the back of her gown and pull the red silk tight against her curvaceous body. As soon as the laces are sufficiently slack, she drags the lovely, bright garment over her head and places it carefully over a clothing chest that stands stoutly by the bed. Ivo is naked now, and she finds the sight of his hairy chest, flat belly and obvious strength very arousing; he is the very epitome of healthy masculinity. He is a big man. But Helewise is unafraid and she stares at his manhood, reaching out her hand to touch. As her fingers begin to caress, Ivo lets out a moan of desire and, pulling off his bride's chemise, picks her up, lays her on the bed and sets about celebrating their marriage for the very first time under his own roof.

★   ★   ★

Helewise, Abbess of Hawkenlye, lay in her narrow, solitary bed and shivered. Fighting the past, fighting the seductive pictures and sensations that tried to pull her back to the woman she used to be, she gave up trying to sleep and, getting out of bed, fell on her knees on the floor. She prayed, as hard as she had prayed for anything, for the strength to overcome her own memory and the grace to remind herself that she was now and would ever more be a nun.

It was hard, so hard.

It was not until the night was pitch black and perfectly still – even the owls had fallen silent – that peace of a sort fell upon her and at last she fell dreamlessly asleep.

9

Josse, stretching on his straw mattress, reached out and gave the fire a poke with a length of firewood; it had died down to embers but he thought he could re-ignite it. The morning air was bitterly cold. Daylight, as Josse and no doubt the Abbess too had suspected, had brought no sign of any arrivals during the night.

He wondered how the Abbess had slept. She had seemed distracted yesterday and that did not bode well for sound sleep. The upper chamber would have been cold, too, because although the efficient Wilfrid lit a fire there as soon as he knew his guests were going to stay overnight, a small fire lit only a short time before retiring did not do much to warm a stone-walled room.

He had hoped so much that she would find her son here or, failing that – and with hindsight he realised that it always had been unlikely – that Leofgar and his wife and child would have got home during the night and be there now this morning, greeting the Abbess with smiles and saying, *Oh, you weren't worried, were you? No need for anxiety, it's all very simple really!*

The more time that passed with no sign of the young family, the more certain Josse was that there was plenty of cause to be worried and that it wasn't simple at all.

He watched the Abbess as she came gliding across the hall towards him from the stair that led down from the guest chamber. Her face was composed but she looked as if she had passed a restless night. Standing up to greet her, he said, 'The excellent Wilfrid is preparing breakfast for us, my lady, and he reports that our horses can be ready as soon as we give the word.'

She bowed her head slightly. 'Thank you, Sir Josse. I suggest that we eat sparingly and swiftly and get on our way as soon as we can. I do not think—' She broke off.

But he knew what she had been about to say. 'No, I agree,' he said softly. 'I don't think they're coming here either.'

They did not discuss what was obsessing them until Wilfrid had brought their small breakfast – some dry bread, a rind of cheese and a very faintly flavoured drink that seemed to consist mainly of hot water – and gone off to bring the horses round. But as soon as they were once more alone, Josse said in a low voice, 'Where are they, then, my lady? Have you any idea? Can you say where your son might go if for some reason he could not come home?'

She frowned. 'I have been thinking about little else since I awoke,' she confessed. 'I do not know very much about Rohaise's kin, the Edgars, although I recall being told that Rohaise was brought up by her godmother, who is now dead, and I conclude that she is not close to her own parents. It is possible that they too are dead; I cannot be sure. But in any case I do not know where they live.' She gave a faint shrug.

'What of your other son?' Josse asked. 'Might Leofgar have sought sanctuary in the household where he grew up?'

She turned dark-circled eyes to him. 'You think then that Leofgar seeks a place of sanctuary?' she whispered.

Mentally kicking himself for the blunder, he said hastily, 'Indeed no, my lady, it was but a figure of speech.'

But he could tell that she was not convinced.

After a moment she said, 'Dominic was brought up in his uncle's household. My brother Rainer,' she explained. 'Ivo's parents predeceased him and Ivo himself was an only child;

my sons have neither uncles nor aunts on the paternal side of the family. Dominic came to treat his cousins as brothers and indeed he is as another son in that household, or at least he was until he went abroad and I am sure that he will resume that position when he returns home.' She paused. 'Although Rainer would have made Leofgar welcome, I do not think that he has gone there.' Looking up and meeting Josse's eyes, she said, 'There always seemed to be so many people in my brother's cheerful home – open, friendly people – and I just can't see it as being the place for somebody hiding a secret.'

There was a brief and, on Josse's part, surprised silence. Then he said softly, 'That is your conclusion, my lady? That Leofgar has something to hide?'

'Yes,' she replied. 'I wish it were not so but it is surely the only explanation. Let us think back,' she said, and a little colour crept into her face as she leaned towards him. 'Leofgar brought his wife and son to us at Hawkenlye because he was worried for Rohaise's health, in particular her state of mind. There also appears to be something amiss with little Timus, who is unnaturally quiet.' She flashed a brief smile at him and said, 'Or *was*, that is, until he had the good fortune to meet up with a certain large and friendly knight who managed to make him laugh.'

Embarrassed that she should refer to his tricks, Josse waved a dismissive hand. 'It was nothing. Really. The lad was ready to laugh again, that was all.'

'Then you do my family another great service,' she went on, relentlessly ignoring his protestations of modesty, 'by extracting from Leofgar the admission that his priest believes Timus to be a changeling who must be removed from Rohaise's care in order that he be given back to the place where he came from and the true child brought home again. Time passes and, in Hawkenlye's healing atmosphere, Rohaise begins to improve. Perhaps, as she returns to her right mind, she sees this tale of changelings for the nonsense that it is. But then something happens and Leofgar takes the decision to run away in the middle of the night, taking his wife and child with him. But *what* happened?'

Josse paused. But there was no point in prevaricating since she must surely be thinking exactly the same thing. 'De Gifford came hunting for a man known to be violent and whom there was evidence to suggest was making for the Abbey. And then the man's brother is found hanging by the neck.'

'My son saw this man,' the Abbess said slowly. 'And that same night he fled from Hawkenlye and went we know not where. Sir Josse, surely there has to be a connection!'

'Not necessarily,' he said, trying to use his most positive tone to convince her that there was yet room for doubt. 'For one thing, I find it hard to think what reason there could be for your son knowing a man of Teb Bell's nature and habits. Why should their paths have ever crossed? For another, we know what Rohaise – and therefore Leofgar – were afraid of, and it had nothing to do with some Tonbridge ruffian looking for his missing brother.'

The Abbess hesitated, and then said, 'Unless this priest that Rohaise feared was so anxious to locate Leofgar and the family that he employed one or both of the Bell brothers to search for them.'

Josse thought it most unlikely. Nevertheless, he said, 'Perhaps we should speak to the priest before we head off for Hawkenlye.'

And she simply said, 'Very well.'

Wilfrid, his son and the blonde young woman he shyly introduced as his wife saw them on their way and Wilfrid told them where to find Father Luke. Josse and the Abbess rode in silence. They carefully followed Wilfrid's instructions and in time found themselves outside a small and immaculately kept stone cottage that nestled beside the church.

Father Luke was a short and round little man with twinkling blue eyes set in laughter lines and curly grey hair clinging tightly to his bald head as if afraid of being swept away. His black robe was as neat as his cottage, the mud carefully brushed from the hem and only a couple of rusty-looking stains down the front, where the cloth stretched over his protruding stomach. He greeted the Abbess with elaborate and formal good manners, clearly impressed by her title; Josse noticed with amusement that he was not nearly so moved by a mere knight. He offered them what hospitality his humble home might provide but the Abbess, with an impatient shake of her head, declined.

'I am grateful, Father Luke,' she said, 'but Sir Josse and I must be on our way back to the Abbey. I have sought you out merely to ask after two of your flock: Leofgar Warin and his wife Rohaise.'

The priest shook his head. 'Ah, yes, a sad little family,' he said. 'The young wife is deeply troubled and I fear for her child.' Leaning closer, standing right beside the golden mare's shoulder, he elongated his stubby neck so that his face rose closer to the Abbess's and declared, 'I suggested to her that her child was a changeling and said I would take him away and put him in the care of the monks!' He smiled and nodded, as if expecting their amazed and delighted approval.

But the Abbess said, 'What possessed you to do something so cruel?'

All pleasure and pride left his plump face. He exclaimed, 'But my lady, my intention was to *help*!' Hurrying on before she could interrupt, he said, 'I reasoned that perhaps the lady Rohaise herself was uneasy with the child – well, I could see very well that she was – and I came up with the idea of the changeling for her sake. I thought that if I took the little boy away for a time and then brought him back, I could tell her that a miracle had happened while he was with the monks and that, thanks to their prayers, her own boy was returned to her. Then she – all of us – could adopt the pretence that she hadn't been happy with the child before for the very good reason that he wasn't hers! *Oh,*' he pleaded, 'do you not see? I thought to give her a fresh start! I really was trying to help!'

'Yes, I see,' said the Abbess. Josse thought that her tone was marginally less stony. 'And you do not in truth subscribe to the possibility of changelings, Father Luke?'

He laughed, only a little uneasily. 'Of course not, my lady Abbess! Superstitious nonsense!'

Josse, who remembered why they had come to see the priest even if the Abbess appeared to have momentarily forgotten, gave her a swift glance and then said, 'Father Luke, you are not aware, I believe, that Leofgar and Rohaise are not at the Old Manor?'

'Not . . . No, indeed, sir knight, although in fact they were not there when I called a few days ago and I imagined they were merely off on a ride somewhere getting some fresh air. I was planning to visit them today or perhaps tomorrow and—'

Before he could continue and possibly ask any questions that Josse and the Abbess would not wish to answer, Josse interrupted. 'So you did not send two men out to look for them?'

'I did not!' Father Luke's astonishment was written all over his puzzled face. 'As you rightly surmise, I did not know they were from home!' His frown deepening, he said, 'And why should I send someone out to find them?'

Josse shrugged. 'To implement this plan of yours of taking Rohaise's son away from her, perhaps.'

Father Luke had the grace to look ashamed. 'No, indeed, for I—' But then a thought apparently occurred to him, by his dismayed expression not a pleasant one. 'Oh, dear sweet God,' he whispered, 'oh, you think that Leofgar has fled because I was going to take Timus away? Oh, but I was trying to help them!'

He looked as if he were about to weep. The Abbess, Josse noticed, was staring at him with the first signs of compassion on her face which he thought, under the circumstances, was generous. He said, 'Aye, Father, we understand that your intentions were good, even if—' No. He would not go on. Father Luke's conscience was already troubling him quite enough. 'We must be on our way, Father,' he said instead, 'for we wish to reach the Abbey by dusk fall.'

Father Luke nodded vaguely, eyeing the Abbess uneasily. She wished him a fairly distant good day and turned Honey's head, kicking the mare's sides and heading off down the path. Josse, pitying the priest staring miserably after her, said, 'Thank you, Father, you have been very helpful.'

'But I don't understand!' Father Luke cried. 'Why should the Abbess of Hawkenlye ride all the way over here to ask about Leofgar Warin and his wife?'

Josse wondered if to tell him. But then he thought, *she* didn't, and he decided to follow her example. Instead he shrugged and said, 'She keeps her own counsel, Father. You know how it is.' He gave the priest a man-to-man grin and, before Father Luke could say anything else, hurried away after the Abbess.

'The man is a fool,' said the Abbess as she kicked the mare into a canter, 'and his *good intentions*' – the very way in which she spoke the words was a mockery – 'may have cost my son dear.'

'Aye.' Josse had to agree with her. But, knowing her so well, he knew too that quite soon her anger would fade and she would begin to see the matter from the priest's viewpoint. Then she would regret having spoken unkindly about him, confess her impatient and bitter first reaction and no doubt be given penance for it.

Hoping to take her mind off Father Luke and his blundering attempts to help, he said brightly, 'Home to the Abbey and your own bed tonight, my lady!'

But she turned and gave him a severe look that had the effect of preventing any further such conversational attempts. And, for the rest of the journey back to Hawkenlye, they rode in silence.

As they led the horses into the stables, Sister Martha came out to meet them. She gave the Abbess a low and reverential bow and then, just as Josse spied the extra horse already tethered in one of the stalls, said, 'My lady, Sir Josse, Gervase de Gifford is here. He has been shown to your room, where he awaits you.'

'Very well, Sister Martha.' The Abbess turned on her heel and strode off towards her room, Josse following close behind. He was about to make some remark to the effect that Gervase's business with her must be pressing, for him to have waited even when there was no guarantee that she would be returning to the Abbey today, but something about her straight back and the determined set of her shoulders suggested that she had also realised this and did not want to talk about it.

She preceded him into her room, where de Gifford stood up and greeted them with his usual smooth courtesy. 'Good day to you both.'

The Abbess returned his greeting. Moving around her table and seating herself in her chair, she said without preamble, 'I understand that you wish to speak to me?'

De Gifford, emulating her directness, said, 'A man named Arthur Fitzurse has been to see me. He claims to be a friend of the Bell brothers and, apparently unaware that I am already doing so, he has asked – demanded – that I instigate a full-scale search for Walter Bell, whom he is very afraid may have met the same fate as Teb.'

Josse asked swiftly, 'Is this Fitzurse the man who was overheard talking to Teb Bell in the tavern?'

De Gifford turned to him. 'Yes.'

'And what do you know of him?'

'Very little,' de Gifford confessed. 'Personally I have never met him and my man who saw him with Teb Bell will say only that Fitzurse looks "vaguely familiar" and that he "could have seen him once or twice afore". Fitzurse is in middle age – perhaps in the mid-thirties – and dresses well. When seen in the tavern he wore a dark woollen tunic with good, bright trimmings and his boots were of supple and probably costly leather and when he—'

'Your man keeps his eyes open,' the Abbess interrupted.

'He does, my lady,' de Gifford agreed. 'When Fitzurse came to see me, he was dressed in a different tunic and also a thick fur-trimmed cloak. As I said, he is a man who likes to dress well and has the means to do so.'

'We were going to search for Walter Bell ourselves,' Josse said. 'When you left us two days ago, I was planning to organise the lay brothers into a hunt both among the people staying here in the Abbey and also out into the fringes of the forest.'

'And did you find anything?' There was a strange eagerness in de Gifford's tone, Josse thought uneasily, as if it were very important that Josse gave him a positive answer.

Josse glanced at the Abbess. 'Er – we were called away on another matter and, as you see, have only just returned. I will speak to Brother Saul presently and ask if he has news for us.'

'I see.' De Gifford frowned. Then, turning to the Abbess, he said, 'My lady, I have been fervently hoping that Walter Bell would turn up alive and well, with no mischief done either by him or to him. But my own search party has found no trace of him. He is known to frequent the tavern in Tonbridge, just as his brother did – in fact they were regularly to be found there, heads together as they plotted their various schemes. Nobody has seen Walter for some weeks. The last positive sighting was reported by Goody Anne, who had an argument with him one market day at the start of the month.' He paused. 'She is a reliable woman, I have always found, and I am inclined to believe her.'

'So am I,' Josse agreed. Turning to the Abbess, he said, 'I have met Goody Anne on several occasions, my lady, and she is both intelligent and shrewd.' The Abbess nodded. To de Gifford he said, 'What was the argument about?'

De Gifford smiled. 'Walter Bell complained that his dish of pie was cold and Goody Anne said it was his own fault for drinking two mugs of ale on an empty stomach and getting so garrulous that he forgot to eat his dinner.'

'Garrulous,' murmured the Abbess. Both men turned to look at her. 'If he was garrulous, he was talking to somebody, perhaps more than one person,' she said. 'Would she, do you think, Sheriff, remember who?'

Looking at her approvingly as if in appreciation of her astute remark, de Gifford said, 'She does. He was talking with his brother and with Arthur Fitzurse and, according to Anne, they were very intent on whatever it was they were saying – *plotting* was her word – and they kept their heads close and their voices down as if they didn't want to be overheard.'

Josse, picking up de Gifford's urgency, said to the Abbess, 'My lady, with your permission I will seek out Brother Saul and ask if the search party has come up with anything.'

She nodded. 'Of course, Sir Josse. Send someone to find him.'

He bowed briefly and hurried to the door. Opening it, he saw a lay brother crossing the cloister towards the refectory and called out to him; once he had the young man's attention, he asked him to find Brother Saul and send him up to the Abbess's room.

Returning into the room, he found de Gifford answering
some question of the Abbess's about the Bell brothers: '. . . live
in a hovel out on a track leading off the coast road,' he was
saying, 'and neither had a wife, although for a time there was
apparently some – er, a woman who lived with Teb and kept
house for them both, although I understand that they've
always lived in such squalor that her efforts can't have
amounted to much.'

'They live by theft?' she asked.

De Gifford shrugged. 'So it appears, although nothing has
been proved against them.'

'And you told me yourself that one of them is a murderer,'
she murmured.

'Yes.' He lowered his eyes. 'Walter is a dangerous man.'

There was a brief silence. We are all waiting for Saul, Josse
thought, hoping against reason that he will come in with a big
smile to tell us that Walter Bell has seen the error of his ways
and has come to Hawkenlye to be shriven of his sins and is
even now down in the Vale selflessly helping the monks tend
the pilgrims . . .

There was a gentle tap on the door and, in answer to the
Abbess's 'Come in', Saul entered.

He bowed to the Abbess and to de Gifford. He was looking
anxious and so, having glanced at the Abbess and received her
nod of encouragement, Josse hastened to reassure him. 'Saul,
please excuse this abrupt summons but we need to ask you if
anything came of the search for Walter Bell,' he explained
quickly.

Saul was already shaking his head. 'No, Sir Josse. We have
asked everyone presently within the Abbey whether they know
of him or have seen him here and all yesterday afternoon me
and Gussie and four of the other brothers hunted through the
nearer stretches of the forest. We found no sign that anyone
had been camping out there, no sign at all.' He gave a

reminiscent shiver. 'It's too cold for skulking out of doors,' he remarked, 'leastways, not without a very good reason.'

'Aye,' Josse said. But Walter Bell, he thought, may *have* a very good reason for skulking if he's hunting for his brother's killer and does not want anyone to know it.

De Gifford must have been thinking the same. 'You are sure, Brother Saul?' he asked. 'You really do not think that anyone could have been hiding up there in the forest and spying on the comings and goings in the Abbey?'

Saul paused as if giving the question careful consideration. Then he said, 'I can't say as that we'd necessarily have spotted a man who was intent on *hiding*, sir, because that would be the purpose of his hiding, wouldn't it? To make sure anyone who came looking didn't find him?'

'Yes, Saul.' De Gifford smiled faintly.

'But I'm as certain as I can be that there weren't anybody about, nor had been since the heavy frosts began,' Saul continued, sounding more confident now, 'because the ground's set hard up there under the trees and we didn't find any sign in the frozen grass that anyone had been by. Animal tracks aplenty – boar and fox and maybe a wolf – but you'd expect to find them.'

'Thank you, Brother Saul.' The Abbess gave him a warm smile, to which he responded. 'That will be all.'

Saul bowed to them and backed out of the door, closing it carefully behind him.

'Walter Bell isn't here,' Josse said neutrally. 'Nobody can find him.'

'It appears that you are right on both counts,' de Gifford agreed. He looked at the Abbess, then, as if he did not want to continue watching her, turned to Josse. 'In which case it seems I have no option but to reveal to you both what else Arthur Fitzurse said.'

'What?' Josse and the Abbess spoke together and he wondered if she too felt the sudden frisson of alarm.

De Gifford's eyes were still on Josse. 'He claims that there was trouble between the Bell brothers and a third party. The brothers were in dispute with this man, although Fitzurse says he does not know the details of the disagreement. He says that Walter Bell went to visit the man to gain some resolution that the Bells would find satisfactory, and he maintains that Walter has not been seen since. Teb Bell believed that the man whom his brother went to see came to Hawkenlye Abbey. Fitzurse says that Teb followed the man here and would have challenged him, only someone strung Teb up before he could do so.'

'Do you believe him?' Alarm had grown swiftly in him and Josse found as he spoke that his throat was dry.

De Gifford sighed. 'I do not know what I believe,' he admitted. 'Somebody murdered Teb Bell, that is certain, and Walter is still missing. Fitzurse is positive that Walter too is dead, killed by the same hand that slayed his brother.' He paused, then added softly, 'The hand of the man with whom the brothers were in dispute.'

'And you are sure that man is here?' To Josse's admiration, the Abbess sounded quite calm.

Now de Gifford faced her, making himself meet her eyes. 'Yes, my lady. The man is your son.'

10

She thought for a moment that she was going to faint.

Her imagination escaped from her control and she saw them hunting him down, capturing him, taking him and imprisoning him in some dark dungeon; putting him on trial, finding him *guilty* and leading him out to be hanged.

She saw his face.

Stop! she commanded herself. Stop this now!

She took a breath, then another. Fighting for calm, to replace the panicked images with logic and good sense, one thing refused to be banished from her mind: she knew, deep in the intuitive part of herself, that Leofgar was guilty.

Not of murder! Oh, no, not of cold-blooded, vicious murder! Please God that her instincts were right over that, for she just could not see her son as capable of such an act. But he had done something very serious and all this that had happened afterwards was because of it.

But she must not speak any of that to Gervase de Gifford . . .

Raising her eyes, she met his interested gaze; out of the corner of her eye she saw Josse make a move to come to her side and, with an almost imperceptible shake of her head, she stopped him.

'My son is no longer here,' she said quietly. 'He left us two nights ago. He is not at home either; Sir Josse and I went to look for him. It is from there – the house is called the Old Manor and is situated beneath the North Downs – that we have just returned.'

De Gifford watched her closely. 'Forgive me for asking, my lady, but was his nocturnal departure anticipated?'

'Of course not,' she said briskly. 'Something must have happened to make him flee without telling anyone.'

'And this flight occurred the night following the discovery of Teb Bell's body?'

'Yes.'

There was a pause. Then de Gifford said, 'There is no need for me to draw the obvious conclusion that suggests itself.'

'But surely we should mistrust it purely *because* it is the obvious conclusion?' Josse burst out. 'If someone wanted to throw suspicion on Leofgar, what better way than to commit a murder and then come along afterwards and say, oh, Leofgar Warin had an argument with that man and I bet you a barrel of ale that it was Leofgar's hand that killed him!' To make quite sure that neither de Gifford nor Helewise had missed the point, he added, 'We have only this Arthur Fitzurse's word for all this!'

Looking at him, fighting so valiantly for her and her son, Helewise felt a rush of love for him. But de Gifford was speaking; she made herself listen.

'That is true, Josse,' he said, 'and I have told Fitzurse that he must either support his accusations or else withdraw them. He says he will find evidence to support his theory and he promises to discover what it was that the Bell brothers argued with Leofgar about. He also claims that he can prove that Walter Bell went to the Old Manor.' De Gifford glanced quickly at Helewise and then, turning back to Josse, said, 'He wants me to go there with him.'

Helewise bit back her protest. I cannot prevent this, she thought; this man Fitzurse has every right to search for his missing friend and if indeed Walter Bell *did* go to the Old Manor, there will not necessarily be any proof of that.

Every instinct in her demanded that she accompany the

sheriff to Leofgar's manor. But it was possible – in her case absolutely necessary – to deny her instincts. She had just absented herself from Hawkenlye for a day and a night and there was no justification for doing so again. Especially when she had a loyal friend who could go in her place.

Turning to Josse, she said, 'Sir Josse, would you be prepared to ride out with the sheriff? After all, you know the way to the Old Manor, having just come from there.'

His eyes met hers. She tried to put her pleading into her expression – *Josse, please do this for me! I need someone to protect Leofgar's interests and there is nobody I trust more than you!* – and straight away he said, 'Aye, my lady. I would be happy to go, if Gervase is agreeable.'

'I am,' de Gifford said. 'And right pleased to have your company, Josse.'

They set out at once. A horseman was waiting for them at the top of Castle Hill and as they drew level with him, de Gifford introduced him to Josse as one of his men. 'Go and find Arthur Fitzurse, Matt,' de Gifford ordered him, 'and tell him to meet Sir Josse and me at the Old Manor.'

Matt gave a curt nod then turned his horse and cantered off down the track. De Gifford went as if to follow him but Josse said, 'We can go by a route that does not pass through Tonbridge, if you wish; it is the way that the Abbess took me and, as she said, it avoids the attention of the curious.'

De Gifford smiled. 'I do not mind that sort of attention, but I am happy to be shown another way. Lead on!'

Josse was relieved that the sheriff had been so amenable. His reason for suggesting that they take the alternative route was to avoid any chance of Arthur Fitzurse coming to join them on the ride to the Old Manor; he very much wanted the chance to talk to de Gifford alone. Recalling with only a little effort the tracks along which the Abbess had led him, he wondered how to go about raising the matter he wanted to discuss and concluded that, given de Gifford's intelligence and perception, the direct approach was probably best.

So, soon after they had crossed the river, he turned in the saddle and said, 'This tale that Fitzurse has spun for you seems unlikely to me, Gervase. From all that you have said, it sounds as if the man is of a very different quality from the Bell brothers, and yet he claims to know them well enough to be aware of this hypothetical quarrel they have with Leofgar Warin. You have told us that the Bells are villains and that Walter is a killer, and should that not tell us something about Fitzurse? If a man associates with dishonest men, is not his own honesty open to question?'

De Gifford had moved up to ride beside him. 'Yes, Josse, I have been thinking much the same thing,' he agreed. 'Indeed, there can be no question about the nature of the Bell brothers. Although I know I should not express pleasure at any man's death, I have to confess that I felt no grief upon seeing Teb Bell lying dead in the Abbey infirmary, and I cannot entirely suppress the hope that his brother stays missing and never turns up again to cause trouble and pain to innocent people.'

'Then—'

But de Gifford held up a hand. 'Josse, I know what you would say and in my heart I agree: why bother to try to find out what has happened to Walter Bell? But his brother has been murdered and now Fitzurse makes this accusation that implicates Leofgar. For all that Leofgar is the Abbess Helewise's son, I cannot do other than investigate to the best of my ability.'

Josse let out a gusty sigh. 'Aye, Gervase. I know that.' He grinned grimly. 'It was worth a try.'

De Gifford returned his smile. Then, kicking his horse to a canter, said, 'Come on. Best to get this over with.'

★

They reached the Old Manor in advance of Fitzurse. Wilfrid came out into the courtyard to greet them and Josse introduced de Gifford and was on the point of explaining why they were there when the sheriff interrupted.

'I must ask you, Wilfrid, whether you recall a visit from a stranger, round about the beginning of the month?'

Wilfrid's calm expression did not alter. 'No, sir,' he replied. 'I can't say as how I do.'

'A stunted, skinny sort of a man, rough-looking, gingery, unkempt?' de Gifford persisted.

Wilfrid said, 'No, sir.'

'What of the other servants?'

'There's not many of us, sir, not who spend their days mostly up here at the Manor, leastways. There's my lad who tends the yard and the stables and my wife who cooks and keeps house. There was a wet nurse but she was gone ages back, long afore the start of the month.'

'Will you ask your wife and son to come and speak to me, please?' de Gifford asked politely.

'Certainly, sir. My lad'll see to your horses.'

He strode off around the side of the house, returning a few moments later with his fair-haired wife and his young son, both of whom gave shy bows and greetings to Josse. Wilfrid said, 'Now, Anna, now Simeon, just answer the question.' Turning to de Gifford, he said, 'Sir?'

De Gifford asked again. Both the woman and the boy solemnly shook their heads. Then the boy put out his hands for the horses' reins and led them away. The woman, with a swift glance at her husband, bobbed a curtsy and hurried away, muttering something about fetching the visitors something to warm them up.

'Will you come inside, my lords?' Wilfrid asked. 'I will light the fire for you.'

Josse, who was feeling increasingly awkward at what he felt

to be an imposition on these courteous and welcoming people of Leofgar's, spoke up. 'We await another man, Wilfrid. We will remain out here, thank you, and please tell your wife that we do not need any refreshments.'

De Gifford apparently picked up his unease; he said with admirable brevity, 'Wilfrid, the man about whom I've just been asking is missing and there has been a suggestion that he came here to see your master a while ago. We have come here to see if there is any trace of him. The fellow we're expecting is a friend of the missing man and, indeed, it is he who is pressing us to search here for him.'

'I see,' Wilfrid said. 'Please let me know what assistance I can give you, sir. I know the estate well, having lived here all my life.' He glanced briefly from de Gifford to Josse and then back again. 'I'll be in the stables giving Simeon a hand. Call me when you are ready to begin your search.' Then, with a bow, he turned away and walked off in the direction in which his son had led the horses.

It was cold. Josse was beginning to regret his embarrassed rejection of Wilfrid and his wife's offers of hospitality and, from the way that de Gifford was shifting from foot to foot and wrapping his arms around himself, Josse guessed he probably felt the same. But then there came the sound of horse's hooves on the hard ground and presently a man rode into view.

He was dressed in a heavy fur-trimmed cloak over a black tunic and his horse was a good one. He removed his hat to reveal a head of brown hair going grey. His eyes were dark in his sallow face and his mouth had a grim, discontented set to it as if he found it difficult to smile and perhaps, despite his apparent wealth and good health, considered that he had little to smile about. Taking all this in, one thing struck Josse more forcefully than any other detail: Arthur Fitzurse rode into the courtyard of the Old Manor staring around him with the proprietorial air of one returning to his own home.

De Gifford stepped forward to greet him. 'I have brought with me Sir Josse d'Acquin,' he added, turning to present Josse. 'Josse, this man is Arthur Fitzurse.'

'Sir Josse d'Acquin,' Fitzurse repeated, with a twist of his mouth that seemed to suggest he knew very well who Josse was and why he was there. 'Well, sheriff, shall we be about our search? You have questioned the servants, I imagine?'

'I have.' De Gifford watched Fitzurse dismount. 'They have no recollection of any stranger visiting at the start of the month.'

'I see.' Fitzurse looked around haughtily, as if expecting someone to have appeared by now to take his horse. He yelled, 'Groom! You are needed!' and, after several moments, Wilfrid appeared and without a word took the reins from Fitzurse's gloved hand.

Fitzurse stared after him as he led the horse away. 'Feed and water him!' he commanded.

There was a faint, 'Aye, sir,' then Wilfrid was gone.

'Where do you propose we begin?' de Gifford asked.

'In the house.' Fitzurse strode off to the steps and mounted them, opening the door into the main hall. It was empty and smelled faintly of the dried rushes on the floor.

'There's nobody here,' Josse pointed out.

Fitzurse was staring around him, peering beneath the rushes, looking behind hangings, prodding at the shield that hung on the far wall, kicking at the charred logs in the great hearth and, picking up a kindling stick, poking through the mound of ashes. Then he turned his attention to the long table, running his hands over its surface and feeling underneath it.

'What are you looking for there?' de Gifford demanded curtly.

Fitzurse turned to him, his eyes bright in the dim light. 'I told you that the Bell brothers had a dispute with Leofgar Warin,' he said. 'There may be some evidence of this concealed within the hall.'

'Evidence?' De Gifford sounded as incredulous as Josse was feeling. 'What, do you speak of some written document, some incriminating manuscript? But good God, man, the Bells are surely illiterate! What could they possibly have to do with *evidence?*'

Fitzurse barely paused in his search. 'I cannot answer that unless and until I find something,' he replied smoothly. 'In the meantime, let us proceed with our hunt.'

De Gifford gave an impatient sound. 'We will look in the solar,' he announced. 'Josse?'

Together the two of them went up the stone stair to the solar and looked in the two sleeping chambers and the small chapel. Other than the family's possessions – of good quality but few in number – there was nothing to be seen. Nor was there, Josse reflected, hating this imposition even more now that he was having to trespass into the private areas of the house, anywhere that a man could hide. Or – he tried not to think of it – where a body could be concealed.

De Gifford came out of the small chapel. 'There's nothing here,' he said in a low voice. 'Josse, I think we're wasting our time. And I feel badly about doing this. Hunting through the house when its master and mistress are not here, for no better reason than because a man like Fitzurse has demanded it, does not feel right. Come, let's go down again.'

They found Fitzurse on his back under the table. 'Have you found your evidence?' de Gifford asked coolly.

Fitzurse stood up, brushing down his tunic and arranging his cloak. Instead of answering, he said, 'Anything amiss above?'

'No,' Josse said, just as de Gifford said, 'Nothing.'

'Then we must search outside,' Fitzurse declared.

★

For a long time they did so. They kept together – at Fitzurse's insistence – and searched kitchen, stables, storehouses, undercroft and even the room behind the kitchen where Wilfrid and his family lived. The blonde woman stood with eyes cast down as Fitzurse poked about in the blankets and covers on the narrow bed and raked through the piled ashes around the hearth; Wilfrid stared off into the distance as if his mind were far away. The child, after a scared glance, had disappeared in the direction of the stables.

Then they began to search the ground around the Manor, looking under the winter-bare trees and along the track that led off into the forest. Finally, as Fitzurse stood staring down a faint path probably made by wild boar, de Gifford had had enough.

'Do you propose that we dig up the forest?' he asked grimly. 'Or may we now admit that, even given that Walter Bell did come here, which I propose is unlikely since none of the servants saw him, then he left no trace of his visit?'

Fitzurse turned and glared at him. 'He came here,' he insisted in a strangely forceful tone. 'I know he did. And he has not been seen since.'

'We have only your word for that,' de Gifford said.

'Do you accuse me of lying?' Fitzurse demanded. 'Is that it?' He turned his angry eyes to Josse. 'And you, sir knight, is that what you think too, you who are such a close friend of the lady Abbess?' He nodded as if to say, yes, I know all about *you*. Then, with an abrupt movement, he said, 'Oh, have it your own way then. I'll carry on the hunt alone!'

'It will do you little good if you do find evidence,' de Gifford pointed out, 'since, without a witness, there is nothing to say that you did not bring it here yourself. Furthermore, use of the forest that stretches out before us is permitted to all at this time of year and so it would be virtually impossible to link anything that you did happen to find with Leofgar Warin and his household.'

Fitzurse stared at him as if he would have liked to punch him. Then, lips tight, he hissed, 'I have not done with this matter yet, sheriff. Just wait. Just you wait.' And, leaving behind him a feeling of disturbing unease, he strode off under the trees.

After a moment, de Gifford said, 'Josse, I am unhappy over this. There is *something* . . .' He screwed up his face as if trying to extract what he felt from the chilly air of the forest fringe. Then, shrugging, he added, 'But it will not reveal itself, I fear, to two cold men who wish they were somewhere else. Come, let us fetch our horses and return to the Abbey. The lady Abbess will be relieved that nothing has been found.'

Aye, she will, Josse silently agreed. Remembering how she had looked when de Gifford had revealed who it was that Fitzurse sought, he added to himself, she'll be relieved, even though she may very well also be surprised.

It was late when they finally reached the Abbey. All was quiet and still within the high walls but, as he and de Gifford rode off in the direction of the stables, Josse was aware of Sister Ursel diligently pushing home all three of the stout bars that secured the gates as if she too felt the vague sense of menace that seemed to hang in the air. The two men saw to their horses and then Josse led the way out of the smaller gate that opened on to the track leading down to the Vale. Once more the porteress secured it behind them, bidding them both a soft goodnight.

The monks, lay brothers and the few visiting pilgrims who were staying overnight in the Vale's sparse accommodation appeared to have settled down to sleep. Moving quietly to his own habitual corner, Josse found a bedroll and blankets for de Gifford and the two of them made themselves as comfortable as they could. There was a fire still burning in the central hearth and its warmth was very welcome.

Leaning close to Josse, clearly anxious not to disturb the sleeping people nearby, de Gifford whispered, 'Fitzurse will go on with his search, I am thinking, despite the fact that I implied that anything he managed to turn up would not necessarily count against Leofgar.'

'You think that he will find something?' Josse whispered back.

De Gifford sighed. 'I hope not, although I confess that I fear the worst.'

Aye, Josse thought, and that was why you were at such pains to discount any incriminating discovery that Fitzurse might make even before he has made it.

Listening to the rustling of the straw palliasse as de Gifford turned over and lay down, Josse reflected that, like the Abbess, the sheriff too seemed almost to be expecting trouble . . .

It was not a comfortable thought on which to try to get to sleep.

II

Josse reported to the Abbess early the next day. She was clearly very relieved when he told her that nothing had turned up at the Old Manor to prove that Walter Bell had visited Leofgar there. Josse did not think it either kind or necessary to add that there had been no sign of a body either, although he was quite sure she had been dreading that there might have been.

'What will Gervase de Gifford do now?' she asked. Her appearance of serenity, Josse decided, was costing her considerable effort. Her face was pale and he noticed that her strong hands were clenched so tightly that the knuckles showed white. As if aware of his sympathetic eyes on them, she tucked her hands away in the opposite sleeves of her habit.

'He has returned to Tonbridge,' Josse replied. 'He intends to carry on the search for Walter Bell as he suggests that finding the wretched man would be the best way of answering Fitzurse's accusations.'

'But even if Walter Bell should be found alive,' she said slowly, 'his brother Teb has been murdered.'

'By an unknown hand,' Josse countered swiftly. 'De Gifford has no suggestions to make on the matter, my lady; at present he has no idea what the motive can have been and therefore he hesitates to speculate who might have killed the man.'

'That is wise,' she murmured. 'I wish that I—' But whatever she wished was to remain known to herself alone, for she folded her lips on the rest of the remark. Then after a moment she said, 'And you, Sir Josse? What will you do?'

He had been thinking about this and had made up his mind; it was partly in order to tell her what he had decided to do that he had come to see her. 'I shall go out into the forest,' he announced. 'Aye, I know that Saul and the brothers carried out a thorough search, but I want to see for myself.' He smiled grimly. 'They are capable and I do not doubt their diligence, my lady. But the forest has secrets, as you and I well know, and it may be that I can find my way into hidden places that other eyes, no matter how well intentioned, would not see.'

She watched him. Then she said softly, 'Be careful.'

'I am always careful.' He tried to smile at her but he did not think he made much of a job of it.

He bowed to her and turned to go. He thought he heard her say 'Thank you, my friend', but he could not be sure.

He decided to walk up to the forest. Horace was a big horse and not renowned for moving silently and, besides, the trees grew low above the lesser paths and tracks and Josse would pass along beneath the bare winter branches more easily on his own two feet than high up astride his horse. He went to collect his sword and dagger and then strode quickly out through the Abbey gates and crossed the track, hurrying across the grass and increasing his pace as he drew nearer to the fringe of trees that circled the main forest. As always, he began to feel the unique atmosphere of the Great Forest reach out to embrace him and he hoped – prayed – that its touch was not hostile.

You could never be sure . . .

He followed the main track through the trees for some time. Memories sprang up to haunt him. Over there, down that smaller path, was the old charcoal burners' camp, long disused by the charcoal burners but a refuge for others in times of crisis. Up along that path the ways branched and one led to a clearing where a woman had hanged herself. And dead ahead, deep in the forest's heart, was the mysterious place that he and the Abbess had stumbled across and where they had witnessed something that he was still inclined to believe had really been nothing more than a disturbing vision.

And then there was Joanna.

He dreamed about her often. But he had not consciously thought about her for some time other than the fleeting images that he always tried to suppress whenever he saw the Abbess riding that beautiful golden mare. For Honey had been Joanna's horse and she had left the mare in the Abbey's keeping when she went away. Josse sometimes had the impression that people *knew* about Joanna but refrained from telling him; there had been one or two hints to that effect and Sister Tiphaine had once muttered that he wasn't to worry about the lass, she was doing all right, whatever that meant. Sister Tiphaine, it was widely rumoured, had dealings with the strange and elusive Forest Folk, that self-contained band who appeared like the sunrise and vanished like the morning mist. Did that mean that the Forest Folk had taken Joanna in? Or merely that they knew where she was – *how* she was – and somehow contrived to pass word on to the Hawkenlye herbalist? Josse had no way of finding out; Sister Tiphaine had never said anything further and Josse wondered if perhaps the duty of obedience that she owed to her Abbess made her keep any knowledge she might have had strictly to herself. Sister Tiphaine might, as they often said, have one foot in the pagan past but her loyalty to the Abbess was, Josse guessed, born out of respect and quite possibly love and therefore unbreakable. The Church – and so it followed, went the reasoning, also the woman who ordered the comings and goings of Haw-kenlye Abbey – would seriously disapprove of a nun even thinking about pagan forest dwellers, never mind having clandestine dealings with them, and so if indeed it were true that Sister Tiphaine had mysterious ways of contacting them, she was not going to boast about the fact and she would probably do her utmost to make sure her superior did not know.

Now as he tramped along the forest tracks he wondered if he could find his way to wherever it was that Joanna lived. If, that was, she were still there . . .

Then he decided simultaneously that there was no possibility of his finding her hiding place and that he wasn't really sure he wanted to anyway. Squaring his shoulders, he reminded himself what he was doing out there and turned his full concentration to the search for Walter Bell.

It was hard to judge the time when deep inside the forest, for the thickly growing branches and endless network of almost leafless twigs above made it difficult to get a proper idea of the sun's position. But, judging from the way in which the light was starting to fade, it must have been quite late in the day when Josse finally turned for home.

He was coming to the conclusion that Brother Saul was right: only the animals were at present living in that corner of the Great Forest. He found many traces of the brothers' passage and he noted, impressed, just how carefully they had searched. My day has been a waste of time, he thought; I should have taken Saul's word for it and done something more fruitful than obeying my own proud voice telling me to go and check because I know the forest better than the lay brothers. Well, I'll just have to—

He heard something.

He stopped stock-still, hardly breathing, ears straining.

Nothing.

He began to walk cautiously on. The path just there circled a shallow dell bordered on its steeper slopes by thick brambles and overshadowed by a large beech tree whose roots curled out from the dell's banked side. There were a few coppery leaves still adhering to the beech's branches and the ground in the dell was thick with beech mast.

I have disturbed some small creature picking through the beech mast, Josse told himself. Even so small a noise sounds loud in this uncanny silence.

Bracing his shoulders – his hand on the hilt of his sword for good measure – he walked on.

He had gone no more than a dozen paces when a voice just behind him called, 'Sir Josse!'

Whipping round, drawing his sword, he would have lunged towards his assailant except that the man made no move to attack. Instead he spread his arms to indicate that he held no weapon and, in a voice just tinged with amusement, said, 'No need for your sword! I am not your enemy.'

It was Leofgar.

Pushing his sword back down into its scabbard, Josse let out his breath and felt his fast heartbeat gradually return to normal. 'Leofgar,' he said, 'oh, that glad I am to see you.'

Then, without thinking about it, he put his arms around the younger man and gave him a hearty embrace. Returning it, Leofgar laughed shortly. 'I did not expect this sort of a greeting from my mother's good friend,' he observed as Josse let him go.

Josse shrugged. 'You have worried her gravely, I'll not deny it. But you've come back, so I would guess that whatever went wrong to make you run off as you did must either have been put right or cannot have been too serious in the first place?' He tried to make the remark a statement and not a question, but he did not think he had succeeded.

Leofgar shook his head. 'Oh, Sir Josse, I wish that were true! But I must first say that I have not come back, if by that you mean that I am on my way to the Abbey to give a full explanation of my actions.'

'Then why are you here?' Josse spoke more gruffly than he

had intended; to see the happy outcome that he had envisaged for the Abbess disappear without so much as a farewell was hard to bear.

'I have to talk to you.'

'To *me*?'

'Yes, don't sound so surprised.' The note of amusement was back. 'My mother trusts you absolutely. Here I am, in dire need of a reliable confidant and adviser, so what better, I thought to myself, than to hide away in some place where the great Sir Josse d'Acquin is bound to come looking?'

'You can't have known I would search the forest!'

'I admit I was downcast when the lay brothers made their hunt – very thorough they were too, let me tell you, and one of them almost found me. He would have done had I not climbed up a very large old yew tree and hidden till he had gone. But still I believed that you would come, for I judge you to be a man who is not satisfied until he has seen for himself.'

'You judge right,' Josse muttered. 'Yet it was a dubious plan, for all that.'

Leofgar shrugged. 'Dubious or not, it was the only plan I had.'

Suddenly Josse thought of something. 'You have not forced your wife and child to share your vigil, have you?' he exclaimed. 'It's *cold*, man, and—'

'Of course not.' Leofgar's tone was almost scathing, as if to say, you cannot believe I would do such a thing! 'They are safe in a warm and welcoming refuge.'

Josse studied him. He was well wrapped-up against the weather and he looked clean and, although his face was anxious, he did not have the pinched, shrivelled look of someone who had spent any length of time starving out in the cold. 'You too have been staying in this refuge,' he said.

'I have. My days I have spent here, waiting for you. By night I return to my hiding place.' His eyes fixed to Josse's, he said with a smile, 'And do not try to follow me, Sir Josse. I ask for your word on this.'

Josse hesitated and then said reluctantly, 'You have it. I shall not follow you.'

Leofgar laughed. 'The promise was not to *try* to follow me,' he corrected. 'A man should not boast of his own abilities but I doubt that you could pick up my trail if I did not want you to. You missed me in the dell there and I believe that I took you by surprise when I spoke your name just now?'

'Aye,' Josse acknowledged. 'You merge well with the woodland, Leofgar.'

'I learned when young how to use the cover of the forest,' he said. 'So would you have done if you'd had to live with a gang of boys all bigger than you who were intent on giving you a hiding for every real or imagined misdemeanour.'

Josse guessed he must be speaking of the household where he had lived while he learned the duties of page and squire. 'You were not happy in the place where your mother put you?'

'Happy?' Leofgar appeared to consider. 'I'm not sure that I expected happiness, Sir Josse. I was well fed, well clothed, my duties were no more than those of any other boy. And when I was one of the older ones, I dare say I was not above making some smaller lad's life a misery from time to time. It's the way of things,' he concluded. Then, with a flash of anger in the grey eyes that were so like his mother's, he hissed, 'Don't you dare tell her!'

Josse almost laughed. 'I won't,' he said. 'You have my word on that, too.'

They had moved away from the dell, walking as they talked, strolling a short distance back down the path that would eventually emerge out from the trees just above the Abbey. Now Leofgar stopped and, putting a hand on Josse's sleeve, said, 'I will not come any further. Will you stay here with me while I tell you what I have to say?'

'Aye, lad. That I will.' But then a thought struck him; he said, 'Just now you implied that you expected me to come looking. But I wasn't looking for you; I'm searching for somebody else.'

'I know who you're looking for. My mother told me about the search party.'

'You know who he is, then?'

'Oh, yes.' Leofgar's face was grave. 'You won't find him, Sir Josse. Nobody will, or I pray that they won't.'

'But you—'

'Please,' Leofgar said urgently, 'let me tell my story. Then all will become clear.'

With an ironic bow, Josse said, 'Go on. I will try not to interrupt.'

Leofgar had snapped a length of twig from the beech tree and his long hands were steadily peeling off the bark. Intent on this small action, he began to speak. 'My wife Rohaise, as you observed, is not well. She suffers from unaccountable miseries and she thinks things – bad and terrible things – that are not true. As I told you at the Abbey, we have sought help from various sources and our parish priest encouraged us to pray. When that did no good, Father Luke decided that Timus was a changeling and must be taken away to the monks, where hopefully the real Timus would miraculously appear to replace the spirit child.'

'But Father Luke did not really believe that!' Josse burst out. 'Your mother and I have been to see him and he told us he made that up to try to help Rohaise! He hoped that if he took Timus away and then brought him back again, explaining to Rohaise that *this* was her real child, it might just put everything right!'

Leofgar was nodding. 'I wondered if that might be his thinking,' he said. With a brief self-deprecating smile, he went on, 'Perhaps I should have tried to argue with him. But if he made Rohaise believe there was a reason why she felt she was failing with her son – the reason being that he wasn't in truth her son but a changeling – then she might feel as if she had been offered a new beginning when her so-called real son was returned to her.'

'Aye, that's it!' Josse said eagerly. 'Almost exactly the priest's words!'

Leofgar looked questioningly at him. 'You think Father Luke did right?'

'No, of course not! He utterly misread Rohaise's distress and his attempt was at best blundering, at worst deeply damaging. But your mother and I felt him to be more a fool than an intentionally cruel man.'

'Yes, I agree,' Leofgar said, 'although it is difficult to maintain a charitable view when someone is threatening to return very shortly and take your child away.'

'I understand,' Josse said gently. 'Your troubles have been grave, but—'

'You have not,' Leofgar cut in, 'heard the half of them yet.'

'Oh.' His heart sinking, Josse said, 'Very well. Tell me the rest.'

Leofgar went back to his bark stripping. 'I have explained all this,' he said, 'as a prelude for what follows, because it is a reason for— Well, hear it for yourself and judge. When Father Luke had gone, I left the house and went out. I was angry with the priest and also, I am ashamed to confess, angry with Rohaise. God forgive me, I should have stayed there with her, comforting her, but I feared for a time that my anger would spill out and I would shout at her, the last thing I should have done. So I saddled up my horse and went for a ride until I was calm again. Then I went home.'

His face had paled, Josse noticed. Whatever he was remembering clearly had lost none of its power to distress.

'Someone else had come to the house in the short time that I was away,' he said, his voice low. 'I think now that the man was waiting his chance and entered the hall soon after I had ridden away. I am not sure what he was after – although I can make a guess – but poor Rohaise, in her distress, believed that he had been sent by Father Luke to take Timus away. She heard him coming and hid behind the hangings at the far end of the hall.'

'Were not your servants there?' Josse broke in.

'No. We were enjoying a bright spell of weather and Wilfrid and Anna were in the habit of taking Simeon out into the forest most days to collect wood. Again, the man who sneaked into my hall must have seen them go out that morning and known that his chance had come. Nobody at home but a frightened woman and a little child. How brave, not to be scared off by them!' Anger coloured Leofgar's voice but after a moment he calmed himself and resumed. 'Rohaise peered round the wall hanging and saw a short, scrawny man creep through the doorway and across the hall. She was puzzled because at first he looked at the big table at the end of the room, feeling underneath it and up and down its legs as if looking for something. Then he went to the chest and, finding it locked, took out a knife and forced the clasp, splitting the wood. He rummaged through the contents – there were some blankets and some clothes of Rohaise's – throwing them on the floor.'

'I recall that chest,' Josse murmured, half to himself. 'I remember noticing a recent repair.'

'You keep your eyes open,' Leofgar observed. 'Rohaise was too terrified to ask herself why this man who had come for Timus should be searching through our furniture. She stood there, trying not to breathe, trying to keep Timus calm, but, understandably, he was as frightened as she was and he let out a sob. The man heard and came lunging across the hall with his knife in his hand. Rohaise was beyond any coherent thought but instinctively she did the best thing that she could have done. As he approached she leapt out at him screaming at the top of her voice and he was so shocked that he stepped hastily back. She kicked out at the hand holding the knife and managed to knock it out of his grip, then threw herself on him, punching his face and raking him with her finger nails. He recovered very quickly and got hold of her hands, then ripped open her bodice and threw her on the ground, pulling up her skirt. But she wriggled out from beneath him and got to her feet, racing off down the hall and away from Timus, still hiding behind the wall hanging. She could hear the man thudding after her and she turned to look at him. He was holding the knife and it was aimed at her. She picked up a silver jug that he'd found in the chest and cast aside and she flung it at his legs. It caught him right on the knee and he tripped and fell heavily, cracking the side of his head on the stone flags.'

'The fall killed him?'

'No,' Leofgar admitted. 'Better for him had it done so,' he added in a murmur. Then, eyes at last meeting Josse's, he said, 'Rohaise feared for her life, Josse. She believed this man had come to take Timus away but it seemed to her that for some reason he wanted to rape and kill her. I say this not to gain your sympathy' – he must, Josse thought, have noticed the instinctive compassion that the story was arousing – 'but to explain what she did next.' He paused, took a breath and said flatly, 'She fetched Timus from behind the wall hanging and put him safely away up in the bedchamber, telling him that he must hide, he'd got to hide and not be found, and she barred the door so that he could not get out.'

Hide, Josse thought. Hide. Aye, that was what the child had said when he'd snuggled inside Josse's cloak that day. Great God, the poor little lad had seen the man attack his mother! No wonder he'd turned dumb.

'Then,' Leofgar was saying, 'she went for my hounds and let them into the hall.'

'Your hounds,' Josse echoed, his heart still overflowing with pity for the damaged child.

'Yes, my hounds,' Leofgar sounded impatient. 'They are big dogs and they are trained to go after wounded creatures that get up and try to crawl away. They go for the throat, you know, as that way the kill is accomplished quickly.'

'And—' Josse swallowed. 'And they attacked the intruder?'

'Rohaise shut them in the hall and went a little way up the stair, leaving them there with the body. She thought she heard some sounds, although she is not sure what they implied. She waited, but there was nothing more. Then she crept down again and opened the door a crack. The man was lying exactly as she had left him and one of the dogs was sniffing at the blood pooling on the floor beneath his head. Rohaise tiptoed closer, then closer, until she was standing right over him. Suddenly he leapt up and lunged at her with his knife. She screamed and flung herself out of his reach and at the same moment one of the hounds leapt at him and took him by the neck. Great arcs of scarlet flew out all over her as the dying heart beat its last – Josse, she was *covered* with his blood.' Leofgar's eyes were wide with remembered horror. 'Then the hounds padded off towards the door and she stood staring down at the man.' Leofgar paused. 'Soon after that I came home and found them. Rohaise had crept away to hide on the stair, shaking with shock and trying pitifully to pull the ripped pieces of her bodice together to cover herself. Timus was weeping hysterically up in the bedchamber and the man was on the floor of the hall. He was quite dead. He no longer had a throat.'

Josse waited while his shocked reaction abated slightly. Then he said firmly, 'Your wife was threatened, Leofgar. She feared that this intruder had come to take her child, and furthermore that for some reason he meant to assault or even kill her. When a man armed with a knife attacks an unarmed woman whom he has just tried to rape, anyone would surely agree that she is within her rights to defend herself!'

'Perhaps,' Leofgar said dully. 'But I dared not take that chance.'

'So you came to Hawkenlye.' But no, that could not be right, Josse thought, for there had been no bloody body lying in the hall at the Old Manor when he and the Abbess had arrived.

He looked enquiringly at Leofgar and said, 'What did you do with him?'

'I stripped him, burned his foul and filthy clothes in a big fire on the hearth and hid him in an outbuilding,' Leofgar said tonelessly. 'I buried his knife, his belt buckle and the remains of his boots. Rohaise and I tried to comfort Timus and finally we got him to go to sleep up in our bed. Then we cleaned every inch of the hall and she put her torn and bloody gown on the fire with the blood-soaked rushes from the floor. We had to make sure there was no sign left to give us away when Wilfrid and his family returned and when I asked him – Wilfrid – to mend the broken chest I told him a lie about having lost the key.' Leofgar looked sad, as if it had hurt to treat his faithful servant this way and he still regretted it. 'While we cleaned the hall I had worked out what to do with the body,' he hurried on, 'and when the light began to fail, I slipped out to make my secret preparations. I penned my swine up in a lonely place where nobody goes, leaving them without any food, and then two days later I took the dead man out into the forest and fed him to them. What was left of him when they were done, I buried.' His anguished eyes suddenly raised to meet Josse's, he said, 'Rohaise tried to stop me. Even after the horror of knowing for two whole days that his – that the corpse was hidden away on our land and what would happen were it to be discovered, still she said it was wrong to deny the man Christian burial. We—' He stopped, drew a breath and then said softly, 'We almost fought over it. She was beside herself, but I was determined.'

Josse could well imagine Rohaise's state of mind. How on earth had she borne it? Great God, but the poor lass had suffered! He was on the point of saying as much but a glance at Leofgar stopped the words before they were uttered; it had quite clearly cost the young man dear to tell his story.

So instead, realising even as he spoke that he already knew the answer, Josse said, 'And you now know who this man was?'

Leofgar sighed. 'Yes, for he was very like his brother whom we found hanging from the tree.' He summoned a very faint smile. 'I thought for one dreadful moment that he'd survived having his throat torn out and being eaten by my swine and had got up and come after me. But I was wrong.' He paused, throwing his head back and for a moment screwing his eyes up tight, as if trying to rid himself of the images of violence that he could not help but see. 'It was Teb who was hanged. The man who died in my hall was Walter Bell.'

12

After a long time Josse said, 'What do you want me to do?'

Leofgar turned to him, his eyes alight with some emotion that Josse could not identify; it occurred to him later that it was probably gratitude.

'I must find out what Walter Bell was after and why he attacked my wife,' he said. 'I want you to help me.'

'Aye. I will.'

There was silence for a moment. Then Leofgar gave a cough and said, 'Thank you.'

Josse, who also felt the need of a little recovery time, said after a pause, 'I may already be able to offer something for you to think about. We have been led to understand that you knew the Bell brothers, moreover that there was some sort of a dispute between you and them and that this was the reason for Walter Bell having sought you out.'

'Who told you that?' Leofgar demanded. 'It is a lie, I swear it! I had never seen him before the moment that I looked down on his dead body in my own hall!'

'Aye, and I believe you,' Josse hastened to reassure him. 'Me, I always doubted it anyway. Said as much at the time,' he added, half to himself. 'Earlier you said you had some idea why Bell had gone to the Old Manor. What was it?'

'Theft,' Leofgar said simply. 'Rohaise is insistent that the first thing he did was to have a thorough look at our table, as if it were his aim to search for—' He gave a helpless shrug. 'I cannot say. Then, as I told you, he broke open the chest.'

'Was there anything of value in the chest?'

'Oh – some pieces of silver. Quite valuable, I suppose, but we keep them put away because the bright shine of the metal is such an attraction to Timus and Rohaise is tired of constantly having to polish off his sticky finger marks.'

Josse waited, and after a moment Leofgar said slowly, 'Walter Bell must have seen the silver, for he scattered the entire contents of the chest on the floor. Yet he made no move to steal anything . . .'

'I think,' Josse said gently, 'that we may rule out theft as a motive. Could it . . .' But this was delicate ground and he had no wish to arouse the young man's ready anger again. 'Perhaps his intention was to do what he tried to do to your wife,' he said as tactfully as he could.

Leofgar shook his head impatiently. 'I thought of that too but a man intent on raping a woman while her man and her servants are from home is hardly likely to rummage through the household belongings first. I have always understood rape to be a crime of hot blood and swift implementation.'

The fury was there, simmering beneath the surface, but at present Leofgar was keeping it under control. With a flash of insight, Josse thought suddenly that perhaps Walter Bell's death had been relatively easy after all, compared to what Leofgar might have done to him had he come home to find the man raping his wife.

'I think,' Josse said after a brief silence, 'that it is my turn to tell you something, Leofgar.'

'What would that be?' Leofgar turned to glare at him, his emotions clearly still running high.

'I ought to explain to you that we have learned a little about the Bell brothers from Gervase de Gifford. When Teb Bell was found hanged close to the Abbey, we postulated that perhaps he had been on his way to Hawkenlye to look for Walter. He had been overheard down in Tonbridge saying that he was going up the hill to hunt for somebody. Now that phrase *up the hill*, in Tonbridge parlance, is usually taken to mean Hawkenlye Abbey, and we all surmised that Teb Bell was intending to go to Hawkenlye to find Walter, who was missing.'

'Of course he was missing,' Leofgar said coldly. 'My wife set my hounds on him and they had just killed him.'

'Aye, I know.' Josse waved an impatient hand; he was trying to follow a twisting path of a tale and did not want to be interrupted. 'Then, when another piece of the pattern was revealed, we thought that Teb Bell had a very different quarry in mind. We – or rather Gervase de Gifford – thought that Teb was probably aware that Walter was dead and was in fact on his way to Hawkenlye in pursuit of his brother's killer.'

'Me,' Leofgar supplied.

'You did not kill him,' Josse said swiftly.

Leofgar shrugged. 'He died in my house and we have but the word of my wife that she killed him to defend herself and her child.'

'Her word is good enough for me.'

Leofgar gave him a bright look. 'Thank you, Josse.' Then: 'But if Teb Bell was in truth coming to Hawkenlye to look for me, who strung him up on that branch?' His face darkening with sudden realisation, he said, 'Josse, I swear to you that *I* didn't, although by this reasoning anyone would conclude that I had abundant motive.'

'That is true,' Josse agreed, 'but I do not believe you killed Teb Bell.'

'What makes you say that?' Leofgar appeared genuinely curious. 'I hope,' he added with a small laugh, 'that it is not your feelings towards my mother that are speaking.'

'Your mother—' No. Josse really did not want to discuss Helewise with her son. 'No,' he said instead. 'It is merely that I recognise an honest man when I see one. You, Leofgar, would hold your head up high when accused of something that you had truly done and shout yes, I did it, so what?'

Surprisingly amid that grim conversation, Leofgar burst out laughing. 'How long have we known one another, Josse?' he asked, still amused.

'Oh – a matter of days, and not closely at that.'

'What a good judge you are,' Leofgar murmured. 'Pride and a tendency to run my head straight into stone walls were ever my devils.' Then, his face straightening, he said, 'Who, then, murdered Teb Bell?'

Instead of further surmise, Josse said, 'There is another man in this tangle of whom I have not yet spoken. He was probably an associate of both the Bell brothers; certainly of Teb, with whom he was observed talking in the tavern at Tonbridge, when Teb spoke of coming up the hill. This man has demanded that Gervase de Gifford organise a hunt for Walter Bell, whom he claims was last heard of making his way to your house to try to resolve this rumoured dispute between you and the brothers.'

'There *is* no dispute! I never met either Bell alive!'

'I know,' Josse reassured him. 'I realise now that the whole business of the dispute is but a diversionary tactic to hide from us the true heart of this business. But for the life of me, I have absolutely no idea what that true heart can be!'

'Who is this man who makes up lies about me?' Leofgar said, an edge of menace in his voice.

'His name is Arthur Fitzurse.'

'Arthur Fitzurse.' Slowly Leofgar shook his head. 'It means nothing. What does he look like?'

Josse brought the man to mind. 'His age is perhaps in the mid-thirties; he is well dressed, greying dark hair, dark eyes and a thin, discontented sort of a face.'

'No,' Leofgar said. 'No, I do not believe I know him.'

Why, then, Josse wondered, staring hard at Leofgar, should he know you?

It seemed that Leofgar was thinking much the same thing. 'It must seem strange to you, Josse, that this man who makes up such fictions about me is unknown to me?'

'Aye, it does,' Josse agreed. 'I would guess that Fitzurse is behind the activities of the Bell brothers. It is his hand, I am certain, that directed Walter Bell to search your house.'

Leofgar sighed. 'We come back to our starting point,' he said. 'We must find out what Walter Bell was looking for.'

Josse glanced up at the darkening sky, in which the first stars were appearing. 'It grows late,' he observed, 'and high time you and I were making our way to the safety of our lodgings.' He glanced at Leofgar, who gave a faint twist of a smile, as if to say, no, I'm still not going to tell you where we're hiding. 'I will return to the Abbey,' Josse continued, 'and tomorrow I will speak to Gervase de Gifford.' He hesitated. 'Have I your permission to reveal what you have just told me?' he asked gently.

'I have been asking myself the same question,' Leofgar said. 'To my mother, yes. For one thing' – he shot Josse a penetrating look – 'I would guess that you and she have few secrets; for another, I did not feel easy when we were together at the Abbey for I was all too aware that she knew I was hiding something from her, something very grave. So, to have her know the truth would be a relief to me.'

'Very well. I shall tell her exactly what you have told me.'

'Thank you. As for de Gifford – Josse, what do you think? You know the man far better than I, I imagine?'

'Aye, and I judge him to be decent, incorruptible and fair.' He paused – for in truth this young man's life or, worse, his wife's, might well hang in the balance and Josse did not want to be responsible for delivering either of them to a judgement that they did not deserve – then he said, 'I believe that it is safe also to tell Gervase de Gifford. He will not rush to accuse you of deeds that you have not done and will, I think, view with compassion and understanding the events that took place in your hall.'

'You believe,' Leofgar murmured. 'You think. Josse, can we take the risk?'

'Aye,' Josse said firmly. 'Although I will not speak to him if you ask me not to.'

Leofgar thought for some time. Then he said, 'I put myself in your hands, Josse. Do what you think best.'

Then, leaving Josse staggering under the weight of that awesome responsibility, Leofgar gave him a graceful bow and, turning, hurried away down the track. In next to no time he had vanished from view.

Slowly, thoughtfully, Josse made his way back to the Abbey.

Although it was fully dark and quite late by the time he was safely within the walls, Josse went to find the Abbess. She was sitting in her room, working as usual on the big ledgers and now by the light of a pair of candles. As she looked up with a welcoming smile, the soft light threw shadows on to her face and he read the worry and tension in her as easily – more easily, for he was an inept reader at best – than words on a page.

'I have not found Walter Bell,' he said as soon as the door was shut fast and their greetings exchanged, 'but' – he dropped his voice to a whisper – 'I did meet your son.'

Her eyes widened and a hand flew to her mouth. 'Is he all right?'

'He is well, my lady. He has taken Rohaise and the child to some safe place whose whereabouts he would not tell me but he assured me they are safe and are being well looked after.'

'He – but what if Walter Bell finds him? With Teb dead and the distinct possibility that he was coming here searching for Leofgar, it is surely—'

'There is no danger from Walter Bell,' Josse interrupted quietly. 'He's dead.'

Then, as succinctly as he could, he told the Abbess what had happened that awful day in the hall of the Old Manor.

When he had finished – it did not take long, mainly because she heard him out without one single interruption – she said, looking uncannily like her son and using exactly the same words, 'We must find out what Walter Bell was looking for.'

'Aye. It seems certain that his purpose in sneaking into the Old Manor was to hunt for something.'

'And that Arthur Fitzurse gave the order to search and told him what to look for,' she added.

'We cannot be certain,' he protested. 'Walter Bell might have been a thief who, once Leofgar and the servants had all gone out, spotted an opportunity and took it.'

'No.' She shook her head firmly. 'If that were true, why should Arthur Fitzurse have made up this story of the Bell brothers' dispute with Leofgar? No, Sir Josse. Fitzurse has a purpose at which, as yet, we may only guess. He sent Walter Bell to search in the Old Manor and, when he did not return, guessed that something had happened to him, quite possibly while he was carrying out his search. We know that this is what he thought because of the pressure that he has been putting upon Gervase de Gifford to search the Old Manor; he is quite certain that Walter Bell went there and probably believes he died there too.'

A memory stirred in Josse's mind. 'My lady, when I was at the Old Manor with Gervase and Fitzurse, I noticed that Fitzurse seemed preoccupied with searching the hall. He raked through the ashes in the hearth – maybe he was looking for evidence that Walter's clothes had been burned there, as indeed they were – and then he started peering closely at the furnishings in the hall. Gervase demanded to know what he was doing and he said something about looking for evidence of this imaginary quarrel between Leofgar and the Bells. But' – eagerly he leaned towards her, hands on her table and face close to hers – 'what if in truth he was searching for whatever it was he had sent Walter Bell to seek out?'

She nodded slowly. 'It seems highly likely,' she agreed. 'So, Fitzurse and Teb Bell discuss what might have happened at the Old Manor and Teb, believing that Leofgar must surely know something about Walter's disappearance, is all for racing up to the Abbey to confront him.'

'How did Teb know that Leofgar had left the Old Manor to come here?' Josse asked. 'Could someone have told him?' It was something that had been puzzling him on his walk back to the Abbey.

He watched her face. Her frown gradually clearing, she said eventually, 'I don't know how he knew *when* Leofgar left,' she said, 'unless somehow he heard it from Wilfrid, but I can guess how he knew Leofgar had come here.' Her eyes on Josse's, she said quietly, 'Because Teb knew that Leofgar is my son.'

'More likely Fitzurse knew,' Josse suggested. 'I do not think, my lady, that the wide gap between your son and the likes of the Bell brothers would allow them to have any knowledge of your son's lineage.'

'Very well,' she agreed, 'let us say instead that Fitzurse, on finding that Leofgar had left his home, said, ah, I bet I know where he's gone, he'll have taken his family to Hawkenlye Abbey where his mother is Abbess!'

Josse accepted that. 'Aye, it's possible,' he said. 'Teb Bell sets out for the Abbey, perhaps with murder in his heart because he thinks Leofgar killed his brother. But he never gets here because someone apprehends him and hangs him.' Before she could speak, he said, 'My lady, please be assured that I do not believe your son murdered Teb Bell. I am convinced that he is as ignorant as he claims to be of these two men and whatever business they said they had with him.'

She studied him for a moment and then said, 'I am glad of that, Sir Josse. I have never thought of my son as a murderer although, in all truth, I think that under certain circumstances he could and indeed would kill.'

'Which of us would not say the same?' Josse countered.

She inclined her head. 'Indeed,' she murmured. Then, as if deliberately turning her thoughts from that unwelcome concept, she said briskly, 'Arthur Fitzurse, then, knows of my son. He knows who his mother is, presumably also the identity of his father.' She broke off suddenly, eyes wide as if at some extraordinary thought. But, whatever it was, she appeared to dismiss it for, when she resumed, it was in the same tone: 'Fitzurse is interested in something that he believes to be in my son's possession. Not something valuable such as Leofgar's modest amount of silver, for Walter Bell found that and ignored it. No. Something of quite a different nature. He wants to look for it within my son's home and he employs a local ruffian to break into the Old Manor and hunt around.'

'Why not go himself?' Josse put in.

'Because if he were to be discovered there, apprehended and arrested, then whatever purpose is driving him would come to an abrupt end,' she said. 'The Bell brothers, on the other hand, are not only expendable, as far as Arthur Fitzurse is concerned, but also, according to Gervase de Gifford, experienced thieves. Perhaps Fitzurse thought it better to employ a professional. By using another to do his dirty work, Fitzurse could distance himself from whatever might happen.'

'Then why come forward now that the attempted theft went wrong and Walter Bell ended up dead?'

She thought for some time. Then she said triumphantly, '*Because* Walter Bell ended up dead! Oh, don't you see, Bell failed in his task and didn't find what Fitzurse sent him to find! And it is as you just said – Arthur Fitzurse is desperate to get his hands on this *thing*, whatever it is, and so he goes along to Gervase de Gifford, spins a tale about Walter Bell having set off to the Old Manor to resolve a fictitious quarrel with

Leofgar and not coming back. He knows it's quite safe to make up this tale of a quarrel because both Bells are dead now and neither can deny it; the only one who can is Leofgar, but presumably Fitzurse reckons that it will be a case of Leofgar's word against his. He uses Walter Bell's disappearance as an excuse to demand that de Gifford make a search of the house and grounds. But Josse, Fitzurse didn't care about Walter Bell! You were right; what he wanted was an opportunity to hunt through the Old Manor himself!'

Josse saw again Fitzurse's face as he strode about the Old Manor's hall; saw the eager, darting hands, the intent expression in the cold eyes. Aye, he thought, I was right.

'Employing the Bell brothers did not turn out to be such a bright idea after all,' he said thoughtfully. 'Walter did not find what he was sent to find and got himself killed for his troubles. Teb took up the role of avenger and came storming up here to Hawkenlye to demand the truth from Leofgar. Now as I said I do not think for a moment that Leofgar killed Teb – apart from anything else, he had no idea of the man's existence and certainly did not know that Teb was on his way to find him.' He watched her face, wondering if she were thinking the same thing. 'No. My candidate for the role of Teb Bell's killer is someone who knew both Teb *and* what he intended to do when he reached Hawkenlye and found Leofgar.'

'Arthur Fitzurse.'

'Aye.'

'But why would *he* kill Teb Bell?'

'Because he did not want him to confront Leofgar. Just imagine, my lady, a furious Teb bursting into the Abbey demanding to speak to your son and accusing him of having killed Walter! Questions would be asked, and if Teb's fury got the better of him and, God forbid, he had attacked or even killed Leofgar, then it would have been very difficult to cover up such an occurrence and there would have been a full investigation. And Fitzurse is not ready for that. He does not welcome anyone looking too closely into his affairs, certainly not before he has found whatever he is looking for.'

'Yes.' She was nodding her agreement. 'And I would judge also that he prefers others to dance to his rhythm,' she said. 'He needs to be in control.'

'Aye, and the danger that Teb Bell might make very loud and public trouble by accosting Leofgar here at Hawkenlye was a risk he could not take.'

'So he followed him, jumped him and murdered him,' she finished. 'Sir Josse, it is possible, is it not?'

'More than possible,' he said. 'I would say it is highly likely.'

She had been watching him but now her eyes seemed to slide away from his and become unfocused, almost as if she were entering a reverie. 'What is it, my lady?' he asked, and heard the concern in his voice.

'Hm?' She returned her gaze to him but still she looked distant.

'What are you thinking about?' he said gently. 'Can I help?'

Now she smiled. 'Dear Josse, I expect so. You usually can.'

He grunted an acknowledgement and then waited while she assembled her thoughts. Then she said, 'Just now we surmised that Arthur Fitzurse knew of Leofgar's parentage. He knew who I was and therefore he probably knows about Ivo. I'm just—' Again she frowned, then gave a half laugh, as if she were amazed at her own thoughts. Then she said, 'Josse, it's probably nothing more than a coincidence and I'm being foolish even to consider it.'

'I have never known you to be foolish,' he said gallantly.

Her smile widened. 'Thank you. That is only because you know me only as a sedate nun and not as the girl and the woman I once was.'

'But even then, *foolish* was surely not the right description.'

'I am not so sure . . .' But whatever image she had been

seeing she must have closed off, for the soft, indulgent expression abruptly left her face. Then she said, 'It is his name.'

'Whose name?'

'Arthur Fitzurse's. Urse surely derives from *ursus*, the bear.'

'Aye, and his forename is that of a legendary hero who fought under the banner of the bear.'

Her eyes studying him were full of emotion. 'As do the Warins,' she said quietly. 'Did you not notice the shield on the wall of the Old Manor's hall?'

He cast his mind back and saw it again. Images and vocabulary rose up from his own fighting past and he thought, aye, I noticed it. Bear salient on an azure ground. A stirring image, for despite the shield's age the rearing creature maintained its ferocity. 'I did,' he said. 'I can picture it clearly.'

'Fitzurse,' she repeated. 'Son of the bear.'

'A not uncommon name,' Josse observed. 'Borne, amongst others, by one of the four knights who murdered St Thomas à Becket.'

'Yes, yes,' she said dismissively, 'but I'm not talking about all these others.'

Then he saw what she meant. 'You believe Arthur Fitzurse has a connection with the Warins?' he demanded. 'An illegitimate connection?' Suddenly very embarrassed by the direction in which they seemed rapidly to be going, he protested, 'But that would mean—' and found he could not go on.

She must have picked up his awkwardness. 'Sir Josse, I have to think about this,' she said kindly. Standing up, she came round her table and approached him. She put a light hand on his sleeve and murmured, 'You must be very tired, as indeed I am. Let us try to have a good night's sleep and then, given time to dwell upon all that we have discussed, speak again in the morning. Yes?'

'But—' He wanted to protest that at that moment sleep

suddenly seemed an unreachable dream; tired though he was, both physically and mentally, the matter at which she had just hinted had set his mind spinning. Could she really be hinting at what he thought she was? God's boots!

She was tidying the ledgers on her table, setting everything out neatly in preparation for the morning. She seemed quite serene, although he knew her well enough to realise that this might be a pose adopted to conceal inner turmoil.

But it was quite clear that she was not going to be persuaded to speculate any more tonight.

'Aye,' he agreed, with a gusty and regretful sigh. 'Aye, let us talk again tomorrow.'

Then she blew out the candles and together they left her room and went their separate ways to bed.

13

Trying to follow her own advice and lose herself in much-needed sleep, Helewise found that it was quite impossible. She had tried so hard to rid her mind of her preoccupations, to remember that she was first and foremost a nun, Abbess of this place that she loved so well, for she knew that she had no right to spend so much of her waking time worrying about her son. He's safe for the time being, she told herself reassuringly. Thanks to Josse, I now know that. But still I cannot stop thinking about him.

And, as if that were not enough to make her conscience far too active to allow her to relax, there was the question of her memories. Not just of her son – and his brother – as children, as, before this visit of Leofgar's, she had known them last; also, and possibly even more vividly, of her life with Ivo. Oh, and the visit to the Old Manor had been the summit of it all! To have gone back there, where she lived so happily with Ivo, when already her mind had been full of the past, had been almost too much to bear.

Now there was this business of Arthur Fitzurse and what might turn out to be a true claim on the Warin family. Josse, dear Josse, had realised what he was about to say and stopped, but she had guessed. His extreme embarrassment was because he had been about to speculate that Arthur might be Ivo's illegitimate son.

He couldn't be. Well, he could, but, if he were in truth in the mid or late thirties, then Ivo would have to have begotten the boy when he was about fourteen or fifteen . . . Actually, she thought now, it was entirely possible.

But she did not think it was true. When they had fallen in love and exchanged those precious first confidences, Ivo had made no secret of the sexual encounters he had enjoyed before meeting her. She had not taken it amiss; he had been thirteen years her senior after all and she would hardly have expected him to be totally inexperienced! But he had never mentioned having left any of these women with child. Would he necessarily have known about it if he had? She would have to think it over; it was only right.

But, right or not, she knew she would not dwell for very long on the possibility of Ivo having had a child about whom he had known nothing.

No.

Not when there was another very much more likely candidate for this hypothetical child's father . . .

She gave in to the power of the past. Settling herself comfortably in her bed, she closed her eyes and, with no effort whatsoever, conjured up in her mind the day she had first set eyes on Benedict Warin.

★   ★   ★

It is spring. It is the year 1167, and the youngest son of King Henry and Queen Eleanor is four months old; his name is John. The kings of England and France have fallen out and there is fighting in France, but then there is usually fighting somewhere and it is of no great concern to the young girl who dances in the bright rays of the early April sun that shine down into her small bedchamber.

Helewise feels like singing. Her beloved father, Ralf de Swansford, is coming home! Oh, Helewise gets on perfectly well with her strong-willed and forthright mother; loves her dearly, in fact; but she is her father's elder daughter and soul mate. And Father has promised to bring home presents for everyone . . .

Helewise's mother is the great Emma Caedwalla, and it is said that in her youth her beauty was such that they called her another Helen of Troy. Nobody carried her off with him and started a war, but the stories tell that her poor parents were besieged with lovesick young men desperate to win Emma's hand until, having enjoyed herself hugely for a couple of years, she settled on her second cousin Ralf and put the rest of them out of their misery. She could, as it happened, have done this far sooner, for she had known Ralf all her life and nobody made her laugh like he did.

Ralf and Emma are both great-grandchildren of a pair who were almost legendary in the history of the region: Cerdic Caedwalla of Sussex and his wife – an heiress in her own right – Hildegarde of Wadehurst. Cerdic was the lord of Swansford, a manor whose lands spread far over the rolling hills in some of the most beautiful country in the land. He claimed proud descent from an ancient British line and said that his ancestor was Caedwalla, the West Saxon king. Nobody knew whether or not this was true but most people found themselves liking Cerdic so well that in the end they didn't much care. The popular Cerdic had, in choosing a wife, made what to some was a surprising choice. Hildegarde was highly intelligent – as was Cerdic, in a different way – and also both literate and very musical, neither of which talents her husband shared, unless the ability to scratch out your name meant that you were literate and by musical you implied capable of carrying a tune and singing bawdy choruses in a loud baritone. Hildegarde composed hauntingly beautiful holy songs in her spare time and, rare in a largely illiterate age, insisted that each of her four children learn to read and write. She extracted promises from them that they would similarly instruct any children with whom God saw fit to bless them and also take steps to ensure that these children did the same, and so on down through the family, which was why Helewise and her brothers and sister are each the possessors of the rare gift of literacy. The ability to read and write is, as Helewise's mother says when Helewise tries to avoid her lessons, her great-great-grandmother Hildegarde's gift, adding that she knows full well that Helewise will be very grateful for it one day.

Cerdic and Hildegarde's eldest child, a boy, was christened Egfrith and he died of a flux of the bowels when he was eight years old. His two younger brothers, William de Swansford and Eadgar Caedwalla, both had sons who married and in time begat children, two of whom were Ralf de Swansford, grandson of William, and Emma Caedwalla, granddaughter of Eadgar. The marriage of these two produced a quartet of lively, healthy, intelligent and capable children in whom the blood and the energy of the Caedwallas runs strong . . .

Helewise's elder brother Rainer is, at the time of this sunny spring morning, now sixteen years old and a squire. He has already achieved his full height, the beginnings of a beard and a manly breadth of shoulder; they mature early, Ralf and Emma's children. Rainer has bedded several cheerful and very willing kitchen maids and is now moon-eyed over the pretty daughter of a neighbouring knight. Helewise's younger brother Eudo, aged eleven, is also undergoing the training deemed suitable for a knight's son, although reports suggest that his heart does not seem to be in it and that he is proving quite a handful. Both brothers are presently away from home, although the households in which they live are not far away.

The last of the four children, Helewise's sister Aeleis, is ten years old and the beauty of the family, with thick, glossy hair the colour of chestnuts and clear grey eyes fringed with dark lashes. Her wide mouth smiles readily and the skin of her heart-shaped face is creamy and smooth. Everyone tries to pet her, dress her up and spoil her, but she usually manages to slip through even the grasp of her nurse and, dressed in cast-off boys' clothing that once belonged to her brothers, loves nothing better than to spend the day with the horses and her father's hounds. Aeleis loves all animals and her devotion to the stable cat means that this large and indolent creature is now too spoiled and well-fed to earn its keep as a mouser. (When Aeleis grows up, this big-hearted and apparently endless well of love will be turned to humans when, after giving birth to her one and only child, she will set about opening her home to foundlings and proceeding to give food, warmth and the hope of a chance in life to many who would otherwise have died young.)

This is Helewise's family. She loves them and, at fourteen, has sufficient wisdom to understand that her childhood has been singularly blessed. Not only is there the very comfortable cushion of her parents' wealth; there is also the unusually tolerant and wide-minded attitude of her mother and father. They have treated their offspring as young adults from an early age, stretching their minds with talk usually reserved for times when the children are not about, so that the four young Swansfords have a wider view of the world than most of their contemporaries. This is one reason why Helewise is so eager to see her father: he has been to London – oh, the very name is exciting! – and has promised to bring back the latest gossip. He will, he whispered to her before he left, save the juiciest morsels to tell her first . . .

The gifts with which Father will present his wife and children (and the most senior of the household servants) will be splendid; they always are. He may well bring Helewise some parchment and a new stylus, or a beautifully written sacred text produced by the monks. He will undoubtedly bring

her a length of yellow French silk, because she asked him to
and he never lets her down.

Helewise's dancing is interrupted by the arrival in the bedchamber of her nurse, Elena. Elena is dark-haired and dark-
eyed and has the perpetually tanned skin that suggests she has
ancestry from the south. Whatever the truth of the matter,
Elena tells her own version: that her grandfather went off to
fight in the First Crusade and brought back a slave girl from
Antioch. Helewise, enchanted by this story as a child, now has
her doubts as to its veracity but loves Elena nonetheless. Elena
is wise and at times too perceptive for the children – especially
the girls – whom she has had in her charge since they were
born; Helewise and Aeleis frequently accuse her of having
good friends in the spirit world who keep her informed, for
how else would she know what is happening out of her sight
and away from her keen ears? Elena is also skilled in herb lore
and has been of service as nurse and healer to the Swansfords
on so many occasions that they have all lost count.

'Hurry up, my girl!' Elena says as she bustles into the room
with Helewise's bluebell-coloured gown carried carefully in
her arms. 'Your father's nearly here and he has brought a
friend with him. You're to go down when your mother calls
you and make a nice curtsy to the man.'

'Is he old?' Helewise is struggling out of her everyday linen
over-gown – a little grubby around the hem and with a blotch
on the bosom where she spilt her barley water – and her words
are muffled.

'Old enough,' Elena replies unhelpfully. 'Now let me look at
this under-gown.' She pauses to drag the fine linen shift down
and straighten it; Helewise is full-figured and the garment is a
little tight over her firm and rounded breasts. 'I ought to let this
out again,' Elena mutters, 'but there's no time now, it'll have to
do. Come, let's see what the blue looks like.' She drapes the silk

over Helewise's head – it smells faintly of lavender; Elena is skilled in the care of fine clothing – and pushes her arms up over her head so that she can fasten the laces down each side of the gown. 'There!' she exclaims as she ties the last bow. 'I'll tidy your hair' – she smacks Helewise's hands away and skilfully twirls the reddish-blonde hair into long braids and attractive curls that frame Helewise's flushed face – 'and I reckon you're done.'

Helewise stands still under Elena's scrutiny. 'Will I pass inspection?' she asks with a grin.

'Aye.' Elena gives a satisfied nod. 'That you will.'

Helewise waits impatiently for her mother's summons. When at last it comes she makes her way through the upper chambers of Swansford – it is a very big house – and descends down the narrow, curving stair that leads into the huge hall. Her father is standing by the long table in front of the hearth and there is another, older man with him. Both are in the act of drinking a toast to one another, as if in celebration of business satisfactorily concluded. Her father would no doubt tell Helewise what that business was if she asked. Nothing, in fact, is further from her mind, because she is quite captivated by the tall, broad-shouldered and handsome man who stands at her father's side.

He is older than her father, considerably so; his face bears strong character lines but these lines give the impression that they all radiate upwards, suggesting that they have been formed from a lifetime of laughter. His eyes are brilliant blue. His mouth is wide and when, as now, he smiles, it is to reveal good strong teeth, the eye teeth long and sharp like a wolf's. He is dressed in a dark blue tunic richly decorated with gold braid and his head of long, thick, white hair is uncovered.

She walks towards the two men. She approaches her father first and receives his kiss and his loving embrace. Smiling up at him, she whispers, 'I'm glad you're home!' Then her father gently disentangles himself and, twisting her round, says, 'Helewise, you must greet our guest.' Turning to the tall man, he says, 'Benedict, may I present my elder daughter Helewise. Sweetheart, this is Sir Benedict Warin.'

Helewise turns to him and makes a low and graceful curtsy, one hand laid on her breast as she bends low and modestly casts down her eyes. She feels his strong fingers take hold of her other hand and he raises her up. She lifts her head and meets his blue eyes. He is smiling at her as delightedly as if her presence has just made the sun come out, and she cannot help but respond.

'You and Emma have produced a beauty,' he says to Ralf. 'Why did you not warn me that, before ever I entered your hall, I should put a guard on my heart?'

He is joking, she knows full well; she is used to this kind of light talk. She laughs and he turns back to look at her again. 'You think I speak in jest?' he murmurs and, at this sudden low tone, something seems to stir deep within her, something that she has half-felt in her dreams and which she knows, without being quite sure why, is something dark and secret . . .

Ralf is apparently unaware of this subtle exchange but his wife is not; Emma Swansford has been watching from the doorway and now she comes gliding across the shiny flag-stones of the hall floor, moving with her trademark grace, her arms extended in greeting as she says, with apparently un-mitigated delight, 'Benedict, my dear! How very good it is to see you again!'

Good manners demand that Benedict withdraw his fasci-nated eyes from young Helewise's breasts and turn them upon his hostess. Graciously he embraces Emma, kissing her on both cheeks and exclaiming that, for all that it is a year or more since he has seen her, she does not look one single day older. Helewise, watching the ease with which this fascinating man turns his charm from her to her mother, feels a quick stab of resentment but soon it passes. Once out of the beam of his eyes she can see that he is in fact quite elderly and she wonders what the attraction was.

In that brief time she has learned a valuable lesson about a man's powers of seduction. And, indeed, about how quickly a man who loves women can flit from one to the next.

In due course Emma leads them all to the meal table. They are joined by Aeleis, face and hair still damp and cheeks still red from Elena's vigorous washing, laced into a gown at which she keeps pulling, as if it does not feel comfortable. The conversation ranges over many subjects and Helewise and her sister are regularly invited to join in. Benedict, seated opposite to Helewise, frequently glances her way although she tries not to meet his eyes. He is, she thinks, rather like a hot-blooded horse: exciting but potentially rather dangerous.

The meal ends. The girls are dismissed and Aeleis hurries to take off her gown and dress herself in her old house gown (Elena will not permit her to wear her usual boys' clothes when there is a guest in the house) and she returns to whatever she was doing in the stables. Helewise wanders off and goes up to her room. She is thinking.

Some time later her mother comes to find her. She sits down beside Helewise on the long wooden bench and takes her daughter's hand in both of hers.

'Benedict Warin,' Emma says without preamble, 'is what is known as a womaniser. Do you know what that means, Helewise?'

'I can guess,' she replies.

Emma smiles. When she does so, Helewise thinks she is still the most beautiful woman in the land. 'What did he say to you?' she asks.

'That he should have put a guard on his heart before he met me.'

Emma nods sagely as if this were no more that she had expected. 'I see.' She studies her daughter. 'And you were flattered, of course?'

'I was while he held my eyes,' Helewise admits. 'But then you came over and he looked exactly the same when he gazed at you, and I realised that it was just something he does, rather as Father would slap a good friend on the back or make a specially deep bow to a woman he respected.'

Emma squeezes Helewise's hand. 'Good girl,' she says approvingly. 'You are wise beyond your years, daughter.' She studies her, taking in the grey eyes, the smile, the strong shoulders and the deepening bosom. 'Although in truth,' she adds, half to herself, 'the sum of your years is adding up almost without my noticing it.'

But Helewise wants to hear more about Benedict Warin. 'He likes women, Mother? Sir Benedict?'

Emma hesitates as if she is pondering the wisdom of discussing with her young daughter the ways of such a man. But then, perhaps reasoning that Helewise is on the cusp of womanhood and ought to know what the world is really like, she starts to speak. 'He does, Helewise. And women like him too, for he is a well-favoured man, despite his limp; did you remark it, daughter?'

'His limp? Er—' Helewise thinks back. 'No, I do not believe that I did, but in truth I did not see him move more than a few paces. How did he come by it?'

'He fell from his horse's saddle but one foot remained lodged in the stirrup so that he was dragged when the horse bolted. They say that it was only the swift intervention of his companion that saved Benedict's life. But that is beside the present point.' Emma tightens her grip on her daughter's hand and, eyes fixed to Helewise's, says urgently, 'Helewise, Benedict likes women too well for his own good. He was married to a fine woman whose name was Blanche. She was lovely,

talented and skilled in the womanly arts. Most men would
have been more than satisfied and, moreover, considered
themselves lucky to have won such a goodly soul to be their
wife, particularly when Blanche gave birth to a son. But there
were troubles in that household.' Emma shakes her head sadly
and slowly. 'It is said that Benedict did not lose his – er, his
adventurous spirit. He travelled widely as a youth and fought
for his King in faraway places where many knights, I am afraid
to say, consider that bedding as many women as they possibly
can is as much a part of their task as slaughtering the King's
enemies.' She sighs. 'Marriage calmed Benedict for perhaps
five or six years or, at least, if he was engaging in – er, in his
philandering ways, then he hid it from his wife. Then when his
son was still a babe in arms, he took off on his travels. There
was always an excuse – to see this man or that, to seek out
some man of influence who would advance the Warins, to visit
some former comrade who had fallen on bad times. But
always, always, there was a woman at the bottom of it and
invariably she ended up in Benedict's bed.'

Helewise, thinking of her own father and of his devotion to
his home, hearth and family, says, 'But what of his children?
Did he not want to be with them?'

'Child, not children. Blanche gave him but the one son. It
was rumoured that she became barren after that.'

'Became barren?' Helewise does not understand. 'I have
heard of women being barren, but not of becoming so. How
can that be?'

Again Emma hesitates. But this daughter of hers is ripe for
marriage and there is no reason to keep such things from her.
'As you say, Helewise, it is quite common for a wife to be
unable to produce children and that would seem to be God's
will and there is little point in demanding to know why.' She
looks sad for a moment, then, perhaps thinking of the ease
with which she has conceived and borne her own four chil-

dren, a sort of thankfulness fills her lovely face. 'But sometimes a woman gives birth to one child and then it is as if her womb sours and will not bear fruit again. Perhaps the experience of the first birth has been traumatic; perhaps there has been damage to the woman's fruitful parts. Sometimes it happens for no apparent reason. But, believe me, daughter, it does happen.'

'Poor Blanche,' Helewise murmurs. 'To go on hoping that another baby might bring her wandering husband back to her and yet to be constantly disappointed must have been hard.'

'It broke her heart,' Emma says quietly. 'Or so they say, and I see no reason to doubt it.'

'Yet you and Father welcome Sir Benedict to our home!' Helewise is indignant.

'It is your father's choice to invite him and we must accept it. That is how it is,' Emma says firmly. 'What a man does in his own hall is his own business and nobody else's. Your father and Benedict have been friends for a long time and it is not for us to query their friendship.' She fixes her daughter with a frown. 'And I do not want you to breathe one word of this conversation to anybody else,' she commands.

'But—'

'Helewise, that is my wish,' her mother says. 'Do as I say.'

She lets go of Helewise's hand and stands up, graceful as ever. Then, relenting, she smiles down on her daughter. 'There is so much for you to learn,' she says kindly. 'Remember that I am always here and that it is I who am the rightful recipient of your questions. I am always prepared to talk over any matter that puzzles you.' A new urgency enters her eyes and, leaning closer to Helewise, she says, 'I want you to be a good wife, my sweet. Your father and I love you dearly and we wish you to make a fine match, as all parents wish for their daughters. But in our case we also want you to be happy.'

Moved, for her mother is rarely so outspoken, Helewise

stands up and gives Emma a hug, which, after an initial slight resistance, is then lovingly returned.

As Emma turns and, with another smile, walks away through the doorway, Helewise reflects that she is now taller than her mother.

She obeys Emma's dictates and speaks to hardly anybody about this new and fascinating knowledge of men, women, wives, mothers and the business of marriage. The exception is Elena, but Helewise reasons that she has always talked over everything with Elena and that her mother must know this and accept it. Anyway, even if she does not, Helewise cannot help herself. And she learns a very great deal more from her nurse than she has done from her mother.

Elena has a wide circle of friends, relations and acquaintances spread throughout the knightly classes of Sussex and Kent. She hears far more gossip than her mistress and she is able to tell Helewise all about Benedict Warin's women. She also supplies some fascinating facts about how women have babies and the things that can go wrong to prevent conception or the birth of a living, healthy child. Elena tells Helewise almost too much about this mysterious and fascinating subject and Helewise has to work quite hard to rid her mind of images of naked and terrifyingly bulging women screaming and straining in childbed, or being forced to lie with some demanding and son-hungry husband over and over again long after desire has gone. From some undisclosed source, Elena seems to know exactly how the body is put together and she shares this knowledge with Helewise. Before she has come anywhere near seeing a human male organ, Helewise has been told exactly what it looks like and what it does when aroused.

Helewise absorbs this knowledge and thinks about it. She understands now that human beings are much like any other animal in their breeding habits and, with a shock, realises that her own parents must have engaged in activity similar to that of the hound on the bitch in season or the big horses out in the paddock who cover the brood mares and insert those huge members into their bodies. She is inclined to be horrified; childhood is, after all, not that far behind her. But her fast-awakening womanhood comes to her aid and something in her – perhaps the same something that responded to the sexual demand in Benedict Warin's eyes – tells her that this is right, this is how it is and how it will be for her.

She finds, after a while, that she is not afraid.

Elena has let slip that this son of Sir Benedict's is a very handsome man. Helewise wonders why nobody has told her this interesting fact before. And she also finds herself wondering – rather too often for comfort – what it will be like to meet Benedict Warin's son and whether or not she will take his fancy. Or, even more important, whether he will take hers.

She has absolutely no doubt that she is going to meet him. It is just a matter of time . . .

14

She does not have to wait very long to find out what she thinks of Sir Benedict's son.

It is one of those uniquely English spring days when April feels like midsummer. Helewise has told her mother that she is going out to collect young nettles for Elena's hair tonic; she has told Elena that she is expected to exercise her mother's palfrey. Neither her nurse nor her mother has in fact asked Helewise to do anything but, since she cannot seem to sit still and very much needs some time on her own, she has inferred to each of the two women who order her days that the other has sent her out on an errand. To ease her conscience, she rides out on her mother's fine-boned bay mare and gets her hands and wrists stung picking a basket of nettles for Elena.

She rides to her favourite spot: a small pebbled beach in the bend of a shallow stream that comes down off a low hill to disappear into woodland. The stream just here runs between a shoulder-high bank on one side and an ancient willow on the other and, once she is under the high bank with the palfrey tethered beneath the willow, Helewise believes herself to be hidden away in her own private place.

For some time she sits on the sun-warmed stones of the little beach, occasionally picking up a stone and flipping it across the water. The stream runs too swiftly to make the stones bounce more than once or twice, but then she spots a place under the bank where the water is deep, dark and apparently motionless. She does better here and makes a stone bounce three times.

She feels . . . she tries to analyse it. Stirred up, is the best she can come up with. Were she to have asked practical, down-to-earth Elena, the nurse would have said, 'You've turned into a woman, my girl, and your blood's up! It's spring and you're as lusty as every other fertile creature on God's good earth!' But, even without Elena's wise words, Helewise has a fair idea of what is the matter with her. She knows about what men and women do together and, even though she is a virgin, she feels a powerful, mysterious hunger inside her that she does not quite know how she is to assuage.

She picks up another stone. Skims it. It gives one feeble bounce and she mutters a word that she heard the stable boy use.

And from up above her, on the top of the bank, somebody laughs and a male voice says, 'Very ladylike!'

She turns, horrified but, at the same time, strangely excited. And sees a man on a big horse, silhouetted against the bright spring sky and clearly large and broad in the shoulder. For an instant an image of Benedict Warin flashes into her mind – she has just been thinking about him – then the horseman disappears. But only for as long as it takes him to dismount, tether his horse somewhere out of sight and then return to the bank; he jumps down and stands before her on the little beach.

She has leapt to her feet and is staring at him; she is tall but he is taller, and she has to look up. Again she thinks of Benedict, for this man resembles him a little although he is much better-looking; she thinks she knows who he is.

Her heart is beating faster.

He says, 'You, I believe, are Helewise of Swansford. Yes?'

'Yes.'

His eyes are dancing. They are not the same blue as his father's; as the sun catches them, they appear sometimes green, sometimes grey-blue. 'My father told me all about you,' he goes on. 'I had to come and see for myself.'

'Oh.'

He laughs again. 'Are you always this talkative?'

'I do not know your name!' she protests, as if the lack of a formal introduction were the reason for her dumbness.

'Ivo,' he says softly, his eyes on hers. 'Ivo, son of Benedict Warin of the Old Manor.'

'I see.' Oh, how prim she sounds! With an effort she says, 'How did you know I was here?'

'I've been looking for you these past three days,' he says with disarming honesty. 'You did not wander far from home yesterday or the day before, but today I was lucky. I watched you ride out and I followed you.' Leaning down to whisper in her ear – a highly disconcerting sensation – he adds mysteriously, 'I've been calling to you and finally you came.'

His exciting remark stirs her strangely, even though it is not strictly accurate. Many thoughts battle for her attention. This man is an accomplished seducer. He is probably a womaniser, as they say his father is. He's been waiting for me for three days! He's been calling to me and I came. And, most powerful of all, oh, he's so handsome and when he stares at me like this I feel as if I were melting.

Her mouth suddenly dry, she says, 'I have brought my mother's palfrey out for some exercise.' She points to the bay mare under the willow tree, calmly swishing away flies with her long tail. 'My mother has not enough time in her day to give her horse sufficient attention.'

He nods sagely. 'And you have taken a tumble in the nettles, I see.' Her takes her hands in his, very gently, and slowly inspects the backs of them and her strong wrists, then turning them over to look at the palms.

She sees the line of nettle stings that looks like a pink bracelet. 'I was gathering the young nettle tops for my nurse,'

she says with what she hopes is dignity. 'Elena – that's my
nurse – makes a tonic for the hair.'

'Does she, indeed.' Now he has dropped one of her hands.
With his free hand he carefully takes up a strand of her long
hair, pulling it so that the curl straightens out and then letting
go, allowing it to spring back. Then he takes out a small knife
and, without so much as a raised eyebrow to ask her permission, cuts off the curl and stows it away inside his silver-grey
tunic.

She is aware that her mouth has dropped open and hurriedly she closes it.

They stand staring at each other. She senses something in
the air and wonders vaguely if a storm is approaching. Almost
unthinkingly – she is a child of the country – she looks up
quickly to see if clouds are gathering, being blown up against
the wind. But the sky is clear, perfect blue and there is scarcely
a breeze. She looks back at him; to her surprise, he too seems
puzzled.

He holds her eyes a moment longer, then says, 'I can skim
stones better than you can.'

His cheerful, everyday remark breaks the tension. 'Go on,
then,' she invites. He picks up a handful of stones and skims a
couple of them expertly over the still waters under the far
bank. Five, six. 'Very good,' she says, in the tone she uses
when her little sister manages to do her needlework without
pricking her finger and spotting the cloth with blood.

He is instantly aware of it and he turns to her, dropping the
remaining stones. Very quietly he says, 'Do not play with me,
girl. I am not your puppy or your baby brother.'

The tension is back and now it crackles between them, all
but visible. He has taken a step and now is very close. 'How old
are you?'

'I shall be fifteen in three months' time,' she declares
proudly. 'My birthday is on the last day of July.'

'I see.' He frowns slightly. 'I am twenty-seven and shall be twenty-eight on the first day of December.'

'You do not look as old as that,' she says, eager, she does not quite know why, to lessen this gap between them.

He smiles, and the expression enchants her. 'And you, girl, are a woman, for all your tender years.'

'I am,' she agrees. She thinks she knows what he means and, although she has been brought up to consider such private feminine matters a secret to be concealed from men, somehow this training no longer seems relevant at all.

There is a moment of perfect stillness. They do not touch; their contact is through their eyes and through their senses, each seeking the other. Then he raises a hand and, with his finger, outlines the curve of her lips. He murmurs, 'My father was quite right.'

She knows she should not ask but cannot prevent herself. 'What did he say?'

That smile again. 'He said that Ralf de Swansford has a beautiful daughter, who has her wits about her and looks as if she enjoys life and who is ripe for the plucking. He advised me to get in first before some other lucky man finds you.'

'Oh!' She is speechless; are men normally so bold?

As if he reads her reaction, he takes a step back, away from her, and he says, 'Lady, I mean no disrespect. It is not fitting for us to be alone and for me to speak such words to you; believe me, I honour you.'

He looks so earnest, puts such stress on the word honour, that she does believe him. 'You do not offend me, sir,' she replies, eyes modestly cast down. Still looking at the ground, she adds, 'Normally I am not permitted to ride out unaccompanied, I do assure you, for my father guards me well and likes me to be in the company of either my family or one of the servants.'

It is a prissy little speech and she is not at all surprised when he bursts out laughing. 'Oh, Helewise!' he says, still laughing. 'You are a cherished and unblemished young bud; yes, I know that full well.'

She feels herself blush. Cross with herself – for her carefully nurtured virgin state is surely something she should be proud of? – she lifts her chin and says, 'I have been raised to be a lady, sir. There is no shame in that.'

Instantly he is once more apologetic. 'No, no, of course there isn't and I am delighted to hear it. Please, forgive me for my laughter and for what you seem to perceive as my mockery – the laughter I cannot deny but I intended no jeering criticism and I am truly sorry if I did not make myself plain.'

Make myself plain . . . Her disordered thoughts prompt the comment, you could never be plain, but this is not, of course, what he meant.

'Very well,' she says politely. 'I accept your apology.'

He bows. 'Thank you, lady.'

She is tingling from the effect of his nearness – without her having noticed, he seems to have stepped closer again. She meets his eyes. Now he looks solemn, almost anxious. 'I must go!' she cries. Suddenly she wants to flee from him; she is afraid – of him, of herself; she does not know – and running back to the safety of home seems like a very good idea.

He bows again, as if in acknowledgement. 'Yes,' he says. Neither of them makes a move. Then he says in a rush, 'Will you come here again? Tomorrow?'

Without one single second's thought she says, 'Yes.'

She spends a hectic night, her pounding blood not allowing her to rest. When at dawn she slips into an exhausted sleep, it is only to dream of him, a dream from which she awakes sweating and heavy with some strange sensation that seemed to promise more joy, more pleasure than she had imagined could exist.

She meets him the next day. They talk endlessly about themselves, each coming up with question after question, as if they would know the story of each other's life from first memories to the present moment. He keeps his distance – he sits down on the pebbles an arm's length from her – but, when they get up to leave, he takes her hand and kisses it. She is not sure but she thinks she feels his tongue touch against her hot skin. The sensations of the night tickle faintly through her body, an echo of their dark nocturnal power, and she has to turn away before he sees her confusion.

The next day they talk again. This time, when they part, he kisses her mouth. And, just as she had thought she would, she melts into him.

There is to be a celebration in the manor because it is May and, despite England's Christian religion, the country people still honour the Old Ways and they do not forget. The Swansford family are all eagerly chatting about the arrangements for the day. Ralf de Swansford has, as he always does, offered the large meadow bordered by oak trees and a birch copse as a venue and already the villagers have erected a May Pole. A cooking fire will be built in a sheltered corner and a hog will be roasted. The Swansfords will provide most of the victuals but the peasants and the tenants will each bring what they can. Even in the poorest homes, men, women and children feel the thrill of the feast day and it costs nothing to pick wild flowers and make a garland.

Ralf has invited friends and neighbours to the celebration. He is delighted to say, he mentions with an attempt at casualness that does not fool his daughter for one moment, that Benedict Warin is coming. 'And he tells me he is going to bring his son, Ivo,' Ralf adds.

Helewise drops her head and meekly says, 'Oh, that will be nice.'

As soon as she can she races away to find Elena. She has her recent gift of the length of sunshine-yellow silk and she wants Elena to help her make the most gorgeous gown that a girl ever wore. Elena, aware that something has happened to her young charge and pretty certain what it is, falls in readily with the plan. Helewise strips to her under-gown and Elena studies her through narrowed eyes. 'You're blossoming, young Helewise,' she observes. Then, with a lascivious wink that makes Helewise laugh and, at the same time, sends her blood pounding, she says, 'Blooming like a flower beneath some man's scrutiny, is that it?'

Helewise does not answer. Instead she picks up the bolt of silk and lifts her arms in a wide gesture, spreading the lovely fabric and letting it settle around her. 'What do you think, Elena?' she asks. 'Tight bodice and flowing skirt?

Elena goes 'Mmm,' in the sort of tone she has always used when aware that Helewise knows something that she doesn't. Then, apparently giving in, she says, 'Aye, my girl.' With a grin, she adds, 'Show off your assets, eh?'

They make a gown that is the most beautiful that Helewise has ever possessed. The silk – imported to France from Genoa and spun in Paris into a cloth that has a subtle self-coloured pattern of flowers and ivy leaves – is heavy and shines like the sun going down in the evening sky. It has a square, deep neckline that shows off the upper curves of Helewise's smooth white breasts. The sleeves are narrow at the shoulder and flare widely at the wrists. The waist is tight-fitting and, at the hips, the glorious fabric flares out to a generous hem. Over the gown Helewise will wear a little bodice embroidered with pearls. Elena also makes an under-tunic in a deeper shade of yellow that is almost gold; it will show at wrist and neckline and it echoes the colour of Helewise's red-gold hair.

On her head she will wear, just like the peasant girls, a garland of flowers.

For the two days before May Day she does not see Ivo. After a fortnight in which they have – unknown to anybody else – been together for a part of every day, the waiting seems endless. But inevitably, time goes by – with infinitesimal slowness – and at last it is May eve. Helewise bids her family a decorous goodnight and retires early to bed. She looks hungrily at the yellow gown spread on her clothes chest, at the garland of flowers that rests in a shallow bowl of cool water to keep it fresh. She imagines herself dressing in the morning. Imagines Ivo when he sees her.

It is almost too much to bear.

The day is sunny and warm and everyone is thrilled to think that the gods are blessing their celebration with such perfect weather. The cooking fires are lit early; benches are lugged out of the house for the ladies and straw bales for the better class of men; everyone else will sit on the good green grass. Ivo's steward is busy organising games for the older children – races, both on their ponies, if they have them, and on their own two feet – and hunts for favours. His wife is looking after the smaller children and Elena has set aside a quiet, cool place in the shade of the oak trees where overwrought toddlers and babies can sleep when necessary. The May Pole has been decorated with ribbons and a small band of musicians are practising their tunes. There will be other dancing too, in addition to the traditional slow measures around the pole that symbolise the Sun's course; groups of men bearing sticks are going through their moves, anxious to get everything perfect so that the people clap and the lord and his lady are pleased.

Helewise has put on her gown and her flower garland. She cannot eat and uses the excuse that her dress is tight and she wants to have room for the feast later. Her mother nods without comment; Elena shoots her a look. The family leave the house in the middle of the morning – it has been a tense wait for impatient Helewise, trying to appear only as excited as she usually is instead of filled with this nervous, thrilling sensation for which she has no name – and, with Ralf and Emma in the lead, they make their slow and stately way down to the meadow, greeting people as they go.

It is some time before Helewise spots Ivo. She has already spoken to his father and been introduced to Benedict's companion, a silent man named Martin who bears a slight resemblance to his master; she wonders if they are related but such is her state of mind this day that the matter slips from her consciousness almost as soon as it has entered it. Benedict gives her a beaming smile and then a wink, as if to say, I know full well what *you're* up to! Then he engages Ralf in a conversation about wool export and Helewise, blush fading, scuttles away. She circles the field, slowly, trying to appear leisurely and graceful, and her sister Aeleis bounds around her, drawing her attention to the horses, the ponies, the hounds – 'Oh, look at the puppy! Isn't he sweet? Do you think Father would let me have him?' – although Helewise hardly hears.

Then she sees him, leaning against one of the great oaks, arms crossed over his broad chest. He wears a tunic in dark green with a lighter green border in which there are touches of rich gold embroidery. His brown hair shines with health and there are bright streaks in it, as if he has been riding bareheaded beneath the sun. He smiles at her and in that moment she knows that he loves her just as she loves him. She walks slowly up to him.

'Hello, sweeting,' he says softly. 'I have never seen you look more beautiful.'

She glances down at herself as if she has forgotten what she is wearing, hardly likely since she thought ahead to this moment, dwelling on its infinite possibilities, with every stitch that she sewed. 'Thank you.'

Their eyes lock again. Then he says, 'I think that I should be presented to your parents, with your permission. My father has suggested that he be the one to do it.'

'Yes, oh, yes,' she agrees. 'Shall we find him and take him to my father and mother?'

Ivo hesitates. It seems that he does not know how these things are accomplished any more than she does. 'Perhaps my father should perform this presentation with me alone,' he suggests. 'If you and I are both there, may it not appear that we have – I mean, that there is a degree of acquaintance between us that your parents have not known about?'

She understands. 'Yes. Very well, then. But we shall be together again later?' She cannot bear the thought that he is to slip off into the crowd and that will be that.

But he is smiling, gently, lovingly. Promisingly. 'Of course we shall,' he says. He blows her a kiss and then he is gone. She watches him stride away. He walks well. She hungers for him.

Time passes. To Helewise in her frantic impatience it feels like hours. Then she is summoned to her father's side and finds him standing with Benedict Warin, the watchful Martin hovering nearby. Ivo is to his father's right, a pace behind. Ralf says, 'Helewise, you have already met Ivo, I understand.' He gives her a keen glance but she makes herself stare back straight into his eyes; she has done things that he does not know about but, she tells herself, nothing terrible. Nothing more than passionate kisses that she has wished with all her heart, soul and body would go on into whatever comes next.

But that is not a thought to share with her father.

Ralf is drawing Ivo forward and, taking Helewise's hand, places it in Ivo's. 'Ivo, son of my dear friend, this is my daughter Helewise.' There is a pause. Then Ralf says, 'Perhaps, Ivo, you would care to escort her around the fair?'

And Ivo says, with admirable self-control, 'Indeed, Sir Ralf. Nothing would please me more.' Tucking her hand under his arm, he says, looking at Ralf, 'I will take care of her, sir.'

Ralf mutters a reply; it sounds like, 'Aye, I know you will.'

Helewise and Ivo stroll off. She can feel the tension in him echoing her own. Now that the correct procedures have been performed and they are together with their fathers' knowledge and consent, they do not need to be furtive but may stroll among the stalls and the entertainments quite openly. Many people watch them; some give them an indulgent glance. Husbands, wives and lovers recognise the look that the pair have. Older and wiser heads know full well what is going to happen before the day is out.

Ivo and Helewise eat their meal on the grass with their families. They watch the dancers circling the May Pole; they dance on the grass to the squeaky fluting and rhythmic tabor beat of the rustic band. Ivo squeezes her as they dance. He holds her hand every moment that he can.

In the end, hand-holding is not enough.

The long day draws to its close. Dusk is falling fast and torches are lit, their flaring, dancing light making swift-moving shadows as people continue with the celebrations. The cooking fire is stoked up and blasts heat and light out into the deep black of the night-time woods and fields. In the happy, disorganised crowds and the kindly darkness it is easy to slip away. Ivo and Helewise hurry to Helewise's secret place and, in the springy grass beneath the willow tree, she sits down and he kneels before her, gazing in adoration.

'Helewise,' he murmurs. He touches the garland of flowers on her hair. 'My Flora. My Queen of the May.'

Tenderly they remove each other's clothes. Staring at his mature male body as she helps him strip off tunic, undershirt and hose, she is aware at the same time of his hands on her, pulling at the laces of her gown, dragging at her under-gown with an impatience that all but tears it from her. Then, in the cool and fragrant stillness of a May night, naked and unashamed, at long, long last they make love.

15

Ivo and Helewise are married in July, a week before her birthday.

She has spent a fraught few weeks.

May is traditionally the fertile month. According to the Old Ways, it is the season when the Goddess and the God, mature and ripe for each other, mate in the greenwood. Their fertility echoes and rebounds with that of their creatures, animal and human; with the flowers, the trees, the crops; with the very land, Mother Earth herself. Some of the old folk who live under the skirts of Swansford still call the May feast by its ancient name of Beltane and the god whom they honour is not the Christ or His Holy Father but Bel, God of the Sun.

Sexual magic was abroad in the night after the feast. It worked on Helewise and Ivo; it worked within Helewise, and Ivo's seed sought out her egg and she conceived out there beside the stream under the soft light of the distant stars.

She does not realise this for several weeks. Ivo formally asks Ralf for her hand in marriage and Ralf, having noticed his elder daughter's new expression that is incandescent with joy, hardly needs to consult her to enquire whether this is what she wants too. This is, however, a necessary step since officially a marriage would not be considered legal without the free consent of both parties (although, as Emma and Ralf have often remarked when considering in private the marriages of the great and the not necessarily very good, sometimes this is hard to credit). Ralf accepts Ivo's suit and consent is given; the families think ahead to the practicalities. Benedict and Ralf get their heads together to discuss the financial settlement, a procedure which, as Emma tartly remarks, seems to require the consumption of rather a lot of the Swansford household's best Rhenish wine. Whether or not the wine is instrumental, a happy compromise is reached regarding Helewise's dowry and the rights she will be able to expect as a wife in her husband's home. Soon afterwards the families hold a small betrothal ceremony, and the priest who will marry Helewise and Ivo attends and gives his blessing. He will read out the banns in church three times over the following weeks and issue the formal invitation for anyone who has a legitimate reason to argue with the match to step forward. In order to give the couple – and Helewise in particular – plenty of time to make the necessary preparations for her new life, the marriage is set for late August; Ivo and his bride are to meet at the church door on the last day of the month.

There is a small and very beautiful house on Benedict Warin's land into which he will move, leaving the Old Manor, traditional home of the Warins, for his son and the new bride. Benedict will continue to be attended by his quiet manservant, Martin; Helewise has learned that the two men are not in fact related although she hears it said that they are as close as brothers and have been companions for a long time. Ivo undertakes to prepare the marriage bed and the priest promises to go along and bless it, praying that the couple's union may prove fruitful.

The trouble is that, as the weeks go by, Helewise knows that this blessing of fruitfulness has already been bestowed. She has missed her courses: she is pregnant.

When she realises this and there is no longer any room for doubt, she seeks out Elena and, dropping her head on her nurse's generous lap, tells her.

Elena gently strokes the wild red-gold hair; Helewise has been pacing her room gathering her courage for this moment and grooming has been the last thing on her mind.

'I know,' Elena croons.

'You know I'm pregnant?' Helewise sits up.

'Aye, my girl. You've been showing the signs. And who is it washes out your menstrual rags, which have lain unused in the chest since April?'

Slowly Helewise nods. 'Of course,' she murmurs. It has always been impossible to hide very much from Elena's sharp eyes, especially something that has apparently been so very obvious.

Elena gives her a little dig in the ribs. 'Why didn't you come to me, girl, before you ran off into the wildwood to mate with your man?'

Helewise is puzzled. 'Why should I have done that?' She adds, with a faint haughtiness that covers up her shame, 'I didn't need your permission.'

'None of that tone!' Elena says spiritedly. 'What I meant is that, if you'd only asked, I could have told you how to enjoy yourself without conceiving this little one.' She puts a large hand on to Helewise's lower belly.

'You—' Helewise does not understand. 'You could have prevented this conception? But how? Babies come from God and it isn't for us to choose whether or not we accept them.' Even to herself she sounds horribly self-righteous and pious.

'Oh, dear, dear, dear!' Elena chuckles. 'I admit you took a real chance, making love under the stars on Beltane night, because isn't it the very time when the Goddess and the God are abroad and giving you every encouragement? Why, the souls of the unborn are flying in the warm air just longing for an invitation!'

But Helewise is hardly listening. Fascinated by this extra-ordinary idea that a woman might choose whether or not she wished to conceive, she wants to know more. Elena readily obliges; indeed, she is planning in any case to have a word with Helewise before the marriage to enlighten her about certain things. Now, thinks the wise old nurse, is as good a time as any.

'It's said,' she begins, 'that a poultice of hemlock applied to the man's testicles prevents the shedding of fertile seed, but I've known that fail and in my opinion it's not to be relied on, besides being a mite uncomfortable. For the man, anyway!' She chuckles. 'Anyhow, best, I always say, for the woman to take care of herself in that way. Now, here's what I suggest . . .'

For the next few minutes Helewise listens to her nurse's contraception advice. Some suggestions are reasonably acceptable: wearing a crown of myrtle to delay conception, or chewing raspberry leaves to make the womb 'clench', whatever that means, and thus render itself unwelcoming. Secreting walnuts in her bodice, one nut for every month that she wishes to delay conception. Then Elena describes several potions which, when drunk, cause temporary sterility. She finishes by telling Helewise how to make a pessary that will reject male seed before it has a chance to sow itself, but the ingredients sound so ghastly that Helewise cannot imagine that its use would be entirely painless.

She absorbs all of this new information, storing it away for possible future use. Then, returning to her present predicament, says, 'But it's too late to prevent this conception, Elena.'

'Aye, my girl.' Elena sighs. Then: 'D'you want to keep the child?'

'Of course!' Helewise is shocked.

'Very well and right glad I am to hear it.' Elena gives her young mistress an encouraging hug. 'You'll not be the first bride to stand pregnant at the church door. I only asked because there are ways, you see, for a woman to slip a child from her womb.'

'I don't want to hear them,' Helewise says firmly. 'Now, what are we to do, Elena?'

Elena still has her strong arms around Helewise. Now, dropping a kiss on to the unruly hair, she says, 'It's simple. We bring your marriage forward by a month. You'll not be showing that early and there's no need for anyone else to know. We'll tell them you'd forgotten it was your birthday at the end of July and you've set your heart on being a wife first.'

'Why should I do that?' logical Helewise asks.

'I don't know!' Elena cries, exasperated. 'Make something up! Be fanciful and silly for once!'

Helewise grins. 'I'll try.' Then, gratitude flowing through her, she flings her arms round her old nurse and says, 'Will you come with me to the Old Manor, Elena? I'll be needing you early next year when he's born.' She points to her stomach.

'You have decided it's a boy?' Elena raises an eyebrow.

'I know he is.'

Elena puts her hand on Helewise's lower belly again, this time leaving it there for a few moments. 'Aye, aye, happen you're right.' Removing her hand, she says, 'As to coming with you to your husband's home, I would like that, my girl. But I'll speak to your mother; see what she has to say.'

Helewise has leapt up, restless energy evident in her very stance. 'Where are you off to now?' Elena demands.

Helewise smiles sweetly at her. 'I'm going to find Father and tell him that I must have my marriage date brought forward because I can't restrain my excitement and I *do* so want to be Ivo's wife before I'm fifteen.'

If anybody suspects the reason for Ivo and Helewise marrying in July rather than August, they never say. As far as Helewise is aware, it is a secret known only to herself, Ivo and Elena. When Leofgar is born the following February, nobody thinks to comment that he is large for a seven-month child; they are all too busy being thankful for a safe birth and welcoming a healthy infant into the world.

In the short time between betrothal and marriage, Helewise gets to know her new family. Benedict is a widower; his late wife Blanche died three years ago from some mysterious swelling in her breast. Helewise tries to encourage Benedict to speak of her; since Helewise is destined never to meet the woman who would have been her mother-in-law, she wants to find out something about her. Benedict speaks of Blanche as if she had been a veritable saint: patient, kind, long-suffering, always considerate of her husband's well-being and reluctant ever to mutter so much as a word of criticism. Her health was never robust, according to Benedict, and he manages to imply without actually putting it into words that he was a considerate husband and did not insist on his marital rights with any great frequency. Blanche, he tells Helewise with an expression of deep regret, took to her bed at the onset of her illness and stayed there for the year that it took her to die. Meanwhile— But Benedict shuts his mouth firmly and does not speak of meanwhile. It is as if he suddenly remembers to whom he is speaking and, clearly, he wishes his son's future bride to think well of him.

As an aid to this good impression that he wishes her to form, Benedict presents Helewise with a dazzling array of gifts. He has told Ivo that he will leave the best items in the Old Manor for their use; his small house is quite adequately furnished for a solitary man, he informs his son. Besides this bounty he has ordered new things for the betrothed pair: thick and costly wall hangings to keep out the draughts; a beautiful chest in which to store unseasonable garments and the like; heavy silver candle holders; a new mattress for the marriage bed. For Helewise herself there is a length of brilliant scarlet silk and a gold circlet to wear to secure her veil.

She feels it is disloyal to this most generous of fathers-in-law but still she cannot help herself trying to find out more about him, specifically the things that he is holding back from telling her himself. Ivo can reveal little more than she already knows so she enlists Elena's help. Elena uses her subtle skills and puts the word out among her many friends and relations that she would be pleased to hear anything they may know of Benedict Warin.

The results are surprising.

Most of her contacts, it is true, perceive Benedict as he paints himself: open-hearted, fond of his meat and drink, a good friend and a cheerful companion; loyal and truthful, a fair master and a generous host. People pity him for the loss of his wife and for the ill health of that wife that prevented her from giving Benedict more than the one child, fine man though this son might be. Benedict likes women; yes, of course, what red-blooded male does not? He flirts with them, praises them, pays them extravagant compliments and makes them feel beautiful and beloved. Yes, indeed. Where is the harm in that?

But some people – quite a few, it seems – know the truth behind this comfortably harmless image. One woman – she is the sister of someone who nursed poor Blanche in her dying weeks – knows very well what Benedict Warin is really like. He uses his easy charm, says she, as a sort of double bluff to conceal his true nature. He is a flatterer and a charmer, but he is more than that: with rather a lot of young women he goes further, seducing them, enjoying them and then abandoning them. While Blanche was alive, or so goes the ugly tale, Benedict always had his excuse ready: my sweetheart, he would say to the girl he was about to discard, how I should love to keep you with me always, care for you as you deserve, make you mine in the eyes of the world as well as in the privacy of our precious moments of intimacy. But what would it do to my poor suffering Blanche if I follow where my aching heart leads me and stay with you? No, no; although it will break me, I must give you up. And, with a tear in his eye and a last tender kiss, off he would go, leaving the poor girl to rearrange herself as best she could, brush the dust from her skirts and pull the hay from her tangled hair.

Since Blanche's death – a happy release in perhaps more ways than one – his excuse is that he must honour her memory. The fact that honouring a dead woman who is surely past caring means that he dishonours many living ones seems to have escaped his notice.

This is what Elena's cousin's friend's sister reports. Elena tells Helewise, who goes away to think about it. After some time she concludes that, first, it may not be true. Second, is it really any of her business? Third, she likes Benedict and she is hardly going to be affected personally by whatever he gets up to in private. Fourth, she is far too happy and excited to worry about it anyway.

She puts Benedict's infidelities to the back of her mind and, for a quarter of a century, that is largely where they stay.

Amid the happy splendour of Helewise and Ivo's wedding day, one small disturbing incident occurs.

The sun has shone since early morning, the bride looks quite exquisitely beautiful and the handsome groom clearly can hardly restrain his impatience to get her alone. Family and friends shower the bridal couple with flowers and the tenants and peasants turn out to wish them well.

The small incident occurs during the splendid feast that Ralf de Swansford throws for his daughter and her new husband in the flower-bedecked hall at Swansford. Helewise, flushed with happiness, is momentarily separated from Ivo as the two make their separate ways around the hall, pausing to talk to their guests, thanking them for the gifts they have brought, encouraging them to eat, drink and enjoy themselves. Helewise is wearing her new scarlet tunic whose silk is so stiff and heavy that it rustles, and Elena has helped her to cut it so that the fullness of the wide skirts begins slightly above the natural waistline; at nearly three months, Helewise's pregnancy is just beginning to show and this wise precaution has been taken just in case anyone is sufficiently impolite – sufficiently curious – to take a close look at the radiant bride's belly.

Helewise dances up to an elderly but still handsome couple who are vague relations of Benedict's and engages them in cheery conversation. They are friendly, affectionate, and they have just given her a beautiful little ivory statue of the Virgin for the private chapel at the Old Manor. Martin, Benedict's man, comes up to join them.

The four of them, even the taciturn Martin, are laughing, happy. But in the midst of these pleasant exchanges, Helewise suddenly feels as if someone has run icy fingers down her spine. She breaks off in mid-sentence, spinning round, and sees that a malevolent, black-clad and dark-aspected woman of about thirty is glaring at her ferociously, her expression suggesting she would have willingly stuck a knife in Helewise's back. Helewise catches her breath, shocked to the core by this sudden discordant element in her blissful day.

It is as if the bad fairy has turned up at the feast.

The wife of the elderly couple has caught Helewise's arm and is turning her away from the awful fascination of the dark woman's stare; she has seen too and she mutters something that sounds like, 'Take no notice, my dear, she is nothing to you.' She gives Martin a nudge – quite a sharp one – and he nods his understanding. He strides off, the old woman's husband following him, elbowing his way through the crowd until he stands beside the black-clad woman. He leans down to say something to her – he leans really close so that he speaks right into her ear – and then he takes hold of her and hustles her away, the old man following, until she has been escorted out of the hall.

'Who is she?' Helewise asks nervously.

The elderly woman sniffs. 'That? That's Sirida. She should not even be here . . .' And she stares worriedly after her old husband, as if suddenly anxious for him.

Helewise tries to laugh. 'She's quite slight; she won't hurt them!' she says jokingly.

But the woman replies, 'She might. Oh, she might.' She shakes her head, still looking anxious. Then she leans closer to Helewise and whispers, 'They say she is a witch.'

Then the old husband comes back – Martin has disappeared – brushing his hands together as if he has just ejected an unruly hound from the house and, before Helewise can ask any more questions about the dark woman, Ivo comes to find her.

Very relieved to see him, she snuggles up to him, feeling his strong body close to hers as he draws her against him. For the first time she realises that he is, in all ways, a man she will always be able to lean on. She raises her face and starts to tell him about the black-clad woman but he misinterprets her intention and, thinking she is demanding a kiss, obliges with such robust enthusiasm that the people standing around clap their hands, laugh and call out encouraging remarks that verge from the cheerfully ribald to the almost obscene; this is, after all, a wedding. Ivo's passion instantly infects his bride and Helewise's brief fear is drowned out by the flood of sensation flowing through her. Then Ivo grabs hold of her hand and, amid the cheers of their friends and relations, spins her away into a dance.

They dance, feast, drink, laugh, dance again, late into the night. Everyone there is having a good time. Everyone there, now, is happy.

Helewise's wedding day ends in joy. In the flurry and the hundred different impressions and memorable images of newly married life, the one unpleasant moment from her wonderful day is forgotten.

Almost.

*   *   *

Helewise lay in her austere nun's bed in the dormitory of Hawkenlye Abbey. Her memories had come back with the force of a rain-flooded river bursting its banks and she had recalled things she thought she had long forgotten. In the chilly darkness she found her face hot with shame as she remembered Leofgar's conception and her total lack of contrition, not only at having lain with Ivo before they were wed but also at the way she had lied to her dear father over the reason why she must bring forward her wedding day. She pictured his face, frowning at first but persuaded by her enthusiasm and her determination and not wanting to question her further in case he put a damper on her joy.

And Elena, Helewise thought, what would I have done without her? The old nurse had been given permission by Emma de Swansford to accompany Helewise into her new life and from the moment she and her young mistress had set foot in the Old Manor, she had been quite invaluable. It had been Elena who had provided the potions and remedies that helped Helewise through two pregnancies that came a little too close together; Elena who had twice turned midwife, capable and loving, easing Helewise's pains by her quiet confidence and by her very presence. And, after each baby boy was born, it had been Elena who had given Helewise the sensible advice that allowed her confidence as a mother to grow until she no longer needed her old nurse's support.

But it was not Elena whom Helewise now needed to think about. It was Benedict Warin.

Could it be possible? she wondered. Could one of Benedict's many infidelities – if indeed *that* accusation were also true – have led to some young girl conceiving his child? Helewise frowned as she considered the possibility. Ivo had been a virile man who, she reminded herself, had set a child growing in her as easily as look at her; why should his father not have been the same? Yes, it was true that Blanche Warin had given Benedict but the one child but then they all said she had been in delicate health and that she had become barren after Ivo was born.

It *was* possible, then, that Benedict could have fathered an illegitimate child. The more she considered it, the more she had to conclude that it was not only possible but probable.

As at last she closed her eyes and tried to compose herself for sleep, Helewise wondered how on earth she was to go about trying to find out whether this *probable* event had ever really happened.

16

Down in the Vale, Josse had an early morning visit from Gervase de Gifford's man, Matt. He brought the sheriff's greetings and the request that Josse come with him down to Tonbridge as soon as he could manage it because de Gifford urgently wished to speak to him.

Josse knew better than to ask what it was about; Matt was a taciturn sort of a man and in any case it did not seem wise to discuss the sheriff's business in an open-sided shelter with all manner of strangers wandering around outside. In fact there were only four pilgrims in the Vale at present and one of those was a baby, but the monks themselves were not above accidentally overhearing muttered discussions and then speculating wildly afterwards on what they thought they had heard and what it was likely to mean.

He told Matt to wait for him while he sought out the Abbess to inform her where he was going and Matt gave a wordless nod of acknowledgement. Then he raced up the path to the Abbey and, pausing to ask Sister Martha if she would kindly get his horse ready, set about trying to find the Abbess. She was not in her room but one of the novices pointed him in the direction of the retirement home which the Abbey ran for aged nuns and monks and that was where he found her.

Sister Emanuel, who was in charge of the retirement home, greeted him calmly and pointed into one of the two long and narrow rooms where the elderly folk lived out the last of their days, nuns to the right, monks to the left. The Abbess was kneeling in prayer by the narrow cot of a very old nun who, Sister Emanuel whispered, had died in the night. Josse waited. After a short time the Abbess rose to her feet and, bending to bestow a last kiss on the wizened forehead of the tiny nun lying so still on the cot, turned and came towards him.

'Good morning, Sir Josse,' she said. He thought there was a suggestion of tears in her eyes. 'Mother Mabilia was our oldest resident; she said she was almost eighty years old.'

'I am sorry for her passing,' he said formally.

The Abbess managed a smile. 'Do not be,' she murmured, 'for dear Mabilia was more than ready to leave us and go to meet her Lord. I have just been giving thanks that her death was easy and painless. She slipped away in her sleep.'

'May the good God above grant us all such an end,' Josse said in the same low voice.

'Amen.' There was a brief silence and then, taking his arm and steering him out of the retirement home, the Abbess said, 'What can I do for you?'

Swiftly he told her about de Gifford's messenger. She watched him, the anxiety flooding her face, then said, 'What does this mean, Sir Josse?'

'I do not know,' he admitted, adding, for he well knew what she was thinking, 'but, my lady, we must not instantly fear the worst!'

'But what if—' she began, then, with an obvious effort, stopped herself.

Josse put out his hand and briefly touched her sleeve. 'My lady, this may have nothing to do with – er, with the matter that preoccupies us.'

She smiled thinly. 'Now that, Sir Josse, I find hard to believe.' Then, leaning closer to him and lowering her voice, she said, 'What will you do if he has – if there is evidence that appears to incriminate my son? Oh, Josse, will you tell him what Leofgar told you?'

He looked at her, in pain himself at watching her anguish. 'Only if I am quite certain that I can persuade him that it's the truth.'

'How could you know that he would be persuaded of that before you had told him?'

It was a reasonable question and he found that he had no answer. 'My lady,' he said firmly, 'I know that Leofgar is innocent of murder. I will do all that is in my power, should it become necessary, to convince Gervase de Gifford that the story your son told me is what really happened that day at the Old Manor.'

He felt that he had sounded less than reassuring but there must have been something in his words – or possibly the way he spoke them – that comforted her. She said softly, 'God bless you, Sir Josse. I will wait to hear your tidings as soon as you are able to return.'

Feeling oddly uneasy – he was touched but also weighed down by her faith in him – he bowed briefly and hurried away.

Josse and Matt rode down to Tonbridge together without speaking a word. When they reached the town Matt said, 'This way,' and led Josse down a turning off the main track that led at first through mean hovels packed closely together but then opened out on to fields that sloped gently down to the river. Some fifty paces past the last of the town's dwellings, standing by itself beside a semicircle of willows, was a stone-built house of modest size with a stout wooden door studded with iron. There was a courtyard in front of the house with rings for tethering horses – and possibly prisoners – and a small stable block. Between the stables and the house was a single-storey building with a door as strong as that of the house and four tiny windows set high up. It did not need much intelligence to surmise that this was the gaol.

Matt dismounted and Josse did the same. Then Matt took

Horace's reins and said, nodding towards the house, 'You'll find the sheriff within.'

Straightening his tunic and throwing back his cloak, Josse strode over to the house and banged on the door, which was almost immediately opened by de Gifford. He greeted Josse and ushered him inside to where there was a fire blazing in the hearth. Looking about him while trying not to make his curiosity apparent, Josse noted that the room was well furnished and spotlessly clean; he had not heard that de Gifford had a wife – in fact he was sure that he hadn't – and so guessed that the woman's touch evident in everything from the highly polished surface of the long table against one wall to the clean rushes on the stone floor must be the handiwork of some efficient and hard-working housekeeper.

De Gifford said, 'Josse, I have asked you here because Arthur Fitzurse has been to see me again. He says he has found something and wants us both to see it. He is coming here later this morning.'

His heart dropping, Josse said, 'What has he found?'

'Bones.'

Oh, God! 'Where?'

'In the forest above the Old Manor.'

Casting round frantically for some sort of counterattack, some factor that would remove the power of this ominous new development, Josse said, 'But you said yourself that anything he came up with would not be proof that—' That Walter Bell went to the Old Manor and died there? Was killed there? No, no, he must not say that! Must not put that thought into de Gifford's mind!

But it was there already, for the sheriff said calmly, 'I know what I said, Josse, and I stand by it.' With a reassuring smile, he added, 'Let us wait and see what Fitzurse brings us.'

★

They did not have long to wait; in fact Arthur Fitzurse followed so closely on Josse's heels that Josse wondered if the man might have been in hiding somewhere watching for Josse's arrival. He came striding confidently into de Gifford's hall, giving the two men the most cursory of greetings, then he brought out from under his cloak a parcel wrapped in sacking and flung it down on the glossy surface of the table. Unwrapping it to reveal a short length of curved bone and another, stouter bone, he said, 'There! I found these half-buried in Leofgar Warin's woods. Tell me now that you don't believe Walter Bell went there, because *I'm* telling *you* that these are the remains of Walter's murdered body and that Leofgar killed him!'

Josse and de Gifford moved closer and stood in silence gazing down at the bones. They were yellow with age and any flesh or marrow adhering to them was long gone.

Josse felt relief coursing through him, as potent as if he had just drained a mug of some strong drink. After what he felt to be a reasonable amount of time for consideration, he said, 'Walter Bell went missing at the beginning of November, I believe?'

'Yes. Just before Martinmas,' Fitzurse replied. Josse turned to look at him; there was a gleam in his dark eyes like that of a starving man bidden to a feast.

'Then these bones do not belong to him.' Josse made sure to remove any hint of *I do not believe that* or *in my opinion* from his bald statement of fact; he wanted both de Gifford and Fitzurse to realise that he was absolutely sure.

'How do you know?' Fitzurse demanded furiously. 'This is his leg bone' – he held up the larger bone, pointing to a small bump about halfway along – 'and there's a notch where he had a break when he was a lad!'

'It may well be somebody's once-broken leg,' Josse allowed, 'but it's not Walter Bell's.' He took it from Fitzurse and put it back on the table. 'It's been in the ground for years.'

Fitzurse's expression went from shock to a devastating disappointment, then swiftly to fury. 'How can you be so sure? *I* say it hasn't!' he shouted. 'It was in a shallow hollow under a scatter of earth and some dead leaves!'

'No doubt a fox left it there to return to later.' In the face of Fitzurse's rising anger, Josse kept his voice level. 'But I do assure you that it takes a long time in the ground to turn bone to a shade as dark as that.'

De Gifford was picking up the smaller, curved bone. 'I would have to check with someone such as a butcher, who is more experienced with animal bones than I am,' he said, adopting the same reasonable tone, 'but I would say that this is the rib bone of a pig, or possibly a boar. Josse?'

Josse took the bone from de Gifford. 'Aye.' He looked at it carefully then, lifting his tunic, held it over his shirt at the level of his own rib cage. 'Too small to belong to a grown man,' he said, 'and the curve is wrong.'

He put the smaller bone back on the table beside the leg bone and wiped his hands on the piece of sacking.

There was silence in the hall. Josse was aware of Fitzurse just beside him and he could feel the man's rage emanating from him like body heat after exertion. De Gifford began to make some remark to conclude the visit but before he had uttered it Fitzurse spun on his heel and strode out through the door. He turned on the top step and said, 'Walter Bell was killed by Leofgar Warin and his body is at the Old Manor. I will find it and take you there and you will believe me!' Narrowed eyes on Josse, he said in a hiss, 'Your precious Abbess Helewise will not be able to help her son then. He'll hang, and I shall be there to watch!' He paused. With unbelievable venom, he added, '*Then* we shall see!'

With that he flung himself away and they heard his rapid footsteps striding across the courtyard.

De Gifford placed the bones on the sacking and wrapped

them up, his movements economical and tidy. Then he said, 'I have found no trace of Walter Bell, Josse. My men have searched all his known haunts and nobody has seen him since the day that Fitzurse claims he went off to seek out Leofgar at the Old Manor.' The parcel of bones tied up to his satisfaction, he turned to Josse and, greenish eyes catching the firelight from the hearth, said, 'Where do you think he is? What has happened here?'

It seemed to Josse that the moment ached with tension. With no idea how he was going to reply, he hedged and merely said, 'It's a mystery all right.'

De Gifford smiled quickly, almost as if to himself, then said, 'Perhaps we shall aid our attempts at explanation if we make one or two guesses. Let me start by suggesting one possible set of circumstances.' He moved away from the table and went to stand over the hearth, eyes watching the dance of the flames. Then he said, 'Let us pretend that Walter Bell really did go to the Old Manor but we'll say that it was not for the reason that Fitzurse claims, for we know that there was in truth no quarrel between Leofgar and the Bell brothers; he did not even know them. Oh, and we must add that this visit was made when the servants of the Warin household were away from home because neither the man, his woman nor their boy recalls a man answering Walter Bell's description coming to the Old Manor.'

He paused, frowning slightly. A log collapsed in the hearth and one end of it fell outside the hearth stones; de Gifford kicked it back with his booted foot. Then he went on, 'Leofgar too is out and his wife and child are alone in the house. Supposing Walter Bell's real reason for sneaking into the Old Manor when everybody but a woman and a little boy are away is something far less honest and open than an attempt to resolve a quarrel. Let us suppose that he has come with theft in mind or, perhaps, a worse crime.' Bright eyes suddenly on Josse, he added quietly, 'The Bell brothers have a bad name, as I have told you. Nobody would think it out of character for Walter to have spotted a house where he might steal some silver and, in addition, rape a lovely and defenceless young woman before making his escape. I am right in surmising that Leofgar's wife is lovely?'

'Aye, she is,' Josse confirmed, 'and she's of slim build and has been unwell, so obviously he didn't expect her to put up such a fight.' Realising even as he spoke the words what he had said, he hurried to correct them: 'That is, he *wouldn't* have expected it, had this imaginary scene really taken place.'

Some flash of understanding shone in de Gifford's eyes, there and gone in a blink. Then, nodding slowly, he said, 'Quite. Very well, let me continue with my description of this *possible* course of events.' The emphasis was impossible to miss, as was the brief urgency in his voice, as if he were compelling Josse to be more careful what he said. 'We'll say that Walter Bell spies his chance and goes into the Old Manor. He finds Leofgar's wife playing with her child in the hall and, although at first she is just an obstacle that he must get rid of before he can steal the candlesticks, or the platter, or the wine jug, it suddenly occurs to him that she is comely. So he pulls his knife and perhaps threatens to hurt the child, forcing Leofgar's wife – what is her name, Josse?'

'Rohaise.'

'Thank you. He forces Rohaise to bundle up the silver candle holders while he holds a knife to—?'

'Timus.'

'To Timus. Then he throws aside the child and attacks the mother, pulling up her skirts, tearing her bodice, but somehow she finds a desperate strength and pushes him off. Swooping down and catching up the knife that he has dropped, she thrusts it at him, blind in her panic, and it goes into his neck. He falls limp to the floor and is still. After a while, when he does not move, she approaches him and realises that he is dead. Leofgar comes home and finds her hysterically weeping and he does what he can to comfort her and his shocked and terrified little boy. Later he disposes of the body, perhaps burying it out in the forest. In an area of the forest,' he adds, enunciating every word clearly, 'that is open and that in early November is used by everybody in the immediate vicinity for the fattening of their swine.' Just to make quite sure Josse has not missed the point, he says, 'So that, were bones – or indeed any other evidence – to be found that could be linked to Walter Bell, then there would, as I have said before, be no proof that Leofgar buried them there.' Green eyes fierce, he demanded, '*Would there?*'

Josse did not answer immediately. He was going through this fictitious scenario of de Gifford's, trying to work out how he should respond. God's boots, but the sheriff had very nearly got it right! Rohaise had not stabbed Walter Bell in self-defence; she had escaped from his grasp and managed to trip him up. Then, when he had tricked her into creeping up to him, he had attacked her again and one of Leofgar's hounds had bitten his throat out. But did not all that mean that in fact Rohaise was even *less* quilty of murder than she was in de Gifford's version?

Dare he risk telling de Gifford the truth? His instincts born of many years' experience of men told him that he could. But then it was not his own freedom – perhaps his own life – that was at stake. It was Rohaise's and, by reason of his involvement and the fact of his having concealed a death, Leofgar's. And what would the Abbess do if her daughter-in-law were hanged for a murder that was no murder and her beloved son strung up beside her because he had helped her?

I cannot tell him, Josse decided. He is a man of the law and an honest and moral one; despite what I feel is a friendship between us, he may consider it his duty to act on what I reveal to him. I dare not do it!

De Gifford was still watching him, waiting for a reply.

Josse had made up his mind. Taking a deep breath, praying he was doing the right thing, eventually he said, 'Let us go on with our pretence a while.'

'Very well.' De Gifford sounded cautious. 'But this is still just a story, Josse. Be in no doubt whatsoever about that, and also remember that whatever is said here is just for our ears.' He grinned briefly. 'We are two men puzzled by a mystery and we pass a chilly morning in idle conjecture.' He paused. 'It is on that basis and that basis only that I will hear you out.'

'Aye, of course.' Josse spoke with false cheerfulness. 'Then let me make one or two suggestions of my own. I find your version of events plausible and I'm going to suggest what might have happened next. We know that Leofgar took his wife off to Hawkenlye Abbey because he was worried about her state of mind – this is fact, not conjecture. But let's pretend that he had an ulterior motive; not only did he want the nuns to help him make Rohaise better, he also wanted to distance himself from the body he had just – er, he'd just buried in the woods. Then while he's there with the nuns and the monks watching Rohaise slowly begin to improve, the inconceivable happens and a man who looks just like Walter Bell is found hanging in the forest not two miles from the Abbey. Somebody announces that the dead man is Walter's brother Teb and Leofgar instantly fears that Teb had somehow found out that Walter lies dead close to the Old Manor. Leofgar leaps to the conclusion that Teb was on his way to kill him in revenge because Teb thinks Leofgar murdered Walter.'

'But if that's so then who killed Teb?' de Gifford exclaimed. 'In this story of ours, that is,' he added quickly. 'I accept that it makes sense for events to have developed as you suggest, Josse, but there is something else: how would a rat such as Walter Bell have known of the situation at the Old Manor? He might, I suppose, have happened upon the place whilst out riding and remarked to himself that it was the sort of household that looked as if it would contain valuables to steal and a pretty woman to assault. But it is extremely unlikely because for one thing Walter Bell does not own a horse and it's quite a walk from Tonbridge to the Old Manor. Also both the Bells habitually restricted their villainy to their immediate neighbourhood, only venturing further afield at another's behest.' With a grim smile he added, 'And probably riding that someone else's horse.'

He paused, staring eagerly at Josse as if in confident expectation of the right response. Which, after a moment, Josse made. 'You think someone sent him to the Old Manor?' he said, trying to sound as if he had only just thought of this possibility. 'Someone said, go and break in while the master and the servants are out and steal the silver?' He made it into a question.

'Yes,' de Gifford said. 'And I'll tell you who it was: Arthur Fitzurse.'

Rapidly thinking it through to see if he would be giving away anything that he should keep to himself, Josse said cautiously, 'Yet the Warin family treasures remain at the Old Manor. Either Walter Bell was prevented from taking them . . .' Deliberately he stopped.

'Or family treasures were not what Bell was after!' de Gifford finished for him. Smacking his first into his open palm, he said, 'We must find out what it was that Fitzurse really sent him to find, Josse, for therein lies the secret that lies so well hidden at the heart of all this!'

And Josse, triumph singing silently through him, said wonderingly, 'Great God, Gervase, I believe you are right!'

He reflected, as the sheriff began to pace to and fro, muttering to himself as he laid his plans for the next move, on his promise to Leofgar. 'Find out what Walter Bell was after,' the young man had begged, and Josse had said he would do his best. Well, now finding the solution to the mystery – and thereby fulfilling the promise – all of a sudden seemed a very great deal more likely; Gervase de Gifford was hunting for the same thing. Watching him, Josse could detect de Gifford's impatience to be moving; it was evident in his brisk step. Closing his eyes for an instant, Josse sent up a prayer of thanks for the gift of such a capable man by his side.

17

Two things pressed on Josse's mind. First, he must get back to Hawkenlye and tell the Abbess what had happened; he would be able to reassure her that, although Arthur Fitzurse had brought what he claimed was evidence to prove that Walter Bell lay dead in the woods above the Old Manor, not only had Gervase de Gifford rightly dismissed this evidence out of hand, he also seemed more than ready to believe that even if Walter Bell had indeed died there, then it was as a result of Rohaise exercising her legal right to defend herself against a violent attack.

The second thing he must do – or at least try to do – was to speak again to Leofgar. Something kept niggling at him, one small detail of the story that Leofgar had told him, and he could not quite bring it into focus. It was something that Walter Bell had done, something that Josse knew was important and that he must remember, but he was damned if he could think what it was . . . Reasoning that Leofgar must want to speak to Josse almost as urgently as Josse wanted to consult him – wouldn't he be desperate to know what was happening? – and that when the two of them had previously met, it was in that dell in the forest where Leofgar had been lying in wait for him, Josse decided to ride back to the Abbey via the woodland paths.

Soon after he entered in under the trees he dismounted and, leading Horace, made his tortuous way to the place where the beech tree hung over the dell. It was too much to expect

Leofgar to be there waiting for him but after a short while the young man appeared, as silently and unexpectedly as before.

'I have been watching for you,' he said, grasping Josse's hand and holding it tightly. He looked drawn and his words fell out in a rush. 'I thought you would come back. Have there been developments? Have you discovered anything?'

'Steady there,' Josse said, trying to calm him. 'One good thing has happened: Gervase de Gifford believes in your innocence.' Leofgar made to speak – Josse guessed he was about to demand if Josse had repeated his story to the sheriff – but Josse held up his hand. 'I have not told him the full tale that you told me,' he said gently, 'for in truth it is not my secret to tell. But de Gifford is an intelligent man and, knowing the foul reputation of the Bell brothers as well as he does, he has worked out for himself a possible course of events that is as near the truth as makes no difference.' Wanting to make certain that Leofgar realised what he was being told, Josse added, 'De Gifford does not see any crime in a woman defending herself from an attacker wielding a knife who bursts into her house with the aim of stealing her goods and raping her.'

As Leofgar sagged with relief, Josse suddenly remembered what it was he needed to ask. Giving the young man a few moments to recover, he then said, 'Leofgar, when we talked before about that terrible day, we concluded that whatever Walter Bell was sent to find – and de Gifford also suggests that Arthur Fitzurse was the man who sent him – it was not your family valuables.'

'Yes, I remember,' Leofgar said. Then, impatiently, 'That's what we have to find out! What it is he's really after!'

'Aye, I know,' Josse said soothingly. 'What I'm asking you is with that end in mind. You told me, Leofgar, that when Rohaise was watching Walter Bell – before he knew she was there – she saw him searching somewhere within the hall. Where was it?'

Leofgar frowned as he tried to recall exactly what his wife had said. 'She was hiding behind the hangings, clutching Timus to her and trying to keep him quiet . . .' Then, as if the remembered scene had suddenly clarified, he said decisively, 'Walter Bell went straight over to the table. That was where he searched first.'

'The table.' Josse was nodding. 'Aye, it always did sound an unlikely place for a thief to begin, unless, that is, someone had told him to look there first.' A smile spreading across his face, he thumped Leofgar on the shoulder and said, 'Thank you. Now I know what to do next.'

Grinning back at him, Leofgar said, 'Go and search my table?'

'Exactly that, because Rohaise did not report that Walter Bell succeeded in finding anything in, on or under that table.' And, he thought, I saw with my own eyes that Arthur Fitzurse met with no more success when *he* looked. But he did not voice the thought; there seemed no need yet to add to Leofgar's worries by revealing that Arthur Fitzurse had also searched the Old Manor. 'So,' he concluded, 'whatever Bell came hunting for—'

'—is still there!' Leofgar gave a whoop of joy. 'Go, Josse, be on your way, I beg you, and God's speed,' he said more quietly. 'May you meet with success.'

'I have a feeling that I will,' Josse said. 'Tell that to your pretty wife, Leofgar, and make sure she keeps her hopes up and her heart high.'

'I will,' Leofgar assured him. 'Come back soon. I will watch for you.'

With a grunt of assent, Josse clicked to Horace and, leading the horse down the narrow track, set off in the direction of the Abbey.

He was so eager to tell the Abbess what had happened and about this thrilling and promising new prospect of searching for the precious thing that Walter Bell was sent to find that, as soon as he could, he mounted and kicked Horace to a canter. Arriving at the Abbey gates in a thunder of hooves, he drew to a halt, slid off Horace's back and, after the most perfunctory of greetings to Sister Martha and Sister Ursel at the gate, he ran off to find the Abbess.

'She's not there!' Sister Martha's voice called after him.

He stopped dead. 'Where is she?' he asked, turning to look at the two nuns.

They looked at each other and then back at him. Then, in a voice that reflected her puzzlement and the very beginnings of anxiety, Sister Ursel said, 'Isn't she with you?'

He got the tale from them in time. Plunged almost into panic by their dread, they both kept trying to talk at once and for a while he could make no sense of what they said. Some man had come up from Tonbridge and told Sister Ursel that he had been sent by the sheriff and would the Abbess Helewise please go down with him to join Gervase de Gifford and Sir Josse d'Acquin there as something had happened and they wanted her to know of it and to give her opinion. Sister Ursel had thought it a little odd, but then hadn't another of the sheriff's men come up to the Abbey earlier with a similar message for Josse, and hadn't he set off without a qualm in answer to that summons? Anyway, odd or not, the Abbess, bless her, hadn't hesitated but had ordered Sister Martha to prepare the golden mare so that she could be on her way. 'And it wasn't for either of us to question her actions, was it, Sir Josse?' Sister Ursel asked tearfully. 'She's our Abbess and we must do as we're told!'

Full of pity for the two distressed nuns, Josse agreed that it was for the Abbess to order her own comings and goings, and he reassured both sisters that it wasn't their fault and nobody would hold them to blame.

'That's all very well, Sir Josse,' Sister Martha said after waiting patiently for him to finish. 'But if she's not with you, where is she?'

Trying to keep his own fears under tight control, he said, 'What was the man like, the one who claimed he had come from the sheriff?'

The two nuns looked at each other, then Sister Martha said, 'Dark sort of aspect to him. Rode a decent horse and although he wore a cheap, thin cloak, I thought I caught a glimpse of a fine tunic beneath it. And there was something else . . .' She broke off, frowning as if trying to search for the words to describe a fleeting impression. Then, apparently finding them, said, 'The man who came for you, Sir Josse, who I sent down to the Vale to find you, he sounded like what he was, if you understand me. This other fellow, he sounded as if he were putting on a voice. Speaking with words he didn't usually use.'

'Could he,' Josse said cautiously, not wanting to lead her, 'have been just pretending to be a sheriff's man?'

Sister Martha shot him a quick look. 'Aye, Sir Josse, he well could. I reckon there was a man of quality hiding under that dirty cloak, or at least a man who habitually puts on the airs of one, and he didn't much like having to act otherwise.'

A man who habitually puts on airs . . . Aye, Josse thought. A shrewd assessment of Arthur Fitzurse, if ever I heard one. Wondering what on earth this meant, what Fitzurse could possibly have been trying to do in luring the Abbess away from Hawkenlye, he did his best to reassure the two nuns that it was probably a simple mistake that would soon be cleared up. 'I'll go straight back down to Tonbridge,' he said, taking Horace's reins back from Sister Martha and swinging up into the saddle, 'and I'll have the Abbess back here before you know I'm gone!'

His words sounded cheerful and optimistic. But his last glimpse of the two worried faces as he cantered away suggested they were no more confident of this rapid success than he was.

He went straight to de Gifford's house. Gervase was still there, or perhaps had been out and returned; he was sitting down to a hasty meal as Josse flung himself into the hall.

'Arthur Fitzurse has taken the Abbess Helewise,' he said breathlessly. 'He went up to Hawkenlye and claimed to be one of your men sent to fetch her down to join us here.'

'Fitzurse?' De Gifford was standing up even as he spoke. 'Why? What does he want of her?'

Josse shook his head impatiently. 'I cannot begin to guess. Where does he live? Do you know?'

'He lodges in rooms in the town. A mean sort of place; I should have expected better from the man's manner.'

Josse heard Sister Martha's voice again. Aye, it seemed more than one person had gained this impression of Fitzurse: he was a man who had the air of someone of more means than he in fact possessed. In that moment Josse saw the man again as he had first watched him ride into the courtyard of the Old Manor, looking as if he owned the place.

'We'll go and look for him,' de Gifford was saying, reaching for his cloak that he had spread before the fire to warm. 'Come on!'

Needing no encouragement, Josse followed him. They mounted their horses and hurried off and after a short time were outside the dilapidated building where Fitzurse had his lodgings. To the surprise of neither man, he was not there and neither was the Abbess.

'Where has he taken her?' Josse raged as they returned to de Gifford's house. Trying to keep his voice low, he demanded, '*Why* has he taken her?'

Reading his anxiety, de Gifford spoke calmly. 'I will summon all the men at my disposal and set them hunting for her.

My men are good,' he added, eyes on Josse's, 'believe me, Josse, they know their way around the dark corners of this town very well and they will not give up until they find her.'

Only a little reassured, Josse watched as de Gifford sent out the summons and, as his men began to arrive, quietly issued his orders. When the last man had gone, he turned to the sheriff and said, 'What do we do? I cannot just sit here and wait, man, I—'

'I understand,' de Gifford said gently. 'You need to be doing something, and so do I. What do you suggest?'

Josse tried to think what he had been doing before this new and dreadful thing had happened. He'd been desperate to see the Abbess because he wanted to tell her something . . .

Aye. He knew what it was, and he also knew what he and Gervase must now do. He said – and he was pleased to hear that his voice sounded brisk and decisive and the terrible anxiety didn't show – 'We'll ride out to the Old Manor.'

De Gifford looked surprised. 'Do you think to find Fitzurse there?'

Josse shrugged; it was possible, he supposed, although he did not see quite why. 'Maybe. But there's something else that we must look for.' And, as they rode out of the courtyard and set off along the road northwards, he explained what it was.

Helewise had been riding along behind the sheriff's man who had come to fetch her down to Tonbridge for some time before she was sure. As soon as she was, she called out to him, 'I thought you said we were to join Sir Josse and the sheriff at the sheriff's house? Is that house not in the town?'

The man turned to her and she caught a glimpse of his sallow-skinned face under the concealing hood. He muttered something about the sheriff living out a way into the country and for a time she had to be content with that.

But her unease grew.

She could not have said why; the man treated her courteously enough and, even if he was bluff of speech and not
inclined to talk unless he had to, those things alone were not
sufficient to explain her vague fear.

They were deep out in the wilds now, riding along what
appeared to be a little-used track that wound along just above
the marshy ground that lay on the river's margins. There were
willows and alder and, underfoot, a sort of wiry grass grew
in tussocks. Here and there smaller paths – perhaps animal
tracks – led off to right and left. The very air smelt wet from
the nearness of the water.

She was about to question her guide again but then, pointing forward to what looked like a length of tumbledown hurdle
fencing extending from a wildly overgrown bramble hedge, he
said gruffly, 'We're here. That's the sheriff's house up ahead.'

She strained to see but the dwelling was as yet still concealed
by the bramble thicket. It could, she thought, be but a single
storey, hardly a house for a man such as Gervase de Gifford.
And why on earth did he opt to live in such apparent neglect
and squalor out here in this moist, misty, damp wilderness?

As if her guide felt that her unspoken question required an
answer, he said, in the same low and slightly husky voice,
'Sheriff has his official residence in the town, see. He likes to
get away here whenever he can a'cause of it's quiet and folk
don't come a-knocking on his door.'

Well, that made sense, Helewise thought. Didn't it? Gervase
de Gifford would very likely be at everyone's beck and call in
the course of his day's work so why should he not choose to
have a house right away from the hurry and bustle of Tonbridge and get away to it when his duties permitted?

Yes, she thought, chewing at her lip, but why has he brought
Josse here? Why did Gervase choose this place for our meeting?

Again the man seemed to read her mind, for his next remark
gave her the explanation she needed. Turning round in the

saddle to look back at her – he was now a short distance ahead – he said, 'Sheriff's brought that Sir Josse d'Acquin along here to show him something what some man's brought him. It's evidence, they say, and nobody's to see it as doesn't have to.'

Ah, now she understood! Somebody had found something – oh, dear God, let it not be anything to incriminate Leofgar; amid her tension, the old familiar dread reared its head – and, since this something, whatever it was, had to be kept from prying eyes, de Gifford had wisely had it brought to his house out here. What a diplomatic man he was!

Trustingly, in anticipation of seeing Josse and the sheriff again very soon, Helewise kicked Honey's smooth sides and hurried to catch up with the man.

Three things happened almost simultaneously. Riding on had meant that de Gifford's house came abruptly into view and instantly she knew it could never have been a dwelling of that fastidious man for it was little more than a hovel, the damage of years left unrepaired, the walls breached and bowing outwards, the reed thatch of the lowering, overhanging roof rotting and dark with age. And, just as she cried out and would have turned Honey's head and put heels to her, galloping off in her fear back along the way they had come, the man leaned out and put a strong hand on Honey's bridle.

Then as he led her captive around the end of the bramble hedge and across the filthy, rubbish-strewn and mud-ridden yard to the low door of the dark little hut, she realised what it was about him that had not been right. It was when he said Josse's name, as he had done when first he came for her and as he had just done again now. Other than the educated, people usually referred to him as 'That Sir Josse' or, if brave enough to make a stab at the rest of his name, 'That Sir Josse Daikin.'

Why, then, should a sheriff's man with dubious grammar and a common man's speech know how to say 'D'Acquin' with perfect intonation and be careful always to do so? It was almost as if, despite the disguise, he would not lower himself to the depths of pretending to be quite that ignorant.

Her heart thumping with fear, Helewise heard the man give her a curt instruction to dismount. He grasped her wrist in a firm hand and took Honey's reins, tethering the mare with his own horse to a post set in the mud of the yard. Then, still holding Helewise's wrist, he opened the door of the hut and pulled her through into the odorous darkness beyond.

Josse and de Gifford reached the Old Manor in record time. It was as if, Josse thought, feeling Horace's great strength beneath him as the horse stretched himself to a full gallop, we expect to find her there and cannot bear to wait an instant longer than we have to for the reassurance that she is safe.

But the Abbess was not at the Old Manor. Wilfrid came out to meet them; he would have heard us coming, Josse realised, for we made no attempt to ride quietly. Wilfrid reported that no visitors had been received since Josse and de Gifford last came by and no word heard from the master. Josse put out his hand and briefly touched the man's shoulder; 'I cannot tell you much,' he said softly, 'but be assured that your master is well, as I believe are your mistress and the child.'

Wilfrid did not utter a word but the expression in his eyes was answer enough.

De Gifford was speaking to Wilfrid now, explaining that they had come to look for something that might well help to put matters to rights so that everything could return to normal. Josse gave Wilfrid a wink behind de Gifford's back – the sheriff had sounded a little pompous – and was rewarded with the first real smile he had seen on Wilfrid's handsome face.

De Gifford strode on into the hall, Josse on his heels. They approached the long table and de Gifford ran his hands over its smooth surface. 'Oak, d'you think, Josse?' he asked.

'Aye,' Josse agreed. 'Plain but well made.' He bent to look at the frame that supported the table top but if there were any concealed drawer or space there, he could not see it. Then, lying down on his back, he looked up at the under surfaces; again, nothing.

De Gifford was feeling up and down the table legs. They too were plain and unadorned; this was a workmanlike piece, there to serve a purpose and do its job, and nobody had wasted their time beautifying it with carvings and mouldings. Nevertheless the sheriff went on looking and so did Josse.

It was de Gifford who was first to speak the obvious. 'There's nothing, Josse,' he said. 'If this damned table holds a secret, then it keeps it too close for us to find.'

Josse was looking around. 'Perhaps there's another table,' he said hopefully. 'Do you remember noticing one when we searched the house with Fitzurse?'

De Gifford shook his head. 'No. On the contrary, I recall thinking how little the young Warins possess. The Old Manor is but sparsely furnished.'

Josse privately agreed – he had received the same impression – but all the same the two of them had a quick look around the other rooms of the house.

They did not find another table.

'The trouble is,' de Gifford mused as they set about a desultory hunt of the chest in the hall and the hangings on the walls, 'that we don't know what we're looking for and so may very well have missed it.'

'Fitzurse knew, if we surmise aright,' Josse replied, 'and he did not find it either, although both you and I watched him search.'

'Hmm.' De Gifford straightened up, rubbing at his back. 'What now, Josse?'

'I confess I am very disappointed,' Josse said. 'I had really thought that we should find a hidden drawer or panel and within it some object to explain what Fitzurse is about.'

'Well, we didn't,' de Gifford said somewhat curtly. 'We should return to Tonbridge, Josse. There is nothing more we can do here and we may get back to find that there is news of the Abbess.'

With that hope high in his heart, Josse followed him outside. Wilfrid came to see them off; observing their expressions, he remarked, 'You didn't find what you came looking for, then.'

'No,' Josse said. With an optimism he was far from feeling, he added, 'But we will!'

Then he kicked Horace and rode off behind de Gifford back to Tonbridge.

18

Inside the hut it was as dark as midnight. The man put a flame to a wick lying in a shallow bowl of animal fat and in the small amount of light that it gave off, Helewise looked about her.

There was just the one room and it was crammed with the detritus of years. A narrow bench was set against one wall and, towards the back of the room, there was a small hearth surrounded with stones, although it looked as though nobody had ever cleared away the ash and it had spilled out in a wide area extending well beyond the circumference of the circle of stones. A black cooking pot rested on a trivet beside the hearth. Along the walls, piled up quite high in places, were what looked like bundles wrapped in sacking and on a shelf set up under the roof were bunches of dried herbs and leaves. On a panel of wood that had once been painted white someone had drawn the rough outline of a bulky and indefinable animal. In a rear corner was a thin straw-filled mattress and some pieces of sacking, presumably a bed, and over this hung a strange cross with equal arms, roughly formed and made out of wood that was almost black. Belying the filth and the unkempt air of the hut, a besom stood beside the door, its twiggy hazel brush pointing upwards and the smooth handle stuck into the beaten earth floor. The room stank of burning fat from the oil lamp and, beneath that stench, Helewise's sensitive nose could detect the smell of unwashed bodies and human waste receptacles that had been spilled and were habitually not emptied before they overflowed.

This man lived *here*?

She turned her head to look at him. He had paced the length and breadth of the small room almost as if looking for something and, from the way he darted back to the door and peered outside, she wondered if he had expected to find someone here waiting for him.

Oh, had it only been Josse!

She was afraid. But I shall not show it, she resolved firmly; seizing the initiative, she said frostily, 'You are not who you pretend to be. Why have you brought me here?'

He spun round and stared at her. He was slightly shorter than she was and she felt a moment's pride at this small advantage. Not that it would do her any good, she realised, for he would no doubt prove the stronger if she tried to wrestle with him and make a break for freedom.

He did not answer her question. But, after a moment's scrutiny, he said, 'No, my lady Abbess, I am not a sheriff's man. I serve nobody but myself.'

'Who are you?' she demanded.

'You do not know?' He looked amused. 'You are an intelligent woman, I have been given to understand; I had thought that you might have guessed my identity.'

Swiftly she thought. Someone was threatening her son, someone who seemed to know that he *was* her son and who had sent a vicious man to Leofgar's house to search for something that had not been found. This someone was presumably still desperate to finish what he had set out to do and must feel that taking captive the Abbess of Hawkenlye was in some way going to help . . . There was really only one person who this man could be.

'You are Arthur Fitzurse,' she said coldly.

He pulled off his dirty cloak, revealing an expensive-looking tunic whose braid, she noticed when the light briefly caught it, was actually of poor quality and beginning to fray. And now he has brought me to this – this *place*, she thought, which, even if not his home, must be the best that he can find to fill his need, lowly and foul though it is. This man, she thought, with what felt like a surprising stab of compassion, tries too hard to achieve his illusion of respectability, education and wealth.

She wondered why. She thought she could probably guess.

'Please, my lady, be seated.' He stepped forward and flicked at the surface of the narrow bench and she moved towards it and sat down as elegantly as she could manage, back straight and head held high, spreading her wide skirts gracefully around her.

He watched her closely for a moment. Then he said, 'I would tell you a tale, my lady, if you have ears to hear it?'

He sounded as if he could only just control his eagerness. Feeling again that strange impulse of pity, she inclined her head and said, 'You have employed deception to bring me here, from which discourtesy I deduce that your motive, whatever it may be, is of great importance to you. Very well, I will listen. What would you say to me?'

He watched her for a moment longer then, as if he needed to concentrate and the sight of her was a distraction, turned away and, staring out through the mean little door, began to speak.

'I am the only child of my mother,' he said, 'and for much of my life believed my father to have been a soldier killed in battle before I was born. As young fatherless children are wont to do, particularly if they are imaginative and male, I formed a secret picture of this man. He became in my eyes a hero, an Achilles, a Lionheart, and I told myself tales of his exploits in the Crusades and before the gates of Troy. I saw him as very tall, broad of shoulder, deep of chest, with a noble face like a Greek god. He was honourable, brave, modest in victory and considerate of his enemies and, naturally, he never lost a battle in his life.' Arthur smiled briefly. 'You will appreciate how childish was the mind that made up this comforting story, for had my soldier father truly never lost a fight, how was it that he came to die before I was born? I revised my tale as I grew older and decided that he had died of a single and totally painless sword thrust through the heart while in the act of saving the lives of an entire company of his loyal men, and that they gave him a hero's funeral out in some beautiful oasis where the soft wind sighed in the trees and a huge moon rose over a flat plain.'

He paused. Then, his voice tight, went on, 'I took great comfort from these imaginary scenes, for in truth my childhood was wretched. What paltry wealth there was soon disappeared and the triple spectres of poverty, hunger and disease stalked me constantly. There was never enough to eat and we – I did not spend my youth as do other boys, for I was a solitary child and had no friends other than the creatures of the wild.'

Again he paused. Helewise burned to question him – who looked after him? Where did they live? Surely not here! – but she held back. Intuitively she knew that the telling of his story caused him pain and she was loath to interrupt and perhaps risk irrevocably halting the flow of words.

Presently he resumed his tale. 'This is an unwholesome place, for it is permanently damp and the river seeps underground, turning firm green grass to a quagmire whenever there is rain; and rain, it seems, falls ever more frequently here than elsewhere. The mists creep about like living things and the very air is wet and foul, bringing phlegm to the throat and rheum to the chest. One's bones ache, my lady, almost all the time. But this place has one advantage: nobody comes here unless they must. For certain, nobody but the outcast and the desperate would choose to live here.' He sighed. 'For those like me who are both, it is . . . convenient.'

'Then this is indeed where you live?' she whispered.

He turned to consider her. 'It touches you, that this might be so?' he asked.

'I – it is an unwelcome thought to think of anyone making their home here,' she replied guardedly.

He smiled faintly. 'It is, isn't it? Well then, my lady, be assured that I do not in fact live here; not all the time, at least, although it is, as I have implied, a most convenient place when one is concerned with matters of a clandestine nature.' Again, she observed, that careful use of words and of grammatical constructions, as if he were very keen to demonstrate that he was – or was pretending to be – an educated man. 'Which, of course,' he was saying, 'brings us to my purpose in bringing you here.'

'It does,' she agreed, ice in her voice.

'Soon, my lady, soon,' he soothed. 'Let me first continue my story.'

She seemed to have no choice but to listen and so she gave him a curt nod of encouragement. Smiling again, he turned back to his contemplation of the dismal scene through the door and picked up the thread of his narrative.

'The word that was most often used to describe my lot in life,' he said slowly, 'was *unjust.* I certainly employed it myself in my thoughts, for I was the son of a soldier, a hero, was I not? Did I not deserve better than to live in wretchedness on the very fringes of society? Yet there I was, dressed in rags, sleeping on mouldy straw, always hungry, frequently verm- inous and usually dirty unless I saw to my cleanliness myself which, I might tell you, I began to do as soon as I was able.' With what appeared to be an almost unconscious gesture he smoothed his tunic and ran a hand over his hair. 'By making myself presentable, I was able, as I grew out of childhood, to find myself employment. Nothing much – never the sort of task for which I believed myself fitted – but at least I earned a little money and, by spending it wisely, steadily I improved my lot.' He turned to look at her briefly, then said, 'Not all of my dealings were strictly honest, my lady, for I burned with resentment and did not hesitate to take from those who had plenty. They were living the life that I should have had and I saw no reason why they should not donate to my cause, even though they might not know that was what they did.'

He is a thief, Helewise thought, although it would seem an honest one, for here he is confessing to me his past misdeeds.

'I might have satisfied myself with what I managed to achieve,' he went on, 'for I reckoned that, for a boy of my upbringing and with my disadvantages, I had done pretty well. But . . .' He paused. Then, as if he had thought about it and had, after consideration, decided to go on, said quickly, 'But my own thoughts and opinions were not all that I had to cope with. Whenever the edge wore off my hunger for advancement, I was instantly reminded of the place – the position – which I ought to occupy, which it was my *right* to occupy. I was never allowed to forget!' His suddenly raised voice startled her. As if he realised it, he turned and said, 'I apologise, my lady. An honourable and courteous man does not shout.'

She inclined her head briefly but did not speak; she felt that he was on the brink of a further revelation.

After a moment he spoke again, and his voice was now distant and cool as if he needed to detach himself from some strong emotion. 'When I was sixteen I learned the truth about my past. I was not the posthumous son of a soldier. My mother had not even been married to my father; I was the result of a quick and animal mating when a lascivious man's blood ran too hot for him to control himself and he grabbed the nearest compliant female. My mother,' he added, very quietly, 'enjoyed sex.' He shot Helewise a swift and somehow sly glance, as if he knew he spoke of forbidden things. 'Or so they took pleasure in telling me.' Flinging out a hand in a despairing gesture, he said passionately, 'From the taunts and the beatings I received because of who and what my mother was, you'd think she was the first woman who ever sold her body in order to feed herself. But she would not have been driven to it if those who stood in judgement over her had had the smallest drop of compassion in their cold and stony hearts! She had other skills but they persecuted her for those too because they were afraid, and their fear served to increase their cruelty.'

Other skills? Helewise thought. Skills that frightened people? Dear God, could Arthur mean what she thought he meant?

He had brought himself under control. After a moment he went on in a quieter tone, 'But all of that was afterwards. I speak of her coupling with the man who fathered me.' He paused again, and then said, 'She would have welcomed him, I am sure, for even as he entered her, brought her to a climax and sowed his seed, she would have been thinking how she could turn his lust to her future advantage.'

A dark suspicion was filling Helewise's mind. No, more than a suspicion, for was this not what she had feared all along? But to have it confirmed by this man whose resentment had been burning in him for twenty years turned it from a worrying fear to a dread: what did he propose to do? And, even more frightening, how would it affect those that she loved?

'Unfortunately for my mother,' Arthur said, 'the man who fathered me was as unscrupulous as she was. When she told him she was pregnant and stated her modest demands – somewhere to live, an income to support herself and the baby, recognition of the child as his – he laughed in her face and said that since she slept with anyone who asked, what proof was there that it was he who had got her pregnant?' Hot eyes suddenly fixed on Helewise's, he cried, 'He lied! My mother swore that at the time of my conception she had lain with nobody but him and I believed her!'

Helewise held his stare. For reasons of her own she yearned

to support the father's version. But there was a hint of fanaticism in Arthur's dark eyes and she feared what he might do if she appeared to doubt his mother's word. So she said, 'Was no helping hand extended?'

'No,' he said sharply. 'On the contrary, my mother's seducer saw to it that she was shunned by so-called *decent* people.' He laid heavy emphasis on the word. 'And when she fought back, my mother was maligned and ridiculed. They called her a whore and threw filth at her. When she took her revenge on her tormentors – and she was very good at that – they said she was a witch who killed their cows with a glance of her black eyes and made their children cry all night with inexplicable fevers and terrifying nightmares. We were driven out!' His voice rose to a shout. 'She came here, and she's been here ever since.'

'She – your mother is still alive?' Helewise was amazed. If Arthur were indeed the age that Josse had guessed, around the mid-thirties – and now that she was face to face with the man, she was inclined to agree with the estimate – then his mother, even if she had been little more than a girl when she bore him, must be fifty at the least. To have lived for more than thirty cold and hungry years in this damp and fog-ridden hovel was some achievement.

As if Arthur followed the line of her thoughts, he said softly, 'It is her resentment that keeps her going, my lady. Such is her desire for revenge that, even when she feeds on it alone, she claims to feel as satiated as if she had attended a banquet.'

'Where is she?' Helewise asked faintly.

'She will not be far away.' Arthur sounded confident. 'She knows that you were to be brought here. She will soon come back.'

Then, with a glance at her that she could not read, he went outside and closed the door. She heard him push some heavy object up against it and, when after a while she quietly got up and went to try to open it, it would not budge.

She sat down again and waited.

Trying to keep fear out of her mind, she thought about Arthur Fitzurse. It was as she had conjectured, she was sure of it. He was in truth the illegitimate son of Benedict Warin, and that was why he was doing all this; it was why he had sent someone to search Leofgar's house and implicate him in murder, why now he had brought her here. Before dread could take hold of her, she made herself think about something else. Two matters presented themselves for her immediate consideration: first, why should Benedict have fought so hard to deny the son he had fathered? For a man of his station to spread his seed and throw up one or two bastards was hardly uncommon, after all; why, even kings did it! And Benedict had in any case been a well-known womaniser; although people might have thought the less of him, nobody would have been very surprised to know about Arthur.

The other matter for her to think about was the interesting fact that it seemed to be Arthur's mother, not he, who was the driving force. She was just turning over in her mind who this fierce woman might be when there came the sound of voices outside. Soon afterwards the door was thrust open and Arthur came in. Behind him stepped a slight figure dressed all in black, a shawl over its head and pulled forward to conceal the face.

Arthur stood aside and tucked himself away in a corner just inside the door. The shrouded figure moved across the room and stopped right in front of Helewise. There was a husky laugh – a woman's laugh – and then a voice said, 'Young Helewise de Swansford, or I suppose I should call you Helewise Warin. It must be a quarter of a century since last I set eyes on you. To these eyes of mine that see so clearly, you have scarcely changed. Despite the habit of *poverty*' – she seemed almost to spit the word – 'I would have known you anywhere.'

Helewise drew herself up. 'You have the advantage, then. Who are you, and what do you want of me?'

The woman laughed again, a sound that now she managed to fill with malevolence and menace. 'Do you not know? Then I will tell you what happened to me and we shall see if you can guess.' Before Helewise had a chance to comment, the woman pressed on, her voice louder now and the words coming readily, as if she had gone through this story very many times.

'I was the daughter of a widow of spotless reputation but limited means,' she began. 'We lived honestly but we were poor, and when I was thirteen a position was found for me in a large household. I began as the lowliest of maidservants but as the great improvement in my diet took effect I grew comely and men began to notice me.' Her face was still concealed but it seemed to Helewise that she stood straighter, preening herself; perhaps she was remembering her lost looks. 'I was given easier work and a better position, then one day I went with my master and mistress to the Old Manor.' Helewise gave a start. 'Aye, Helewise, you remember the place?' Now the woman was jeering. 'You remember its master too, I dare say. You remember Benedict Warin as he was in his prime. So do I, lady. So do I.'

She stopped. Turning away from Helewise, she strode to the door and back, as if the memory that she was conjuring up was too powerful for her to stand still. 'I liked what I saw, I admit that,' she said, resuming her position in front of the bench where Helewise sat. 'I knew by then how to attract a man, how to make him think he would never rest again until he had bedded me, and I put my spell on Benedict. It's quite easy to draw a man when you know how, Helewise,' she remarked, as if Helewise had asked, 'a simple matter of a love potion slipped into his broth, a spell spoken naked in the moonlight and the exquisite scent of your own lust on your fingers when your hands are close to his face. He came running, I can tell you, quicker than a hound on a hare.

'Then when I found I was with child I sought him out and asked him what he was going to do. I told him what I wanted—'

'Yes,' Helewise interrupted, 'I already know the sum of your demands.'

'Oh, you do, do you?' The woman's mocking tone had returned. 'Reasonable, were they not? The pity of it was that Benedict Warin did not agree. He claimed the child wasn't his and when I insisted, he threw me out. I kept coming back and he blackened my name, hounded me wherever I went, and I was driven to trying a few little ruses of my own to keep body and soul together. I was pregnant, mind, and you know, don't you, Helewise, how that state makes the appetite grow? Especially when it's a healthy boy who kicks in your womb?'

'Little ruses?' Helewise demanded sharply. 'You speak of spells and witchcraft, do you not?'

'Perhaps, perhaps.' The woman drew out the words. 'Folk are superstitious, no matter how the church tries to beat it out of them, and if they prefer to trust in the old ways when they perceive a threat instead of running to that meek and mild saviour whom their priests value so highly, why should I care?'

'What did you do?' Helewise whispered.

The woman smiled. 'Oh, I poisoned a well and when the people fell sick I told them they'd offended the spirit of the spring and that only my charms would save them. Then when they had all paid up I stopped putting the potion in the water – don't look like that, Helewise! It wouldn't have killed them, for I know my herbs better than to kill where I don't intend to – and miraculously the people recovered.' Leaning closer, she said softly, 'That was a trick. But I have the Sight and the power to see and to influence things that are veiled from others. You would be surprised to know how many folk crept to my room by night and begged me to make this person fall in love with them, or that person's crops fail, or tell them what some secret enemy was saying behind their back.'

Despite herself, Helewise was fascinated. 'How can you see these things?' she asked.

The woman contemplated her for a long moment. 'Does your bible not speak of visions?'

'Yes, but—'

Sirida sighed. 'But such things are allowed among the holy but not for witches? Helewise, witches are but the holy of an earlier religion! Are you so blind that you cannot see?'

Closing her eyes and her mind to what this terrible person would have her see, Helewise fell silent.

Presently the woman spoke again. 'What if I did use my talents? I had to help myself, seeing as nobody else was going to. But they turned that against me too and drove me away, accusing me of making magic, of putting the evil eye on their livestock and turning their bawling brats sickly. I promised I'd make all well again if they'd give me what I wanted but oh, no, even my small requests were too much for those smug and self-righteous folk who had once been my neighbours and my friends!'

She was spitting with anger, all the passion of her rejection returning in full force. Her thin body shook with the force of her rage and the concealing shawl slipped slightly; with an impatient hand, the woman pulled it back in place.

Trying to speak calmly, Helewise said, 'And so you came here and brought up your son alone.'

'I did,' the woman agreed, quieter now. 'Aye, I did.' She turned and, for a brief moment, stared into the dark corner where Arthur still stood, his head bowed. Facing Helewise again, she said, 'But I did not let him forget his roots. He's a Warin, never mind that he was conceived out of wedlock. Yet

look at him and look at your own son, Helewise!' *Son*, Helewise thought with the first stab of relief; this woman, whoever
she is, does not know as much as she believes she does! She
does not even know that I bore *two* sons. 'Look at Leofgar in
his splendid house,' the black-clad woman was saying, 'lovely
wife and handsome child, food on the table, servants to attend
to his every wish, doting mother who conveniently hears the
call from God and vacates her marital home so as to leave it
free for her son!'

Indeed she does not know everything, Helewise thought
jubilantly. She knows nothing of Dominic and she is only
guessing at how I came to leave the Old Manor and enter
Hawkenlye Abbey. Eyes down lest the woman read her expression, she said meekly, 'Leofgar has lived a blessed life, in
truth.' Until you came along to spoil it, she wanted to add. 'But
what of it? What is it to you?' She made her voice sound
puzzled and indignant, as if she truly had not grasped what
was happening.

The woman gave a sound of annoyance; hard, abrupt.
Then: 'They do not require intelligence of their nuns up at
Hawkenlye, then.' Helewise held her peace. 'It's obvious,' the
woman hurried on, eager now. 'Leofgar has what Arthur
ought to have. Leofgar has it *all*, Arthur has nothing. I am
old now and I will not live much longer, yet I would see my son
come into his inheritance before I die.'

'Your son is illegitimate and has no legal claim on the
Warins,' Helewise stated flatly. 'That is the law. It will not
be changed to suit you.'

'No legal claim, perhaps.' The woman pretended not to
have heard the rest of Helewise's remark. 'But he has a moral
claim, do you not agree, Helewise? Your father-in-law used
me cruelly and flung me away when he was finished with me,
and my son and I have lived wretchedly ever since. Why
should not Leofgar give some of what he has in such abun-

dance to improve Arthur's lot?' When Helewise made no reply – she had no intention of doing so – the woman cried out, 'I do not ask for much! But what I demand I will have, I swear to you, or else it will be the worst for Leofgar! You think he has suffered already? Well, you wait! If you do not give me what I want, you'll learn very quickly the terrible things I can do when I'm *really* angry!'

The threat was awful. But Helewise's own anger had burned up through her; leaping to her feet, towering over the woman, she shouted, 'You will not succeed! You have sent a thief to my son's house and tried to make it appear that my son killed him, and now you have taken me captive, but neither measure will avail you! I am not afraid of you – you will *not* succeed!'

The echo of her words rang out in the hut and, as they faded, there was silence. A horrible, creeping silence, as if the last word in the world had been spoken. Alarmed, wondering why she should suddenly feel such dread, Helewise stared down at the woman.

Who, with agonising slowness, drew back her dark shawl so that Helewise could at last see her face.

It was very white, as if she seldom ventured out, and thin, the cheekbones stark and sharp. Her wide mouth was tight and surrounded by small outward-radiating lines, deep-etched as if from constant pursing. It was a dead face, sucked dry of all joy and of all generous impulse. In it the only living things were her eyes.

Her eyes burned with fire.

And she was muttering under her breath, continuously, repetitively; it was a spell, and the terrible sense of malice in the hut was the result.

When at last she stopped and Helewise was released from her thrall, the woman spoke in her normal voice. 'Know me now, do you? They told you I was a witch the first time you saw me, didn't they?' She laughed. 'They were right.'

Helewise, transported back twenty-six years to her wedding day feast as easily as if she were flying on the besom in the corner, saw the woman as she once had been. And she said, with a calm that cost her dear, 'Yes, I know you. Hello, Sirida.'

19

Sirida's black-eyed stare was horribly discomfiting and Helewise was desperate for her to speak and dispel the frightening
tension. But, as if the woman knew this full well and wished to
enjoy the power of the mood that she had created, she held her
silence.

Finally it was Helewise who spoke. 'If—' But her mouth was
too dry to make the words. She coughed, swallowed and tried
again. 'If by threatening me you seek to force my son to give
you what you claim is your due, then, Sirida, you will not
succeed.' She hesitated, her resolve weakening; were Leofgar
to receive some extravagant demand in return for his mother's
safe return he would, Helewise well knew, accede instantly;
both her sons had been brought up to respect and honour her
and Leofgar would not permit her to remain captive for a
moment longer than necessary if it were in his power to buy
her release. Whatever the cost.

But Sirida must not be allowed to know this . . .

So Helewise shifted her argument. 'If what you say is true
and Arthur is indeed the son of Benedict Warin—'

'I speak true!' Sirida hissed.

'—then he is, as I said just now, illegitimate and has no claim
on my family.'

Sirida studied her for some moments, dark eyes narrowed.
Then, with a slow nod, she murmured, 'We shall see. Oh, yes,
we shall see.' Then, as if long-pent venom were abruptly
breaking out, she put her face close to Helewise's and said,

'You thought you were so fine, didn't you, the day you wed Ivo Warin? They took you into their home and their heart, those two, father and son, and I was ordered from the house! I, who had borne Benedict a child and who, now that the saintly Blanche was dead, should have been invited to take my place at his side, in his bed and by his hearth as his lawful wife! It should have been I who danced at my wedding feast, and yet I was supplanted by a strip of a girl who was no better than I was!'

Sirida paused dramatically. Then, as Helewise had known she would, she said softly, 'No better, Helewise, for I know what was under your beautiful scarlet tunic the day you wed Ivo. You had not waited for the Church's blessing on your union, had you, any more than I did?'

Furious protests sprang to Helewise's lips: you cannot compare your situation with mine! Ivo loved me, wanted from the first to make me his wife! It was love that made my son, not lust!

But she held back the passionate words.

For one thing, she wore the habit of a nun and she was Abbess of Hawkenlye; the dignity of her office forbad exchanging heated words with the likes of Sirida as if the pair of them were fishwives in the market. For another thing, could she truly claim that it had in fact been love and not lust that led to Leofgar's conception? If her memory served her right, it was not easy to say where one left off and the other began.

Straightening her back, she summoned her dignity and said coolly, 'I demand that you let me go from here. I must return at once to Hawkenlye and if you insist on keeping me from my duties there, you will be punished.'

'Oh, I'll be punished, will I?' Sirida gave an unpleasant laugh. 'Well, my lady Abbess, I reckon I'll take that risk. I have not much time left to me on this earth and I am quite determined to see this affair that I have begun through to its finish. I'll keep you safe here with me while Arthur seeks out your son and dictates the terms of your release.'

And with that, before Helewise could say another word Sirida spun round and walked swiftly out through the door, taking hold of Arthur's arm and pulling him with her. Then the door was pushed shut and once more there came the sound of that heavy object being set against it.

Helewise strode furiously across the floor, once, twice, restraining only with difficulty the urge to shout aloud with frustration and anger. But had she not only a moment ago been reminding herself who she was? She was no longer the carefree child Helewise de Swansford, no longer the wild and lusty girl who had married Ivo Warin. Those identities were far behind her; she wore the habit of obedience and no more was she free to act as impulse dictated.

Slowly Helewise sank down on the bench. Quieting her breathing, using her will to impose calm on her tumultuous thoughts, she began to pray.

Josse and Gervase de Gifford arrived back in Tonbridge to be greeted by the dismal news that there was no sign of the Abbess nor of Arthur Fitzurse. One of the search parties was still out but all the others had returned and the men were scratching their heads and wondering where to look next.

Pacing up and down in de Gifford's hall, Josse felt the frustration of inactivity; making up his mind, he announced to de Gifford that he would ride up to Hawkenlye and see whether any word or clue had arrived at the Abbey to explain where the Abbess had gone. It was a slim hope, he knew, but he did not know the Tonbridge area well enough to be of much help to the search parties and at least riding up to the Abbey was *something*.

'Very well,' de Gifford agreed. 'I will come to find you there if there is any news.'

★

There were no reassuring, optimistic tidings awaiting him at Hawkenlye. Far from it: the nuns looked stunned, as if the unthinkable had happened and they did not know how to cope with it. Sister Euphemia, informed of Josse's arrival, came to seek him out.

'Where's he taken her?' she demanded. 'And why? What does he want with her, Sir Josse?'

Josse wondered if it was really necessary to share his suspicions with her; was it not enough for him to have to bear his dreadful thoughts without the infirmarer having to do so too? But then, realising that in the Abbess's absence Sister Euphemia was one of the most senior nuns, he decided that she had a right to know and so he told her.

'I fear,' he said gently, 'that this has to do with the Abbess's son and the reason for his disappearance. Someone' – he did not want to use Fitzurse's name – 'is attempting to make trouble for the Warin family and I believe that this someone thinks to influence matters by holding the Abbess captive.'

Sister Euphemia looked horrified. 'But she—' Then the fear left her face, to be replaced by anger. 'If he hurts so much as her little finger, I'll—'

'He will not hurt her!' Josse said swiftly. 'In truth, he will not!'

He was not sure, in that moment of dread, whether he was reassuring the infirmarer or himself.

It did not take long for Sister Euphemia's practical mind to turn from her anxiety to concern for Josse; noticing that he was drooping with fatigue and looked cold and drawn, she suggested that he go across to the Abbess's room, where she would order a fire to be lit and food and drink to be brought. He was reluctant to accept – it would sit ill on him to be warm, well-fed and comfortable when the Abbess was possibly being deprived of all of these happy states – but in the end he agreed for, as Sister Euphemia wisely remarked, his strength might well be needed soon and he would be of far more use if he were fully restored.

He sat himself in Helewise's high-backed chair and his mind was filled with thoughts of her. I'll not stay here, he told himself; I'll eat, drink, warm myself and rest for a while, then I'll go out again and I won't stop till I've found her.

But he was exhausted. The simple meal that he was served combined with the warmth and he relaxed in the throne-like chair, propping his elbow on one of the arm rests and resting his head on his hand. In no time he was fast asleep.

It was dark when he woke abruptly from his deep sleep and for a few moments he could not remember where he was. Then the sound that had wakened him came again: someone was tapping on the door. Then he felt the hard chair beneath him and, stretching out his hand, knocked over the wine cup on the table. There was a candle on the table somewhere – he passed his hands to and fro until he found it – and, taking it to the brazier, he put the wick to a faintly glowing ember and, blowing the ember to a small flame, lit the candle.

Then, standing up straight and hoping he did not look like a man suddenly roused from a slumber he should not have taken, he called out, 'Come in!'

For a moment nothing happened. Then the door opened very slowly and quietly and a cloaked and hooded shape slid through the narrow gap and into the room, carefully closing the door again.

'Who are you?' Josse demanded, for some reason picking up the figure's soft-footed and furtive manner and speaking not much above a whisper.

The figure put back the hood.

It was Leofgar.

Hastening to put down the candle and take the young man's

hands – they were very cold – Josse said, 'Leofgar! What are you doing here? Did anyone see you come in?'

Answering the second question first, Leofgar said, 'No, I made sure that I was not spotted; my black cloak and the darkness helped, and the good sisters were not expecting me.'

'But why have you come?'

Leofgar rubbed his hands over his jaw and Josse studied him. He looked as tired as Josse felt and his face was pale. Then the young man said, 'I have been to the Old Manor. Wilfrid told me that you and de Gifford were there, hunting for something. I knew you had gone to search through the table and I realise that you did not find anything. He said – Wilfrid said you were both very anxious – there was a dread about you, he said, and I just—' He stopped, apparently unable to go on.

'You just had to know what is happening,' Josse finished for him. 'And so you come here and, instead of finding your mother sitting in her usual place, you find me. Aye, Leofgar,' – he sighed deeply – 'she is not here.' Taking a breath and looking the younger man straight in the eyes, he said quietly, 'It appears that Arthur Fitzurse has taken her captive. Gervase de Gifford's men are even now searching for her but so far without success.'

Leofgar's white face had paled yet more. He tried to speak, swallowed and then said quite calmly, 'If he harms her I will kill him.'

You'll have to beat me to it, Josse thought. Aloud he said, 'We must not speak of harm, Leofgar. There is no reason to suspect that he intends to mistreat her or indeed wishes her any harm.'

'Then why,' Leofgar said with cold logic, 'has he taken her?'

'I do not know,' Josse said gently.

'Where *is* she?' Leofgar said, although it seemed to Josse that he spoke more to himself. 'What does Fitzurse want with us? With her?'

'I believe,' Josse said carefully, 'and indeed it is the opinion of your mother, that this all has to do with your family's past. That, whatever it is that Fitzurse was trying to find at the Old Manor, it is likely that it concerns a claim that the man believes he has on the Warin family. He—'

'Fitzurse,' Leofgar cried suddenly, interrupting him. 'Son of the bear. Why did I not remark it before? The bear is the traditional device of my forefathers.'

'Aye, lad, I know,' Josse murmured. Not wanting to elucidate – it was a matter of extreme delicacy – he simply said, 'So, now you have it.'

Leofgar nodded slowly. 'Fitzurse claims to be a bastard son of – of whom, Josse? Of my father?'

'I could not say,' Josse answered. 'Your mother – well, I do not know what she thinks of this suggestion for she has not discussed it with me. Not that she should!' he added hastily. It was, after all, he reflected, far too personal.

'My father loved my mother greatly,' Leofgar said. 'I was but a child of six when he died but I understood well enough that he had eyes for no woman but her.'

'He would have begotten Arthur years before he met your mother,' Josse pointed out gently. 'If it proves to be he who fathered the man, then it will not detract in any way from your father's love and loyalty to your mother.'

'No, I see that,' Leofgar said slowly. 'Yet—' He shrugged. 'It is not easy, Sir Josse, for a grown man to face the possibility that he may have a half-brother whose existence he has never even dreamed of, and who is a rogue into the bargain.'

'Do not forget that it *is* but a possibility,' Josse urged him. 'There is a tale yet to be told here, and we should make no assumptions yet.'

'Good advice,' Leofgar said. 'I will—' Again he broke off, as if struck by a sudden thought.

'What is it?' Josse demanded.

Leofgar frowned. 'Something you said keeps coming back into my head.'

'What?'

'You made a remark about all this being to do with my family's past.' He was wrapping himself in his cloak again as he spoke. 'If you are right – and I confess that I think you are – then there may be something that I can do to help. Wait here, Sir Josse, I'll be back as soon as I can.'

'Help in what way? Where are you going?'

But Josse found he was speaking to empty air; Leofgar had hurried out through the door and, when Josse looked out and along the cloister, was already racing for the gates.

There was nothing to do but obey Leofgar's order and wait for his return. Closing the door, Josse went back to the Abbess's chair and sat down again.

He did not know how Leofgar was getting into the Abbey; the first time he appeared, he had presented himself alone at the door of Helewise's room, and this suggested to Josse that he had not entered via the gates for, had he done so, then Sister Ursel or one of the other nuns would probably have escorted him across the courtyard and along the cloister. Or perhaps even then it had been late, and the good sisters all abed.

When Leofgar returned, it was well after midnight and the gates were shut fast.

He was breathless and red in the face, his cloak bespattered with mud; noticing Josse's eyes on him, he gave a quick smile and said, 'I apologise for my appearance but I have been riding hard.' Then, excitement bursting from him, he cried, 'I think I know where she is! Will you ride with me to fetch her home?'

Josse leapt to his feet and went to embrace the young man. 'Aye, and gladly!' he cried. 'Give me but a moment to fetch my horse and collect my weapons, and I'll follow wherever you lead!'

The stables were night-dark but it did not take Josse long to put saddle and bridle on Horace; it was not the first time he had made a hasty departure in the small hours. He led the horse out to the gates, easing back the bar that held them fast and slipping out on to the track. Leofgar, behind him, fastened the gates again and soon afterwards reappeared on the track leading his own horse.

'You have your own private means of access, I see,' Josse remarked drily.

'Yes.' Leofgar grinned. 'A convenient tree bough and a branch to which to tether my horse.'

Both men mounted, then Josse said, 'Right, lad.' Excitement coursing through him, he added, 'Lead on!'

Leofgar took them down the track towards Castle Hill but, before it began its descent into Tonbridge, he branched to the right along a narrower path that led off at an angle to the main track, entering an area of sparse woodland and then, after quite a time, emerging into the open. They had come down into the river valley – Josse could sense moisture in the air and there were dense pockets of low-lying mist – and were somewhat to the east of the town.

Leofgar drew rein and Josse came up beside him. 'Where are we going?' he asked, keeping his voice down.

Leofgar turned to look at him. 'I am sorry, Sir Josse, I should have explained. Thank you for following where I have led, even though you did not know where we were bound.'

'It is of no matter,' Josse replied, 'but I would like to know now.'

'Of course.' Leofgar considered, then spoke again. 'Your speaking of my family's past made me think of a person who is, I would guess, the best source of knowledge on that subject. She is, indeed, the person with whom Rohaise and Timus are now lodging, the good soul who understood our grave need and, without a single question, took us into her home.'

Although he thought hard, Josse found he had no idea whom this could be. He asked, 'Who is she?'

'Remember Wilfrid, my manservant?'

'Of course.'

'Wilfrid is the son of the man who filled the same office for my father as Wilfrid does for me. This man – his name was Fithian – had as wife a woman named Magda, who had served the Warins all her life, being herself born to a servant of the household. Magda was housekeeper when my mother first came to the Old Manor and, so I am told, loved her from the moment she set foot through the door.'

Frowning, Josse tried to work out why Leofgar was telling him this. 'Had Magda and her husband other sons, then? Has one of them – one of their wives – taken you in?'

Leofgar shook his head. 'No. She has.'

'*Magda?*' Josse was astonished. 'But if she was a mature woman when your mother wed Ivo Warin, then by now she must be elderly indeed!'

'She is well advanced in years, yes, but her age has not made her feeble,' Leofgar replied.

Understanding at last, Josse said, 'And she has been able to help you.'

'Yes. She did not explain – I did not give her the time – but she told me where she believes my mother will have been taken.'

'You are confident that she is right?'

Leofgar smiled. 'You don't know Magda, for if you did, you would not have asked that. Yes, Sir Josse, I am quite confident.'

'Then let us hurry and go there,' Josse said with sudden impatience, 'for your mother is waiting!'

But Leofgar took a long time finding whatever path he was

looking for. Trying to restrain his impatience, Josse held Horace on a loose rein and waited while the young man followed this track and that. The sky was clear and there was a bright moon; by its light, Josse was able to make out that some of the paths down which Leofgar was searching were surely no more than animal tracks.

Finally he found the right one. Returning along it, beckoning silently to Josse, he said, as Josse approached, 'The hut is down here. All is dark and I imagine they are asleep. We should leave the horses here, I think, and make our way quietly on foot.'

They tethered the horses to the branch of a hazel tree and set off along the path. The ground was waterlogged and sometimes one of the men's feet made a loud squelch as it was withdrawn from the mud. The air stank of foul, rotten vegetation and curls of malodorous mist seemed to attack nostrils and mouths. It was a desolate place.

After some time they came to a clearing. Putting out a warning hand, Leofgar whispered, right in Josse's ear, 'There's the hut.'

Josse peered into the clearing and saw the hut at one side, its back to the encircling trees. Drawing his sword, he said, 'Then let us break the door down and see what we shall find.'

Together they strode across the wet grass and up to the door of the hut. There was a large stone set against it and they moved it away. Leofgar flung back the door and they both rushed into the room.

The Abbess sat straight-backed on a bench, her skirts spread around her, calmly eyeing them. She said, 'I have no idea how you found me, but I am most grateful.' Standing up, she added, 'My mare is somewhere close, I believe. Shall we find her and be on our way?'

'My lady, are you hurt?' Josse asked, taking her hands, just

as Leofgar, an arm around her shoulders, demanded to know
what Fitzurse had done to her.

'I am quite unhurt and, beyond bringing me here and
making me stay here against my will, they have done nothing
to me,' she said. 'Nevertheless I wish now to return with all
speed to the Abbey. I have been too long away and far too long
preoccupied with matters that are not the business of an
Abbess.' She glared at them both as if it were all their fault.

With a courteous bow, Josse said, 'Aye, my lady. The
sooner we have you back in your rightful place, the better.'

They left the hut. Leofgar, staring about him, spotted a
roughly made corral consisting of little more than a few rotten
hurdles lashed together and, hurrying across to it, called out
softly that he had found the Abbess's mare; he brought her
forward out of the concealing shadows and, tightening the
girths, helped his mother into the saddle.

'Where are your horses?' the Abbess demanded in a carrying hiss. 'I do hope we shall not have to return to Hawkenlye at
a walking pace.'

'No, indeed, my lady,' Josse assured her. 'We have left them
up the track. We wanted to approach as quietly as possible, so
as not to alert Fitzurse as to our intention.'

'I do not believe that they are here,' she said. 'I do not know
where they have gone, but they judged that barring the door of
the hut was enough to keep me prisoner.' With a sudden smile,
she added, 'They reckoned without the two of you. Thank
you, both of you. You are—'

But she was not to finish her remark.

There was a sudden rush of sound, an impression of urgent
speed, a wild cry. Then Arthur Fitzurse stood on the path
before them, his sword tip at Leofgar's throat freezing both
Josse and the Abbess into immobility.

When he saw this and knew that, for Leofgar's sake, they
would not rush at him, Arthur gave a slow smile. Then he said,

'Did you think I should leave my bargaining tool unattended? Oh, but I should not be so careless!' Then, turning, he called, 'Mother, show yourself. They are all here now, the Abbess, the son and the knight. I have them safe – come out and finish the tale.'

And as Josse watched, his eyes ever returning to the sword point that had now drawn a speck of blood from the flesh of Leofgar's throat, a small and black-cloaked figure detached itself from the reeds lining the path and came to stand beside Fitzurse. Pushing back her hood, the bent and ageing woman looked first at the Abbess, then at Leofgar. She murmured something – it was, Josse thought, barely able to make out the words, an observation that now both she and the Abbess had their sons at their sides – and then she turned to Josse.

As she stared at him, her black eyes seemed to glitter in the moonlight. It was as if her gaze held him in a vice: for a frightening moment, he felt he could not move even if he tried. He seemed to hear her muttering, chanting, although when he put it to the test, there was no sound on the still night air. She tries to bewitch me, he thought wildly.

And, despite the fact that she was tiny, old and probably as weak as she looked, he felt a terrible stab of fear.

20

Arthur made the Abbess and Josse walk ahead of him back to the hut; the Abbess had been curtly ordered to dismount, and the old woman was leading the mare back to the corral. All the time that Arthur holds a blade to Leofgar's throat, Josse thought – Arthur had exchanged his unwieldy sword for a short-bladed and wickedly-pointed dagger – we cannot risk disobeying his orders.

Josse pretended a docility that was only superficial; beneath it he was tense, alert for the smallest opportunity. Should Arthur make the least mistake, then Josse intended to be ready . . .

They entered the hut and, by the light of a couple of rush lamps, Arthur told the Abbess and Josse to sit down on the bench. He made Leofgar kneel in front of him, the knife blade still against his flesh. Presently the old woman joined them.

'Sir Josse, this is my mother.' Arthur nodded in her direction, keeping his eyes on Josse. 'Her name is Sirida and I am the result of her union with Benedict Warin.'

Leofgar's head shot up and he met Josse's eyes. Despite the situation, still he managed a look of triumph, as if to say, my grandfather! See, I told you my father begat no bastards!

'So, Arthur,' Josse said, looking at Fitzurse, 'it is the identity of your father that is the reason for your pursuit of Leofgar's family.'

'*My* family,' Arthur corrected him. There was a profound, black anger there not far beneath the surface, Josse thought; it showed in the man's burning dark eyes. 'I have been the outcast for too long, Sir Josse. It is time for this family of mine to make amends.'

Josse looked across at the old woman. Standing in the doorway, she was a silhouette against the steadily lightening sky. It's almost morning, Josse thought absently. He said, 'Sirida, why have you waited so long?'

She stepped down into the hut and approached him. The face that she turned up to his was painfully thin, so that the bones of the skull stood out with clarity. 'I am dying,' she said simply. 'I have foreseen my own death and now it draws near.'

'The time of our deaths is for God alone to know!' the Abbess protested.

Sirida turned to her. 'Your God is not the only power in the universe,' she said calmly. 'And I tell you this, Helewise Warin: were I to describe to you the day and the circumstances of my end, when that time comes you would look back to this moment and know that I had spoken the truth.'

Josse seemed to feel an icy finger on the back of his neck. Did she really have such power? he wondered, an awed fear filling his mind at the thought of being in the presence of one who saw the future with such certainty.

The Abbess was saying something – telling the old woman again that such matters were not for humans to meddle with – but Josse thought her tone lacked conviction and he guessed that, even if she pretended indifference, she too was affected by the strange atmosphere inside the hut.

With the intention of bringing them out of the realms of magic and back to the all too real – and menacing – situation they were facing, he said, too loudly, 'But why, Sirida, does the prospect of your death force you to do what you are doing?'

She gave a hoarse laugh. 'Is it not obvious? Because I am the last person alive who can prove who fathered my son. This is my final chance. I am determined that the Warins recognise Arthur for who he is and act accordingly.'

'What do you want of us?' Leofgar demanded. Even on his knees and with a blade at his throat he managed, Josse observed, to sound fierce and unafraid.

Sirida looked at him. 'Not much. Arthur must be allowed to use the family name and –' she paused, apparently thinking, '– and be given assistance in setting up a modest household for himself.'

'Perhaps he'd like to move into the Old Manor with Rohaise and me!' Leofgar cried furiously. 'You'd like to sleep in a real bed, wouldn't you, Arthur? Better than that filthy heap of straw down there in the corner!'

Josse held his breath as the knife point dug infinitesimally into the skin of Leofgar's throat. Be careful, lad, he pleaded silently; it may be brave but it is not wise to antagonise a man who holds a blade to your neck.

But Arthur controlled himself. 'This is my mother's dwelling,' he said, his voice cold and distant. 'I was begotten in something very similar, so she tells me, and, because of Benedict Warin's intransigence, neither she nor I have ever managed to better ourselves.'

As if this reminder of her sufferings had loosened some restraint within Sirida, she suddenly spoke. 'He used me and he abandoned me,' she said, the cold, detached tone somehow more powerful than anger. 'He took me to his hut in the woodland above the Old Manor, him and that Martin of his, the man who was his constant companion after the accident.'

Leofgar and Josse said together, 'What accident?'

The Abbess, eyes vague as if she looked back into the past, said quietly, 'Although he tried to disguise it, Benedict Warin walked with a limp. He had a bad fall from his horse and he was dragged for quite some way before his companion managed to get hold of the horse and bring it to a halt. Martin was that companion; the two men had been close since boyhood. After Benedict was hurt, he used Martin as a sort of body servant, someone to prop him up and help him move about when the pain from his old wounds became bad.'

'Yes, yes, that was Martin,' Sirida said impatiently. 'But listen now and forget about Martin, because it's Benedict I'm telling you about. He knew I was with child for I told him so and yet he refused his help. But there was *something* that he did.' She paused, looking around the circle of listeners to make sure she had their full attention.

Unable to bear the suspense, Josse said, 'What do you mean?'

She turned to him, a soft smile on her thin lips. 'When my baby was born I sought out Benedict and I showed him the child. I hoped that Benedict's heart would soften when he saw the fruits of his seed – he only had the one son, you know, by that barren wife of his. But even then, staring down at my pretty babe in my arms, he would do nothing for me. I pleaded, I swallowed my pride and I begged. I said, ignore me and my plight if you must but do something for your little son! In the end – I suspect just to get rid of me – he said that he would help.' She paused dramatically, staring around at each one of her listeners. Then she said, 'He told me that when his time came he would leave proof of Arthur's paternity.' Her eyes on Arthur, she added quietly, 'I made him promise to make it right for you in the end.'

There was a brief shocked silence.

Then Leofgar broke it. 'And it is this *proof* that you have been searching for in my house?' he burst out. 'For which you sent that foul villain Walter Bell prying and hunting?' He tried to crane round to stare at Arthur, but Arthur increased the pressure on the blade and he had to stop. 'Your *thief*,' Leofgar said, spitting out the word, 'attacked my wife and terrified my little son so badly that he was struck dumb.'

Sirida turned on Arthur. 'I told you not to send Walter Bell,' she said coldly. 'He can control neither his lust nor his anger and he forgot all about his mission once he set eyes on the woman.'

'I had to send him!' Arthur shouted.

'A man like Bell?' his mother countered. 'You fool, Arthur! Involving the likes of him and that worthless Teb was an invitation to trouble.'

'You knew the Bell brothers, Madam?' Josse asked her courteously; if he could appear to side with her and alienate Arthur, perhaps dissension between mother and son might come to his aid . . .

'Yes, I knew them.' She was watching him, a slight smile on her face, and he was certain that she knew what he was trying to do; for a strange moment he thought he was hearing her voice in his head saying that it was a fine idea but not one that stood any chance of working. *Nothing comes between me and my son* . . . 'They are both dead and I judge that they are no loss.'

Josse shook himself as if it were possible in this way to throw off her spell. Did she but know it, he thought, forcing himself to concentrate, she echoed the words of Gervase de Gifford. She knew of the deaths and Josse wondered how. 'Your son has told you what happened to the Bells?' he asked.

'He did not need to,' she said wearily. 'I saw Walter go for Rohaise Warin with his knife and I saw how her quick wits gave her the presence of mind to throw that jug at him and trip him up. I saw him lie as if dead and then, when she approached, lunge up at her. I saw the hound that bit out his throat and took his life and I saw what Leofgar did with his remains.'

'You were there?' Leofgar asked, the astonishment evident in his voice.

She smiled. 'I was – a witness, of a sort,' she said, 'although nobody else knew of it.'

'But—'

She did not allow Leofgar to continue with his protest. Instead she said, 'So much for Walter. And many people as well as I saw Teb Bell hanging from his tree.'

'Do you know who strung him up there?' Josse asked.

'I saw,' she replied.

'It was not I!' Leofgar protested.

'No, indeed it was not,' she agreed. 'Teb Bell was on his way to find you, Leofgar. He knew that his brother had been to the Old Manor and he thought that you had killed him. He wanted to beat the truth out of you but he could not be allowed to approach you. Had he been apprehended – which was surely likely, given that Teb had fewer brains and even less subtlety than his brother – then he would have blurted out the truth of the matter and our hopes of achieving our ends quietly and harmoniously would have come to naught.'

'So he had to be stopped,' Josse said. Aye, it was as he had thought; even if Arthur did not admit to it, it seemed certain that it was he who murdered Teb Bell.

'Teb was of no further use,' Sirida said dismissively. 'It was a mistake to involve him and his brother in the first place.'

'You have not managed to find this alleged proof for which you have been searching,' the Abbess suddenly said, the authority in her voice filling the small space so that, as one, they turned to her.

'It is not there to be found,' Arthur said in disgust. 'According to my mother, Benedict said he would secrete the document that he promised to write in a hidden place in his table. But I searched that table myself and it is not there. There *is* no hidden place!'

'But—' the Abbess began.

Leofgar interrupted her. 'If this document of yours cannot be found, man, then it is because it is not there!' he shouted. 'It does not exist! Benedict never wrote it because, Arthur

Fitzurse,' – he laid heavy and sarcastic emphasis on the name – 'he did not acknowledge you as his son!'

'I am his son! *I am!*' Arthur protested, his body tense with rage.

'I was bedded by Benedict Warin!' Sirida cried. 'His man Martin helped him into the hut where I awaited him! He blew out the lamp and took me in his arms and he penetrated me! I conceived and bore him a son, and that son is Arthur!'

'Without Benedict Warin's word, you cannot persuade any of us that this is the truth,' Josse said, making his voice sound very firm. 'It is hopeless, Sirida.' He stepped closer to her, his eyes never leaving hers although he could not read the expression in their dark depths. 'Let us go,' he said gently. 'Tell your son to remove the knife from Leofgar's throat now. No harm has been done and we can all be safely back in our homes this day if you relent.'

There was a moment of perfect stillness. Then slowly Sirida nodded. 'You speak wisely, Sir Josse,' she said. 'We achieve nothing by this, for the one man who could have supported my story refused to do so in life and now is dead.' She bowed her head and gave a long sigh.

For a triumphant – and very brief – moment, Josse believed that she meant it.

But then Arthur's anguished shout broke the silence.

'*No!*'

As one they turned to stare at him, even Leofgar twisting his head around as far as the knife blade allowed. Arthur's face was contorted with passion and his eyes bulged.

'Thirty-five years of misery!' he cried, intent only upon his mother. 'A few moments of lust in a filthy shack and what did it advance us? You gave up the poor but honest life of a serving woman because you saw your chance to grasp something better and, for as long as I can remember, you've forced me to share your ambition! Look at Benedict, you used to tell me, that man is your father. Look at his son and that pretty wife who hides a secret, you said. Look at Benedict's new grandson, who will grow up to have all the things that are rightfully yours handed to him on a silver platter! Oh, I looked, Mother, again and again, for you would not let me stop. I looked and then I came home to you in this *sty'* – he spat out the word – 'and even then there was no respite for I loved you and my heart would ache to see the life that you were forced to lead.'

He stopped, panting, and Sirida made a small moan, stretching out a hand towards her son.

But he ignored it.

Stepping back a pace away from her, dark eyes still fixed on hers, he said, 'You suffered, well I know it. But so did I, Mother. Bastard, son of a whore, witch's brat, devil's spawn; those were some of the less offensive names they called me and I will not sully the delicate ears of this company with the worst ones. I endured the taunts and I endured the missiles that the boys flung at me, endured being daubed in animal dung and having my hair shorn with sheep shears. I endured because you promised me it would end in time. You told me I must be patient because one day the world would know me for who I am and honour me for my name.'

'Son, I—'

He would not let her speak.

'When is that day to be, Mother?' he asked. 'I wish you would tell me, for I am heart sick of waiting.'

Josse found that he was holding his breath. The tension between Sirida and Arthur was almost visible. Arthur had backed off another pace, almost as if he did not dare risk physical contact with his mother's outstretched fingers in case it made his love for her triumph over his anger and caused his resolve to collapse.

And the knife blade, Josse noticed, feeling sick with the anxiety of helplessness, was no longer pressed right against Leofgar's throat . . .

Sirida was staring into her son's eyes. 'Arthur, the day will come, for despite all that you say, I know full well that Benedict's document is where he said it would be, for I have seen it with my inner eye and I *know* that he kept his promise to me.'

There was a gasp – from the Abbess, Josse thought – quickly suppressed, as if, like him, she too could not bear to make any sound or movement that might affect the mood between the mother and son enacting the dreadful drama before them.

'I can't find it, Mother.' Arthur's voice hardly rose above a whisper.

'We *shall* find it, son,' she crooned, closer to him now, eyes still on his. 'And there will be no more talk of *relenting*,' – she put venom into the word – 'I promise you, for—'

She stopped.

She stood there in front of Arthur, looking deeply into his eyes, and then her mouth opened and her face contorted in anguish. Shaking her head, muttering, 'No, oh, no!' at last she managed to grasp Arthur's free hand in both of hers.

Half to herself, she muttered, 'It shall not be! Oh, but I will not allow it to happen that way!' and then, pulling herself together with a visible effort, she said decisively, 'Benedict's letter exists and it will be found. Then my son will stand beside his blood kindred and he shall be—'

But whatever scene she was envisaging was never to be revealed. For just then, seizing the chance while the knife blade wavered and perhaps finally driven over the edge by the thought of accepting this desperate, driven man as his uncle, Leofgar acted.

It was only to be expected, for Leofgar had suffered the most. He had seen his wife and his precious son traumatised by the villain that this man had sent to disturb their happiness. He had been forced to flee his home and seek the help of the Hawkenlye community; had been pursued there too and driven to hide himself away like an outcast.

He had, for the past interminable time, been forced to kneel in the dirt with a dagger at his throat.

He launched himself up off the floor as if his knees were springs and, spinning round as he rose, hurled himself on Arthur. At the same moment Josse leapt up from the bench and grabbed Sirida, who, the instant that Leofgar moved, had shot out her hand towards some object hidden on a shelf set high under the hut's roof. She could not be allowed to grasp what she sought, Josse thought wildly, for it just might be a tool of magic and they had quite enough to contend with already . . .

Leofgar and Arthur were struggling, Leofgar's hand tight around Arthur's right wrist, trying to twist it and squeeze it so that he dropped his knife. But Arthur had recovered swiftly from the shock of the attack and was resisting; suddenly he brought up his knee and caught Leofgar in the groin. With a groan, Leofgar doubled up and Arthur hit him hard with his left fist, knocking him back and to the side.

Furious grey eyes on his adversary, Leofgar glared up at him with murder in his face. 'You are no Warin,' he gasped, contempt like poison in his voice, 'and there is no letter from my grandfather stating otherwise. You're a bastard, just as they—'

With a howl of rage Arthur threw himself on Leofgar. But some precious instinct of preservation came to Leofgar's aid and at the last possible instant he spun himself round, twisting out of the way, and Arthur's momentum carried him on into the space where Leofgar had just been.

He fell heavily.

There was an instant's silence. Then he gave a great cry and, rolling on to his side, put both hands to his chest.

The handle of his own knife was sticking out from between his ribs.

Sirida wriggled out of Josse's arms and fell to her knees over her son, the Abbess crouching beside her. Arthur's eyes seemed to roll up in his head and he fell quiet; Sirida unfastened his tunic and undershirt to reveal the knife and the wound.

'It has not penetrated as deep as I feared,' the Abbess said, 'look, Sirida; the blade has gone in at an angle.'

Sirida had her hand on the knife handle. 'I will pull it out,' she said.

'*No!*' Hastily Josse dropped down beside them. 'No, leave it where it is, for I have seen men pull out the weapons that have wounded them and thereby release the fatal flow of blood that the blade holds back.' Meeting the Abbess's eyes, he said, 'My lady, we must get him to Hawkenlye. We will put him up on the mare, with your leave, for she has the gentlest gait. You may ride with me on my horse, if you will.'

She was nodding her agreement, already hurrying to get up. 'Yes. Leofgar, are you fit to ride?'

'I am.' Leofgar spoke stiffly.

'Go and collect your horses,' the Abbess ordered. 'Sir Josse, if you and Sirida will bear Arthur out of the hut, I will fetch Honey. But we must be swift and not waste a moment, for Arthur—'

She did not finish her sentence – in truth, there was no need to do so – but, lifting her wide skirts, ran outside and across the open space to the corral. Sirida padded Arthur's wound as best she could – she used some green mossy stuff from a wooden box on one of the shelves in the hut, fastening it in place with lengths of thin, grubby linen – and they got him outside and on to the mare. Leofgar returned with his horse and Horace and helped the Abbess on to the big horse's broad back, where Josse got up behind her.

Sirida stood looking up at them.

'Will you not come with us?' the Abbess asked her gently.

'We will care for him to the best of our ability, you have my word. But do you not wish to be with him?'

Sirida's eyes were on her son as slowly she shook her head. 'No, Helewise. I do not leave my hut any more. The source of what strength remains to me is here.' She bowed her head. 'Were I to leave, I would not get very far.' She lifted her chin and gave a brave smile. 'I have not left this place for twenty years.'

Leofgar had hold of the mare's reins but he was finding her hard to control; she sensed the burden on her back and must have been disturbed by the fact that Arthur, barely able to sit in the saddle, was clearly not in control. 'We must go, Mother!' Leofgar said urgently. 'The mare smells the blood and she is uneasy. It will be better if I can get her moving.'

'Yes, of course,' the Abbess said. 'Sir Josse?' She half-turned to him. 'Let us be on our way.' Josse clicked his tongue to Horace and the horse set off down the track. As they left the glade, Leofgar riding ahead, the Abbess turned from her seat in front of Josse and looked back. She called, 'Goodbye, Sirida.'

The response came softly on the breeze that had come up with the dawn. 'Farewell, Helewise.' And, like a whisper that might or might not have been spoken, 'You *will* find that letter . . .'

In silence they set off along the track that would lead them to Hawkenlye.

They took Arthur straight to the infirmary. Sister Euphemia examined the knife wound and complimented whoever had had the wits to leave the blade in place. Josse would have modestly kept quiet but the Abbess was having none of it: 'That was Sir Josse,' she said.

The infirmarer gave him a glance. 'Old soldier,' she remarked. 'Maybe you should give me some lessons, not that we

get many blade wounds here. Thank God,' she added under
her breath, for she had just extracted the knife and even as she
spoke was pushing wadded lint into the wound to stop the
blood.

'Do you need us, Sister?' the Abbess asked her.

'No, my lady. I can manage here. The wound is long but not
too deep and, provided I can stem the flow of blood, he'll not
die of it.' Without looking up she said, 'I'll send word when he
recovers his senses.'

'Yes, please do. Thank you.' Then the Abbess turned to
Josse and said, 'Sir Josse, let us go outside and find my son.
There is something I must do.'

Bowing his agreement, he followed her out of the infirmary.
She beckoned to Leofgar, waiting outside, and in silence led
them across the cloister and along to her room. She opened the
door – someone had kept the brazier stoked and the heat was
like a blessing – and went round the table to sit down in her
chair.

Then, looking at them both with a strange excitement in her
eyes, she said, 'I know where it is.'

'What?' Josse and Leofgar said together.

'Benedict Warin's proof.' So eager that the words raced out
of her, she said, 'Benedict told Sirida that he would hide the
document in his table and she told Arthur, who sent Walter
Bell to the Old Manor. Walter looked but presumably could
not find the hiding place.'

'Neither could Arthur and neither could I,' Josse agreed.
'De Gifford and I searched every inch and came up with
nothing.'

Now the Abbess was smiling. 'That was because,' she said,
'it was the wrong table.' Patting the wide oak surface in front of
her, she said, '*This* is Benedict Warin's table. Benedict left it
for Ivo's use when he moved from the Old Manor to his new
home, shortly before Ivo and I were wed. It became Ivo's

possession permanently after Benedict died, although in truth I had more use of it than ever did Ivo.' She looked down fondly at the table and added softly, 'I became rather attached to it, and it was the only item from my home that I brought here to Hawkenlye with me.'

But neither Josse nor Leofgar were giving her their full attention; at her first words, both had shot forward to start examining the table, feeling over its surface, underneath it, up and down its stout legs. 'Where's the hiding place?' Leofgar demanded. '*Where is it?*'

Josse, his hands flat on the table top as he ran his fingers over the smooth wood, was watching the Abbess. Frowning, she murmured, 'I am not sure . . .' Then she knelt down and her head disappeared under the table.

Suddenly she exclaimed, 'Yes! I do believe . . .' Grunting with effort, her voice coming from under the table and strangely muffled, she said, 'Help me, Leofgar, the catch is stiff,' and he too knelt down so that only his rump and legs were visible. There was a grating sound, then suddenly Leofgar shot backwards and sat down heavily.

The Abbess straightened up. In her hands was a small wooden box, dusty and dirty. 'It was fixed to the central support of the frame,' she panted. 'You would never have found it unless you knew where to look.'

'And even then it did not come away without brute force,' Leofgar added. Getting up, he came to stand beside Josse. Then, voicing the question that Josse burned to ask, he said, 'Is there anything in it?'

The Abbess had raised the lid, whose hinges gave a screech of protest. As Josse watched her face, she put her hand inside and extracted a piece of parchment, rolled up tightly and bound with frayed, faded ribbon.

She put the box down and, resting the parchment on the table, gently began to unroll it. There were a few lines written in brownish ink in what Josse thought was a cleric's hand; silently the Abbess read through them, moving her lips as she digested the words.

Then slowly she raised her head and looked at her son. 'Benedict Warin was not his father,' she breathed. Then, joy spreading over her face, 'Oh, dear God, but I am so relieved!'

Leofgar was picking up the parchment. But Josse, still watching the Abbess, said softly, 'Why such relief, my lady? It is not that rare for a man with a barren wife to lie with another woman and beget a child on her.'

But she shook her head. 'No, I know that. It is not the reason for my reaction.' She paused as if weighing her words. Leofgar, Josse thought, casting a glance at the young man, was too enthralled in his inspection of the parchment to listen. Then the Abbess said, 'Sir Josse, I loved my father-in-law. I knew him to be flawed, for he was in truth a womaniser. But had he known that Sirida had borne his child and yet done nothing to help her, that I should have found hard to forgive.'

'Aye, and—' Suddenly Josse caught sight of Leofgar's face. 'What is it, lad?'

Leofgar looked at Josse, then at his mother. 'Before you exonerate my grandfather,' he said slowly, 'I think you had better look at this.' He held out the parchment. 'There's more written on the reverse side. My Latin is not as good as it should be and neither is my skill in reading' – he gave the Abbess a swift and rueful grin – 'so perhaps you would be kind enough to read it for us, Mother.'

For all the courtesy of his words, Josse observed, there was authority in his voice; Leofgar was in truth very like his mother.

The Abbess picked up the parchment again and read what was written on the other side. Her expression altered and hardened. When she had finished there was a short pause. Then she said, 'So that is how it was.' Glancing at Josse, she added, 'The first side of the parchment states simply that Benedict is not the father of the child borne by the woman Sirida. But this,' – she lightly tapped the other side – 'this is rather more expansive.'

Then she began to read.

' "I, Benedict Warin, confess my sin and record it so that after my death the truth be known. Ivo, my legitimate son, is and remains the one true fruit of my loins, for the damage I suffered when I was dragged by my horse robbed me of my manhood and I was never more able to satisfy a woman. In my pride and my shame I told no man of my condition save my faithful Martin, who acted as my substitute in those actions that I could no longer perform for myself. Being full of pride at my reputation as a man who loved women, I could not bear for the shameful truth to be known and so I continued to pursue pretty girls and persuade them to come with me to my shelter in the forest. It was dark there and they did not know that it was not I but another who serviced them. It was of no great import; for Martin was a considerate and I believe a skilful lover and the girls were not heard to complain. The subterfuge was, I believed, harmless and it allowed me to retain that part of my former identity that I could not bear to give up.

' "But then there was Sirida. She told me that she had conceived that day in the shelter and she asked for my help. The material things she requested I would gladly have given her but to do so would have acknowledged that she had a just claim on me and this would have meant that I accepted her son as a Warin. This was impossible. The Warin blood runs true and goes back far; to accept the son of my body servant, fine man though he be, as my own flesh I simply could not do.

' "I am truly sorry for what I have done. I offer in mitigation the fact of my accident, which caused me to suffer every day for the rest of my life. Physical discomfort I endured without complaint; what I could not bear was men's pity for a eunuch. May God have mercy on my soul." '

The Abbess looked up. 'It was written by his confessor,' she said softly. 'The date at the bottom is April 1172, a month or so before Benedict died.'

Nobody spoke for some time. Then Leofgar said, quietly but vehemently, 'I *knew* Arthur was not one of us.'

The Abbess turned to him. 'So you said in Sirida's hut and it all but cost you your life.'

There was, Josse thought, a reprimand in her tone and Leofgar must have heard it too, for he had the grace to look ashamed. 'Yes, I know. But the thought of him as a kinsman became too much. He has caused me and mine far too much grief, the jumped-up fool!'

Josse repeated the last three words silently to himself. Compassion flowed through him; poor Arthur, he thought, for he has been struggling all his miserable life towards one impossible end only to be dismissed in such demeaning terms. As if, all along, he had been no more of a threat than an importuning beggar or an over-eager puppy.

But the Abbess was speaking and he made himself listen.

'I sympathise with you for your trouble,' she was coolly saying to Leofgar, 'and indeed I am more relieved than I can say for matters to have been concluded as they have. But, son, can you find no pity in your heart?'

'No,' Leofgar said. Josse could well understand the young man's firm denial.

But the Abbess had not finished. 'Well, I can,' she said firmly. 'Arthur Fitzurse had been told he had a fine, noble, wealthy man as father, yet through no fault of his own he has lived the life of the outcast.' Flinging out her hands, she cried, 'Are you not touched at the sight of him in his cheap clothes that he wears as if they were fur and fine linen?'

'No, I'm not,' Leofgar said stubbornly. 'He acts as if he's one of us and he isn't.'

'Do not,' the Abbess said warningly, 'fall into the sin of arrogance, Leofgar, for none of us chooses our parents and some are luckier than others. Where we are born is for God to decide.'

'Yes, but—'

'Hear me out!' the Abbess commanded. Turning to Josse, she said, 'Forgive me for my insistence, for indeed I sense that perhaps you are inclined to agree with my son.'

'I—'

But she did not allow him to speak either. 'I confess I too am relieved that Benedict did not father Sirida's child, yet I perceive that he committed a scarcely lesser sin in what he did do. To salve his wounded pride, he allowed another to – er, to do the deed of which he was no longer capable, and the deception was so thorough that we all believed it. All of us, without exception, thought that Benedict Warin was a womaniser until the day he died.' Her astonished eyes went from Josse to Leofgar. 'He did this rather than simply confess that his accident had rendered him impotent!' Shaking her head, she added, 'I just cannot understand it!'

'But you, my lady,' Josse said gently, 'are not a man.'

'I—' It was her turn to be rendered silent. Again she looked at the two men standing before her, one after the other. Then in a small voice she asked, 'Is it that important?'

Josse and Leofgar looked at each other. Then together they said, 'Yes.'

21

Helewise sat in her room waiting for word that Arthur Fitzurse was well enough to talk to her. Leofgar had gone: he had asked her permission to ride off and fetch Rohaise and his son back to Hawkenlye and she had gladly given it; she still did not know where they had been hiding. Too much had happened too quickly for her to think to ask him. The Bells were dead, she reasoned; Sirida would never again leave her hut, Arthur lay wounded in the infirmary; in truth, there could be no further threat to her son's family from that quarter now, at least not until Arthur had recovered his strength . . .

Josse, leaning against the door post, was staring absently across the room, a slight frown on his face. She had just announced to him that she intended to tell Arthur the truth about himself and Josse had argued that this was neither kind nor necessary, and therefore she should not do it.

'It may not be kind but it is the truth, and every one of us must have the courage to face the truth, no matter how cruel!' she had cried.

'Arthur Fitzurse has built his whole identity upon a lie!' Josse had replied, as heated as she. 'To remove the very foundations of what he perceives to be his essence is a cruel truth indeed, my lady!'

'It is also *necessary* that he be told,' she pressed on, ignoring his protest, 'for it is only by learning who his father really was that he will drop his pursuit of my son and his family!'

'Surely he would not risk another approach to them!'

'How can you be so sure?' she flashed back. 'He set Walter Bell upon them and, but for Rohaise's desperate action, that dreadful man might have slaughtered both her and her child! Arthur is a driven man, Sir Josse, and I would not be able to forgive myself if I held back from telling him the one thing that would stop him dead in his tracks!'

He had stared at her for a long moment, breathing heavily. Then he had said coldly, 'You will do as you wish, my lady, as you always do.'

He is sulking, she thought now, looking at him out of the corner of her eye. He knows I'm right and he doesn't want to admit it.

But as her anger died she was ashamed of herself. Here's dear Josse, she thought, at my side in my time of need as he has so often been. I have always trusted him and, since first we met, he has never let me down. And he's right: it will indeed be a terrible moment for Arthur Fitzurse when I reveal the truth to him. But do it I must, for my first allegiance is to my son and I would do anything in my power to protect him and his family.

'I am sorry that I spoke so heatedly,' she said quietly. 'Please forgive me, Sir Josse.'

He turned his head and his brown eyes met hers. A grin slowly spread over his face and he said, 'You are forgiven, my lady. I would never—' He stopped. From the slight flush that briefly rose in his cheeks, she guessed he had been about to make some remark that was rather too intimate for a knight to say to an Abbess.

Despite the instant of keen regret, she was quite relieved that he had held back.

After a moment he straightened up from his relaxed pose and said, 'Gervase de Gifford should be notified of your safe return to Hawkenlye, my lady. With your leave, I will ride down to Tonbridge and tell him.'

'Shall you reveal what happened?'

'That you were taken captive by Arthur and held against your will?'

'Yes.'

He hesitated. 'Would you have me do so?'

Slowly she shook her head. 'No. Arthur has suffered enough. And once I have told him what Benedict's letter contains' – she gave Josse an apologetic look – 'he will have no reason to come after any of us again. And—' She stopped.

'And you feel sorry for him,' Josse finished for her. 'Aye. I know.' His voice was soft. 'But,' he said, 'it is almost certain that he murdered Teb Bell.'

'He did not actually say so!' she protested.

'No. Maybe not. But a man is dead and we both believe that we know who killed him.'

She thought for a moment. Then she said, 'Should Gervase de Gifford ask me about Teb Bell's death, then I shall have to tell him what I believe to be the truth. He will have to act upon that truth, Sir Josse, for despite our pity, Arthur is very likely a murderer and the sheriff will have to bring him to trial.'

'Aye. And I—' But then a look of astonishment filled Josse's face and he said, 'My lady, how did Sirida know about the deaths of the Bell brothers if, by her own admission, she has not left the vicinity of her hut for twenty years?'

'Yes,' she said with a puzzled frown, 'I have been pondering over the same thing.' Slowly she shook her head. 'She told me that she has the Sight. If she speaks true, then it can only be that she has ways of seeing that are outside the skills of ordinary folk.'

For a moment it seemed that neither of them wanted to – could – speak. To break the strange mood – after all, this was an Abbey and she its Abbess; this was no place for superstitious nonsense! – she said rather too heartily, 'Well, they always said Sirida was a witch!'

The echoes of her falsely jovial tone died away. There was an odd little silence in the room and she felt suddenly chilly. Then Josse gave a quiet cough and said, with what sounded quite an effort, 'If you are quite sure that you do not wish to make a worse case against Arthur by adding abduction to murder, then I shall tell de Gifford that Arthur asked you to ride down to meet his mother, whom you knew of old, and that you went willingly but stayed longer than you should. Will that serve?'

It was very nearly the truth. 'It will serve very well,' she said. 'Thank you, Sir Josse.'

With a grunt and a swift bow, he was gone.

Presently there was a tap on the door: Sister Euphemia had sent one of her nursing nuns to fetch the Abbess, since Arthur Fitzurse was conscious.

Helewise followed the young nun across the courtyard and into the infirmary. Sister Euphemia was waiting for her. 'I've stemmed the bleeding at last,' she said quietly, 'but he's weak. Only a brief word, my lady, if I might suggest, for he needs to rest.'

'Very well, Sister,' Helewise agreed.

Arthur Fitzurse, bedded down in clean linen, looked very pale and somehow diminished. His dark eyes turned to her as she approached. Moving to stand right beside his bed, she leaned down and said softly, 'Sir Josse has ridden to Ton-bridge to speak to Gervase de Gifford, but I want you to know that you are not to be accused of any crime in relation to having spirited me away to your mother's house.'

Arthur stared into her eyes. 'That is generous, my lady Abbess.'

She made a grimace. 'Not really,' she muttered. 'I have bad tidings, Arthur,' she went on. 'The proof for which you have searched so hard has been found, although it is not what you

think. The table in which Benedict Warin hid it is now in my
possession and the document that he wrote was still in the
hiding place where he put it.'

Arthur struggled to sit up but, with a gentle hand, she
pressed him back. His eyes alight, he said eagerly, 'Then you
know that I spoke the truth! I am his son! I'm a Warin!'

'No, Arthur,' she said softly. 'Benedict played your mother
false. The injuries he received when he had his accident
rendered him impotent; his manservant took his place and
it was he who fathered you.'

The shock was easy to read in Arthur's face. 'But – but I
cannot believe this! She would have known, surely she would!'

'Apparently not, unless—' Unless your mother has been
lying to you all this time, she almost said. But that was too
cruel. 'She was very young,' she said instead. 'And consider
the circumstances: the thrill of the forbidden, the danger of
slipping out unseen to meet him, the dark little hut, a naked
man. And Benedict and Martin were of similar build and not
unalike. It is possible, I believe, that Sirida truly did not know
that it was Martin and not Benedict who penetrated her.'

But Arthur was not to be readily convinced. 'No,' he said
firmly. 'She told me what she wanted me to believe. What she
wanted to believe herself, perhaps.' He looked up at her. 'My
lady, she is clever, my mother. She would have calculated that
Benedict Warin might have felt guilt over his deception. Even
had she realised what he did, she would have gone on pretending she believed it was he who had her in that hut. It would
not have served her interests or mine to confess to knowing
what really happened.'

Helewise could not but think that he was right. Just as she
was starting to admire him for the fortitude with which he was
receiving this shattering news, his manner changed. His face
seemed to crumple and, despair in his eyes, he said, 'But to
withhold the truth from me! To have me believe I was a Warin

and to sit back and watch my efforts to prove it, knowing all
along it was all make-believe!'

'I am not convinced that Sirida deliberately misled you!'
Helewise protested. Dear God, the poor man had just been
told that the man he had believed to be his father was no such
thing; let him not also have to contend with his mother having
lied to him!

But Arthur did not answer. He turned away from her and,
as he closed his eyes, she saw tears leak from them and drop on
to the spotless pillow.

There seemed nothing else to do but tiptoe away.

In the middle of the day Leofgar returned. Sister Ursel had
been looking out for him and when the party came in sight, she
sent word to Helewise, who hurried to the gates to meet him.
With him came Rohaise – a smiling and suddenly beautiful
Rohaise – and Timus, sitting in front of his father and
whooping with delight.

Behind them, grumbling about her aching bones, was a very
old, very plump woman on a sturdy bay pony. The years fell
away and Helewise was a new bride, full of nervous excitement
at taking on her husband's household and servants; yes, dear
old Elena had gone to the Old Manor with her but Elena, she
had well known, loved her already; Magda was the one she'd
had to win over . . .

She had succeeded. She'd grown to love Magda dearly,
especially after Elena had died, and she knew that her feelings
had been fully reciprocated.

Now, her eyes opening wide in amazement, Helewise cried
out, 'Magda! Is it really you?' and, as the old woman's round
face creased into a joyful smile, Helewise ran forward to
embrace her.

'Looking every inch the Abbess, I might say,' Magda
observed as Helewise helped her down from her pony.

'Thought I'd come and see for myself, young Helewise, whether all that I hear of you is true.'

'And is it?' Helewise asked, grinning.

Magda gave her a reverential bow. 'Indeed, my lady Abbess.'

But Helewise heard her add, not quite sufficiently under her breath, 'Still my Helewise underneath that black habit, I'll warrant.'

Helewise greeted Rohaise and swept Timus off his feet into a cuddle, managing to hug him for at least the count of five before the little boy wriggled to be released. Laughing, Rohaise said, 'Do not take it amiss, my lady; he is lively and restless from spending days shut away inside and he has energy to spend!'

Leofgar came to stand beside his mother. 'We have been lodging with Magda, who has a little house in Tonbridge, on the edge of the town,' he said quietly. 'We could not go home when we left here in the middle of the night, for I feared that whoever had killed Teb Bell might find us there and could set out to harm us. So I went to Magda and she took us in. We have been there ever since.'

Helewise turned to the old woman and hugged her close. 'Thank you,' she whispered.

Magda nodded. But her smile was an indication of her pleasure and satisfaction. 'All's well now, Helewise,' she whispered back. 'See how the young wife looks? They've grown close, she and her husband, while they have been under my roof. She'll do very well, now.'

The simple statement was enough, Helewise thought, studying the laughing, happy Rohaise as she chased Timus and then, pretending to be afraid, let him chase her. Something profound had altered; whatever malaise had sat so heavily upon her had lifted. And, with the threat to her husband and child gone, the true woman was emerging.

Yes, Helewise thought. She'll do very well.

★

She made the time to tell Leofgar of her conversation with Arthur Fitzurse and, when Josse returned late in the afternoon, she told him too. He in turn reported that Gervase de Gifford sent his compliments and was delighted to hear that the Abbess had been returned safe and unharmed to Hawkenlye. 'But he's not satisfied that no crime has been done, my lady,' Josse added with a frown. 'He cannot see why these events have happened. I did not explain to him, for the secret is not mine to tell.'

'I will explain, if necessary,' she said. 'If he comes asking, I will tell him what I must. Although when I think of Arthur's despair, I realise how very reluctant I am to broadcast his shame further than I have to.'

'De Gifford is discreet,' Josse remarked. 'He would not use against Arthur Fitzurse something that was not the poor man's fault. Considerations such as that, however, would no doubt become irrelevant were de Gifford to accuse Arthur of Teb Bell's murder. It is his duty as sheriff to bring to trial those believed to be guilty of such serious crimes and de Gifford would be failing in that duty if he allowed our pleadings for clemency to affect him.'

'We could speak in Arthur's defence, could we not, if he comes to trial?'

'Indeed we could, my lady.'

'But let us hope that de Gifford does not accuse him,' she said fervently.

Josse was watching her. 'He may suspect but he has no proof,' he said. 'He will not make an accusation, I judge, unless and until he has.'

'Hm.'

Josse spread his hands expansively, a smile on his lips. 'My lady,' he said winningly, 'your son and his wife and child are back here with you and the young woman, I would dare to say, looks bonnier than ever. Will you not forget your cares for a while and simply enjoy their company?'

It was, she reflected, the best suggestion she had heard all day. 'Yes, Sir Josse,' she said. 'I rather think I will.'

Leofgar and his family remained at Hawkenlye Abbey for another two days and Magda stayed there with them. Helewise, able to relax now, enjoyed being with them all even more than she had thought to. In particular she loved to be with Leofgar, walking, talking; quite often, just being quiet together.

She realised something about herself. Spending these past days as she had done, with such extensive and clear thoughts of her past, had led her to see that she had been carrying considerable guilt, particularly since she came to Hawkenlye, over the manner of Leofgar's conception. She was a nun now and it seemed to her that her sin in having lain with Ivo before they were wed still stained her soul. She had never confessed it to Father Gilbert lest he think the less of her for her past.

She wondered now whether this guilt had led to her not wishing to see her son. He was, after all, a constant, vital reminder of her life with Ivo and she saw his father in him all the time, for all that everybody else said he looked just like her. I have been too hard on him, this beloved son of mine, she told herself, and on Dominic too; for I have not allowed myself contact with the younger brother all the time that I denied it to myself with the elder. But it is time for a change.

She went to see Father Gilbert and told the astonished priest the full story of meeting Ivo, falling so deeply and passionately in love with him, making love with him and conceiving Leofgar before their marriage. Father Gilbert gave her penance – he seemed to realise that she could not forgive herself if he did not impose a token punishment – but she thought that his kindly manner suggested strongly that he thought she had been making a lot of fuss about nothing very much.

Straight away she felt better. And, with the removal of the

dark lens imposed by the long burden of her guilt, at last she was able to see her own past through open, honest eyes.

When the time came to bid farewell – a temporary farewell – to Leofgar, Rohaise and Timus, Helewise opened her heart and let them see how much she loved them. 'We shall meet again soon,' she promised Leofgar, who looked surprised and then, very quickly afterwards, rather pleased.

Magda held Helewise against her as they said goodbye. 'Come to visit me in my little house,' she urged. 'Leofgar'll tell you where I am – it's not far away. I would like to think that I shall see you again before I go, Helewise. It would comfort me.'

'Then I shall,' Helewise promised, smiling. She had over-heard several of her nuns suggesting politely to Magda that she refer to Helewise as my lady Abbess, but the elderly servant still saw the young bride and not the stately nun; Helewise was destined to have Magda call her by her name until the day that the old woman died.

Magda beckoned for Helewise to bend down so that she could whisper in her ear. 'There's another one on the way,' she said softly, nodding in Rohaise's direction, 'unless I'm mistaken, which I never am. They've found each other again, Helewise.'

Helewise, who discovered that she had a lump in her throat and could not speak, instead made her response by silently returning Magda's hug.

Josse stood with her as they waved the party on their way. He too had announced that he was leaving; he was planning to set off the following morning. The Abbey would seem quiet without the visitors but, as for herself, Helewise thought that she would quite welcome a return to serenity . . .

That serenity would have to wait a while longer.

At first light the next morning, when the nun on duty in the infirmary went on her rounds, she found an awful sight.

Arthur Fitzurse must have turned too violently in the night, for he had managed to open his partly healed wound. It had gaped wide, almost as if its edges had been forced apart, and the infirmarer, instantly summoned, realised as she inspected it that he had been bleeding for some time; Arthur's bed was soaked in his blood.

He was dead.

They gave him full funeral rites and nobody mentioned the possibility of suicide. Sister Euphemia held her peace: she had seen his face and recognised the expression. She knew that where life holds nothing, a man may well choose death.

Helewise suspected. She realised that she had probably brought about Arthur's final despairing act – if indeed it had been a deliberate act and not an accident – by revealing the truth to him. She cried her woe to Josse, who heard her out and then, once she had eventually finished with her self-accusations, said calmly that even if Arthur had decided to end his own life, it was not her fault for having told him the truth but the fault of those who had done those deeds that she had been driven to reveal to him.

Still she was not convinced.

Finally Josse said that if Arthur had sincerely wanted to die, then who were they to hold on to him and make him remain alive? She had started to say that only God had the right to make that choice, but something in Josse's expression had stopped her.

'Do not be so hard on yourself,' he said kindly. 'None of us is perfect, even you.'

He waited until she was calm again, bless him, before he set out for home. He went to the Abbey church with her for Sext and then they returned to her room, where she sent for bread, salted fish and a draught of weak ale to fortify him for the journey. Then, aware that he was still giving her the occasional glance as if to reassure himself that she really was all right, she walked with him to the stables and saw him on his way. As always, she said, 'Come back to see us soon' and as always he replied, 'Aye, I will.'

Back in the privacy of her little room, she thought about what he had said and she loved him for the determined way in which he had tried to talk her out of her guilt over Arthur Fitzurse's death. She still felt the echo of that guilt, however, and a part of her knew that she always would; she would have to learn to live with it. I did what I thought best, she thought, but perhaps I got it wrong.

But then, as Josse had said, *None of us is perfect, even you.*

She smiled. When she thought about it, it was not a bad summing-up.

POSTSCRIPT

Midwinter 1193

In her lonely hut down in the mists by the river, Sirida mourned for her son.

They had come to tell her he was dead.

That Helewise had not turned out too bad after all, Sirida had to admit; she had made sure that the lay brother with the kind face who had brought the message – more than a month ago now – had told Sirida a gentle version of Arthur's last hours. But Sirida hadn't needed to be told: she knew what had happened.

I could not help you, Arthur, she said to his shade as it flowed around her, the greyness moving to make a vague human form, briefly coalescing only to disperse again. I have always done what I thought was best for you, and I know now that what I believed to be right was probably wrong.

But how could I tell you that you were born from a fumble in a shack with a man who performed another's duty?

Benedict Warin hid the secret of his impotence so well, my son, that I never suspected the truth until it was too late. My senses were dulled by lust, otherwise I should have probed into his mind and seen him for what he was. But I did not think I had any need for such precautions. I wanted him and I used every trick that I knew to make him want me; I set my trap and he fell into it. He summoned me and I came to him. I lay in that hut, wet and hungry with desire for him, for he was a splendid man and knew well how to make women – girls – love him and want him. He was kind, appreciative, generous with his compliments and with his little favours. I could not resist him, and the thought of what he might do for me if I pleased him – as I knew I would – ran ever a short second in my mind to how much I wanted to bed him.

I lay naked in the straw and he came in. He too was naked and his shadow loomed over me, although there was scarce any light and I was not able to study him as I wished. He lay down beside me and took me in his arms, and I felt the smooth flesh of his cheek – he was ever a clean-shaven, fastidious man – and I thought that I smelt the characteristic scent of him. Then passion took me over and I stopped thinking.

He entered me quickly but then he slowed his pace and it seemed to me that those precious moments lasted for a small eternity. He was wonderfully skilled in the ways of the bed-chamber and I remember having the fleeting thought that Benedict Warin's reputation as a lover of women was well founded. He gave me delight such as I have never experienced again.

Afterwards – he too was spent and satiated, as pleased as I with the delight we had made between us – he relaxed. And forgot, I believe, just for an instant, that he was meant to remain quiet and not speak a word. He whispered in my ear, kissing my cheek and my hair as he did so, 'Oh, Sirida, what a woman you are!'

I knew, even from those few soft-spoken words, that he was not Benedict.

I never told anyone.

Until now, my son, when it is far too late, that I am telling you.

It had come as a terrible shock to Sirida to discover what Benedict had written in the letter that he had left for others to find after his death. He had promised her that he would see to it that Arthur would be provided for in the end and she, fool that she was, had believed him. But then why should she not, when she had used her inner eye and *seen* the letter hidden away in the table? It had been but a fleeting glimpse and she had never managed to repeat the vision; she had not known that the table had long been removed from the Old Manor and that it now sat in Helewise's room at Hawkenlye Abbey.

She had never dreamed that in death Benedict would undo all his carefully built subterfuges and tell the truth about Arthur's conception. It had simply not entered her head that he would do such a thing, when for so many years he had taken such pains to pretend to the world that he was still the virile seducer that he had always been. His reputation meant so much to him; it was surely not Sirida's fault that she had not suspected.

She had *seen* the letter; she knew full well that it existed.

It was just a pity that Sirida had never learned to read . . .

Her thoughts were full of her son. She saw him as a solitary child, desperately hurt by the casually cruel taunts of the other children but determined not to show it. She saw him quietly bathing a bruised back where some wretch of a man had beaten him for trying to steal a couple of eggs – poor lad, he'd been hungry for most of his early years – and hoping that she wouldn't notice. Saw him growing up, fierce and resentful, and saw him on that fateful day when she told him that he was the son of Benedict Warin.

Saw him finally as he had been that last day in her hut. You were so angry, son, when you believed that I was about to give up, she thought, seeing the scene repeat itself in her inner vision. Perhaps I might have done, even then, but for that moment when I stepped forward and looked into your eyes.

Then I knew that there was no other way for me but to

continue along the path on which I set my feet all those years ago. For I *saw* what would happen to you if ever you knew what really happened.

I knew then that the truth would kill you.

And now it has done so.

Her mind wandered back to the past.

She thought of Benedict, dead these many years, and of Martin, who survived by only a few months the master to whom he had given a lifetime's loyalty. Benedict had gone to his grave with his reputation intact – they said that he was still chasing petticoats until shortly before his death and that it was one cup of wine too many and a last rowdy chorus with the woman sitting on his lap that brought on his final collapse. He had never contacted Sirida again, although sometimes she had sensed his thoughts tentatively turning her way, seeking her out as if, knowing what he intended to do, perhaps – just perhaps – he wanted to tell her he was sorry.

Sirida had lain with Martin only that one time, but Martin could not forget any more than she could. He had not helped her, nor had he given her any support for Arthur, his son, although Sirida did not hold it against him for she understood that his allegiance to Benedict Warin overrode any other attachment. She understood and forgave him for, of all the people in her long life, he was the only man ever to have shown her true kindness.

Just once he had made his way to the marshes to seek her out, coming by night to her hut and creeping along in the shadows as if he feared curious eyes were upon him. He slipped into the dark little room, glanced quickly at the young Arthur asleep by the hearth, then blurted out in a hoarse whisper that he had tried to put her out of his mind but could not do so and would she ever consider accepting him as her friend, her lover, her husband, even, if she'd have him?

They had stood face to face in the soft light of the dying fire and she had felt again an echo of the passion that this man had sent burning through her. For an instant she was tempted and she had felt her body lean towards his as if her own flesh recognised a soul mate and would cleave to him.

But her head had overruled her heart, her soul and her body; if she admitted that she knew it was Martin and not Benedict that she had lain with and accepted Martin as her man and the father of her son, then she must forget all about her claim on Benedict Warin.

She might just have done it had there only been herself to consider.

She turned Martin away and he did not come back.

But he had made one further attempt. She saw, as clearly as if it had just happened, that day in the great hall at Swansford, when the young Helewise had stared at her from frosty grey eyes and that old aunt of Benedict's had called Sirida a witch and commanded Martin to kick her out. I had every right to be there, Sirida mused, or so I had to make them all believe. Martin could well have gone along with the majority and treated me cruelly, but he did not. He took my arm – gently – and, once we were outside and alone, he asked in a soft voice how the boy was doing and if I was managing all right.

Oh, but how she wished she had told him then that she knew the truth! Was that what he had been asking her, on that miserable and unforgettable day of other people's celebration? Was he subtly probing to see whether she would relent and confess at last that she knew it was he and not his master who had lain with her and begotten her son?

What would he have done, she wondered, had I admitted that I knew? Would he have quietly slipped from Benedict Warin's orbit and come to me? We could have been wed, for he had already asked me and I knew that he would take me as wife if I said the word. We could have made a good life together and provided Arthur with two devoted parents.

But I was ambitious for my only child. I thought then that worldly position and wealth were the only things that mattered. I looked him in the eyes, shook my head and said, 'I do not need your help, Martin.'

She had never forgotten his face. His half-smile had slowly faded and it was like the light dying at the last moments of the day. He leaned close to her for a precious instant and said, 'I am sorry, Sirida.' Then he had made a sound – she had thought it might be a sob – and muttered something before turning and quickly hurrying away.

She had never forgotten those words, either. Because he had told her he would never stop loving her.

She sighed, deeply, painfully. 'Oh, Martin,' she whispered, 'I'm sorry. I was proud, I thought I deserved better than to be a manservant's wife. I thought that the only fit role for me was lady of the manor.'

Now, she thought, I know different.

Now that it is far, far too late . . .

Sirida felt death approaching.

Arthur had gone ahead of her, and she sensed that his spirit was not far away.

Was there physical substance after death? She wondered – more often now that she was about to die – but she did not know. She hoped there was. She would like to hold her son once more and tell him that she loved him.

And, perhaps, somehow she would find Martin, and the best lover she had ever had would lie with her again.

She lay down in her hut, wrapped herself in her thin coverings and closed her eyes. Death came and it seemed to her that she was borne off upwards inside a great beam of light.

She thought she saw Arthur and, behind him, another.

Arms open in greeting, a smile on his still-handsome face, Martin stood there waiting for her. And, an answering smile on her own lips, flying across the misty ground as if she were a young woman once again, Sirida ran to meet him . . .